Accordance

A Significance Series Novel
Book Two

Shelly Crane

Editing services provided by Jennifer Nunez.

Printed in paperback September 2011 and available in Kindle and E-book format as of September 2011 through Amazon, Create Space and Barnes and Noble.

Printed in the United States

10 9 8 7 6 5 4 3 2 1

More information can be found at the author's website
http://shellycrane.blogspot.com

ISBN-13: **978-1466344440**
ISBN-10: **146634444X**

"Far away, I feel your beating heart. All alone, beneath the crystal stars. Staring into space, what a lonely face. I'll try to find my place with you

What a beautiful smile
Can you stay for a while?
On this beautiful night
We'll make everything right
My beautiful love, my beautiful love."

- The Afters

This book is dedicated
to my family, my support system, who always keep me connected and
down to earth. You give me everything I need to be happy and I love
you more than life, A, J, N.

One

"Dad, I can't believe you thought it was a good idea to send him here," I said, fighting to keep the bite from my voice.

"Now, Maggie," he rebuked. "He really missed you. I'm sure Bish is not that bad."

"He could find out about us, Dad, about what we are."

"We - Peter and I - thought it would be better to send someone who had no powers or...whatever, there to watch you and keep everyone else here. They are planning a lot of things and need all the hands they can get. So Kyle insisted on going and Bish said he'd go too and be a chaperone to you all. He doesn't know what he's doing, just that he's keeping watch over a bunch of teenagers. Give him some slack, Maggie. He's having a hard time. He quit his job, you know."

"I know. He told me and he wouldn't have if not for me. None of this would be happening if not for me."

"Don't be like that." I could hear him shuffling papers and imagined him putting the newspaper down to further focus on me. "These people care about you. That's evident from the time I've spent with them."

"What do you mean you spend time with them?"

"Yes. I met them at Kyle's or Peter's for those meetings they have and have eaten dinner with them more than once. Rachel is a fantastic cook."

I balked. What?

"Why?"

"Why what? Why would they want me hanging around?" he asked wryly.

"No. No, that's not what I meant. I meant, why would you want to? I thought you'd be...more upset or cautious of them, because of the abilities and all."

"Maggie, you are one of these people now. It's not ideal and I still have some things to work through but I want to know everything there is to know about them and their history. Plus," he cleared his throat, "you and Caleb aren't going to have some big break-up anytime down the road, are you?"

"No, Dad," I answered and almost smiled.

"Well then I need to like these people. I need to know all about them and be around them, to get used to them. They're going to be my family one day, right? One day a long, long, long, long, time away."

I laughed and tangled my fingers in my long hair, still wet from the beach.

"Ok, Dad. You're right. And I'm glad that you're getting along. It was more than I could hope for."

"Good. Well, be nice to Bish. And just be careful around him. I'm afraid he's not as enthused about Caleb as you are."

"I can tell," I said, not even trying to tamp down on the sarcasm.

"Love you, baby girl. Thanks for calling your old man."

"Love you, too, Dad. See you soon."

We hung up and I blew a settling breath, leaning back on the white chaise in the library of Caleb's aunt and uncle's beach house in California. This was our second day here. We'd gone straight out to the beach once Bish and Kyle had shown up, unexpectedly, this morning.

We had padded our way out past the back gate and into the white sand. I flung my towel out and began to take Caleb's shirt off that he had gotten for me to wear when Kyle wasn't being shy about his looking or thinking about me in my bathing suit. Bish had immediately come up and said I should leave it on. It was a little chilly with the wind, he said. I had scowled at him while I peeled it off and threw it in the sand. Then I sank down, laying back and closing my eyes to the warm bright sun just like any normal day.

Though I couldn't see him, I could hear his thoughts. He was pissed. He thought I was being reckless with my life and with this guy who was apparently some kind of swindler to have convinced everyone to like him and let him take me away to the beach alone. The slutty bathing suit was just icing on the cake. I gasped at his thoughts and sat up to glare at him, forgetting that he hadn't said it out loud, but his back was already turned.

Caleb sat down in the sand beside me, his shirt off too, and placed a soothing hand on my seething back as he spoke softly to me.

"He's your brother, Maggie. He's not gonna be happy unless you're wearing a sweater."

"He used the word 'slutty'," I whispered harshly so Bish wouldn't hear me. "I can't believe him...ugh. I just thought this trip was gonna go differently. And I have no idea why Kyle's here either. What the heck is that about?"

Caleb grunted unhappily in agreement.

"Dad said they couldn't spare anyone else."

"Boo," I complained.

"Hey, why don't you let me teach you how to surf in the morning? It'll take your mind off things. There's a stash of boards at the house. If we come out early the surf should be good."

"Yeah," I agreed, a gleaming spot of hope seeping in. "I always wanted to learn to do that."

"Good. It's a date."

"So," I said and snuggled against his bare sun-warmed side.
"Are you going to take me on a real date while we're here?"

"I have quite a few places I intend to take you before we leave, actually," he said smugly.

"Good."

He smirked and went to bend his head to kiss me, but did a quick peek at Bish and decided against it. He leaned back onto the towel on the sand beside me, his arms under his head, his foot rubbing mine, and we stayed that way until we came back into the house a while later. Kyle had spent the entire time in the water and Bish had stayed an annoyingly close distance to Caleb and me.

And here we were now, me, sulking on the phone with my dad, complaining. Caleb was trying to fix something for supper in the kitchen. Bish was taking a shower upstairs and Kyle was playing video games on the TV in the den.

I placed the phone on the table by the chair and lay my head back in frustration. I closed my eyes, crossing my ankles and pulling Caleb's t-shirt further down over my thighs.

I thought about everything that had happened that day. About everything I wanted to do while we were here. About what Caleb and I had been doing when we were interrupted by Bish and Kyle.

To my unbeknownst dismay, I drifted off to sleep.

I was sitting on the porch in the plush cushions of the swing, watching the ocean by myself. I felt utterly content and safe there, even though Caleb wasn't with me. I wondered why he wasn't.

The ocean was so blue, the waves were so white, and the trees in the backyard were so green. It was like a...dream. Crap! No!

"Oh, yes."

I turned to see Marcus, smirking from the doorway. He had an elbow leaned into the doorjamb, making his upper arm muscles stand out. He was wearing a gray t-shirt with jeans and black boots. He had gotten his black hair shorn seriously short, except for his bangs that hung choppy over his forehead, and a small gauge placed in his earlobe since the last time I saw him.

"Maggie," he crooned falsely sweet. "I told you lover boy wouldn't be around forever, didn't I? The beach, huh?" he said as he looked around. "Didn't go very far did you? Sikes' thought you had fled somewhere far away like little cowards."

I realized then that he thought I was still near Tennessee. He came to lean back on the railing in front of me and crossed his ankles and his arms.

"What do you want?" I asked, trying to keep my voice steady.

"What do I always want?"

"I'll call Caleb," I warned and started to carry out my threat when he shook his finger at me.

"Ah-ah-ah, I wouldn't do that. If you do, then you won't find out what I've come to tell you."

Despite it all he had my interest peeked. "What?"

"First, you're going to do something for me."

"What?" I repeated warily.

"Nice shirt," he said with a little smile that made my stomach turn. I looked down and saw that I was still in Caleb's t-shirt over my bathing suit and it was barely covering my legs at all. I yanked it down over my thighs and he laughed. "Oh come on. I was enjoying the show!"

"Marcus. If this is what you wanted me to stay for-"

"You are going tell me what your ability is. Sikes wants to know and I want to be back in his good graces."

"No way," I said like he was crazy. "Why would I tell you that?"

"Because then I'll tell you why Sikes is so upset about you and lover boy ascending. It's not just jealousy because the Jacobsons are imprinting. There's a prophecy."

"A prophecy," I scoffed. "What is this, Harry Potter?"

"No. This is very real and I'm willing to make a trade," he said seriously.

I thought about it. I wondered if Caleb would be upset if he knew what I was about to do. Of course he would. He would hate the thought of them knowing something about me, but we need to know what to be on the lookout for, right? What could he do with the knowledge of what my ability was? What would it hurt? Then I had a revelation. I hadn't read any of Marcus' thoughts since the dream started. I hadn't heard anything streaming from his mind to mine. I focused on him. I tried to read him. I tried to see his past thoughts, but received nothing.

Crap. My ability didn't work in echo dreams.

But I wasn't about to tell him that. So I sat up straighter and made my decision to tell him.

"A Seer. That's my ability."

10

His jaw dropped and then he made an ugly noise in the back of his throat. "You're lying," he accused with a grimace.

"Am I?" I asked and pretended to be smug. He suddenly looked very ready to be out of this echo. "Now it's your turn."

He wasted no time in giving it to me. "There's a prophecy, that there would be a time of great tribulation. No one knew what that meant until the imprints stopped. That meant the ascensions stopped and we understood that this is what it had been talking about. The prophecy says this:

'Two will come forth to become one. That one will end what was done. One will possess power to birth, a new day of justice, strength and mirth. Then two to keep our spirit pure and strong, start anew, end the wicked and wrong.'

"It's dumb, but that's what it says. And Sikes is set on believing it. I'm sure it's not hard to see who would be viewed as the wicked in this prophecy," he spouted, almost proudly.

"How did you get a prophecy? Did it miraculously appear on a hamburger bun in ketchup?"

"No, smarty pants. It was foreseen and written down by another seer over seventy five years ago. We've kept it safe and hidden."

"So, you want me to believe that Caleb and I are the one? The two become one?"

"That's what Sikes believes. From the first second he heard of your imprint with Caleb he was dead set on stopping your ascension. Set on stopping you from becoming the 'one'."

"Why are you telling me this?"

"You thought I'd skip out without telling you the truth, huh?" he said with a malicious little grin.

"Yes."

He laughed at my honesty. "Sikes' and my agenda don't end up on the same page anymore I'm afraid."

"What does that mean?"

He made a sound like a buzzer on a game show. "Ehhhh! That's all the time we have today folks, but thanks for playing. Now if you'll excuse me, I've gotta be getting back before Sikes knows what I'm up to."

"Wait, how can you use Sikes' gift like that?"

He gave me a droll look. "You really think *I* care if I hurt his precious feelings?"

"No, no, I didn't mean 'how could you', I mean how can you like, literally? How can you?"

He shrugged, looking really pleased and superior. "Don't know how it works. It's only you though. I can't pick anyone I want, believe me I've tried. So now don't you feel special?" he sang.

I shook my head in aggravation.

He started to walk around me to the door and with me lost in thought I didn't think to be cautious until it was too late. I felt him grab my hair from behind and yank it hard, holding me captive to the chair. He leaned over to speak to me close, but not touching me.

"I can't just leave. Caleb will know that you had an echo and he'll think I've gone soft if I let you leave without doing *something* to you."

I saw the gleam of silver and thought it was a knife. Then I saw it was scissors and cursed my stupidity.

"What are you doing? You told me all that just to kill me?" I said frantically.

And then it hit me. That's probably exactly what he was doing, trying to play nice for kicks.

"No, silly human," Marcus said. "Oh, wait. Dang, I guess I can't call you that anymore, huh? But no, I'm not going to kill you. I'm just going to make it look to Caleb like I still hate your guts. Which by the way, I still do," he growled in my ear and I winced as I saw his arm move.

Maggie! Wake up!

I heard Caleb but it was too late. There was nothing to do. I waited for the sting and pain of the scissors in my chest but felt nothing but the tug of Marcus' hand in my hair.

Listen to me! Wake up now, Maggie!

Then I heard a snip. I gasped awake on the chair and saw Caleb sitting beside me, leaning over me, his face etched with concern.

"Maggie?"

"Marcus," I croaked in explanation.

"I know. You fell asleep on the chair," he chastised softly. "Did he hurt you? What happened?" he asked as he looked me over.

"I don't know, he…he told me some things and then he had scissors and-" I sat up and bits and strands of hair fell all around my shoulders and lap. I realized what he had done with those scissors. That bastard cut my hair! "He cut my hair!"

I felt Caleb digging around in my mind, seeing Marcus.

"What the hell did he do that for?" Caleb said vehemently, knowing exactly what had transpired.

"He's an insane jerk, that's why." I picked at the strands on my shoulders and then felt the hair still on my head with trembling fingers to feel it was cut up

12

passed my shoulders. I felt a sudden loss. I wanted to cry, but jeez, it was only hair...right? "He cut my hair," I repeated softly.

Caleb grimaced and pulled me under his shoulder. "I'm sorry. Let's get you upstairs and dressed before Bish gets out of the shower. Then I'll take you to the salon around the corner and we'll see if they can fix it, ok?"

He rubbed my shoulder and the hair strands showered around us as he did so, making me wince like it was painful.

"Yeah, ok."

Just as we got up from the chair, Kyle rounded the corner. Ugh! He couldn't have waited five seconds?

"Mags, what the hell?" Kyle replied.

"Marcus," Caleb explained. "Now move," he barked.

"But I thought he could only get her in a dream?"

"I fell asleep. It was my fault," I said quietly.

"No, it wasn't," Caleb said. "I'm the one that told you he couldn't reach you when you were this far away. You felt safe. It was my fault that you let your guard down."

"But why did he cut your hair?" Kyle asked me, looking at me closely. "What did that accomplish?"

"He said some things to me. He told me some things about Sikes. Then he said he needed to do something mean to me so that Caleb-" I looked up at Caleb and smiled sadly. "So that you wouldn't think he'd gone soft."

"I could kill him," he growled, his grip tightening on me. "What an evil little bast-" Caleb started in a rage, but I stopped him.

"No, don't, please? This is why he did it." I put one of my hands on his chest and one on his neck to draw off his anger. "He knew you'd go nuts when you saw me and do something crazy. Please?"

He visibly took a deep breath and I heard Kyle's mutter as he walked away. "I'll go clean up the chair before Bish sees it."

"Ok," Caleb said gruffly. "Come on, you've gotta take a shower and wash all that off before we go."

"Ok."

I let him tow me upstairs as I self-consciously stroked the stringy strands left on my head. Once we reached the upstairs bedroom, he pulled my hand away.

"Hey, it'll be ok. We'll fix it. Don't be self-conscious around me."

I glanced up into the hall mirror and grimaced at the mess of my head. "Oh, my-"

"It's ok." He turned me so I didn't look anymore. "Come on. The sooner the shower's done, the sooner we can go."

He yanked my shirt off over my head and directed me into the huge stand up stall shower with my bathing suit still on. He turned on the water for me and shut the glass shower door.

"I'll go get dressed," he said.

"K."

I kept pulling handfuls of hair away as I let the water wash over me. I took off my suit and started to wash what was left of my hair. It felt so different. I'd never worn my hair short before, ever. It felt wrong. I hated it. I knew there was no way to make it right again without having to take more off to even it out. I was so furious I started to cry hot, angry tears. It was so stupid crying over hair, but it was *my hair!* I had been attached to it, literally!

I sat down on the floor with my knees up and let the water rinse me as I sniffled and felt utterly ridiculous. After a few minutes, Caleb came in. I didn't hear him or see him. I just felt him and knew he was here.

"Baby," he soothed and leaned on the glazed glass door, his silhouette showed him there with a hand against the glass. "Don't cry. It'll be ok, and you're not stupid." He'd been reading me and heard my inner rant. I felt even worse. "All right you, come on. We'll get it taken care of, right now."

He pulled open the door and held a big black towel up in his hands. His eyes were closed. I smiled despite myself.

"Cute," I muttered, "but haven't you already seen me naked?"

He peeked and saw I was standing. He looked at my face over the top of the towel that he still held out.

"Yep, and that memory is burned into my mind for life. But I'd rather not see you again until we're ready." I knew what he meant by ready. "I'm trying to be a gentleman here," he joked and shook the towel to get my attention focused on it.

"Oh, sorry," I turned and let him wrap it around me. "So, you don't want to see me naked?" I asked as I turned back around.

That seemed strange to me.

"Of course I do. Don't start your girly insecurities with me, Maggie Masters." He smiled a real smile. "I just don't want the temptation. You saw me before, this morning...and that was with your suit still on."

I blushed, recalling the look on his face. "I'm sorry it's so uncomfortable for you."

"It's ok. I'll contain myself...somehow."

I laughed under my breath as I went to the big bed and opened my luggage, taking something out. I turned to find him gone and the door shut so I got dressed quickly and crept downstairs. I did not look in the hall mirror. I didn't want to see what I looked like.

I focused on Bish and saw in his mind that he was shaving so I swiftly made my way down the stairs to Caleb waiting for me at the bottom, always waiting for me.

"Are you sure they can fix it?" I asked as I reached him and he slipped a blue Tennessee Titans baseball cap on my head.

"Who fix what?" Kyle asked as he came from the kitchen and stared at me. *Crapola, look at that. That sucks. She's gonna be ruined for the rest of the summer.*

"Kyle!" Caleb yelled, reading his thoughts as I read them. "Dude, shut up."

"I'm sorry," he yelled back and shrugged in innocence. "I didn't say it out loud, that should count for something."

"It doesn't. Keep Bish busy while we're gone."

"Where are you going?" Kyle asked as he bit into a green apple and I winced with him as he thought about how sour it tasted.

I could actually feel my own jaws lock with it. Weird.

"There's a salon around the corner. My mom uses them when she's here. They must be good."

Hope they're really *good,* Kyle muttered in his mind as he turned to go back to the den to finish his game of Halo.

"Kyle, if you don't shut-"

"It's ok," I said with a hand on Caleb's arm to stop him. "Let's just go."

He took me to the Jeep, muttering under his breath. We pulled up to the salon and it looked swanky. Much swankier than anything I'd ever been in and I felt underdressed. Caleb opened my door and I mentally focused on him so as not to be overwhelmed once we entered the salon. He glanced at me as if to say 'ready?' I nodded and we made our way into the big glass doors.

"Hi," Caleb said to the receptionist, who was sporty in wire-rimmed black glasses and a pitch black bob hairdo.

Caleb started to spill our situation, but she took one look at me and gasped.

"Oh, no. Did your brother do that to you? My brother chopped off my ponytail when I was sixteen and I was so devastated. But darned if I didn't just chop it all back off when I got older anyway! Ha!" She stood and came around the counter. "Pull it off. Let's take a look see."

I pulled the hat reluctantly off the side and winced at the onslaught of sympathetic thoughts from many others as well as our eager receptionist.

"Oh, honey, he did a number on you." She glanced at Caleb and narrowed her eyes. "Is this the one?"

"No. It was...never mind. Can you fix it?"

15

"Sure we can, honey. Follow me. You need the VIP treatment after what you've been through."

"Um...just the regular treatment will be fine," I said wondering how much the acronym VIP would jack up the bill.

"Give her the VIP," Caleb said and scolded me internally.

You have to stop thinking in dollar signs. It doesn't matter to me.

"Well then," she started again, without a word from me, "let's get you situated. Sugar Daddy can hang in the waiting area," she said, pointing him where to go.

He smiled and waved a one hand salute at me as she pulled me away by looping her arm through mine.

"But he's not my-"

"Oh, it's ok, honey. It's California. Everybody has one and those that don't wish they did."

~ Two ~

I wanted to roll my eyes at the receptionist's too frequent use of the word 'honey' when I barely knew her.

"So where are you from, honey? That accent is the cutest thing I've ever heard."

"Um...thanks?" I was sure there was an insult in there somewhere. "I'm from Tennessee."

"That's a long way from home."

"Yeah."

Then she was shoving me towards another lady with dramatic eyebrows and completely white hair. "Now, Moon will take care of you over here, starting with a buff."

"Moon?" I asked before I could think better of it.

"Yes, Moon, and you are?" Moon asked as she stared at my disaster of locks with her mind blasting all kinds of offensive words.

"Maggie."

"Maggie," she repeated and grimaced like it was painful. "How quaint. Let's get you in the chair."

"Can you fix my hair?"

"I do skin, not hair. Sit," she ordered.

I sat. She leaned me back all the way flat and began to buff my arms and hands with a sugary smelling gritty substance. It smelled heavenly. Like brown sugar and figs or plums. She buffed and polished with vigor in silence as the oriental style music played over the loudspeaker. She had candles lit in every corner and the lights were dim but it didn't change the fact that she was scrubbing

17

off the top two layers of my epidermis. It wasn't hard to make sure I was alert so as not to drift off to sleep.

"You have really great skin," she said matter-of-factly as she started on my legs. "Usually I get woman who've spent eleven hours a day baking in the sun and feel like leather."

"Thanks."

"Just making a statement. All right, you're done. Let's rinse you off and then I'll take you for your Mani\Pedi."

Mani/Pedi. I groaned and sent Caleb a message to his mind. I could see what he saw as he sat in his comfortable chair in the waiting room with two other men watching reruns of 'Dirty Jobs'.

Ooooh. You are in so much trouble.

He chuckled in my mind as I was carted from one room to the other. They sat me in a high-back chair and stuck my feet into scalding hot blue water that fizzed and bubbled. It felt like it was singeing flesh.

Are you not having fun?

If being tortured constitutes as fun, then yes.

He laughed harder.

I somehow doubt that. You need to get out more, Maggie.

I am out. *Are you bored out of your mind?*

Nope. I love 'Dirty Jobs'.

Boys.

He laughed again.

You're so funny. Just have fun, Maggie. Relax. This is supposed to be our stress-free bubble. Remember?

But they haven't even fixed my hair yet.

Maggie, he chastised. *I'm ordering you to relax. Enjoy it. It's all the rage. You are not letting me have any fun at spoiling you.*

Does that mean you'll stop trying?

Nope. I'll just try harder.

I sighed and decided to play along with a big, fake, enthusiastic tone.

Fine! I'm having such a fantastic time! Seriously, just wow. Who knew boiling the flesh from my bones was so. Much! Fun!

I heard his laugh from where I was sitting, his real laugh, from the other room. I bet those guys in there thought he was nuts.

That's the spirit!

I'm not trying to be ungrateful. I really appreciate all this, I do. I'm just not one of those girly girls. I'm sorry.

You are exactly who I want you to be. I love you.

Love you.

A big man with metal rods through his lip and eyebrow with black hair and green spikes finished up my toes and fingers and sent me to have my eyebrows waxed. Once that painful and mentally scarring experience was over, I finally was brought to a woman to get my hair fixed. She was tall and slender with big hips accentuated by her spandex lime green pants, and gold, high, pump heels. Her hot pink button blouse matched her earrings and her completely silver hair was short and shorn at an angle to hang from her forehead over on eye. I wasn't sure if it was Hollywood fashion or not, but to me... she just looked insane.

"Come now, dear. Let's see what you have for me," she beckoned and sat me in the chair. She turned on a mini spotlight of sorts that shone right on me and frowned. "Did you do this to yourself?"

"No, ma'am."

"I am not your ma'am. You may call me Isla. Now, what do you want; Funky, Goth, Chic, Retro?"

"I just want you to fix it without taking off anymore than you have to. I really liked my hair before and don't want anything crazy. Just make it look normal."

I seriously doubted her grasp of normal.

"Normal," she repeated, "fine."

She got to snipping and brushing and spraying. I closed my eyes to the array of disastrous movements I knew were taking place. Would Caleb not like it? Would he be ashamed to be seen with me? What would my dad say? I figured it really didn't matter what anyone thought but me, and I hated it without even seeing it.

So I sat through all her ministrations silently and still as a church mouse. She blow-dried it and I felt her pulling and tugging. And then...

"Alright, you can look now." My eyes peeked open and I gasped in pleasant surprise. It looked fantastic! It was under my chin in length and she'd kept my waves loose and hanging around my face and across my forehead. Yes. It was short. But it was cute, too. And it grew on me instantly. "You like?"

"Yes, I do. Thank you so much. It looks great," I said as I stood and ran my fingers through it.

"Pleasure. The receptionist will see you now. Go, see."

I scrambled as she shooed me away and thanked her again as I left. The receptionist had someone there already so I made my way around the bamboo partition to the little waiting area to Caleb. I saw him at the same time he saw me. He smiled emphatically ecstatic.

"Ah, Maggie," he said sweetly and got up to meet me. "You look so gorgeous. You didn't have anything to worry about."

19

"Thanks," I said and tussled the strands of hair by my chin. "It's really short."

"Not that short." He pulled it back for me like it was going in a ponytail and showed me I could still put it up if I wanted to, barely. "See?"

"Yeah," I said as he released it and ran his fingers through it instead. I shivered and smiled in shy embarrassment. "So, you like it? It's ok, really?"

"I love it. You look more...grown up."

"Thanks."

"Do *you* like it? Are you happy?"

"Yes. I do and I am."

He ran his hands down my arms. "You are really soft and sweet smelling for someone who claimed to have been tortured."

I laughed and pushed his chest a little playfully. "It was torture. Next time you come back with me."

"Next time?" He leaned forward closely. "Are you saying you're going to let me spoil you again?"

"We'll see."

"Hey, that's progress as far as I'm concerned," he said grinning and took my hand to tow me to the receptionist to pay.

I balked when she said my total.

What! Did we just buy a used car I didn't know about?

He laughed and covered it in a cough as he gave her his credit card.

Spoiling doesn't come cheap, my love.

Caleb...It's too much-

Don't start that again. I thought we were making headway here?

That was before I realized you'd have to sell a kidney to get me a haircut.

Maggie, Maggie. Money is just paper.

To you maybe.

He smirked and signed his receipt and we got in the Jeep and headed to the beach house. Bish and Kyle were in the den playing video games together.

"You two aren't supposed to leave without me, you know," Bish spouted, not taking his eyes from the screen. Kyle screamed in battle rage and Bish yelled back as his avatar was decapitated. "Oh! Come on, man!" He threw the controller to the couch cushions. "Yes? I'm waiting patiently for an excuse," he said all smart-alecky as he stood and turned to glower at us. But his glower soon turned to surprise and then a small smile. "Maggie? What did you do? You look...gorgeous."

"That's what I said," Caleb spouted happily.

"You cut your hair?" Bish said and came to stand in front of me. "Why? I mean, I like it but, why?"

Kyle glanced at me over the couch back and did a double take. I immediately blocked his thoughts.

"I just wanted something new."

"Well, you got it, really." He let a few strands run through his fingers. "It looks really good on you, kid."

"Thanks. Ok, how about some supper now? I'm starving," I said trying to steer the thought process away from me.

"Well," Caleb said. "I started supper but it burned when I was...I forgot about it I guess when we were getting ready."

Crap. Was it because of me?

It's ok.

"I'll order a couple pizzas," Caleb said.

"Better order a few. I'm starved," Kyle said, coming to stand beside me. He turned to look at me and smiled. "You do look really great."

"Thanks. I'm just glad they could fix it."

"Fix it? What do you mean," Bish asked quirking a curious brow.

"Uh...just that it was so damaged. They did some treatments on me."

"Is that why you smell so good?" Kyle said and circled me. He smelled my hair from behind. "Mmmm."

"Kyle, stop."

"What?" he said innocently.

I turned and looked him in his eye. My gaze didn't waver. I pleaded with him silently and saw him soften.

"Please, Kyle. It doesn't have to be this way."

I saw him about to speak, but Caleb returned so he sighed and went back to the couch. Bish shook his head at me.

"Ok. Pizza will be here in thirty minutes or it's free," Caleb announced.

"What kind did you get?" Kyle asked, back to playing his game.

"One pepperoni, one pineapple and ham, and two with everything."

"Did you get one everything with no black or green olives? Because Maggie hates them," Bish volunteered.

"I can pick them out, Bish. It's ok," I assured and gave him a funny look.

"Actually," Caleb started and threw his arm over my shoulder. "I got one pizza with no olives. I knew you hated them." He kissed my temple and smirked. "So Bish," he turned to him and nodded his head toward Kyle, "what do you say we kill each other?"

"With pleasure," Bish said but his smile was playful as they both made their way to sit by Kyle. Caleb threw himself on a huge brown suede beanbag and Bish sat in the club chair. "Set us up, Kyle."

21

"Oh, yeah!" Kyle yelled animated. "I haven't whipped you in Halo in too long, my friend."

"In your dreams," Caleb rebutted and looked to me. "Maggie, you in?"

"I don't know how to play."

"Come here." He scooted back a bit and beckoned me to him. I sat between his legs and he wrapped his arms around me to show me the controller. "You can watch me this time and then we'll add you next go round. K?"

"K."

I wasn't about to complain. I had the best seat in the house. They played for a while and then I heard the doorbell. I whispered to Caleb that I'd get it and he muttered a response but was so into the game, I may as well have not been there. I laughed under my breath and grabbed the money he'd set aside on the table to give the delivery man. I opened the door and saw a guy, about seventeen, maybe eighteen.

"Hi. Thirty seven fifty."

Well helloooooo pretty lady.

"Here you go," I said and tried not to roll my eyes at him.

"Need change?"

I got some change for you.

"Nope, thanks."

"Hey, is Caleb here?"

"Uh...yeah. Hold on."

I took the pizza, placing it on the table and did roll my eyes as I heard his next thought.

Even better from the back.

"Caleb. The delivery guy wants you," I called.

"Huh?" he asked still not looking at me.

"He asked if you were here."

He placed the game on pause and looked pensive.

"Oh, it's probably Chris." He went to the door and I didn't follow but I stood where I was. I could hear their thoughts anyway. I didn't need to be close.

"Hey, man. Long time no see," Caleb said and they did some strange handshake, bumping fist and snapping thing. "So is Zeke home from school?"

"Yeah, he's throwing a major rager at the pier tomorrow night. I wanted to see if you'd come." He looked over at me and clucked his tongue in appreciation. "And bring all that goodness with you."

"Hey," Caleb barked, "that *goodness* is mine."

"Sorry. Nice work, man. Kyle here too?"

"You know it," Caleb replied begrudged.

22

"Cool, bring him. Eight o'clock."

"Ok. We'll see. Thanks, man."

"See ya."

Caleb shut the door and turned to see me watching.

"That's Chris. He's the little brother of a guy we used to hang out with when we came here in the summer."

"Uhuh," I gave him a raised eyebrow look and cocked my head in jest. "And...all this goodness is yours, huh?"

He laughed. "You little eavesdropper." He hugged me to him. "And yes. All mine."

I just giggled and went on my tiptoes to kiss him...just as Bish came around the corner with Kyle on his heels.

"I thought we agreed to cut that out," Bish muttered.

"I didn't agree to anything," I said as I handed him a plate and heard him grunt.

We took our plates to the den and they resumed their game, while eating. It was strange to watch them. They didn't even look when they took a bite. It was just mindless automation.

I texted Beck as soon as I was done.

Hey. I'm still fine. I'm actually in California with Caleb. Long story but it was necessary for safety reasons. I'll call you soon, love.

Once Caleb was done eating, he got me to sit in between his legs again and showed me how to work the controls. I received my answer from Beck.

Awesome! California?! Holy cow, Mags, you are gonna be so tan. Call me soon.

Kyle added me as a player and we started again. I was killed in like seventeen seconds. Kyle.

"Dude, take it easy on her," Caleb scolded. "She's never played before."

"No prisoners," Kyle mumbled as he shot someone, poking his control forward with each gunshot. "Oh yeah, take that New York City."

I realized that was Bish's name on the game.

"I'm tired anyway," I said to Caleb. "Can I just sit here?"

"Yeah." He looked down at me. "You want me to go to bed with you?"

"No, you play. If I fall asleep, you'll be here with me. It'll be ok."

"Why don't you just go lie down on the bed by yourself, Maggie?" Bish said and though his eyes were on the game, his voice was puzzled. "Or the couch in the other room? It's not rocket science."

"I'm fine here. Thanks."

"Whatever. Caleb can't be comfortable like that. And I never pegged you as the clingy girlfriend," he said in a mocking tone.

I had no idea what to say. I always looked nuts-so, everything I did, to Bish. He thought I was naïve, immature, and now clingy because of this echoling thing and Caleb not being able to leave my side. I just snuggled into Caleb's chest and tried not to think about it.

"You're fine like this," he assured me.

Don't worry about him. You are right where I want you to be.

Thanks. I'm sorry.

For what?

I am being clingy.

You have to be clingy right now. I'd rather you be clingy than not safe. Besides, I like you clingy. Your being clingy equals you in my lap. What guy wouldn't want that?

I laughed softly and shook my head, knowing he'd feel me doing it.

You're so crazy. I love you.

I love you, baby. His lips skimmed my temple and kissed softly. *Sleep.*

I nodded and did just that.

~ Three ~

The next morning I woke on the couch bed with Caleb. He must have carried me to bed last night after he was done with their game. I had no idea when I fell asleep, but he probably stayed up late. I decided to creep out and let him sleep in. I smiled and rolled over out of Caleb's arms, but Bish was there. Eating a bowl of cereal in the chair and watching me.

Look at them. All tangled up and sleeping together, my baby sister. I never thought she was the type to be like this.

"What are you doing in here?" I asked.

"I could ask you the same thing," he replied as he sat his bowl on the side table. "How is Dad ok with this? I don't understand it. He told me to let the two of you sleep on the sofa bed together and not give you any flack about it. What kinda sense does that make? What kind of Dad approves - no, not only approves, but insists - like it was a rule or something - that his daughter sleep with her boyfriend in the same bed. I don't get it." He eyed me curiously. "Are you sure you're not pregnant? You can tell me, Maggie."

"No, I am not pregnant. Dad must just see that Caleb and I-"

Bologna!

"Oh, don't start all that "We're gonna be together forever" crap." He stood and glowered at me. "Something is going on. Something's not right here with this whole thing. I'm gonna figure it out, be sure about that. I'll crack heads to do it if I have to."

"Bish, times have changed."

"So! The Maggie I knew didn't sleep around!"

Ouch.

"The Maggie you knew wasn't in love. And I'm not sleeping around. We just sleep." He looked unconvinced. "Do I have to say it? I'm the big V, Bish."

25

"Oh! Don't!" He covered his ears. "Don't say that word."

Oh, no. What have I gotten myself into? I wanted to know, but I'm not so sure I can sit here and talk about sex and virgins with my sister.

"What word? Virgin?" I yelled. "I am. So stop bugging me about it."

"Is this because I'm not your real brother?" I gasped at his question. "You think I have no business or no right to-"

"I can't believe you just said that!" I climbed out and stood in front of him as he towered over me. "You know I don't think that," I said softly. "You are my brother. My *real* brother, the only brother I'll ever have."

He nodded and that seemed to lighten him up some. "I just wish you'd trust me to handle whatever it is that you're keeping from me."

I changed the subject. "We could have fun here you know, but instead you're being mopey and morose."

He smirked.

She's so smart.

"Morose?"

"Yes, morose."

"Well, I wouldn't want to be morose, now would I?" he joked.

"No. Please lighten up," I pleaded.

"I'll try. But, Maggie, it'd be so much easier if you just told me what was going on."

"Nothing," I said and tried for convincing.

He didn't buy it, but didn't look quite as upset anymore.

"Ok, I'm going to put on my suit. That shiny pool is calling my name. Are you in?"

"Sure. I'll be out in a minute," I assured and sent him a small smile.

He nodded and made his way to the doors and up the stairs.

I sighed and sat back on the bed. I knew something was going to have to change. Bish was not going to give up on this until he knew and I wasn't sure how he'd handle it all, despite his assurance he'd be ok with it.

I felt a hand on my back the instant before I heard his thoughts.

You're right about that. We'll have to be more careful from now on.

I turned to him, lay my head on his stomach like a pillow and looked at him.

"I don't care if he thinks I'm a loser. I mean it sucks, but I can deal with that. I just don't want him to find out the truth and go berserk."

"I know." He ran a hand through my short locks. "We'll figure something out. So, Chris was telling me about a party tonight at the pier, I know you heard. You wanna go? It'll take Bish's mind off things."

"What kind of party?"

"Beach party. We've known them since I was ten. We always came during the summer and used to surf together. He's good people, just really rich and a bit...unconventional."

"What does that mean?"

"He's a self made rock star. His band started making videos on YouTube. Now they book gigs all over and aren't even signed, but they make a killing. His parents were already rich before that, but now..."

"So what's so unconventional about him?"

"Well...picture Russell Brand and Jonah Hill have a baby."

I burst out laughing. "You're kidding?" I said through a giggle.

"Nope, sadly not. He's a little hefty, but he wears no shirts, ever. He always wears leather pants and has this crazy curly fro hair. It's pretty hilarious, but it's all for his image, to be crazy and eccentric, to keep his music going."

"So will they be playing at the pier?"

"No doubt."

"We can go if you want."

"Good. So, surfing? You ready?"

"Crap, I forgot. I just promised to go swimming with Bish."

"That's fine. I'm still kind of tired. Kyle and I stayed up until almost four." I shook my head at him. "I know. We'll surf tomorrow morning," he promised.

"Ok. Hey, why can't we cure sleep? I mean, you'd think we'd both reenergize each other and not ever be sleepy."

"I wish. It's the one thing we can't cure. That and hunger."

"Alright, well, I'll let you get back to sleep then."

"Thanks, baby. I won't be too much longer. Then I'll make lunch, ok? I make a mean spaghetti."

"Ok." I got up to leave, but he grabbed my hand.

"Hey. Everything is going to be ok, you know that right?" He waited for me to nod. "Good." He kissed my hand and I smiled at him as I made my way out.

I put on my suit and made my way to the pool where Bish was doing laps. I jumped right in and started doing them with him. I was faster than I used to be, I could tell.

We did laps together as he told me about New York some more, though I already knew most of it from listening to his mind. Now, he planned to move back in with Dad, temporarily, find a good job in the city and then find an apartment. He didn't tell me but I knew he was lonely. He hadn't made any friends in New York, not for lack of trying, but literally there was no time to and also no want to. He didn't want to be attached to a city he hated so much. He missed people back home and even though he'd never admit it to himself, he missed having a girl.

He missed something he'd never had.

Though he'd never had a girlfriend, he wasn't a virgin. He had sex once when he was thirteen on a dare with a girl he barely knew and never saw her again. He was constantly in trouble with the law as a kid because of running away or hanging out with the wrong people. His real parents were lowlifes. His dad was a jerk who beat his mom and his mom had been resentful because she was stuck with a kid and a husband that didn't want one.

She beat him, kicked him, starved him, and eventually abandoned him when he was seven. She packed his dad and her things and left Bish there alone in their apartment. After some time a neighbor called the police and they took him to social services. They shoved him into one horrendous foster home after another. Every now and then, he'd get a really good, nice place, but they'd yank him out and move him before he could really have any peace.

I tried not to just sit in his brain all day, but sometimes it couldn't be helped. Some people's thoughts were more loud and forceful than others, I realized.

It was painful to see his memories, to see what he went though before he met us.

His memories of meeting my parents were priceless. They had gone through all the stuff they were supposed to, the classes and home evaluations and decided instead of adopting a child, they'd adopt an older kid because there seemed to be a lot of them and no one else wanted them.

His memory of them was almost angelic; they were glowing and smiling too widely. My mom's hands were too soft when she touched his shoulder. My dad's grip was too friendly when he shook his hand. Once again, Bish's memories were skewed and altered to fit, like a child's dream.

When he met me, he saw a small, helpless, adorable little girl who desperately needed protecting. Like every other good person in his life before me.

I always knew he was protective of me. He was always walking me to school and taking me to the beach, but never letting me go out too far. He was a wonderful big brother and now, I was letting him down. I felt wretched about that, but didn't see a way to change it.

Kyle came out to join us and I was relieved to be free of Bish's thoughts. Until Kyle swam to me, too close.

"Hey, Maggie, you look a little peeved. What's up?"

"Nothing, just...listening," I said low, where only he could hear me, and he nodded.

"Aha. Well, stop it if it's upsetting you. Let's do something fun. Wanna get in the hot tub with me?" he asked and grinned, raising his eyebrows.

"Not really, Kyle. I'm kinda tired already. We've been doing laps all morning.

"Well, the hot tub will do you good then." He moved to stand almost behind me and put his hands on my shoulders. "It'll work out the tension and kinks."

I shrugged his hands off. "Kyle, don't."

"What? I'm just trying to help."

"I know what you're doing," I rebutted and started to swim away. He grabbed my hand to stop me.

"Why are you always running away from me?"

"You're always acting inappropriate."

"You never even gave me a chance," he said hotly and pulled me closer. "If only you had stopped being so stubborn before you met Caleb, and went out with me, we'd be together now. Not you and him." He wrapped his arm around my bare waist, his face on my ear. I tried to keep calm so Caleb wouldn't come running and beat the stew out of Kyle, which is exactly what would happen if he saw him right then. "It should have been me. If only you had touched me first."

I pushed at him, but he held tight. Bish looked at me funny and started to come our way, but I held up a hand to him.

I saw visions, Kyle's memories of him watching me at lunch as I laughed at something someone said. One of when I was dressed as a fairy for some school function. The one time he got to do the spirit cheer with me when Chad was sick.

So many times when Kyle was watching and I didn't know it. So many times he wanted to touch me or call me and was never allowed. I felt bad, but what could I do?

"It doesn't matter anymore, does it? It's too late. There's no point in you acting like this, it doesn't help anything. It just makes us both feel bad." His face dropped as he leaned back, his expression as forlorn as ever so I softened my tone. "Kyle, please. I want to be your friend, but you can't do this. I'm sorry. I wish I could help, but I can't and Caleb isn't going to like this. Let go."

"If I could just make you see. Just once, kiss you for real, and you'd see how much I want you. We'd be good together and you know me. You've known me forever, Maggie," he sighed and touched my cheek.

"Just because we've known each other doesn't mean we belong together," I told him and turned away from his touch.

"You don't have any idea," he said sadly. "All you can think about is Caleb and it makes me sick watching you two all day."

"In all fairness, I left. We came to California. You're the one who came *here*. Stop this, please. Let go."

He did, almost pushing me away, and sighed harshly, letting his head fall back.

I heard Caleb then in the kitchen, so I got out and trained my mind so I wouldn't think about what Kyle was trying to do. Caleb would see it eventually, but I wasn't in the mood to deal with it today.

We ate lunch, as I talked about the beach and avoided Kyle's gaze, and Caleb was right, his spaghetti was pretty good. Then they played video games and I read a book from the library until later on. In the evening, we got ready to go to the pier party.

I put on a long sundress I'd brought. It was blue and white and had little ruffles on the front with halter straps. I slipped on my flops and earrings. I fixed my hair just like the lady had the day before. It was still cute and I still really liked it.

When I came down and saw Caleb in his khaki cargo shorts, flops and green Carolina Liar shirt, I sighed in contentment. He was pretty adorable.

He turned to me smirking, reading me, and beckoned me to come. All four of us, walked down the beach to the pier. It wasn't that far and I could see the party already raging and hear the thump of the music.

You look great.

I looked at him and could see his face barely in the moonlight.

Thanks. So do you. The band t-shirts are really growing on me.

Well, we'll have to start going to concerts. I haven't been to one in a couple weeks. That's like a record or something.

Yeah, we should.

You know, Mutemath is playing here this coming up weekend. I wish Mom was here. She loves them.

Your mom? Your mom loves Mutemath?

Yep, loves 'em.

That's so weird. I like them, too.

Well, we should go.

Sounds good.

We walked up with Kyle and Bish behind us to a wild party. There were already tons of beer bottles littering the beach and it had just gotten started. Kyle took off the second we got there.

"Let's get something to drink," I suggested over the loud music.

"You can think again if you believe I'm going to let you drink alcohol, Maggie," Bish scolded.

"I wasn't," I insisted.

"It's ok. We can't drink alcohol anyway," Caleb spouted and then looked a little bit chagrined.

Crap.

"Why can't you?" Bish asked suspiciously.

"Because we're not old enough," Caleb replied.

Aces can't drink alcohol. Something in our blood doesn't handle it right.

Really? Then a thought came. *That's why you took my drink at that party before?* He nodded slightly. *It wouldn't have mattered. I don't drink anyway.*

Well good because you can't now even if you wanted to. It makes us super, super drunk, like borderline alcohol poisoning. You want a soda or something? I'm sure they have something here.

Yeah. I'll stay with Bish, I guess.

Ok.

"Why don't you-" I started to say to Bish but was interrupted.

"Hey, cutie," a girl with long blonde hair and big blue eyes called to Bish then came to stand by him. "Not dancing?"

"Nope," he said, shifting a little uncomfortably from one foot to the other.

"Well, why not!" she laughed. "You want to dance with me?"

"I'm good here, thanks."

Oh, Lord. Now I have to deal with this juvenile crap just so I can look out for Maggie.

"Oh," she said disappointed. "Oh! You're together?"

"No. No, I just don't want to dance, but thanks."

"Ok," she said shrugged and turned to go.

I could hear her as she walked away.

Dang, I haven't been turned down that cold in a long time.

"Jeez, Bish," I scolded. "Could you be more rude? She was nice. She just wanted to dance."

"I don't want to."

"But you didn't have to be so cold to her."

He pondered that and conceded. "Yeah, you're probably right."

Caleb came back with three drinks. "I got you a Pepsi, Bish. I didn't know if you wanted a beer or-"

"I don't drink beer."

It makes people mean and hateful.

And then it hit me again. His memories, his thoughts flooded to me and overtook me with a rush over my senses.

It all made sense then.

He was the unwanted child, always. He was the troublemaker. He caused people to be stressed, to drink, to hit and to be mean, to hurt people. He had all those caretakers and all those people who took him in. All those people who abused him and beat him and hated him. What did he ever do to any of them except be born?

He was unnatural, he thought. He caused trouble and discord. His father now was in prison for rape and murder, and his mother beat him every day for seven years. And then it followed him everywhere he went. He was cursed.

He didn't drink. He tried to be good and fair. He tried to protect the ones he loved, the first people to ever care about him, and not treat him like he was nothing. And then that mom left, too.

My mom.

He tore my family apart, like everything else. That's why he didn't date.

His blood was spoiled. He had raping, murdering, hateful, abusing blood running through his veins and he was afraid he'd wind up hurting anyone he ever cared about that way. He never looked twice, except for Jen, and that had been a fluke. He pushed it out of his mind and kept to his decision. He would never love anyone. Never get married, never have kids. So the curse and bad blood would stop with him.

I yanked back and realized it was Caleb who'd yanked me back to reality with a hand on the back of my neck. He turned me away and I felt a couple tears on my face. He hadn't wanted Bish to see.

Are you ok?

Yeah. I wiped my face. *I'm ok. Gah, Caleb. I don't know what to do with him.*

I know. I'm sorry.

I wanted to tell Bish everything right then and there. To tell him it wasn't his fault. To tell him I trusted him and loved him, but I couldn't.

I heard Bish start to walk away, but I turned and grabbed his arm. "Will you dance with me at least?"

He looked at Caleb and back to me. "I'm sure Caleb is ready to have you to himself and not have me dragging along."

"I want," I grabbed his hand and started to drag him, "to dance with *you*."

He looked back at Caleb, who shrugged and smiled. "Go ahead. I'm finishing my soda."

I took him to the end of the pier where everyone was dancing and we danced. He was really good. I was clumsy and all over the place, but I danced anyway. It was so much fun. He was hilarious, playful, and actually having a fantastic time. He twirled me under his arm and bent me backwards, being silly, making me laugh hard.

He missed just being able to let loose. We danced for a long while before I was too bushed to keep going. "Come on. I can't dance another second."

"Quitter! You're the one who brought me out here," he said laughing.

"I know. You can keep dancing if you want. I know there's plenty of willing girls."

"Nah, I'm gonna go find a place for the old fogies to sit," he said grinning.

I laughed and went to find Caleb.

I found him by the strangest looking guy I'd ever seen. He was wearing no shirt, black leather pants, no shoes, and his hair was in a wild afro of black curls. I could only assume this was Zeke and I immediately blocked his thoughts and focused on Caleb.

"Hey, you," Caleb called sweetly and pulled me to his side. "Zeke, this is Maggie. Maggie, Zeke."

"This is your Maggie, eh? I say, good work, my man."

"Thanks," Caleb muttered wryly.

"So, lads and lasses, what are we drinking? Refill?" Zeke tipped Caleb's cup towards him and grimaced. "Still a soda man. What about you, Maggie, my dearest? A little bubbly to brighten your night?"

"I'm fine, thanks."

"Zeke and the guys are about to go on stage," Caleb told me.

"Really?" I said enthusiastically. "Great. I've heard a lot about you guys. What's your bands' name?"

"Metal Petals."

"Aha. Nice."

"Well, you two sit right there and prepare to be rocked," Zeke said and pointed his fingers at us as he walked away backwards.

I told you he was unconventional.

I just laughed as he took the stage and introduced their band. Then they began to play. They were pretty good actually. We stayed right there until I felt someone tap me on the shoulder. I turned to see Kyle...with the blondest fakest tanned bimbo I'd ever seen. Her makeup was all bright purple and pink and her blue leather mini skirt couldn't really even be called a skirt - scrap was more like it. I was sure my eyes went wide. She looked me over, too, and her thoughts came to me.

So this is her, huh? Nothing special.

I blocked her out.

33

"Hey, guys. I'm gonna go ahead and take off and go back to the beach house with Amber." He purred her name, making her giggle and flip her hair.

"Kyle," Caleb said, like he was talking to a drunken idiot. Only this idiot wasn't drunk. "What are you doing?"

"What does it look like?" She made playful nipping and biting type moves toward him and he made them back to her. I wanted to gag. "I'm going to go play with Amber."

"I don't think Uncle Carl would want you bringing people we don't know to the house, Kyle, especially with us not being there."

"Well," Kyle leaned in and whispered. "You not being there is kinda the point, cuz. If you know what I mean?" He winked. I must have looked disgusted because he turned to me and frowned. "What's your problem?"

I shook my head. "Nothing."

"That's right, nothing. You don't get a say in what I do, Maggie. I could take the whole party home to screw and you couldn't say one word to me about it!" he yelled angrily, and a few people near us looked to see what was going on.

"Hey!" Caleb yelled back and moved me behind him. "You need to calm down. You don't talk to her like that. Go. Go to the house, whatever, I don't care, but go before you say something stupid and I have to do something about it."

"Whatever," Kyle muttered. He looked at me once more before putting an arm around Amber's shoulders and pulling her away.

They walked down the beach toward our house and I sighed in exasperation. I felt sorry for him too. He was hurt, because of me, and he was trying to get back at me for it.

"He shouldn't have yelled at you like that," Caleb reasoned with my inner thoughts. "No matter how *hurt* he is. He's a jackass."

"Yeah, he is," I agreed and shook my head to clear it. "Come on. Let's get back to Metal Petals."

He smiled sadly and positioned me in front of him. Now we were in front of the makeshift stage. He put his arms around me from behind and kissed my neck before sticking an arm in the air and yelling loudly as the song ended. I laughed at him and we listened to the rest of the set. Once the music ended, that was pretty much it for the party, especially once the beach patrol showed up. He turned to me and yelled over the ruckus.

"Come on. Let's get Bish and get out of here."

Back at the house, you could hear the giggling from the porch. I assured Caleb they weren't doing anything unclothed and we could go in. They were sitting on the couch, she was lying on her back across his lap and laughing as he tickled and nuzzled her.

"Oh, hey, guys. You remember Amber?"

Caleb and I looked at each other and shook our heads.

"I'm going to bed," Bish announced and came to me. He smiled and hugged me to him. "Night, Mags."

"Good night. I had fun," I told him sincerely.

"Me, too." He leaned down to my ear. "I can even overlook the fact that you are an appalling dancer."

"Ha, ha."

I heard Caleb stifle a chuckle. Bish nodded to him in goodnight. Then he called to Kyle from the stairs.

"Night, Kyle. Don't be an idiot."

Kyle scoffed and Amber turned his face back to look at her.

"I'm kind of tired too, actually," I said, "and hungry." I looked to Caleb. "You want a sandwich?"

"Yeah, thanks. Kyle, can I talk to you, on the porch?"

I heard an aggravated noise as I left for the kitchen and soon I was joined by the bimbo.

"Hi! I'm Amber."

"Yes. I know."

"What's your name?"

"Maggie," I muttered.

"Awe, how cute! OMG! Isn't Kyle just delicious? How do you live here with him and not just want to jump him? Though that other guy was pretty hot too."

"Somehow I manage," I muttered as I started to make the roast beef sandwiches.

"So, did you and Kyle used to go out or something?"

"No. Why?" I asked as she moved behind me to go to my other side.

She bumped my arm in the process and I sliced the end of my finger. I huffed and looked at her, but she didn't say anything. I rolled my eyes and grabbed a napkin, wrapping it around my finger.

"Eeew, blood makes me gag," she said as she watched me, her neck wrinkled as she sucked it in.

"I'm fine by the way," I said with sarcasm that she didn't catch.

"Mmhmm. So anyway, back to Kyle. He just seemed very intent on seeing you and that other guy before we left to come here. We looked for you forever!"

"What?" I asked and got a clean knife.

"Yeah, I thought he was parading his rebound or something."

I put the knife aside and looked at her.

"So if you thought you were a rebound, why were you so happy about coming back here with him?"

"Hey." She leaned forward on her elbows and smiled coyly. "Don't knock rebound booty til you try it."

"Eeew," I muttered before I could stop myself and resumed the mayonnaise.

"Hey!" She suddenly seemed a little bristled and stood up with her hands on her hips. "Don't judge me. You don't even know me!"

"You're right, I don't. See ya," I said, unwrapping my finger that had stopped bleeding and grabbing the sandwiches, making my way out of the room. I had to visibly shake the grossness off me. Girls like her gave the rest of us a bad name. "Caleb?"

He was still on the porch with Kyle, all big brother-ish. They were discussing the no-dating rule again and Kyle was explaining basically the same thing as Amber just had to me. A one night stand, no matter if they did or didn't have sex, wasn't a relationship. I tuned them out and went to go sit on our couch bed and wait for Caleb.

He came in shortly after, upset and shaking his head, grumbling about how Kyle was being an idiot and it was stupid how childish he was being about it all, stringing that girl along. I just sat and let him rant, listening, and then lay down with him when he was done and ready for bed. He put his arms around me from behind and spoke his words into my hair.

"Hey, uh," he started, "I didn't get a chance to tell you. Zeke's band wants me to play with them next weekend. Their bassist is going to a wedding in Maine or something."

"Really, you want to do it?"

"Yeah, I do."

I heard his thoughts. He'd always secretly wanted to be in a band or start one but never got the notion to. Plus what good would a band do for his family? He really wanted to do this. Just to say he did it once.

"I think it's awesome. Did you tell him yes?"

"I wanted to talk to you first."

"Why?"

"I didn't know if you'd be...weird about it. I don't know. I mean, it doesn't mean anything, nothing will come of it, but I will have to practice this week if I do it. Like everyday to be ready for this weekend. I'm not thrilled about the idea of leaving you alone...but Bish is here so..."

"I'll be fine. I think you should do it."

"Ok," he said brightly. "I'll call him tomorrow."

36

"What about the Mutemath concert?"

"That's Saturday night. The gig is Friday."

"Great! Wow. I'm dating a rock star," I teased.

"Ha, ha. It's not a big deal."

"It is to me. I like it when you're happy." I snuggled closer. "It makes me happy, too."

"You're still amazing," he murmured and kissed the back of my neck.

We tried to go to sleep. The giggling and loud whispering from the other room lasted for hours. Caleb shouted for them to shut up, but that just seemed to make it worse. He started to get up a few times to tell them to shut up to their face, but I held him back. Kyle wanted to rebel. I refused to believe this was all about making me jealous. He just wanted to do something without being told to.

Eventually, we went to sleep.

~ Four ~

In the morning, we woke early to go surfing. We made our way through the living room and saw Kyle and Amber asleep on the couch. She was all scrunched up in a ball on one side and bed hog Kyle all sprawled out on the other. Both were still clothed, so that was a plus.

After a quick breakfast and changing into our wetsuits, we made it out to the beach, only one board in tow. The beach was empty except for a few other surfers. The sun was low, hanging over the water and making beautiful orange waves. The air was warm and smelled so much like the sea. It was perfect.

I started to have second thoughts.

"Caleb, I've never done this before. It's so cold and the water's deep and there could be something in there," I complained.

"Well, I hope there's something in there. It *is* the ocean," he said all smart-alecky.

"Caleb," I whined. "Please don't make me."

"This whiny side of you is very cute," he said through a wide grin.

"Funny. I'm serious. I'm scared now. Maybe I'll just watch you."

"You," he said tossing his board and grabbing me around the middle to hug me to him, "are not a chicken. I'll be with you the whole time so there's nothing to worry about. It's really fun once you get the hang of it."

I stared up at him. He really thought I was being silly, didn't he?

"Yes," he answered. "Yes, I do."

I smiled and shook my head at him. "Fine, but if I get bitten by a shark," I poked his bare chest, "you are telling my dad it was your fault."

He grimaced, but laughed. "You drive a hard bargain, lady. Deal."

"Deal."

He kissed me on the tip of the nose and we treaded into the surf.

38

"You're gonna ride in like this first. Now wait for the wave and then paddle, paddle, paddle. Got it?" he instructed as he floated beside me.

"Got it."

I was lying on the board on my belly and he was showing me how to start in the surf and watch for waves. He kept a hand on my lower back the whole time and didn't seem to mind too much that my bikini clad behind was right there in his line of vision.

"Ok." He watched behind me. "Wait, wait...Go! Paddle! Paddle!"

I paddled and got swept under when the wave crashed over me. I started again. He gave the same advice and told me what I did wrong. Over and over we did this. Not once did I make it very few feet before some mishap. He was patient and always gentle in his instruction. I still liked it though I hadn't actually done it yet. It was still fun, but I was determined. "I wish your uncle was here. He could teach me and I'd know it all in five seconds," I said as I climbed back on the board.

"He's good to have around, but sometimes...it's good to learn things the old fashioned way."

"So wise, Confucius," I joked and he smacked me on the butt in retaliation, making me laugh.

"Now, focus, babe. Let's try again. Wait for the wave."

When he said "Go" I paddled hard and felt the wave take me up with it to the crest and then back down as it crashed. I steadied and stood up slowly. I rode it all the way to the shore in one smooth glide. This was the first time without falling off in over two hours of working with Caleb. I stood up in the sand yelling and jumping up and down on my toes in triumph. I saw him swimming my way. Then he ran. Once he reached me, he pulled me into a hug and kissed me on my smiling lips.

"You did it! Was it worth all that trouble?"

"Absolutely," I said grinning. "How long did it take you to learn?"

He smiled looking embarrassed, and said, "Five seconds?"

"Cheating hypocrite!" I laughed and poked his ribs. "And after that lecture about not using your uncle."

"Hey, I was seven, ok? I wasn't too keen on the value of hard work, just the result back then," he said pompously, making me laugh harder.

"That was so awesome. Can we do it again?"

"Well, it's getting late and the beach will be filling up soon. Why don't we quit while we're ahead? I'll bring you back out in the morning, ok?"

"Great. I'm starving anyway."

"Surfing will do that. Let's go and get dressed. We can all go get lunch at this place I want to take you to in town."

"Awesome."

We made our way up to the boardwalk. There was a huge pavilion there that was open on two opposite sides for airflow.

"So, how long do we have to be here?"

"Why," he asked, "ready to go already?"

"No way, I was just curious."

"The family is working hard to make sure everything is safe before I bring you home. You are our number one priority."

"I was just wondering if it was going to take a week or a month. I don't want you to spring it on me one day that it's our last day, ya know? You have no idea of a time frame?"

"No. I'll let you know as soon as I find out something. I expect a call from Dad soon."

"How is your tutoring service? Is everything working fine without you there?"

"Sadly, yes. I'm not even really needed anymore," he said wistfully. "I basically just go in during the school year after classes to help out. We have a lot of volunteers during the summer."

I nodded.

"Soooo," I crooned, changing the subject. "Are you just never going to kiss me again until we go home?"

"What?" he asked genuinely puzzled. "What do you mean?"

"Well, you have barely touched me at all since Bish got here, except to sleep. Are you afraid of him or something?" I goaded him.

He let the board fall to the ground.

He smiled and pulled me to him, closing the distance between us. He lifted my arms to wind around his neck and then pulled me up onto my toes with his hands on my sides, letting his warm lips overlap my top one. His hands went right to my hips and his fingers bunched in the strings and material of my bikini bottom.

I could taste the salt from the seawater on our lips, but as he deepened the kiss, it was all Caleb. And I missed him. His tongue brushed my lip and I instinctively pulled him closer and pressed myself to him as close as I could get. He groaned slightly in surprise, his hands on my hips pulled tighter and then his arms wound around my lower back as he lifted my feet from the sandy floor.

I felt the hard pavilion sidewall on my back as he pressed me against it. My legs automatically wound themselves around his sides. He kissed me differently, with a new fierceness and need than before. It was a little scary, but I felt different too, somehow. Something was changing between us, moving forward. There was only going to be so much more time when pecking and kissing would be enough for either of us. I realized that then. Our imprinted bodies were made for each other and mine wanted Caleb like nothing else.

I bunched my fingers in his hair, pulling and smoothing it. Then I tugged to lean his head back. It broke the kiss, but I moved my mouth to wander under his chin and he reacted with harsh breaths. Then he took my lips again even more greedily. His hands moved to hold the undersides of my thighs and gripped tightly as he slid his mouth from my lips to my chin to my neck to my collarbone. His tongue tasted my skin and I heard a wild desperate noise. Me.

I groaned again, unable to stop myself as I grasped at his hair.

"Ah, Maggie, what are you doing to me?" he said gruffly against my lips before taking them once more, hard and furiously frantic.

For a split second I wondered if I'd be able to say no when I'd felt we'd gone too far and wanted to stop, or if *he'd* be able to.

Then I heard the thoughts before he reached us, but it was too late to stop and not be caught.

"Hey!" A beach patrol ranger called from across the pavilion. "Get your butts out of here, stupid kids."

Caleb and I laughed as he let me down, grabbed my hand and we took off running up the wooden planked walkway. He grabbed the surfboard and we made a swift getaway to the house through the back gate. Once there he stored the board in the storage shed and then grabbed me before I could go in.

"Maggie, wait." He pulled me to him and put his forehead to mine. "I heard you. And yes, things are changing, for me, too. I want you...so bad sometimes I can't stand it." He sighed, his breath washing over my face and neck. "But I'm not pressuring you. I know I've said that before, but I want to make sure you understand that I want what I can get, ok? I'm not going to think you're a tease or whatever. I want you to be really, really ready and there's plenty of stuff we can do until you are. Really nice stuff," he almost growled and kissed my jaw making me giggle.

"Thank you. And I want you, too. It's getting worse by the day," I admitted softly.

"Well, I'm glad I'm not the only one," he said and I could hear his relief.

"Definitely not."

"I'm serious." He pulled back to look at me. "Don't feel pressured. Whenever you say stop, we stop. I would *never* do something unless I knew you wanted it. You know that right?"

41

"Yes. I know that. It was just so intense and we were so...I have no idea why I thought that, it was just a flash. I know you'd never hurt me."

"Good." He kissed me quickly. "I love you, baby," he murmured against my lips.

"I love you, too. Thanks for teaching me to surf."

"Anytime."

He slung his arm over my shoulder and we made our way inside.

Amber was gone by the time we got back, which I was ecstatic about. I did find Kyle picking up trash off the floor in the kitchen though. I looked at him questioningly.

"The trash was all over the floor when I woke up," he said shrugging and went back to it.

Bish was more than willing to get out of the house and Kyle was game for anything, so we all got ready and piled in the Jeep as Caleb took us to this little Panini place in the middle of town called Chew Bread.

It was fantastic. It was even more amazing that the people who ran it were gray, had to be in their seventies, and the food was fast and delicious. And of course, they knew Caleb and Kyle. It seemed everyone knew them everywhere we went.

Caleb bought some of their fresh baked bread and we headed back home. He called Zeke and told him it was a go for the show on Friday. Kyle rolled his eyes, his thoughts were along the lines of thinking Caleb was a showoff.

Once home, Caleb had to leave for his first practice.

"You can come if you want," he told me as he played with my fingers. "It'd probably be fun to watch me mess up from being so out of practice."

We stood in the driveway by the Jeep, the sun blaring down on us but the breeze from the beach keeping us a strange cool at the same time. I loved it.

"I'm fine. I'll find something to do."

He sucked his lip in and out in anxiousness. He had wanted to do this but now...having to actually leave me under someone else's protection was making his veins tingle with discomfort.

"I'll call Zeke. Tell him I can't do it, something came up."

"Caleb," I said and put my hand over our hearts in his chest. "I'm right here. You can feel me the whole time. You'll only be up the beach a ways, right? It'll be fine. Bish and Kyle are here and I'll stay in the house with them, ok?"

"You're sure?"

"I'm sure. It'll do you good to do something other than worry about me."

"But I'll just worry anyway," he sighed. "You know that. This gig isn't something I have to do."

"This is something you've always wanted to do. I'll be fine. I won't go to sleep, I promise."

He fingered my shorter locks in reminder and smiled sadly.

"You can't always help it, Maggie."

"I won't. I think I learned my lesson," I muttered dryly.

"If you're sure, I'll go, but promise me you'll stay inside. And that you'll call me if anything *at all* happens."

"I promise. Have fun."

He looked behind me to the porch and saw Bish watching us. He got a sudden grin on his face and I heard his thoughts a second before he pressed his lips to mine. He engulfed me in his arms and lifted my feet from the gravel. He kissed me long and good until I was breathing funny and my cheeks were flushed in delightful confusion.

"Now," he said through labored breaths, "Bish can have something to complain about."

I laughed, remembering me goading him about not kissing me anymore.

"Yeah, I think you accomplished that. Now you're leaving me to deal with it."

"Yep." He grinned wider. "Have fun."

"I will. Knock 'em dead."

He got into the Jeep and left quickly before he changed his mind. I turned to see Bish with pursed lips and crossed ankles as he watched me make my way to the porch.

"So, what is it that Caleb plans to do with his life?"

I rolled my eyes and moved to sit beside him on the Adirondack chairs.

"Oh, so we've moved on to this? Interrogation?"

"No. I'm curious. It's hard to support yourself let alone others. I want to see what Caleb is planning on doing to support my baby sister since she has no plans to get rid of him."

I sighed, but answered his question.

"He's going to school to be an architect. His family owns a huge firm and he plans to work for them."

"Huh."

Hmmm. Pretty good one.

"Kyle is, too. It's a huge deal."

"Hmm."

43

"Caleb also owns his own company." He looked surprised at that, as I knew he would. "He runs a tutoring service for kids that are struggling in school."

"Really?" A pause. "Dang."

"What?"

"Well, I can't really make fun of him for that now *can* I?"

I laughed and bumped my shoulder against his.

"You could just learn to like him. That'd be easier."

"Maybe," he mused, "but it's hard to like people when they keep things from you."

Once again, I pondered telling him, spilling all my beans without Caleb here to stop me, but I stopped myself and sighed instead.

"Come on. I'll make you an iced coffee. I know you like those."

"Sure," he said and followed me inside.

I went to sit on the couch and sipped my coffee with Kyle while we watched a DVR episode of Saturday Night Live. Jim Carrey was the host and I found myself laughing pretty quickly. Bish heard us and peeked in to see what was going on.

"Jim Carrey's hosting again?" he asked.

"Yeah, man. He's such a frigging idiot. He should host every week," Kyle laughed as a segment came on where he was a psychic medium contacting dead relatives and bumped my arm to get me to agree.

"Mmhmm," I mumbled and cringed when he started impersonating Alan Thicke and Kyle slapped my leg as he laughed harder, doubling over.

"Jeez, Kyle," I said and slapped him back. "Have you ever even seen Growing Pains before?"

"Have you?" he rebutted in a sarcastic voice and shook his head in jest at me, his hand still on my leg squeezed once and I glared at him before he grinned and moved his hand away. "Leave me alone. Carrey's the man. I don't care what he does, it's funny."

"I guess. I prefer Jimmy Fallon and Will Ferrell."

"What? But Carrey is classic funny. Like Adam Sandler."

"Oh, come on," Bish complained. "If you want funny, you gotta go back to the source; Steve Martin and Bill Murray."

"Ok, sure," Kyle agreed. "But times have changed. They aren't the same kinda funny anymore. There's a whole new genre of comedy."

"That's true," Bish conceded and sucked down a gulp of the coffee I'd made him.

"Really?" I asked dubiously. "You're really sitting there debating various degrees and levels of funny when SNL is on, right now?"

"Maggie, Maggie," Kyle crooned. "You are so naïve. My friend over here is correct. And if you wanna see true funny, we need to just go rent Greatest SNL Moments of the cast of '85 – '90 off Netflix and be done with it."

And he did just that.

Caleb was back in a couple hours, just like he said and time flew by. After SNL, Bish and Kyle tried, while Caleb was gone, to teach me how to play Halo and Kyle explained how Call of Duty was so much better but he'd left it at home.

I wondered why with all his money he didn't just go buy another one. I sat on the couch with Kyle most of the time and had to push him or his hand away more than once and eventually just made my way to the suede beanbag to sit by myself. Kyle texted Amber to see if they could meet up again, like maybe tomorrow night. I rolled my eyes.

So, after Caleb came home and we ate some chips and chicken salad sandwiches I made for supper we all sat down to watch a movie. Kyle suggested the latest horror flick so that's what he rented. He sprawled out on the beanbag with his hands behind his head after turning all the lights off. Bish sat in the club chair, one foot over his leg, and Caleb and I took the couch.

I snuggled into his side with his arm around me, but pretty soon I was clutching his shirt in my fist and burying my face in his shoulder every few minutes at the disturbing images. Kyle had picked a gory horror movie about a guy who kidnapped people, locking them in a room and making them solve riddles about the bad things they did in the past. They all died in extremely gory and vile ways.

It made my stomach turn.

While Kyle laughed at me, Caleb kept his hand on my arm or neck at all times to draw off my anxiety, but thought it was funny too. Even Bish chuckled once or twice when I let out a girly little gasp or squeak. It was ironic that I had made so much fun of Beck and her scary movies, but I was the one cringing this time. It hit home a little bit too closely to the well and Sikes. I blocked that part from Caleb.

Eventually I fell asleep against him and tried not to dream of sick men hell bent on making me pay in gory ways for my transgressions.

In the morning, we had our short surfing lesson, to which I made three full glides. Then Caleb went ahead and got his practice over with, with Zeke. When he came back, he told me he was surprised how easy it was to pick it back up and he thought it was going to be great. After lunch, all the guys resumed a previous game of Halo.

They asked me if I wanted to play. I didn't. As soon as I said that, it was like I didn't exist anymore.

I laughed to myself and decided to go explore the house. Caleb had given me a mini tour when we first got there but I wanted a full on exploration. I made my way through all the bedrooms and found my way back to the library upstairs. In there was a wall of nothing but shelves. On those shelves were books and about thirty different picture frames and holders.

I went down the line and read the book titles as I glanced at pictures in between them. I didn't recognize most of the faces but some stood out. Most seemed to be from a long time ago, when Peter and Max, Kyle's father, were younger. They were close then too. There were a couple of Kyle, Jen and Caleb as kids, on a tire swing, in the pool, and on four wheelers.

The books were mostly photo albums or fictions novels. Sometimes I'd run across a book on architecture. Then I saw an older book. Leather bound, wrapped with a leather string of some type. I got a creepy feeling that it was an enchantment tome or spell book of some sort.

It wasn't.

It was the historical account of Raymond Jacobson on the Jacobson family line. I was instantly fascinated. I mean, this was Caleb's grandpa, the one who died strangely and unexpectedly. The one who looked so much like him that I had to double take at his picture. This was his family. As I turned the page, I saw a picture of him and Gran, in their slightly younger years. The bottom of the picture had a handwritten date on it. 1998. They stood, side by side, their arms together as they were lining up their wrist tattoos, laughing.

I realized this was the birthday that Caleb had told me about. The day Gran got her tattoo for him. I smiled and felt oddly connected to them. They were so in love, it was plain as day. I turned the page and saw that he had cataloged all the births, deaths, marriages, ascension dates, and abilities of every member of the family.

I read through them all, every page so carefully written and handled. Each name was perfect in its presentation. I saw Peter and Rachel's marriage. Kyle's parents marriage. I saw so many of their cousins and kin marrying and starting lives. Then there was Caleb's birth. The last thing written was Kyle's birth. There was nothing after that. I realized Maria's birth wasn't even mentioned. I wondered why.

I turned the next page, it was blank, but as I ran my fingers down it I began to see flickers in front of my eyes. Then a vision flashed and took over. At first I was scared, but my body understood what was happening. This was ingrained in me now. I calmed down with a deep breath that my lungs demanded on their own accord and let it happen. I was a Seer. And this was my first vision.

~ Five ~

I saw people. People I didn't know, but understood who they were, Aces. I got a feeling of words and actions. An odd salty and metallic taste, like licking a penny, on my tongue as a word made itself known.

Greed was the first one.

I saw them working so hard to have their mansions built, to drive their fancy buggies down the street, parading themselves as self-proclaimed royalty and prophets. I didn't know these people but I knew they were Aces from long ago. Then I was shown them passing others in the street, others who were poor and hungry and not privileged like we were. They laughed and one used her ability to spill a man's cup of shillings to the ground. They laughed harder as the vision faded.

A new word formed and my tongue tasted bitter air, pride.

I saw more Aces, beating slaves and workers, smirking as they used their magic on others in torture to scare them into submission of their ways, feeling they had the right to do so. Then different Aces. One who, horrendously, killed a servant maid for burning a piece of her hair with an iron as she tried to curl it. She held her throat in her hands without touching her until the servant stopped moving. She threw her down to the expensive rug as if it were something that could be replaced, but as if she were nothing.

Another new word formed, ignorance, and my mouth felt like paper and grit.

I saw Aces playing and running, going to school for things only to earn money and be important. They were abusing their gifts to get ahead and claim fortune, never learning, or striving to keep record of their kind, or keep family close. They never felt the need, nor wanted to learn from past mistakes, nor had a desire to avoid making new ones.

A man became a senator by tricking his voters and using glamours. A magician at a vaudeville house using his control of earthly objects to throw food, leaves and other objects into the air and juggle without touching them causing people to call him a messiah or wizard. A woman lured men away with her charm and then stole their money, leaving them penniless and unknowing of what had happened to them when she used her magic on them.

Then, complacency was another word that formed. The feel of my tongue was like water; tasteless, but consuming, like I was drowning.

I saw old and new. It was everyone I knew and didn't know. I saw the Watsons. Their Champion before Sikes standing by and watching his clan become something that went against everything he knew, yet he did nothing to stop it.

I saw another clan, a young girl and her cousins spending thousands a week on trinkets and parties, and giving their bodies and morals away freely to be popular and special in the world's eyes. Their parents watching as they did so and thought it was common teenage behavior, as the times had changed.

Many more clans flashed before me, their transgressions lay open for me as if I were a judge. Then the Jacobson clan came to me and I held my breath. Their only transgression shown to me was not taking charge, not saying something and letting it all happen around them, though they held themselves in check. Many years ago, the Jacobson clan was the leader of all Virtuoso. They organized the meetings in London. They were the historians and record keepers for all. They watched over the years as each family was slowly destroyed by their magic, their use of greed for personal gain, their flaunting it in their pride, their ignorance of how to control themselves and their children...their ignorance of how to use a power that was given *to* them.

The power was a gift, not a birthright. Not a power to parade and abuse for our entertainment and pleasure.

A gift that was taken away because of those reasons and now returned to the one family, the Jacobson's, who were deemed worthy of redemption.

And that was the last word I felt. Redemption. The taste on my tongue was sweet and fluffy, like whipped cream.

It showed me that Caleb and I were the ones to put an end to it all and return the Virtuoso back to what they once were, a selfless, caring, outreaching, helpful people. They were people who were given gifts to help not to hurt, and to build up and prosper each other, not tear down in power play and hatefulness. Caleb and I were to be the key, the new leaders of the new Ace order and keepers of the right way.

In the glimpses, I saw Caleb and I fought side by side, sometimes literally. Hand to hand. Sometimes we mentally fought a battle of wits with others, sometimes, a battle of wills but, always together. The last vision was of us, old and gray and blissfully wrinkled as we smiled at each other. He kissed the end of my nose as he sometimes did now and said he loved me, still.

I gasped as I felt the cold air in the room and I came back to myself. I was oddly tired and drained feeling, but it wasn't in a bad way, just a productive feeling. I was still sitting in the library. I had no idea how long I'd been there but I felt a new sense of something. A purpose. I looked down and saw under my hand there were words written. The page that had been empty before the vision now held the words, written in an old antique pen, the words that I felt so much feeling for.

Greed.

Pride.

Ignorance.

Complacency.

Redemption

Then under that, it read: **The fate of all rest in the hands of all.**

I knew it was a warning, I even felt heat go through my body. If we didn't straighten this out, it would be bad for all of us, all clans, and all Aces. I knew my purpose now, to speak to the Reunification coming up in a few weeks in London. I was supposed to address them, warn them.

My heart beat steady in anticipation of it, and a scared but slow rhythm of having to be the messenger, but nothing to alarm Caleb with. I didn't know if I was ready for all that. I was no one. I was a newcomer. How would they feel with a person who'd only been in the clan for a couple weeks, and only a teenager at that, coming in and telling them to stop being greedy, prideful, ignorant people who take everything as it comes and doesn't fight back?

I was sure that would go over just swell.

I kept the book. I felt like I had some claim to it now. I didn't know if anyone would mind, but for some reason, I felt that it was supposed to be with Caleb and me. I set it on my bag in the upstairs bedroom and made my way downstairs. I was lost. Lost in translation. Trying to figure out how to decipher everything I'd been shown and where to go from here.

I heard the doorbell. I was starving, I knew that, and I didn't smell anything cooking so I figured I must not have been gone as long as it seemed. Maybe someone had called for take out but it had seemed very long. Every vision was detailed and precise. It was like it all happened in real time but that couldn't be true.

As I hit the bottom step, I saw Caleb make his way to the kitchen with boxes in his hands. Kyle was coming from the den and stopped mid-stride in a halt. He stared at me in wonder.

I was puzzled. Could he tell I'd had a vision? His mind was empty.

He came slowly towards me and smiled. He took my hand, kissed the back of my fingers, and then touched his head to them in an odd bow.

"You're the Visionary," he said reverently as he looked at me as if he was seeing me for the very first time.

"What? Kyle, what are you doing?"

"You have no idea, do you?" he asked. "You have no idea what you are."

I shook my head in confusion.

"Come on, guys. Eating...time," Caleb mumbled as he came around the corner. He too stopped and looked at me with a weird new look of admiration. He came forward, just as Kyle had done, took my hand and kissed my fingers, and then touched them to his head before looking back to me. "Oh, wow, Maggie." Cautiously he touched the side of my neck, as if he wasn't sure he had the right to anymore. "You're the Visionary."

"What does that mean? How do you know that?"

His fingers hovered over the side of my neck. "You have a mark here, a symbol indicating who you are."

"And what am I?" I asked softly.

"You are the Visionary," he repeated. "The One who sees all, knows all."

"I don't..." I mumbled. "Caleb, please stop looking at me like that."

"I'm sorry." That seemed to knock him out of his trance. "What happened, Maggie?"

"I was in the library. I found your Grandpa Ray's old record book. It had all your family's births and marriages in it. Then I had a vision-"

"What vision?" Bish barked in. "What are you talking about?"

We all looked at Bish in alarm. We'd been running our mouths, forgetting about our other guest.

"Nothing, it was in a book I was reading upstairs," I half lied and grabbed Caleb's hand to tow him. "Let's eat."

We ate our Chinese at the barstools at the counter. Caleb and Kyle couldn't keep their eyes off me, like I was the queen of frigging England sitting at their table or something. It was really starting bug me. I gave them a look that said so. They both looked away bashfully. I wondered if Bish could see the mark on my neck but I guessed not. He hadn't said anything about it and I figured since the family crest tattoos on the wrist were only seen by Aces that this probably was too.

I was anxious to see what it looked like, but didn't want to as well. Caleb and Kyle's behavior about it all was strange and a little scary.

We heard the doorbell again and Kyle cursed as he shot up to get it. I heard him dismissing Amber with a half-hearted apology and then he came back to finish his meal.

After supper, Bish said he was tired and was going to head to bed. As soon as he was gone, I grabbed both their arms and pulled them into the den, closing and locking the bay doors and pulling the shades down. I turned to look at them.

"What? Explain."

"Well," Caleb said and blew a loud breath as he sat on the ottoman across the room. "We've always been told a story, a bedtime story you could say, about a prophetess who would come. She will be a light in the dark to our people. She would wield the sword of justice and the shield of fortification. She would speak all tongues, know all things, see all, be all that we needed her to be. She would bring a new order." He smiled in awe at me. "I always thought it was just a story, a fairytale."

"Yeah," Kyle chimed. "Nobody ever believed it. It was just fun to joke about. Like the Y2K bug or the supposed end of the world in 2012. But this- you're real..."

"But I'm still me."

"Yes," Caleb assured, "you are. But you are the Visionary *because* you're you."

"What does that mean?"

"You're special. Even more so than we thought before." I sighed and he held his hand up. "Now wait. Just listen. God controls us, watches over us, and has called you. Chosen you to be the Visionary because of who you are, inside. The kind of person you are. It's a position of privilege and responsibility and power."

"We've always been told," Kyle stated, "the person who came would change everything. They would be the most important person we'd ever meet and we'd be lucky to see her in our lifetime."

I nodded and pursed my lips. I was suddenly very upset...and even a little pissed. Things would never be the same now, I could see that. Caleb would look at me with that goofy grin of reverence every day and never touch me again and Kyle would bow at my feet every time I said good morning. I had enough of this whole 'she's special thing' before this, and now...

It's a great honor. You were chosen for this. Not only are you young and human and the first person to imprint in a long time...but you're the Visionary. The one we've been waiting for.

I glared at him. "You are not helping."

It was the first time I could remember being mad at him.

"I'm sorry," he said quickly and actually lowered his head, like in shame.

That lit the fire.

"Ok! Enough! I will not be some deity for you to worship." They both looked stunned that I had yelled so forcefully. I closed my eyes for my admission. "I am this Visionary, ok. I feel it. The things I saw upstairs are going to change the way things are. But that doesn't make me anything special, it makes me knowledgeable. I'm not an angel or a goddess or a prophetess or whatever else. I'm me. I'm still your soulmate. I am the same person I was before all this and if you're going to treat me different just because I...I-" I stopped.

If I said another word, I was going to cry. Burst into tears. I just wanted to be normal, to be with Caleb and now all that was over. I felt the loss of my life as I had known it. I sucked in a ragged breath and buried my face in my hands.

"Maggie, you have to understand. You are special. You're different. Things can't just go back to us sitting, playing Halo with you in my lap everyday, ok? Things are going to change. You're going to have to be ready for that."

I lifted my head and saw them both looking sternly at me like I was a child throwing a temper tantrum. Caleb heard my mind, knew what I was gonna do. I saw his hand snake out to grab my arm but I pulled away forcefully and went right out the front door.

I was livid.

I ran to the Jeep and slammed the door right as I saw him step off the porch. I didn't see the keys anywhere but I searched in a mad rush. I locked my door so he couldn't stop me just as he reached my door and banged on the window.

"Maggie, stop. Where are you going?"

"Away," I said as I looked in the visor and still didn't see them.

I beat my palms on the steering wheel in frustration and the Jeep roared to life. Just like that. It was like I willed it. I looked at Caleb through the window and he was just as stunned. He pulled the keys from his pocket, looked at them and then back at me in wonder.

I didn't wait any longer. I put the Jeep in reverse, no matter how it cranked, it was drivable, and that's all I cared about. I pulled onto the highway with Caleb in my rearview mirror, his hands going in the air in a frustrated move before he ran back into the house. My heart pounded and ached. It didn't want me to leave, not mad, and not like this. We weren't made to fight, I remembered our first fight in Kyle's back yard, how it hurt me, but I didn't turn around.

I had no doubt he was going to call his father. And mine. And then Caleb and Kyle would contemplate on how to bring me back and why I was acting insane. Did he really not know? He was supposed to be my equal, my love, my life. And now he was treating me as if I was someone he no longer deserved and needed to be groomed for a life of privilege. I was someone to be managed and bowed down to as if in obedience.

Maggie, don't do this. You need to come back and face this-

I pushed him out and blocked him.

How dare he treat me like some spoiled prodigy who was on the warpath or something? I was me! I am me! Wasn't that the whole point of everything I was shown upstairs in that vision was that their race was spoiled and unclean in their actions and past thoughts: Greed, Pride, Complacency. Those weren't minor offenses and there they were trying to worship me. This was every girl's dream, right? Not mine.

I hated it. I begged for God to take it all back. I didn't want to be the Visionary, I just wanted Caleb.

I drove for a while and then pulled into an ice cream place off the main highway. I tried to breathe and calm down so Caleb wouldn't call a cab and follow my heartbeat to me.

I got a text from Bish.

Caleb said you left. I heard all the shouting. WTH Mags? Get your butt back here and answer me right now.

Then a call from Caleb came in. I pressed the red button to send it straight to voicemail and didn't bother to listen. I wasn't really angry at him. Not really. I was just angry. I just wanted my life back. My chest begged for Caleb, my fingers twitching. I pushed it away.

I pulled the visor down to look in the mirror. I saw the telling mark they had seen. It was a half sun half moon that put together made a whole with the line where they met blurry and gray, fading into each other. The sun half was white with wide slithering rays protruding. The moon half was black and smooth. It was small, about an inch and half maybe, right on the side of my neck. I ran my fingers over it. It wasn't really a tattoo, it looked more solid than that, but my skin felt smooth to the touch. It was odd.

The two guys behind the counter at the deserted ice cream place were giving me odd looks for sitting it the parking lot and not coming up so I sighed and got out. I had seen Caleb stash a few bills into the ashtray. I retrieved them and went to the counter. It was one of those outdoor places with benches and umbrellas and you ordered through a walk-up window.

"Hi."

I tried to sound normal.

"Hi, there. What can I get for you?"

"Um..." All the flavors were crazy celebrity names. I had no idea what was in them. "Which one is the most like rocky road?"

54

He looked amused.

"Rocky Balboa, of course."

"Oh. Ok, well then I'll take a small Rocky Balboa."

I gave him his money and waited as they made it. He handed it to me and smiled.

"Anything else?"

"No, thank you."

"Are you sure? You look kind of...upset."

"I'm fine. Thank you though."

"Ok. Have a nice night, miss."

I scoffed at the miss. I couldn't be more than a year older than him and he called me miss. It was the ascension's fault that I looked different.

I went to a table and sat down. My phone sat pitifully on the table in front of me. I had two more texts from Bish and Caleb called me three times. Then one missed call from Dad already. Great.

I pushed it aside and ate a spoonful of the gooey goodness in front of me. I was winding down, thinking I had overreacted now that I had a chance to really think about it. But I didn't! They were the ones acting crazy.

They bowed. Bowed to me!

After all my ice cream was gone, I threw my cup away and decided to walk around. I know, it was dark and late, in California no less, but I couldn't go back to the Jeep and head back to the house yet. In fact, I was sure I couldn't even remember how to get to the beach house again.

I saw a cleared area set off to the side of the stand, like it was important. As I got closer, I saw it was a small enclave of big rocks in a circle. The sign said it was a memorial to the men and woman who'd served our country. I sat there on a bench in the middle of those rocks in the dark and cried. I cried for everything, all the right reasons and even the wrong ones; the petty and silly ones. I was already going so I might as well get it all out.

I felt terrible. My heart was fluttering uncomfortably with aching for Caleb, but I tried to breathe through it so he wouldn't think I was in trouble. I decided to see him and make sure he was ok. I focused on him and saw he was sitting on the front porch steps, phone in hand. His hands were shaking slightly. He reached one up to rub his heart and he sighed harshly, wincing. I knew he was hurting like me, worse than me. It made me feel horrible, but I had to stay put for just a little longer.

He jumped when the phone rang.

"Maggie!" he said in panic. "Oh, Dad, yeah, she's still gone." Peter said something and Caleb grimaced. "No. She's blocking me. I can't get through to her and she won't answer her phone." A pause and he scrubbed his face with his hand.

55

"I know that, Dad, ok? I know I messed up, but I can't fix it until she talks to me now can I?...Yes, I'm sure she's the Visionary, she has the mark and she told us she had a vision...I know...She's my number one priority, I could care less about this Visionary crap right now, all I care about is getting her back here safe...No. It's like I was under a spell or something. I was in complete awe. It was strange, like I couldn't control myself...I know that, Dad, but she's my significant, first, before anything else. I don't care if we're married or not. She's mine to protect and that's more important that any of this other stuff. Everyone else can go to hell for all I care if they think I'm gonna step back and let them come in and take her from me. Who better to take care of her than me?" he said in a vehement and upset tone. Then, "Yes, I know, I screwed up already but I won't again. When she comes back I'll...I'll...I don't know. I'll do something. I'll fix it." Then he hung up and beat his fist on the porch steps rail.

I wanted to squeeze him to me, hug him until it all went away but I couldn't move, not yet. There seemed to be something I needed to do first.

Caleb sat up straight and sucked in a quick breath.

"Maggie?"

I watched in awe. Could he feel me there watching?

"Maggie, come back. I'm sorry. Please, baby," he pleaded. "I'm dying here not knowing where you are."

I yanked away before he could read me and figure out where I was. I looked around me to the big stones and saw a figure coming my way. The ice cream guy.

"Hey, what are you doing out here?"

"Just sitting."

"Well, it's not really safe for a girl to be alone at night out here, you know."

I could just make him out in the moonlight.

"I'll be ok," I said and smiled at him in reassurance.

"Are you a black belt or something?"

I chuckled remembering Uncle Max giving me karate 'lessons' in my mind. "Yes, I am actually."

"Oh. Well..." That seemed to take the steam out of his argument. "I still don't think you should be out here."

"I won't be long."

"What's the matter? I knew something was wrong earlier when I asked you."

"I'm just going through some stuff."

"Aren't we all?" he said with a chuckle and sat down beside me on the bench.

"I guess, but my stuff is really, really, scary complicated."

He nodded like he understood. Then he pulled a receipt paper from his pocket and wrote something down. Then he ripped off a piece and gave it to me.

"I'm not trying to be a creepy guy or anything but I've been chewed up and spit out by this city on more than one occasion." I took the paper and saw it was a phone number. "I live across the road, in the crappiest apartment you've ever seen." He pointed. If you ever need a place to crash or someone to...vent to, call me."

I smiled at him.

"That's really sweet, but I'm not from here. I have no idea how long I'll stay."

"Georgia?" he asked.

"Tennessee."

"I could tell from the accent. I'm from Nebraska. Yeah, we can spot the out-of-staters," he laughed. "We all have that open wound look going." He laughed again and I joined him. "I'm serious. You look like a nice girl. I wouldn't let whoever it is you're worried about get you down."

"It's a thing actually. Something...happened to me. And no, I'm not pregnant," I said, when he got the look. "I'm just not ready to be what everyone else wants me to be."

"Aha. Well, at least you have people who care about you it sounds like. Some of us haven't seen our family in a very long time and the friends I have would stab me in the back in a minute for a few extra bucks."

"I'm sorry. That must suck."

"I get by. Life is long and then you're gone," he said sadly and twirled his cell in his fingers. "Alright, well I'll let you get back to...whatever it is you're doing out here. You weren't planning on sleeping out here were you? My offer stands about crashing-"

"No. I'll head home before that."

"You're sure you're ok?"

"Positive."

He shrugged like there was nothing else he could do.

"Ok then." He held out his hand. "Nice to meet you, Tennessee."

I smiled.

"You, too, Nebraska."

And as soon as I touched his hand I was blinded by another vision.

~ Six ~

I saw the boy whose hand I was holding and he was leaving, suitcase in hand. His father was angry, his mother crying and his brother laughing a jealous and vindictive laugh as he watched him go.

What the boy didn't know was that his mother went after him. She watched his beat up car leave the driveway and tried to stop him, but it was too late. He was gone. She yelled at her family for making him go. She slapped his father and packed her bags to go look for him.

He didn't have a cell phone when he left and she had found no way to reach him. That was four months ago. She was still looking and searching.

I pulled back with a gasp and heard him do the same.

"How did you do that?" he gasped out.

"You saw that?" I said and looked at him in surprise.

"Of course! What was that? Are you a psychic or something?"

"No."

"Is it true? Did my mom come looking for me?"

I looked at his young, eager face filled with hope.

"Yes. It's true." I had a feeling like I knew what to do but I didn't want to. Ultimately I sighed and caved, focusing on her face in my mind. She had burgundy hair in a messy bun and her face was worn from wear and worry. "She's...working at a diner. Her shirt says Joe's on it."

"Joe's. There's a Joe's across the railroad tracks."

"She's thinking about you...at a baseball game and you were pitching."

"Oh, my... I used to pitch in high school. What are you?" he said, but it wasn't facetious...it was in reverence.

58

And it made me wonder if everyone, even humans, would be able to tell something was different about me.

"She's there. Go. She's dying to see you," I told him.

"I don't know how you...I can't ever repay you. Thank you."

"You just did."

He got up and started to take off, but stopped. "By the way, I'm Craig."

"Maggie."

"I don't know what you're running from, Maggie, but I get the feeling that you should be embracing it. You can't run from destiny."

Then he took off with a wave.

I felt tingly all over. Destiny? What a strange thing to say. It was destiny that everything had happened up until now, I knew that. Caleb and my imprint visions proved that. One of them had already come true and there was no stopping it. After everything that happened to us, we still ended up where the vision of our future said we would. No matter what we tried to do or how we tried to twist things, we would end up right where we were always meant to be. That meant...I was definitely meant to be the Visionary. Crap! Why'd that kid have to be so darn perceptive?

I took a deep breath, feeling the pain in my chest, and peeked back at Caleb. He was still on the porch but this time he was pacing. In his mind, I could see I'd been gone for over three hours now. He was so worried. His fists were clenched, his jaw tight, and he was running through scenarios of me falling asleep in the Jeep and Marcus doing worse than cutting my hair, or me getting mugged, or me getting a flat tire on the freeway.

Caleb.

Oh, thank you, God. Maggie, are you alright? Where are you?

I'm coming home.

Maggie...

Not now, Caleb. I'll be there in a little while.

I love you. I love you and I'm sorry. Just be careful.

Love you, too.

And then I somehow found my way home. I figured it must have been something supernatural like starting cars without keys or having visions of human mothers, but didn't fight it. In half an hour or so, I was pulling into the driveway. I saw him turn and take a deep breath when he saw me.

I got out and turned to face the Jeep door when I shut it. Now that I was there, I wasn't ready to face him yet. I closed my eyes and knew he was coming, but kept them closed.

I felt Caleb's arms come around me and though I wasn't sure if I was still mad at him or not, I knew I was sorry for how I acted. I couldn't resist him anyway. I turned and wrapped my arms around his shoulders and pressed my face into his neck. I sighed unsteadily and he pulled back. He put a finger under my chin to make me look at him.

"I'm sorry. I mean it. I'm so sorry. I was so caught up in the novelty of it all that I forgot that you were still mine to look after. Forgive me," he whispered.

I looked at him closely. He was sincere and I could feel it rushing through him to me. "I'm sorry, too. I overreacted...childishly."

"No, you didn't. You had every right to drive off." I gave him a look to make sure he wasn't saying I had a right because I was the Visionary. "Not because of anything other than the fact that I acted like a jackass. You're my soulmate." He moved his hand to cup my cheek. "My significant, above all else, and you really needed me to explain it all and help you get through it, but instead I was so caught up in thinking you were special that I forgot. You are special, but you always have been. From the moment I met you, not the moment we imprinted. You were always different for me and I promise you I won't forget it again."

"I need you at my side, Caleb, not at my feet. I'm still the same person-" I started, but he stopped me with a thumb over my lips.

"From now on, you'll be just my Maggie to me."

I was filled with relief and just then realized that his touch hadn't been soothing me, just like after our first fight. Now it was and it was a wash of calm and relief, the tightness in my chest loosened. We both sighed happy breaths into each other's faces. I wrapped my arms tighter and he pulled me as close as I could get to him, pressing me to him.

We stayed like that for who knew how long, just being with each other. I needed him now more than ever and he realized that and was ready to be by my side no matter what.

I pulled back to look at him. His hair was a mess and he looked like he was ready to fall into bed, but he was still gorgeous, and still mine. He was waiting on me again, making sure I really forgave him and wasn't just giving in. So I pulled him down to my lips, angled them to kiss him easily and sweetly under the moon and stars and streetlamps. His gratefulness almost swept me away. The beach wind blew my hair in all directions until I pulled away slightly and chuckled a little.

"You're not gonna believe what I've been up to."

He looked a little scared at that and pulled me tighter to him out of instinct. "What do you mean?"

"Let's go inside. I'll show you."

60

We walked through the door together, hand and hand. Kyle was there pacing, waiting for me. He smiled hugely and took my other hand, kissing it.

"I'm so glad you're ok."

"Kyle, we need to talk," Caleb said pulling my fingers from Kyle's grasp.

Kyle bristled, crossing his arms and twisting his lips.

"This isn't about my feelings for Maggie. This is about my respect for the Visionary. You can't get jealous over that. Get over yourself."

"I know what this is about, but Maggie doesn't want that." He looked back at me with a smile. *Go ahead. Let him have it like you did me.*

I got right to it.

"No more bowing," I said sternly, looking at Kyle. "No more kissing hands, no more gooey-eyed stares like I'm a princess or something. I'm just Maggie, treat me like you always have, ok?"

"What? What do you mean? You *are* the Visionary?"

"Yes, I am and this Visionary says she doesn't want to be seen as anyone but who she is. I'm Maggie, the one who gets to see things but I'm still your friend, the same old me. Promise?"

"Yeah, sure," Kyle said with a hand through his hair. Then he looked up at Caleb. "He doesn't have to promise? You want *him* groveling at your feet, huh?" he spouted bitterly.

"Yes. I promised, too," Caleb said sincerely as he placed a hand on my cheek and smiled at me to prove it.

I saw a change come over Kyle before I heard his pained thoughts. He shook with the rage of it.

"Of course," he sneered and looked at me then Caleb, his eyes blazing. "Not only do you imprint when no one else does, and steal the girl I want in the process, but now you get to put your hands on the Visionary. You're soul mates with the Visionary! What did *you* do to deserve that?" he asked with a hateful voice.

"Kyle," I intervened for Caleb, feeling his shock run through me. I thought of what to say and what to do. "Don't be like this. It's not as glamorous as it seems."

"Says the girl who knows everything."

"I don't know everything! I know a lot of stuff I didn't before, but I don't know everything. I still can't tell you the population size of Lithuania," I said trying to ease the mood.

He actually cracked a small smile and I thought I'd reached him, but he kept shaking his head.

"I'm sorry, Maggie. I'm just so tired of playing second string."

61

With that, he walked away. Flashes of Kyle being benched in football, back-up to Chad, came. Then, following Caleb all through his years and never seeming to get what he wanted before Caleb did, and me, always out of his reach. Caleb tried to go after him, but I stopped him.

"He just needs to cool off," I assured. I felt sorry for Kyle but we had bigger fish to fry. I had a sudden need to speak to Peter. I turned to Caleb and said, "Besides, you have to call your father."

"I already did. Why?"

"I need to speak to the Champion."

"He's on his way already," Caleb said as he closed his phone. "He jumped the first plane out of Tennessee as soon as he heard from me that you...ran off. Sorry."

"It's ok. The sooner he gets here the better."

"What's up?" he asked concerned.

"It's-"

"Maggie!" Bish yelled over us as he descended the stairs. "What's going on? Why didn't you text me back and tell me you were ok?" He turned a hellish look on Caleb. "You knew I was worried sick. How could you not come tell me when she got back?"

"Sorry. We've been a little busy."

"Ah," Bish groaned, "you can keep your little escapades out of my ears, but you should have told me." He came to stand in front of me. "So, you had a fight with your boyfriend and ran off. Really? That's the kind of girl you are now?"

I flicked a glance at Caleb. What could I say? But I hated him thinking those things about me.

"I guess. We worked it out though," I said in a small voice.

"Oh," he said sarcastically and flicked his hands in the air. "I'm so glad because that's what I was worried about." He turned to go back upstairs. A quick glance at the wall clock told me it was almost four in the morning. "I'm going back to bed. I guess I'll see you in the morning if you're still here. Who knows what Caleb might do next," he mocked, his voice dripping with sarcasm and disappointment.

I felt drained and sad and spent. I was ready for bed and Caleb, though in his mind he was anxious to see what I'd done while away and why I needed his father here, he was also tuned into me. He was worried that I wasn't handling it all very well and that I was wearing down. I couldn't argue with him as he lifted me in his arms and carried me to our couch bed.

We lay there, warm and comfortable, and I decided to share with him what had happened at the ice cream place. I didn't want him completely out of the loop once I had to show everyone everything. I opened my mind and pushed my images to him, my forehead to his. My skin tingled and even though I was almost drifting asleep, my body knew just what to do. It was so easy now.

He gasped as we connected and he saw me buy ice cream and go sit in the stones. Then the guy who I showed a vision about his mom, and I saw her and told him where to go. Then I showed him on the porch as he spoke to his father and called to me when he felt my presence. Then I came home.

"I knew you were there on the porch with me. I felt you."

"I remember. Sorry."

"No more apologies." He kissed my neck. "But you can't run out on me like that, Maggie. I was in agony worrying about you."

"I know. I'm sorry about that, too. My chest hurt so badly," I said pressing my hand to my heart, feeling the memory of pressure.

"I know. I could feel you, and me. It was...just please don't do that again," he begged softly. "Ok? You can slam the bathroom door in my face if it helps, but you can't leave. It hurts too much."

I turned to him. I knew he was hurting, like me, but I almost forgot he felt all my pain too. And I felt like a double idiot.

"I'm so sorry-"

He cut off my apology with a kiss. He moved to hover over me, not pressing me, but letting me feel his weight. His fingers slid down my cheeks and neck, caressing me. He nuzzled my nose with his. "How does it feel? Our first *real* fight now out of the way?"

"It sucked."

"Yeah," he agreed with a small chuckle, "but do you feel better? Being able to stand up to me? Not feeling so trapped by our imprint?"

"I didn't stand up to you. I ran away."

"Yes, but you did it knowing that was exactly what I didn't want you to do."

"I'm sorry-"

"No, I'm not scolding you, Maggie," he chuckled. "I'm just saying, I told you it'd get easier, didn't I? To fight? I want you to feel free, not like you have to please me on everything just because your body rebels if you don't."

"I don't like it anyway. I don't ever want to fight, I want to talk. We should be able to talk through anything together. If you had gotten in the Jeep and ran off like that, I wouldn't have been so worried. I'd have been angry. I'm sorry."

"It's ok. Even though it sucked, I was proud of you, too."

"What? Why?"

"Because," he said. He nuzzled my nose once more and then rolled to be back on his side, facing me. "You felt the pain, but fought through it for what you thought was right. I want you to be bound to me, Maggie, don't misunderstand me on that. I want to feel everything in you and be connected, but I don't want to control you. It feels sometimes like I'm controlling you, even though it's really the imprint."

"You're not. I want to be bound to you, too," I assured, wrapping his shirt front in my fist. "It makes me feel safe. Let's just forget tonight ever happened. I'm safe, you're safe. Let's just go to sleep, ok?"

"Ok."

"I love you, Caleb. You're really good to me."

"I love you." He kissed me. "You're the most important thing to me, Visionary or not." He put his face to mine, noses touching, heads touching. "I love you so much it hurts," he whispered.

And I kissed him and he kissed me until we eventually fell asleep.

When we woke late in the morning, Caleb said he needed to go for a swim so I went into the kitchen. I expected there to be tension and awkwardness in the house, but to my surprise, Bish had cooked breakfast and Kyle greeted me with a small sideways hug and a smile.

"Morning, sunshine. Sleep well?" he asked.

"Yeah, I did. I'm sorry I kept you guys up so late. Bish, you too. I acted...childish. I'm sorry."

"Forgotten already," Kyle said and grabbed a piece of bacon that Bish had put on a plate to the side.

Bish growled at him. "If you snag one more piece of bacon, I swear..." Bish turned to look at me. "It's ok, Maggie. I was a little harsh last night, but in my defense, I was sleepy. I'm just glad you're ok."

"I'm fine. It was my fault; I take full responsibility. Sorry."

"Accepted. Now grab a plate and dig in before Kyle eats all yours, too."

I grabbed a plate of bacon and Bish's western hash browns. He used to make these for us when he lived at home. Kyle grabbed a piece of bacon from my plate, too, putting his finger to his lips to shh me when I started to protest. He grinned, winked, and then kissed my cheek before heading off to go play Halo, his mind said.

I sat at the table after pouring a glass of milk. Caleb was still swimming laps, which I felt good about. He didn't feel the need to be with me every second, which meant he believed I was safe here.

"So," Bish sang, coming to sit beside me with his own plate piled high. "What's on the agenda for today?"

"No idea. Caleb's father is gonna be here sometime, probably tonight."

"Why?"

"Because Caleb called him after our fight and he jumped the first plane out," I answered without thinking.

"Wait, what?" He looked at me sharply, setting his fork down to the table with more force than necessary. "Why would Peter care if you and Caleb had a fight and you ran away? Why does that warrant a visit from your boyfriend's father?"

"He's just a really cautious guy," I said through my glass as I took a sip. *Enough of this; it ends now.*

"I'm not buying it, Maggie." He stood up and banged his fist on the table, making me jump in surprise, but I was also a little frightened. He was glaring and leaning over me. "What the hell is going on? Tell me now. I don't care what it is. Be pregnant, be married, be in a cult, whatever! But you better start giving me some answers that make sense!" he yelled loudly.

"Maggie!" Caleb called and I heard his footsteps as he ran, feeling my heart rate jump. "Maggie!" When he saw me, he sighed and came forward, but then saw Bish red-faced, angry, and towering over me with his fist bunched on the table. He came, his swim trunks and a towel around his neck still, and pulled me from my chair to put me behind him. "What are you doing, man?"

"She's my sister. I can yell at her if I want to. What are you doing?" He looked from me to him, and then narrowed his eyes. "You think I'd hurt her?"

"She's terrified, dude. You tell me."

My own sister? Can they see the monster in me?

"I'm fine," I said softly and moved in front of Caleb, which he wasn't too keen about. "Bish, why can't you just accept that I'm in love with Caleb? Everyone knows it. His family is my family. I'm going to marry him and have little Calebs running around one day." Caleb's heart jumped so violently with joy from hearing me say it, I felt it. "You are the only one who hasn't figured out yet that I don't need saving. Not from him and not from his family." Caleb's hands went to my waist from behind and he squeezed affectionately. "I'm fine here, Bish. I want you to stop being so worried about me that you can't even enjoy anything. We're in California! Live a little."

Bish shook his head.

They've got her so in deep with whatever this is that she can't even see it anymore. Maybe I can take her one night. Take the Jeep and get away from them, from everyone, for a while.

"No," Caleb and I both protested at the same time and Caleb pulled me to him as we read Bish.

Crap. There would be no way to cover that up. Crap. Crap.

Bish eyed us both. He shook his head and backed away.

I'm going crazy.

He went upstairs to his room and slammed the door.

I wanted to go after him and tell him everything. I was seconds away from following him. I'd had enough of watching him suffer and fight for me.

Caleb turned me to him and pressed my face into his neck with a hand in my hair.

"It's ok. We'll...I'll tell my father. Maybe we can...I don't know. I don't want to lie to you and tell you it'll work out when it might not, but I can't stand to see you upset either."

I pulled back to see his face.

"I'm not worth all this trouble."

"Yes, you are," he said hotly. "Don't ever say that. Bish wouldn't care so much if you weren't."

"But I'm-"

I was about to say I had caused Caleb and his family a lot of grief too but he cut me off.

"Are you serious? After everything we've been through are we back to this? Do you really not know how I feel about you by now?"

I sighed as he put his hand on my cheek.

"You're right. I'm sorry."

"You apologize a lot lately," he said through a small smile.

"I'm an idiot a lot lately."

"No, you're not. You're just a silly girl," he said and then laughed when I poked him in the stomach. "Ow."

"I just feel so bad about Bish. I wish..." I said and heard the tears threatening.

"I know." He pulled my face up with his hand cupping my cheek and kissed me on my trembling mouth. He smoothed his hands down my arms, my back, my hair, my cheek, soothing me.

"There's a picture of you two in the dictionary under 'get a room'," Kyle said from behind me.

I'd been so focused on Caleb's hands I hadn't heard him come in. We pulled apart and I licked my lips. Caleb smirked and then turned to Kyle, expecting a fight but Kyle was smiling.

"How about we take Maggie and Bish to that sub place on Bradshaw for lunch? I've been dying for a Philly."

"Sure," Caleb said, unsure, "if Bish wants to go. He's not really happy with us right now."

"Because why?"

"Because," I explained, "he knows something is going on and I can't tell him. He knows I'm lying and I've never lied to him before."

He smiled in sympathy and came to put an arm around my shoulder. Caleb cocked his head at him.

"Sorry. I know it sucks, but things are different now, right? You can't just blab to him about everything anymore. You're doing what's best for him. He just doesn't know it. He'll get over it eventually."

Caleb and I both stared at him. What was up with Kyle?

"What?" he said in his defense of our stares.

"Thanks, Kyle. I just wish I could tell him but not tell him, you know?"

"Yeah, I know. Alright, I'm going to go see if Bish wants to annihilate aliens with me."

"Ok."

He left and I was just as stunned as Caleb but let it go. I pulled Caleb with me to the back porch. I lay down on the big soft white cushions of the porch swing and pulled him down with me. I remembered this from the plane. Caleb had shown me a vision of him pressing me into these cushions while he kissed me wickedly. I was ready for some more of our visions to start coming true.

"I agree," he said to answer my thoughts and kissed me softly as we lay side by side in the breeze and shade.

Sometimes we barely pecked or brushed our lips and then other times he'd push and pull me and I could barely breathe under the assault of his lips. After a few minutes, I could hear Bish and Kyle in the den playing their video game and it made me glad that Bish was at least out of his room. We stayed out there until it was time for lunch.

At the restaurant Kyle and Caleb took us to, Bish didn't speak. He just watched us, watched other people. His thoughts were exactly what I expected; wondering what was going on for real. He was mad at Dad for being naïve. He was mad at Caleb for feeling the need to touch me every ten seconds and mad at me for lying to him.

I just avoided his gaze and tried to tune him out.

~ Seven ~

We did a little shopping before going home. Kyle wanted to buy a new game controller and some more swim trunks. We went to this really huge, two-story surf shop. In Bish's mind, I could see that he wanted a new pair of shorts. His were some he snagged from Dad before he boarded the plane and he hated them. He also hated not having any money either. He eyed a few pairs and then went to stand by the door and wait for us to get done.

He was thinking about needing to get back to Tennessee to set up job interviews.

I felt sorry for him as I followed Caleb around the store. He felt me, heard me reading Bish through me. He turned, grabbed a pair of shorts that he'd seen in my mind and put them over his arm. He winked as I started to protest and grabbed my hand, towing me to the t-shirt section.

"I think it's time you got your very own first t-shirt. You can start collecting them at all the places I'm going to take you."

He started pushing and browsing through them, pulling one out and then putting it back.

"All the places?"

"Yes." He smiled and moved his face inches from mine. "I'm gonna take you everywhere. Anywhere you wanna go." He kissed the end of my nose. "Now, how about this one?"

He held up a yellow t-shirt that said 'I Break for Tanned Surfers'. I laughed and shook my head as a 'no'. He shrugged and put it away, looking for another. After many other funny shirts passed our eyes, Caleb - understanding I wasn't a funny shirt kind of gal - decided on a blue shirt with one lone wave on the front. It suited me. We checked out and left the store. We walked down the sidewalk to the Jeep, but Caleb stopped suddenly.

"You go ahead and take this stuff to the Jeep. I'll be right there," he said and he was thinking about surfing so I assumed he was going back to the surf shop. He must've forgotten something.

"Ok," I agreed.

Bish, Kyle, and I made our way to the Jeep and I cranked the ignition, blasting the cold air against the blazing June heat. Bish and Kyle in the back were looking and talking about the game Kyle bought.

"Mags, this is the game I was telling you about. Now you can play with us. I promise I won't shoot you on sight this time," Kyle said and grinned.

"Sounds good. I've never been very good at those things. Remember, Bish, your first Christmas with us they bought us a PlayStation? I don't think I ever won a single game we played."

"I remember," Bish said with a chuckle and I saw in his mind a memory of us sitting on the living room floor together playing. "You were pretty terrible."

"You didn't teach me much back then," I countered.

"You were too busy with Beck. She was over everyday and pulled you away to play dress-up."

"Actually, she pulled me away to talk about you. She said you were dreamy," I sang in a singsong tone to irritate him.

He scoffed and turned to look out the window as Kyle and I laughed. "She did not. You're just saying that to piss me off."

"She did. She was practically in love with you. She used to write your name with little hearts beside it and Mrs. Rebecca Masters," I said grinning.

"You're lying," he said, like he really didn't believe it.

No frigging way.

"Nope. Of course, that was when we were in six grade. By high school, you were just a phase," I said flippantly.

"Well...good," he said uncomfortably.

"Dude," Kyle said with a look. "Beck's hot. I'd go for that if I were you."

"I'm like seven years older than her. It's not cool."

"You're too late anyway," I said. "She's with Ralph now."

"Great. No concern of mine," Bish brushed off and nodded toward my window. "Good. Caleb's back."

"Hey," Caleb said as he got in his seat. "Sorry it took so long."

He was thinking about math; prime numbers, multiples of four, math problems, over and over. I looked at him curiously, but didn't say anything.

We pulled into the driveway and got out. Bish and Kyle ran in together to start the game. I thought what an unlikely friendship that was. Bish was older and

Kyle was pretty immature. It didn't seem like a good match-up but there was no one else, so maybe they were just making do.

As I closed the door, I heard Caleb's mind still running through subtraction. I gave him a weird look and then remembered that he hadn't come back to the Jeep with a package. What had he been doing? Then it hit me. He was using math to keep his head busy so he wouldn't think about something. There was something he didn't want me to see.

"Dang it, Maggie," he whined. "You couldn't let me have my little secret? You are going to be impossible to buy presents for."

"What are you talking about?"

"I-" he started, but the doorbell rang.

He went to answer it and I heard Peter's thoughts of happiness about seeing Caleb before I saw him turn the foyer corner to the living room where I was. And then Rachel, then my dad, then Jen...then Bella, Caleb's Sheepdog, all walked in right behind him.

I gasped in happiness and in dread both. What were they all doing here? Then I blushed in shame. They'd been worried about me running away? This seemed a little extreme.

Caleb petted and crooned to Bella for just a second as he ushered her to the backyard. He was anxious to be with me when we started all this. And it didn't take long.

Peter made his way to me.

"Magnificent."

I knew what he was going to do, but I couldn't muster up the gall to tell him no, though I wanted to. I didn't want to be disrespectful as he kissed my fingers and then touched my hand to his head.

Then to my horror, Rachel did the same thing. I cringed and tried not to pull away, but when Jen made her way to me, I could no longer take it.

"I-"

"Maggie doesn't want you to do that," Caleb explained softly and came to stand in front of me like a guard. "Remember, Dad, on the phone we talked about this. Maggie doesn't want the bowing and protocol; she wants to just be herself."

"I'm sorry, my dear, but you have to understand that this has been foretold since I was a child. It's just such an honor..."

"I know, and I'm not trying to muck up tradition or be disrespectful, but I can't have everyone bowing to me every time they see me. I'm still the same old me. Treat me like the same old me. Please?"

He nodded and smiled slightly. "Whatever you wish, my dear."

"Dad," Caleb protested for me.

"I meant that as Maggie's wish, not a Visionary's wish," he clarified. "Whatever makes Maggie happy."

I nodded in gratitude.

Caleb went to hug his mom and I made my way to my dad. He was holding himself in check, but wanted to grab me the second he saw me. As soon as I got close enough, he pulled me roughly to him.

"Ah, baby girl. I've missed you something fierce."

"Me, too, Dad."

I realized it was true. Then he looked at me and cocked his head. He put a hand up to rub the ends of my hair.

"Peter told me what happened with your hair. It's looks really great this way though."

"Thanks."

Did Peter really bow to you? I nodded. *Is that normal?*

"Apparently."

I hope you're behaving...

He looked at me expectantly with a perfectly arched questioning brown eyebrow.

"Yes, Dad, of course," I obliged.

He smiled and nodded his head to Caleb in hello, then looked around.

"Where's Bish?"

"Playing a video game with Kyle."

"Really? Bish? Strange."

"Yeah, tell me about it. So...what are you doing here?"

"Well, I heard a little rumor that you were a goddess or something."

"Dad, come on," I said more forcefully than I had intended.

"Hey, it's true isn't it? You are this Visionary person? So I figured, it couldn't hurt to have your old man here to keep you grounded. Don't let all this go to your head." He winked.

"Thanks," I said through a smirk.

A sense of urgency came over me. I knew the time had come to show the Champion what I had seen. I could hear their awe and wonder as they looked at me and the mark. They were waiting for something spectacular to happen.

"Kyle, Bish!" I yelled, startling Jen.

"What's up? Uncle Peter! Hey!" Kyle hugged them as Bish came in and he was more stunned than I had been about seeing Dad.

Jen's thoughts slammed into me. She was still just as interested and taken in by Bish as she had been before. He had been on her mind every since that day and it was driving her crazy. She bit her lip and looked at me quickly before looking away, ashamed knowing that I'd heard her thoughts.

"Hey, Dad, what are you doing here?" Bish asked.

"Just checking in."

"Hey, Kyle," I called, "can you take Bish to the store and get some steaks? I'm gonna make some for tonight but I need to talk to Dad about some stuff." He looked around and knew he was being left out of something. He took a deep angry breath. I stopped him before he started. "Kyle, please do this for me? I need you to."

He softened a bit.

"Fine, but you show me later," he compromised and pointed at me.

"Absolutely."

"Show what?" Bish said just as he noticed Jen standing there.

He got a bright look on his face for a few seconds before he fixed on a blank expression.

Oh, what is she doing here? Daggumit! How am I going to keep an eye on Maggie with all these people here? Especially her. Gah, look at those arms... She's just so...

"Hi," he said.

"Hi," she said softly and I felt Caleb tense. "How are you?"

"Good. How was your flight?"

"Good."

"Good," he answered and noticed us all watching so he cleared his throat and spoke to Kyle. "Steaks?" he said happily seeking an out.

"Yeah, let's go."

Once they were gone, I turned to them. Caleb stood next to his father and watched along with the rest of them. He wasn't thinking he shouldn't be with me, just that he would be in the way.

I looked at Peter. "Champion, I have a message for you."

He sighed in wonder and started to kneel.

"No. No, kneeling either. I need you to stand. You're going to need to stand up, literally, for the task we have to do. We all need to. Ready?"

"Yes."

"Dad," I waited for him to look at me eyes, "don't be alarmed."

"Why would I be?"

"Just don't. I'm fine. It's all fine."

He nodded warily.

I closed my eyes and felt completely powerful and in control. This was what I was meant for. I could feel it in my veins. I tried to open myself, but then realized I was forgetting something.

"Caleb," I called and looked at him. "I need you."

He looked surprised as he came forward.

"What do you need?"

"You."

"Does this require a human sacrifice?" he said joking.

"No," I laughed and heard Jen laugh too. "You remember I told you how I needed you at my side? I do, always. I can't do any of this without you. Your touch is the trigger."

"It is?" he said in surprise.

"You are just as important as I am. In the vision, I saw that you and I will be the key, not just me. Everything we'll accomplish, we'll do it together or not at all."

He looked at me with an elated and humble expression. Peter and Rachel's thoughts were so proud and happy for their son and daughter-in-law.

I looked back at him and put my hands on his upper arms as they went around my waist. I pulled him down to lay my head against his.

At my side, not at my feet, remember? Always. Every time I show a vision, every time I have to speak to the our kind, every time I breathe, even, I need you right here. Ok?

He nodded.

I understand. I'm with you all the way.

I grinned.

Good.

I pushed up to kiss him quickly. Then I smiled at him as I lay my head against his again. I saw the energy ribbons before I felt them. It was a little different this time now that I'd had my first vision. As the blue ribbons floated and danced in a circle all around us, I heard a gasp from Jen and Rachel. Peter and Caleb had seen them before and weren't surprised. I focused on Dad to make sure he was ok. He was thinking about some Star Trek episode as he let the ribbons go through his hand, so I assumed he was taking it in stride.

I began to replay the vision I'd seen in the library as they all watched it play out above us in a hazy glow.

I showed them the greed of our kind, the pride seeping in and corrupting us, the ignorance whittling away at our potential, the complacency of our leaders, and finally, the redemption that could be ours if we'd only try. I showed them the book, how the words came to me, and how they tasted as I looked on the people of our past. As this happened I could smell the taste I'd tasted in the vision on the air around us and from their thoughts I knew they did too.

I showed them me helping the guy from the ice cream place.

I then smiled as the vision I'd seen of Caleb and I fighting side by side and then old and gray together played across my eyes, Caleb saying he still loved me.

Caleb laughed happily and quietly into my ear as he pulled me closer to him.

There, written in stone in your very own vision that we'll be together to the end. Do you believe me now?

I always did. I just didn't want to see what was right in front of my face. You love me; I know that now without a shadow of a doubt. And I love you more than I ever thought was possible to love someone.

I smiled at him as he gazed at me in unabashed adoration. His lips turned up slightly and then he put a hand on my cheek, brushing my hair back just like he did that first day; the day I met the love of my life.

The love poured out of him. It was like, for the first time, we both were completely sure of each other, ourselves and our destinies. It didn't matter what was thrown at us, we would weather it together.

He pulled my face up to his, his fingers sending warm calm through me as he kissed me softly. I could hear the thoughts of the others as they watched the energy ribbons dance around us. They were happy, so happy and so proud and rejoicing with us. Even my father was in a complete trance of happiness and humbleness.

I pulled back slightly and we laughed a happy breath with each other before turning to face our family. I knew Peter had questions but so did everyone else. Rachel was crying, tears streaming down her face as she watched her son love his significant. And the fact that I was the Visionary was just the cherry on the sundae.

I turned to look at Peter and waited. He had to understand. He had to see the truth. Our clan was chosen for this task for a reason. And it was up to us to see that it was carried out.

~ Eight ~

"I'm still kind of in shock, actually," Peter continued on. "All those horrible things you showed us, all the terrible things our ancestors did to others. It makes sense why our abilities were taken, but why was our family chosen to be the beacon of reason? Why now? Why us? Our imprints were taken just like everyone else's."

He'd been talking and going over everything we'd seen together at the dining room table for about twenty minutes. I expected Bish and Kyle anytime and wondered how long they all planned to stay. Bish was already so suspicious. I tried to bring up that subject but Peter was stuck on the vision.

"The visions were so precise in purpose. I don't know what I expected but it wasn't that," he continued. "Maggie, what were you doing when you got the vision?"

"I was just sitting in the library, looking at photos and books. I ran across Grandpa Ray's record book and when I opened it I saw the picture of him and Gran on his birthday." I looked at Caleb. "The one you told me about, where she got the tattoo for him." I ran my fingers over his wrist tattoo with envy. He laced my fingers with his as I sat on his lap where he'd pulled me when we first came to sit down. "Then I opened the book and read it to the end. Then the vision came."

"What tattoo?" Dad asked.

As Peter explained it to him, I talked to Caleb, taking a break in conversation.

What are we gonna do about Bish and Jen?

I don't know. He sighed and rubbed his chin. *I'm not sure we should do anything. Maybe better to just leave it alone. Jen would never break the rule.*

Yeah, I know. But I don't want them to start to like each other even more and be stuck with nowhere to take it. You know? Bish has had a...hard enough life without all this.

I started to choke up just thinking about it. He was such a good man and he deserved better than what he got. Caleb put a hand on my cheek to calm me.

I don't know what we're gonna do. We'll keep them busy, keep them apart as much as we can. Don't worry. He's my family now too which means he's my family's family. He'll be taken care of and it'll all work out.

I hope so. I ran a finger down his wrist again as I studied his tattoo. *I hate that Bish will never feel what I feel for you for himself, or Jen for that matter.*

He nodded sadly.

"How are you holding up, Maggie?" Rachel asked as I turned to find her and Peter watching us over the rims of their coffee cups.

"I'm ok. It's Bish I'm worried about." Jen's eyes shot up at his name. "He's not just curious anymore, he's mad. He knows. He doesn't know what he knows but he knows there's something I'm keeping from him."

"Are you two being careful?" Peter said and I saw the worry in his eyes. "Kyle was complaining to his father on the phone that you were flaunting your abilities."

"That rat," Caleb muttered under his breath. "No, we're not flaunting. Besides, you have to have abilities before you can flaunt them." Everyone stared in stunned silence. I rubbed his arm. "It's ok. I'm just saying, I haven't felt any pull or anything. I don't think it's coming, Dad."

Peter shifted uncomfortably in his seat. "Well, son, I've never heard of this. It's unprecedented, but everything with you two has been, so...I'm not sure where to start looking. I'm sorry, but I'm not giving up."

"It's ok. Like I said, I read everything through Maggie anyway. Besides, we have more important things than my measly lack of abilities to worry about."

"I'll work in it, son. I promise."

"Thanks. Now, I have some unrelated news."

He told them all about his gig and how he'd been practicing. Then he said he was going to buy tickets to the Mutemath concert in few days and Rachel gasped and squealed. Peter was laughing and Jen was shaking her head. Caleb just smiled. He had told me she loved them but I thought he was just giving his mom a few extra cool points.

"So, we'll go, whoever wants to. There's this great little band from Florida opening at the venue, Fusebox Funk. I can't wait," Caleb explained.

Rachel clapped her hands and leaned into Peter's side looking at Caleb.

"Oh, thank you, baby. It's been almost a year since I've seen them," she crooned, making me smile just as I heard the front door open.

"Honey, we're home," Kyle yelled loudly to announce to us to shut-up the Ace talk. "Steaks all around."

"Thanks," I said as I took them and dreaded cooking them all. But I started it so I'd finish it. "So, who wants theirs rare?"

"Let me do that, if you don't mind. I'm sure you and your father have a lot of catching up to do," Rachel assured and took the apron from me.

"Thanks, are you sure? I'm sure it was a long flight."

"I'm sure. I live for the kitchen."

"Ok." I started to turn but she touched my arm.

"Your hair really does suit you. It's very elegant that way."

"Thank you," I said sincerely as I absently touched my locks. "It's growing on me, I guess."

Caleb grabbed my hand from behind me. "I'm going to go take a drive with Dad while you catch up with yours."

"Ok. Hey, listen." I felt a fuzzy and gnawing feeling in my belly. I pulled him closer to whisper in his ear. "Everything's going to be fine. I don't know why...but I feel like something's going to happen. Something to do with you and it's important. I don't think you should worry about your abilities."

He pulled back to look at me. "Is this Maggie talking or the Visionary?"

"Does it matter?"

He laughed and shook his head. "Nope."

He kissed my forehead and headed to his father.

Dad, Bish and I sat out by the pool in the loungers with Bella by my side as I scratched her head. Dad told us about the police investigation being called off. The town was buzzing with gossip about me and he'd had tons of calls and people stopping by to check on me. I was floored, actually. I didn't think anybody there really cared about me anymore.

He also asked Bish if he wanted to move back and told him he'd love to have him in the house again. I was grateful to him for that. Then, I could have smacked him when he brought up Jen. No one had explained to him about the no dating.

"So, Bish, Caleb's sister is a pretty sweet girl."

Bish seemed taken aback that my dad would be so blunt but recovered quickly, crossing his ankle over his leg in that grown up, serious way he did.

"I'm sure she is."

"Dad," I butted in. "Um, how's work?"

"It's good," he answered and looked back to Bish. "So, what do you think of my offer?"

"I think I like it. It would really help me out if you're sure you wouldn't mind."

"It would help me too actually. I don't like to live alone."

"Alone? But Maggie will be home soon and..."

He seemed to catch on and I saw his jaw harden.

"I'm leaving for school, Bish," I defended.

"I'm sure Caleb just happens to go to the same school, right?" he said sarcastically.

I rolled my eyes at him, pulling my knees up to my chest and looked over to see Jen coming with drinks in her hands.

"Hey, Mom thought you might want something to drink before supper."

Bish was forcing himself not to look at her and Jen was studiously doing the same as she gave an already sweating glass to me, then Dad, then Bish. I watched closely as their fingers avoided each other to exchange the glasses.

"Thanks," he muttered.

"You're welcome. Have y'all been having fun here? We always loved it here when we came during the summer."

"Oh, yeah," Bish sneered. He leaned forward as Jen stood with her hands behind her back. "Caleb and Maggie have been all over each other. Maggie is acting like a freaking psycho, running off in the Jeep for hours, not caring about who's worried about her and then lying to my face about it all. Kyle is the only sane one in the lot of them."

I locked my gaze with the grass. Jen's thoughts were sympathetic because she thought he had been too hard on me, but still understood where he was coming from. Dad was worrying because Bish and I had always been so close before all of this. I was just hurt. He called me a psycho. I was sure I deserved some form of that word, but to me, knowing the truth of what was really going on, it hurt.

I got up, leaving my glass of tea behind, and made my way out to the beach. Bella trailed behind me to catch up and then walked with me. Jen wanted to stop me but refrained and just went back inside. Bish felt sorry that he had said those things but didn't think they were untrue so didn't really regret them.

I plopped myself down in the sand once I reached near the waves and looked at all the surfers and swimmers. I ran my fingers through Bella's coat and said innocuous and random things that people croon to dogs to keep them happy. The wind was blowing especially hard and I picked up some sand and let it blow away through my fingers, like my life.

I kept my heart rate normal and tried not to feel too upset so Caleb wouldn't come back early and not talk it all out with his father. I didn't hear anyone come up behind me but I heard Rachel's thoughts.

Oh, Maggie. I'm so sorry.

I looked up at her and shielded my eyes with my hand.

"It's ok. I'll just have to let him think what he wants. It's not like I can tell everyone I know about us, now can I? It won't be too long before Beck is asking questions and not speaking to me either."

I felt her sit down beside me in her expensive slacks and silk shirt as hot tears burned my eyelids.

"What bothers you more, Maggie? That Bish thinks you're a silly girl or that you have to lie?"

"I hate lying. It doesn't feel good and it makes everything harder."

She nodded beside me. "I understand that. I'm sorry you're having a hard time."

"It's fine. I can deal with it. I just needed to get out of there."

"Do you miss your mom?" she asked softly.

I started to lie again and say I didn't, but I'd had enough for today.

Poor girl, I wish I could do something for her.

"Yes," I whispered.

"I understand. I miss my mom, too."

"Do you ever see your parents?"

"Sometimes, but for the most part, I only see them every few years or so. Caleb, Jen and Peter have only ever met them a few times. It felt very strange to me in the beginning but each clan is separate. It was just the way things were. You are so young...I can't imagine leaving my parents when I was only seventeen."

"Caleb is here," I reasoned, "what else could I do?"

"Caleb is what you need now. You need to be dependent on him even though it is hard at times."

I nodded and continued to pet Bella before she took off to chase a seagull.

"My dad really needs me, though he'd never admit it, and I still need him. It's strange that you guys just split from your family."

"I just want you to know that no matter what happens, no matter what anybody says, no matter what drama that's going to plague us once the leaders learn of your being the Visionary, you are not without family. I know you have your father but...sometimes a girl just needs her mother. Although I'd never try to take her place, I'm here, if you ever need to talk or vent or whatever."

"Thanks," I wiped my cheeks with sandy fingers. "I appreciate that."

"So, has Caleb talked to you about the ceremony yet?"

"What ceremony?" I groaned. "Don't tell me there's some kind of Visionary ritual I have to go through," I said horrified.

"No, no. I'm talking about the dedication ceremony."

"What's that?"

"Caleb didn't tell you?"

What is he thinking? Why would he not say anything about it? Maybe he just let it go because of everything that's going on.

"Well," she started and stretched her legs out, crossing them and then looked at me. "A dedication is our kinds wedding ceremony."

"What?" I felt my heart speed up and took a deep breath.

"We don't have traditional weddings. It's similar in a lot of ways, but it's only for our families. Humans are generally not involved with it. It just lets everyone know that there's no doubt about you being each other's significant and that you are dedicating yourself to each other and to the clan. It's really beautiful, actually. Some people get hung up on the whole imprint thing, about how our bodies need each other. Well, this is to show that it's not just our bodies, it's our willing hearts, too."

I saw stills of Peter and her at their dedication ceremony in her mind. Rachel was so young, so very pretty and lively. Peter was dashing. They weren't wearing tuxes and poufy dresses and there were no bridesmaids. Rachel was wearing a simple red silk slip dress that had a slight train and her feet were bare, a Malva flower tucked behind one ear. Peter was barefoot as well wearing a red un-tucked, button-up shirt and black pants.

Everyone else wore red too as they made a circle around the two of them. Grandpa Ray was officiating. It was intriguing.

"What's all the red for?" I asked and Rachel laughed.

"Oh," she laughed again. "I forget about your ability. Red is for blood. I know," she said when I made a 'what the' face. "It sounds terrible. We don't use the traditional white for purity because we are binding ourselves together, body, soul, mind, and heart. Significant's blood calls to one another, protects each other and completes one another. It's the basis for a body and it's the basis for an imprint, a bond. Remember back to your imprinting? The very first thing you feel is your blood freezing?"

I nodded, remembering and realizing it made sense.

"So you just exchange rings in front of everyone and that's it?"

"Oh, no, no, your rings are a very private thing. It used to be that your rings were for public display purposes, to show humans you were married, but over the years it's grown into a very romantic and sweet thing. You won't pick your own ring, you see. You'll choose Caleb's ring for him and he'll pick yours for you."

"Really? I like that. That *is* sweet."

"It is. I was so nervous searching for Peter's. Picking out a man's piece of jewelry is nerve racking."

"But don't most people have matching rings?"

"Most people aren't us. Do you want matching rings?"

"No," I answered truthfully. "I think the idea of picking the other person's ring is a great leap of faith. Picking something like that for someone shows that you know them."

"Exactly." She smiled.

She's so perfect for this life. I just wish she'd see what we see. Thank you, God, for bringing her to Caleb.

"You have to conduct the ceremony or the clan doesn't recognize you as a couple?"

"No, you don't *have* to, but I don't see why you wouldn't want to. It shows that you love him and want to spend your life with him and you accept his love, his family and protection for you."

"I just...never thought I'd be married at seventeen," I said in a small voice, almost ashamed of saying it.

She wrapped her small, firm arm around me and pulled me to her side. I could feel her taking deep long breaths beside me. Her mind was filled with sympathy and kind thoughts, but she also worried, like she always did. Caleb was her son and she didn't want to see him hurt, and though she didn't think I'd ever intentionally hurt him, she didn't want to see her son in pain; the kind of pain that losing a significant would cause.

She also worried that we *were* too young, but it seemed that God had chosen us and she was powerless to stop it.

"I would never hurt him," I said with conviction and turned slightly to her, her arm still around me. "I love him." I felt a tear slide down my cheek and saw her swipe a tear of her own. Bella ran over and licked my hand, like she sensed I needed a kiss. "I love him and I'm not going to reject him or your family or your ways. I've seen it. Caleb and I are going to be together and I wouldn't have it any other way. I just don't understand why everything with us has to be so complicated. Why can't we be just like everyone else and be normal teenagers that love each other? Why do I have to lie to everyone about it? Why do I have to be the Visionary?" I felt the sob rising in my throat as I started to cry harder. "I just feel like I have no one to talk to. Sometimes I just...I just-"

"You just need your mom," she finished for me.

"I need the way my mom used to be. I just need someone who would understand."

"I'm afraid there won't be anyone in this world who understands. You and Caleb, no matter how irritating it may be, are one of a kind. I'm sorry, honey. I'm sorry that you feel so torn over this."

"I know it's me, that I'm the Visionary. I can feel it in my blood. I just don't know if I'm strong enough for the fight that's ahead."

"You are or you wouldn't be the Visionary."

"That's what Caleb said," I said laughing through my tears and she laughed, too.

"He's pretty smart, my son."

"He's pretty...everything. I don't know what I'd do without him now," I said more to myself than her.

"I'm so glad to hear you say that."

"I don't deserve him," I muttered. "He's always so sweet and thinking about other people. I'm selfish and naïve."

She chuckled. "I wish you could hear the things that Caleb has told me. When he calls, he talks non-stop about you. I wish you could have seen him tell us that he'd imprinted with you." She got a bright look in her eyes and tilted her head. "I can show you."

She immediately began to replay me a fuzzy, off-kilter playback of Caleb running into Kyle's house, not even shutting the door, and yelling for his parents. Everyone was gathered around in the living room as he ran in. He sank to his knees on the carpet so he wouldn't fall. As he told them he'd found me, they gasped, excited. Everyone scrambled to get out the door to see me. He told them I'd left with Kyle, to give him space to tell them. "You should see her. She is everything I would have thought up for myself. She's sweet and adorable, and took everything so well. I was pulled to her even before the bond, like she already belonged to me."

"What does she look like?" someone asked.

"She's just...gorgeous. She's short with brown curls and freckles."

"Now, come on, Caleb, you can do better than that," Gran complained.

"You'll all see her tomorrow. I'm going to go get her in the morning and bring her here to meet you. Please take it easy on her. I know this is just a...miracle and all, but I don't want to scare her."

"Now, Caleb," Gran drawled, "if she's your girl, she'll be just fine."

"She's mine," Caleb confirmed loudly and then cracked a little embarrassed smile. "I can feel her heartbeat, right now."

There was an explosion of 'ahh's and 'ooh's at that and Rachel grabbed him in a hug with big fat tears dripping from her chin as everyone hooped and hollered behind them. Peter clapped him on the back and looked towards the ceiling with his eyes closed.

Rachel let the memory fade and I wiped my tears away once more and felt her do the same.

"All will be as it should be, Maggie. We can't outrun destiny." I looked at her and wondered why that word kept coming up in conversations with people. "I know you love Caleb."

"I do."

"And he loves you."

"I feel silly for leaving like that in the Jeep," I said and felt a burn of shame on my neck and cheeks.

"He should have been more focused and supportive. We all make mistakes, even Aces, but at the end of the day, you always have each other."

"Have you and Peter ever had a fight?"

She giggled and pressed me harder to her. "Of course, honey. When you've been married as long as I have, you'll have quite a few fights under your belt. You learn to fight. We're not human; we have a lot of the same mundane issues, but for the most part, we're different in just about everything we do. We fight in a constructive way. Heated talking can be very useful."

"I agree," I said and nodded, remembering the conversation Caleb and I had after I got back.

"Caleb is very protective of you, even more so than Peter was with me. It's very endearing to watch. If he's hard sometimes, Maggie, it's just because he loves you. Maybe the reason his protectiveness is so fierce is because you are the Visionary and it is ingrained in him to protect that. It's instinct for him. Rely on it."

"I will," I promised and scratched Bella's head. That dog was very serene for a puppy.

"Alright, I guess we can head back unless you want to stay out here longer?"

"No, I'm ready. Thank you."

We walked back up the beach in easy, comfortable silence as Bella waddled between us. One we reached the back yard of the beach house, I stopped Rachel with a hand on her arm and hugged her tightly as Bella took off toward the house.

"Thank you, really. You helped me more than you know."

"I'll always be here for you. I know it's strange to you, but we love you. And someday, you'll learn to love us, too, Maggie," she said sweetly.

"I already do," I whispered.

"Ah," she gasped. "Maggie, you don't know what that means to me."

I felt Caleb watching us and peeked up to see him standing in the bay windows with a proud little smile quirking his lips. He was happy to see his mother and me getting along, getting to know each other, let alone embracing.

"Alright, let's eat, dear," Rachel said bringing me back around.

"Ok, yeah. I'm starving."

~ Nine ~

Everyone was already seated either at the table or bar by the time we washed up and came to the kitchen. I avoided Bish's gaze, not out of spite, but out of exhaustion. I didn't know if I could handle anymore of his disappointment tonight. I did see, however, that he and Jen were seated across from each other.

Caleb tried to ask me about what had happened with Bish, seeing me thinking about it, but I assured him I was fine now, thanks to his mother.

As I sat in the chair that was left empty next to Caleb, I saw Bish and Jen both doing that little gaze dance. When she looked up, he looked up, and then they both looked away and vice versa. I was concerned and knew Caleb was even more than I was. He didn't want his sister hurt, and I didn't want my brother hurt, so we were on the same page. Though I thought it would be nice if Bish found someone, and Jen, the sweetest sister I'd ever met, would be perfect for him.

I felt Caleb mentally balk beside me. I glanced at him quickly.

I said 'would be', not I'm gonna hook them up. I know it's impossible, I just hate to see them unhappy and it's pretty clear they're attracted to each other.

Yeah, pretty clear. But it's impossible and better not to even entertain the idea of it. It'd just hurt them worse in the end.

I know. Do you know any single girls in their twenties that would go for Bish?

Sure, I know plenty, but would Bish go for it? He doesn't seem to be attracted to anything that walks, talks, eats or breathes except my sister.

I laughed and then covered my mouth with my hand to cover it and faked choking on a piece of steak. Caleb was trying not to laugh beside me. I guess it was obvious to the Aces what was going on because I saw Peter shaking his head in amusement.

After dinner, Peter and Rachel were ready for bed. Everyone was jetlagged and Caleb was supposed to be heading to practice. Only two days left until his show with Metal Petals. So, that left Bish and Kyle and I to our own devices. Bish and Kyle's devices were Xbox, so I decided to take Caleb up on his offer to watch him practice.

We left after a short explanation about where we were going.

"I miss your bike," I said in the Jeep. "The Jeep's nice, but there is something about that bike."

"I hear you. I miss her, too."

"Her?" I laughed. "Don't tell me your bike has a name?"

"What?" he said incredulously. "As a matter of fact, I do have a name for her. I'm glad Lolita's not here to hear you make fun of her."

I laughed harder as we pulled into a massive three-story beach house, right on the beach. "If they're so loaded, why does Zeke's brother work at the pizza place?" I asked.

"Their parents think if they work part time their senior year of high school it'll teach them restraint and responsibility. But they kinda botch the plan when he's wearing his new Jordan's and driving his brand new Lexus while he's delivering pizzas."

I smiled and nodded in understanding.

We parked on the street and walked into the garage. I could already hear them practicing. Caleb pulled my arm.

"Wait. Now, you remember Zeke, he's zealous. He might even act all stupid around you and I'll stop him, but just don't listen to half the things they say, ok?"

Really, they are a bunch of spoiled college dropouts who think they can just do whatever they want. He's been my friend for years and we're helping each other out.

"I understand. I won't jump the gun on the judgment. And I'll be quiet."

"You don't have to be quiet just...ok, yeah. It's probably better for you that way."

I laughed and shook the sand from my shoes before we went inside. "I'm fine. I'll still love you after this, I promise."

He grinned. "That's my girl. And you better shut everyone out before we go in. I'd just spend the whole time busting heads if I knew what they were really thinking about you," he said in a low voice.

I just smirked and shook my head, then focused on Caleb.

Then we entered the garage and I couldn't say anything even if I wanted to. They had Marshall Speaker stacks lined up along the back wall. There were two Zilgdan drum kits, drummers involved. The floor was carpeted, as were the walls, with a plush sea blue. The band was there, five of them, and Zeke in all his tacky rock star glory was there in the middle, no shirt and no shoes. I wondered if he ever wore any.

"Caleb, it's about freaking time, mate!"

"Sorry, the family flew in unexpectedly."

"Really? Well, tell Jen I said hello why don't you. That little kitten still single?"

Caleb groaned, "Dude, shut up." He pulled me to him and pointed me to a leather couch in the corner. "You remember Maggie?"

"Of course," Zeke looked at me and winked. "You just don't forget someone with a sweet, wholesome name like Maggie."

"Here are the rest of the guys," Caleb went down the line, but I knew I wouldn't remember their names, "and this is Maggie."

"Hello, Maggie. You coming to sing backup? You can sit on my lap?" one of the drummers said and smiled cockily as everyone else laughed.

Well, almost everyone.

"Enough. And on with practice," Caleb barked and rubbed his hands together, flexing his fingers.

He picked up a green bass and strummed it a few times before Zeke began making all these weird noises as he warmed up his voice. He just sounded demented. He shook himself out and blew his lips. Then he stood very still and spoke. "I'm ready."

And Caleb opened with a bass line.

I watched his fingers with fascination. He was fast and good; focused. Zeke grabbed the microphone and draped a purple scarf around his neck as he belted out their rocked out rendition of '25 or 6 to 4' by Chicago and then 'Seven Nation Army' by White Stripes. They played many originals as well. I was in awe at the lack of understanding I had as to what any of the songs were about.

During one such song, Caleb glanced over at me and smiled. He kept playing flawlessly as he locked his blue eyes to mine and did one of those slow spreading, heart fluttering, and dimple inducing smiles. Then he winked. I could only stand there in awe. He was wearing some rugged jeans with flip-flops and a plain white t-shirt. His hair was a mussed mess of curls and he'd gotten even more tanned since we'd been in California. It made me bite my lip when I remembered that that beautiful creature belonged to me.

If possible, his smile got wider and he sent me a mental picture of him kissing me senseless on the porch swing, buried in white cushions. It was no longer a vision, it was a memory. My mouth opened slightly in surprise and I scolded him with my eyes for doing that right then. He laughed silently and winked once more before turning back to Zeke, who was coming to shimmy with the bass.

After about two hours, they had played through the set list and fussed with each other about the other's messing up enough. I tried to hide my smile. What a bunch of girls! Zeke was constantly dabbing his face with a lime green hand towel and getting chilled water from the mini-fridge, all the while yelling at the others for dragging or not 'feeling the music'.

He was nuts.

"So, Maggie," one of the drummers said as he passed me and stopped by the door, "where are you from?"

"Tennessee."

"Ah, so that's where Caleb met you. I thought you were just his little beach bunny."

"Nope, I'm afraid not."

"So you go to school with him?"

"Not yet. I'll start in the fall."

"Shame," he muttered.

"What is?"

"You are wasting a good mind on mundane government brainwashing schooling. Think about it. Where has this country been headed in the past sixty years? The pit, that's where!" He pointed to emphasize his point. My eyebrows rose at his vehemence. "A socialist society is where we're headed, my friend. Then The Man will be all over us. You think it's bad now? Ha! Just wait until you can't even grab a burger without Big Brother knowing whether you ate pickles on it or not."

Caleb walked swiftly towards us and leaned forward to whisper loudly to him, "Careful, Spence, they could be listening."

"Ah, come on, man!" He pushed Caleb off and scoffed. "You think this isn't real?" Caleb took my hand and led me laughing to the Jeep. Spence kept yelling after us. "It's real, Maggie! Don't go to school, man. It's just one step closer to the end for you if you do!"

"What is he talking about?" I asked as Caleb put me in my side.

"Conspiracy theory," he laughed as we pulled out.

"Aha. Well, you guys sounded really good."

"Really? I feel so stupid now for agreeing to do this. They are...too eccentric for me. I just wanted to play."

"You did great," I soothed and rubbed his hand on the gearshift knob. "Who cares? It's just one show and you'll have fun."

"Yeah, you're right. Just gotta suck it up. So what was your favorite song?"

"Um...the one about the sun sizzling into the ocean." He laughed hard.
"What?"

"Zeke wrote that song about his cat."

"His cat," I repeated blandly.

"Yep. Peaches, she ran away."

"I'd run away, too," I muttered under my breath, making him laugh harder.

When we pulled into the driveway, I don't know what I expected to find. The house was dark, sleeping bodies inside it. There was a half moon in the sky. I looked at it, comparing it to the Jacobson family crest tattoo that everyone wore on the inside of their wrist. Once again, envy inched its way inside. I wanted one. One day, even if I had to pull a Gran to do it, I'd have one.

"You coming, babe? That moon is just as pretty from our bedroom window," Caleb called and beckoned me to him with a waggle of his fingers.

We made it to the porch before we heard the giggling. I knew that giggle. I peeked around the back porch and saw Amber and Kyle in the pool together. He was shushing her and watching the windows to make sure no one woke up. His mind was racing. He wanted to be in the pool with Amber, what guy wouldn't, but he was still secretly concerned about his aunt and uncle finding out. He had no intentions of this thing going anywhere with Amber, but he didn't want the drama.

Amber's mind was way too dirty and vivid and I yanked out of it immediately uttering an 'Eeew'.

"Ditto," Caleb said and pulled my hand for us to go inside. "Kyle is such an idiot," his whispered as we walked through the dark house.

Once inside our room, aka the den, he turned his back so I could change into my pajamas. These days that consisted of his band t-shirts and boxers or some sleep pants. I know. It was kind of weird. It scared even me. I mean, we'd only known each other two weeks. Two weeks! That was it. It was so strange yet exciting to feel so primed and ready for something. I've never felt more ready to be or do anything that I was to be Caleb's significant.

Now...marriage and living together and kids and joint checking accounts was another story.

But for now, even though this time had been short, we'd grown comfortable around each other. And I loved to wear his clothes. Ever since that night after Marcus's attempt to kidnap me and Caleb changed my wet clothes, putting me in some of his, I couldn't sleep in anything else. And he loved to see me wear them. It was a mutual thing. My camisoles would have to be on hold anyway because we slept in the middle of the living room where anyone could walk in and they often did.

89

We climbed into our couch bed. I was last and forgot to turn off the light. I groaned and banged my head on the pillow, so not wanting to get up and all of a sudden, the lights went off. I sat up quickly in the moonlight.

"Caleb, did you get up?"

"No. Why? What?"

"I didn't turn that light off."

"Okay," he sang, clearly not understanding.

"No. I didn't get out of bed and turn the lamp off. I just..." The thought came to me.

Just like in the Jeep with the keys. I banged my fist and almost...willed it to start. We'd never talked about it since and I'd actually forgotten about it until now with so much going on.

I concentrated and focused on the lamp. I wanted it to turn back on. But it didn't. I laughed at myself for thinking I had some kinda extra special power or something. It was just a fluke, right?

"I saw what happened that day. I'd forgotten about it too. There is something to it, I think. Try again," he coaxed softly and sat up next to me.

I focused and it just sat there. I glared at it in the dark corner and said in my mind for it to come on, flip the switch, burn bright, wished it would do something. It continued to disobey. I slapped my hand down on the bed in frustration.

"Dang it."

The light came on.

Caleb gasped a surprised breath and put a hand on my leg.

"Maggie," he whispered in awe. "Try again, baby. Turn it off."

I tried and once again, it did nothing. Not even a blink. I was completely confused and I could feel Caleb was too. I huffed and the room went black again.

"Why does it only do it sometimes," I asked in a hushed, angry tone in the dark.

"I think...I think it has to do with your emotions or something. It only seems to do it when you're frustrated."

"So what do I do?"

"Get mad."

I blew a breath. Get mad... I thought about Amber in the pool. Girls like that who just burn my...

The lights turned on.

"Ha!" I laughed surprised and strangely giddy.

"You did it! Maggie," he sighed and rubbed his hand on my leg.

"What is this?"

90

"I have no idea. I mean we've had a techno-path in the family before, but this is something different. Try something else."

Kyle interrupted him by tapping on the window gently.

"Will you cut it out?" Kyle hissed a muffled complaint. "You're going to wake everyone up. What's with the light show?"

"Just shut up and go back to your pool date," Caleb sneered, turning his back on him and focusing on me. "Ok, let's try something else, something not mechanical. Um...swing the door open."

"Ok, I'll try."

I thought about how Bish has been such a jerk to me the past few days, warranted or not. I pictured the door opening...right on Bish's big toe. The door swung slowly and silently to a wide-open position.

"I knew it. You can do anything, can't you?" Caleb said in fascination and enjoyment.

"I have no idea what I can do."

"I'm sure Bish would appreciate the gesture, too," he said and grinned. He pulled back the covers and stood up, beckoning me to him with a hand out. I looked at him questioningly. "What? You think I can sleep after that?"

"Where are we going?" I asked but let him pull me up to stand with him.

"Come on. Let's go see what else you can do," he said slyly. We slipped on our flip-flops and a couple of his hoodie jackets.

He pulled me down to the beach and made me practice moving shells, flinging sand into the air, a poor unfortunate crab was probably scared to death as I finally got something to hover in the air between us. I found out I could do just about anything. Things and objects of all kinds obeyed my mental commands if I was angry or upset or frustrated enough. Eventually, it took a toll and I was exhausted.

Caleb sat in the sand and I practically collapsed in his lap. I pulled my bare legs up and wrapped my arm around them. It felt amazing outside. Caleb pulled his hood up and then mine for me. He leaned back a little against the dune and nestled me closer. He was beaming and radiating with pride and love.

He had helped me and encouraged me all night. He would touch me to help keep my emotions in check and then we'd start again as his heartbeat banged away next to mine in my chest from all our melding.

His warm hands came up to rub my legs to keep them warm as I felt my eyelids start to droop. He kissed my forehead and sighed.

My eyes popped open. I looked up at him quickly, remembering something. "Ah, Caleb, I'm sorry I keep doing this to you," I rasped.

He was reading my thought and shook his head back and forth as he said, "Maggie, I'm happy for you. I'm not jealous."

"No, I wouldn't think you're jealous. I just..."

"I know, but you think it bothers me. It doesn't, not that you have so many abilities. I can definitely handle that. I'm not worried about my ability at all right now. I have a place, right here." He squeezed me. "I don't need anything else right now. I'm so proud of you," he whispered and then took my chin between his thumb and finger, kissing me so very gently.

"Gosh, Caleb," I sighed and shook my head and put my hands on his chest. "You have too much faith in me."

"Why do you say that?"

He turned me on his lap to look at him so he could see my face, my legs on both sides of him.

"I just hope...I turn out to be what everybody expects," I muttered softly.

"You will," he said surely. "I have no doubt about that."

"Well, I'm glad one of us believes."

He chuckled quietly before saying, "You're so funny, you know that? It's still my favorite thing about you." I just smiled a wry smile. "Are you tired?" he asked and tucked my hair tighter under my hood.

"Very."

He pulled me back to lie on his chest and rubbed my back. He soothed me with his hands and said, "Sleep, Maggie."

"On the beach?" I asked and it broke with a yawn.

"Yep," he chuckled.

"You've slept on the beach before?"

"We used to camp out all the time when we were kids. You've never?"

"Never."

"Well there's a first time for everything."

Under his warm soothing hands, I fell right to sleep.

~ Ten ~

I woke with overly warm breath on my face. I crinkled my nose and I thought Caleb's breath was awfully bad this morning. My eyes peeked open and I was licked on the cheek by a fluff of blonde.

"Bella," I crooned. "Did someone let you out? Huh?" I said as I scratched her scruff.

"She really has taken to you," Caleb said, startling me.

I didn't know he was awake, but I could tell from his tone he was happy about Bella's and my blossoming relationship.

"Yeah, she has. She's a sweet girl. Us girls gotta stick together, don't we?" I crooned some more to her.

"I'm trying not to be jealous."

"Jealous of me or Bella?" I asked with a little smile and a raised eyebrow.

"Either."

I giggled and accepted his kiss, but Bella was having none of it. She nuzzled her nose in between us.

"Alright, you," Caleb said and pushed her away playfully. "Go lay down." She trotted about six feet away and plopped down on the sand.

"Now," he pulled me back to him with a hand on the nape of my neck. He kissed my lips sweet and long. "Good morning."

"Morning," I breathed in a daze.

"So, did you like sleeping on the beach?"

"Yeah." I pulled my hood down and looked around. Caleb smoothed my hair for me, I'm sure it was a mess. "I love the beach. Can we move here? Buy a little yellow beach house with a wraparound porch and just never leave?" I said and snuggled into his chest, wrapped in my fantasy.

He sighed. It was a very loaded sigh. I realized what I'd just done. I just made plans... albeit hypothetical plans, but plans nonetheless. Caleb had wanted to talk about me moving in with him when we went to school for a week now. And I had studiously avoided it from the beginning.

"I will do whatever it takes," he said softly, "to get you to move in with me. Anything you'll let me do if you'll allow me to take care of you the way I was meant to. I want to buy you a house, and if I have to move to California to do it, I will."

I didn't know what to say to that. It was still scary to think about being married and having my own house. It wasn't that I didn't want to be with him. I wasn't doubtful of our always being together. It wasn't just the being young thing and people thinking I was hillbilly either, even though that was front and center. The label of marriage just brought something different to the table. I wasn't sure what. But my mom didn't honor the vow. She just left. Why couldn't we just be together and not worry about that right now? No, Dad would freak about my living with a guy and that's not what I wanted nor believed in either.

Caleb had a point about living with him, also. It would be impossible for him to reach me with conflicting class schedules while living in the dorm.

Wow, I was being so stupid. The answer was right there in front of me. Marry the man. Live with him, be happy and prosper.

Why was I being such a silly idiot about it all?

I looked up at Caleb from under my lashes to see him watching me work it all out. His face was anxious and hopeful. When I stayed silent and continued to stare into his ocean of blue eyes, he sighed and framed my face with his big warm loving hands. "Maggie, marry-"

A deep, sharp bark interrupted as Bella jumped and bounded up the beach. We looked behind us to see Kyle and Amber coming our way. I looked back to Caleb, knowing full well what he was going to ask me. He looked back at me, smiling sadly and we waited for the annoying giggling to reach us. Only then did we look away.

"Hey, guys. Wow, did you sleep out here?" Amber asked with a high voice, and I glared incredulously at her thoughts.

Mmmm. The beach...maybe tomorrow night Kyle and I should change venues.

Kyle gave me a look for my glare and I rolled my eyes before looking away.

Those two are seriously trying to show me up.

"So romantic," she crooned.

"Yes. It is," I said looking at Caleb, offering a little smile and then leaned my head back on Caleb chest and shut everyone out.

With his arms wrapped around me, I could feel the rumbling deep in his chest as he and Kyle conversed, but I didn't hear the words. I was in a mental state of shock, awe, happiness, fright and most importantly, unbelief. This just couldn't be my life. Sleeping on the beach with warm loving arms around me, being almost proposed to as we snuggled in the sand, blocking out annoying chatter from my mind with just a thought. I was so very lucky and so very scared. I'd always wanted to be special and important and now that I was, I wasn't so sure anymore.

I was the Visionary. It was time I accepted that and learned exactly what that meant. Then it hit me, we had to call the Reunification meeting early. There was no other way around it. I had to meet these people and understand exactly what it was that everyone was doing in the present day that was wrong when they were powerless and without abilities. It was strange to me that the ones who had already ascended got to keep their abilities. It was only the ones who hadn't ascended who were affected. That had to mean something.

I glanced up to see Amber fluttering her hands as Bella tried to lick her hand. "Ooh, ooh, get it away!"

"Come here, girl," Caleb ordered softly and she dropped her head on my leg as she lay down beside us. He rubbed her ears. "She just wants some loving."

"Well, she's way too big and slobbery." She wiped her hands on Kyle's shirt. "My Pomeranian is way cuter and not so disgusting."

Caleb cocked a brow at her and then at Kyle, who just looked at the sky and shook his head. He had nothing to say to that.

"She's not disgusting," I sang to Bella. "You're a sweet, big girl." I looked up at Amber. "She's really sweet and soft and lovey. She can't help it she's so fluffy."

She looked at me, almost as if she was sorry for something, but her mind just flitted right on to the dogs again before I could grasp anything. She seemed like she was trying not to think about something awfully hard, like it hurt her to.

"Well...whatever, I just don't like big dogs. Kyle, are you ready to walk me home?"

"You live like three streets over," he said and looked back at the house. "Can't you just scurry home real quick like, and I'll see you later?"

"You're not going to walk me home?" she asked and put her tan hands on her hips.

I was thinking the same thing actually. What kind of jerk wouldn't walk the girl home after he spent all night with her in the pool, regardless of what they did?

"Yeah, Kyle." Caleb smirked and nodded his head at her. "Walk her home."

"Everyone will be up soon," Kyle said and glanced back to the house again.

"Maybe you should take responsibility for the things you choose to do," Caleb said, not unkindly, just matter-of-factly. "If you're ready to hang out all night and rebel, then you're ready to walk the girl home and make sure she gets there safely."

"Ahh," Amber said and looked at Caleb with new eyes. "That's so sweet."

"Eat me," Kyle said to Caleb, glanced at me, almost shamefully. "Fine, let's go."

"Ok, bye," she said and let him drag her up the beach by her arm.

"Jerk. His daddy didn't raise him to act that way," Caleb muttered sarcastically.

"He just doesn't understand. He doesn't feel anything for her. That's why he doesn't care."

"I know, and that's the problem. How could he be like that to her and not feel like a jerk?"

"He's just a normal, human teenage boy. That's how they act."

"I never did," he countered.

"Yes," I put my arms around his neck, "but you were waiting for me, remember?" I said sweetly, smiling brightly and playfully.

"Mmhmm." He pressed his lips to mine, sucking on the top then bottom before taking them completely. "And now I've got you," he whispered against my mouth and then deepened our kiss.

I felt myself being pulled to his mind, my body wanting to take over and feel everything in him. It felt like so long since I'd been in his mind, when it had been only a few days. I felt his protective barrier, burning even brighter. It almost hurt to feel the flame of it. He was almost angry it seemed, regarding something he was worried about protecting me from; I wondered about it. His need to protect had doubled and it was a full-force wild fire now. Something had happened.

But before I could dwell on that, I felt myself slip in further and saw a new loop of memories. Him watching me at his band practice, my face filled with awe and love and longing. I was shocked by it. It was all over me how much I loved Caleb and he absolutely loved that look on me. Then another one came of us surfing, me taking a glide, and then fast-forwarded to the pavilion. Me pressed against the wall. I blushed at the scene in which I was utterly enraptured in him and he was eating it up, loving it.

Then I was jerked away, seeing the energy ribbons I had completely forgotten about fizzle away in the air. Caleb put his forehead to mine, breathing raggedly.

"You can dig in my mind anytime you want, babe, but not like this," he said sternly, but chuckled. "I want to, you know I do, especially since we were so close last time and were interrupted. I don't think I could stand to start and not...finish again, ok? Let's just wait until we know we won't have any distractions."

"Ok," I sighed and took a deep breath to calm myself.

I wondered what he meant by 'finish'. I wondered what happened at the end of the Mutuality. If it was that amazing during the act, I wondered what in the world could happen to top it off. My skin was hot and flushed from being so consumed by him and seeing the things I'd seen in his mind. He smirked at me and helped me up, standing himself.

"I better get you inside," he said into my ear, his breath in my hair, "before you convince me that the public beach is an appropriate place for such a thing." He nipped my earlobe.

"Caleb," I breathed, "that's not helping."

"I know." He snickered and dodged my swat. "Come on, gorgeous. I'm hungry, for food," he said and gave me a sidelong grin, taking my hand.

I just shook my head and tried to walk straight. Bella trailed us and as we made our way inside she bolted to her bowl and scarfed the contents.

"There you are," Rachel said and put a hand on her hip, spatula in hand. "I was beginning to wonder. You know it's almost ten o'clock in the morning? Wasting perfectly good daylight," she said and smirked.

Everyone was piled in the kitchen around the table or at the bar with plates high of pancakes.

"We were...practicing on the beach last night," Caleb explained and smiled at me.

"Practicing what?" Bish muttered darkly. *I'm sure I don't want to know.*

"Um..." Caleb hadn't thought about Bish being in there, "surfing."

"You're not wet," Bish observed and glared at me over the rim of his coffee cup.

"We changed our minds. It was cold," I lied and went to grab a plate from Rachel.

She gave me a small, knowing smile and then made a plate for Caleb.

"It looks pretty warm out to me."

"So, I was thinking," Dad interjected and glanced at me. I gave him a grateful smile, knowing he was changing the subject for us. "We're in California and I've never been here. How about we head out and do some sightseeing today?"

"Yes!" Rachel said excitedly and took off her apron. "We can show you all the- oh wait, you meant you, Maggie and Bish, of course."

"No, I meant all of us unless you'd be bored. I'm sure you've seen it all."

"Not at all," Peter chimed. "We're usually just content to lounge around and be lazy and...relax." He glanced at Rachel with a smile that made me hide a blush under my hand. I heard Caleb groan in my mind. "We'd love to come if you wouldn't feel imposed on."

"No, of course not," he said.

"I better go get all dolled up then," Bish said and thanked Rachel for breakfast before heading out.

"Peter," I said softly and he glanced at me. "I need you to do something for me."

"You want me to call the Reunification meeting early? Done." He glanced at Rachel, and asked, "Can you hand me a knife, honey?"

"Sure," she said and opened the drawer. A butter knife floated out and went through the air, straight to his waiting hand.

"Thanks," he said as he dug in with my father gawking openly.

"You already called them?" I asked. "How did you..."

He smiled and winked at me as he took a big bite of pancakes. "These are divine, Rae," he said to Rachel.

"Thanks, honey," she replied.

"I'm not even going to ask what a reuni...reunited...whatever meeting is," Dad questioned. "I'm sure it's something with a lengthy explanation and I'm ready to sightsee. I'll go get ready, too." Then he looked at me. "What *were* you two doing on the beach?"

"Practicing," Caleb repeated. "We...discovered something about Maggie last night, something new."

"What...like a new ability?" Peter asked excitedly and leaned forward on the table towards us.

I nodded, and Dad went off...mentally.

Great, juuuust great, more reasons to keep her away from me. More reasons to upset Bish, to lie and more reasons for her to be even more of a freak.

I gasped and felt Caleb wrap his fingers around mine to calm me, but I felt the shock pouring off him, too.

"Dad," I breathed in disappointment.

He looked up and his face blanched a white that matched the china plate his breakfast was on.

Crap, I forgot.

"Baby, I'm sorry. I didn't mean that." He looked between Caleb and me and then over at Peter and Rachel, who had no idea what he'd said, and Jen, who'd been surprisingly silent. I felt my lip tremble and Caleb pulled me to him closer, his hand rubbing small, comforting circles on my back. "Maggie. I completely forgot about your ability. That's not an excuse, but...I'm sorry. This all takes some getting used to." He leaned his elbows on the table towards me. "I'm sorry, really,

98

that wasn't only an insult to you, but to everyone else in this room, and I apologize."

I nodded, but didn't feel much better. "Dad, I know this is hard. Especially being on the outside of it and just looking in all the time. I'm sorry...I mean, I'm not sorry this happened, I'm just sorry that you had to get all wrapped up in it."

He gave me a surprised look.

"You're not sorry this happened? How can you even say that? They hurt you, those men who took you. You've had quite a few close calls. You're saying if you could go back, you wouldn't change anything?"

He did not understand at all. Not like I thought he did. He still saw this as something I was being forced to endure and just making the best of it.

"Dad, you're so clueless. I'm not being disrespectful." I held up my hands. "You have no idea and for some reason I thought you understood. I'm not being forced, Dad. I'm not unhappy. I'm not just enduring Caleb. I'm not just accepting my fate and going with the flow. I *like* my abilities...most of the time." I shook my head side to side in debate. "I like being a part of Caleb's family and I love Caleb. If I could go back and change the day I met him, I wouldn't."

"You said he touched you and then you saw visions and then he was feeling your heartbeat and he's like a drug to you. That's the gist of all this, isn't it?"

Crap, we were going to have to hash this out in front of Caleb's family. I pulled him to the edge of the kitchen to have a little bit more privacy.

"The day Caleb touched my hand and I saw all those things, I was excited. Yes, a little freaked but excited more. I felt like... everything I ever needed was right there. I still feel like that. It's not something you can just turn off and I wouldn't want to. I *want* him more than I *need* him."

"Maggie, being addicted to someone isn't the same thing as real, true, pure love," he said softly, like this was an intervention.

I shook my head and felt my breath leave me in a rush. Even Peter was thinking of saying something now, still being able to hear us from across the room. They all could. Dad was infringing on all our relationships at this point. I thought I saw a few energy ribbons bounce in the air by the window, but when I looked, there was nothing.

"Dad, you have no idea what you're saying," I said. "I'm going to get ready to go."

I expected Caleb to follow me, but he didn't. I figured he wanted to talk to my father or his, but I didn't care. I needed a shower and he couldn't come with me anyway.

As I reached for the doorknob to the bathroom, Bish was coming out. He snorted and crossed his arms over his bare chest. The towel wrapped around his waist.

"No Caleb? This must be a record."

"Shut up!" I yelled, suddenly furious and spent from the morning. "I am so tired of you lately. Why are you always on my case?"

Oh? She wants to fight, huh?

"Someone has to try to look after you, though I question the point now. It's obvious you are so completely different than before and Caleb is just...I don't know, but whatever this is that you won't tell me, I can handle it." He braced his hands in the doorframe and stood over me with a menacing sneer on his lips. "What can it be? It can't be that bad if we've ruled out marriage and babies. I don't get it and it does nothing but insult and piss me off that you feel the need to be petty and lord over me some secret that I'm not allowed to be privy to."

"You have no idea what you're talking about." I tried to go, but he moved over a bit to block me.

Oh, I think I do.

"Answer me, Maggie. Just answer me already and stop this stupidity. I have racked my brain for answers; drugs, joining some cult, moving to China?" I stayed silent looking at the doorjamb behind him and he exploded with anger and cursed loudly, his voice booming. "This is ridiculous! I'm just gonna leave and go home. There's no point in my being here. You don't want me here and I don't want to be either. I can't stand liars and manipulators. You've become a master of both."

His words cut and I couldn't say anything in response, not that he gave me time to. He stomped off and slammed his door behind him making me jump. I heard footsteps coming up the stairs and didn't wait to see who had come to witness the show.

I went in the bathroom, still steamy and hot from Bish's shower. I wasted no time. I pulled Caleb's hoodie and clothes off and stepped into the huge shower in one of the guest rooms. I let the water be as hot as I could stand it as I quickly washed my hair and shaved my legs. Then I sat against the wall, closed my eyes and just cried. So many things going on and I didn't have a straightforward answer nor a response to any of them. It seemed that this Visionary thing just sort of *winged it*. I had no prior idea or knowledge until I got a feeling, and then just went with it. It was annoying.

I took a deep, calming breath to slow my heart so Caleb wouldn't come, but it didn't help at all.

And Dad, what had all that crap been about? Now he was back to resenting Caleb and feeling sorry for me again? And Kyle with his stupid fling and making moves on me, thinking that was somehow going to help things. Bish was a jerk, nothing else to say about him.

I felt the pressure of all of those things....an uncontrollable sob was so close to breaking loose...

Then the shower stall suddenly started to rattle. I looked around and the water got even hotter it felt like, but I didn't touch the knob. It was scalding my skin but wasn't actually hurting me and the fog swirled. I could see a faint haze of energy ribbons starting to shimmer and dance. I wondered what was wrong, but felt all the breath leave my chest as the mirror above the sink shattered, blowing glass all around the floor, tinkling on the tile.

Eleven

I shook, my heart pounding through my chest, wondering what was happening. Then I heard loud, quick banging and I realized that the cabinet doors were rattling. The shower stall door shook so hard it was a miracle it stayed on the hinges.

"Maggie?" Caleb asked through the door. He then banged his fist. "Maggie, open the door!"

I was so scared I could only stare at the door, afraid to move. There was nothing I could do. The more scared I got, the more noise everything seemed to make, the rattling and shaking louder and vibrating the air. The energy ribbons were blinding and writhing all around me until they hummed so loud, my ears hurt. I covered them with my hands and squeezed my eyes shut.

"Maggie!" Caleb yelled and banged again, jarring the door. "Open the door, baby."

I could hear other voices and thoughts outside with him. They heard Caleb's banging and now wondered what was going on.

"Maggie!" Caleb boomed. "I'm coming in."

Their worry, my fear, Caleb's frantic need to reach me; it just was too much for whatever was happening to me.

The glass shower door shattered around me. I screamed as the glass pelted me and that was all it took for Caleb. He busted the door down with his shoulder. I felt the stinging pain in my shoulder from his pain. His eyes were wide at what he saw; me sitting naked with my knees drawn up on the shower floor with glass and blood around me.

"Maggie," he breathed and ran to duck in front of me. He pulled me to him and covered me with his arms as I sat on his lap. "Maggie." *Talk to me, baby.*

"Get out," I heard Dad say as he reached over and turned the water off, but I couldn't tear my eyes from the bloody glass shards on the floor. "Bish, get out now! She's ok."

"She is not ok!" Bish yelled back. "What the hell is going on here, Dad? What happened? Did she do this? How could she break the door like that?"

"Go, Bish."

"I'll call 911."

"No, don't, just go. I'll be there in a minute."

I heard him grumbling and shuffling. I heard the hard bang of fist on wood as he made his way out.

I saw my dad over Caleb's shoulder. He handed Caleb a towel and then knelt beside us as Caleb covered me with it.

"Maggie, what happened?" Dad asked insistently, his eyes wide and searching.

Maggie. Look at me, baby. I tore my eyes slowly from the mess in front of me and looked up to Caleb's blue worry-sick eyes. "Are you ok?" he asked softly and I noticed how Caleb hadn't asked me what happened, he was concerned about *me* first.

I looked down at myself and opened my mouth to speak, but no words came. I looked at him at a total loss and then felt him focus and the scrapes on my arms and legs started to burn and fade away to my normal, smooth skin. I heard Dad's swift intake of breath and mutter behind us.

"God, help us."

"I don't know what happened," I croaked and wrapped Caleb's t-shirt front in my fingers. "Caleb," I rasped and took a deep, shuddering breath.

"Shh," he murmured in my hair and tightened his arms around me. "Shh, I've got you now."

Caleb's questions were floating around in his mind, but more than anything else, he was upset. Seeing me with blood all over me had done something to him and he was shaken.

I heard Peter come in behind us and he was baffled as well.

"Maggie, are you all right? I checked the house and no one was here."

"It wasn't someone else," I answered softly. "It was...me. I don't know what happened. I was just so upset..."

I pressed my forehead to Caleb's and decided to show him everything that had happened instead of trying to form words with my trembling lips. I felt the energy humming around us. The vision started with us on the beach for some

103

reason, me on his lap and then Kyle and Amber, then coming inside and the whole bit with Dad, the hall with Bish as he berated me in the doorway and finally the shower scene. I couldn't even blush or be embarrassed as he saw me take my clothes off and get in and shave. Then the weirdness started and he burst through the door.

Caleb pulled back and sighed as he looked at me with sincere concern. He looked me over, pulling my arms up and then examining my legs for any more cuts. Then he looked back to my face.

"I think it *was* you. Just like the moving things and telepathy stuff, they were tied to your emotions, too. It was just too much, all at once."

"Telepathy?" Dad mumbled under his breath.

"I think so, too," I said. "I'm so sorry," I cried and felt the tears burning my cold face. "I didn't mean to."

"No, no, no," Caleb insisted and pushed my hair back from my face. "Don't you dare."

"What about the door and the mirror?"

"That's just stuff, Maggie. Don't you worry about any of that," Peter assured. I felt so embarrassed that I was naked, had busted up the bathroom and everyone was just standing around.

I heard Peter picking up pieces of glass behind Caleb and the metallic clinking of it hitting the bottom of the trash can.

"What's going on?" Dad asked.

"Jim, I think we should leave them alone for a minute," Peter suggested, putting a hand on his shoulder.

"Maggie, are you ok?" Dad asked ignoring Peter.

"I'm fine. Please just go so I can get up and get dressed," I asked and he grimaced looking at Caleb.

Aha, right, no clothes and Caleb is gonna help her naked self get dressed, huh?

"Dad," I protested with tightly shut eyes. "Please."

He huffed in defeat and took off down the hall.

"I'll get Rachel and Jen, we'll get Bish and Jim out of the house," Peter suggested.

"Good idea. Thanks, Dad," Caleb said, his eyes fixed to mine.

"Take care of her, Caleb."

"Dad," he looked at him over his shoulder, "I know, ok? I've got her."

"I know, son." He put his hand on Caleb's shoulder and then turned to walk away.

Caleb lifted me immediately in his arms, with the towel still wrapped around me, and carried me to the guest room with my stuff in it. He set me on the bed after kicking the door closed and knelt in front of me. He secured the towel around me and continued to look at me closely.

"I'm fine," I said finally, hearing his thoughtful concerns in his mind, "really."

"I know you are. You're strong enough to handle anything, but I hate that this is happening to you. How am I supposed to protect you from something that's in you? Or something that's happening to you?"

"You *are* protecting me, right now. This is what I need; you."

"You know it's not the same thing," he said softly.

"It is to me." I wrapped my arms around his neck and pulled him close to me, between my knees. His arms were warm and soothing around my skin as he pulled me close, crushing me to him as I breathed in the familiar smell of his neck. I felt his calm invading me and I sighed in respite.

"You are still surprising me," he said into my hair. He pulled back to look at me. "You're still amazing." He placed a warm hand on my cheek. "We'll figure this thing out. It's just like everything else we've been through, we'll do it together. I'll always be here."

"I'm scared," I whispered my admission and felt him wipe a tear from under my eye with his thumb.

"I'm not. I know that we'll be fine. You are my life and I won't let anything happen to you." This reminded me of the extra sensitive protective barrier in his mind. I asked him the silent question. "It's just something my dad said. He thinks the council might try to take you from me. Hide you away somewhere for your protection, because you're so important."

"But...they can't do that!" I said in a panic, but he covered my lips with a finger as he leaned in close.

"No, they can't because I won't let them. I'd have to be dead first before I let them take you from me."

"Caleb, don't say stuff like that," I groaned.

"It's true. I will never let them. You're mine. I didn't say anything to you because you already had so much going on, but you don't have to worry."

"Running away is starting to sound really good right now," I mumbled.

He chuckled and kissed my forehead. "You're so funny," he whispered. "Please don't let this get to you. My family would never let anything happen to you and I guarantee my dad has already been on the phone with them to try to figure out the latest puzzle piece."

"Thank you."

"What for?" he asked.

"For always knowing what to say to make me feel right again." I smiled and touched his nose with mine.

"Gah, I love you," he breathed.

"Love you."

He kissed me softly, taking my mouth with gentle pressure that was sweet and loving, not demanding. My eyes closed and I saw the ribbons behind him in the dark. He lifted me into his lap as he sat on the bed and cradled me against him. He moved his palm up and down my thigh in a soothing caress. I felt him run his hand all the way down to my ankle and back up before slowly laying us back on the bed. We stayed just like that with me snuggled protectively against him, breathing steadily and slowly until we heard the doorbell downstairs.

"I'll run and get that, and let you get dressed," Caleb murmured against my forehead.

"Ok," I said and smiled when he got up as he straightened my towel to make sure it stayed secure.

I sat up and was amazed at how much better I felt. Caleb was my drug, Dad was right, but that didn't mean it was a bad thing. He was like my...prescription drug, just what I needed.

I put on my blue puff sleeve shirt and a pair of jeans, brushed my hair in the spare bathroom. I didn't even peek in the one that I had destroyed, and flung on some blue and gold dangle earrings and a slick of makeup. As I walked barefoot downstairs, I heard a girl's voice. She was laughing and giggling, and Caleb was talking excitedly. The voice sounded familiar and at first I thought it was Ashley.

I froze on the stairs.

Then descended slowly, guarding my expression, but then I heard her thoughts and smiled. I turned the corner to see none other than Beck and Ralph standing in the foyer.

"Mags!" she yelled and skipped to me in a girly scamp. "Omgosh, your hair!"

"Beck," I gasped in surprise as she ran into me, forcing all of the air out of me. "What are you doing here?"

"Caleb called me yesterday. He said you could use a friend right now and you missed me, so he booked us a ticket for the first flight out. And here I am."

I balked and turned to Caleb. He was leaning against the foyer wall with his arms crossed, watching me with a little crooked smile, his dimple making a necessary appearance.

"You flew her here for me?"

"And me, too," Ralph butted in grinning.

106

"Of course," I said and went to hug him.

"It's good to see you."

"You, too. Thanks for taking care of Beck."

"My pleasure," he said and glanced at her, winking slyly.

She blushed and giggled silently making me press my lips together to keep from smiling.

Caleb continued to stand there watching. I was completely in awe and enraptured by his easy smile and eyes that followed and caressed me from across the room. He winked at me and I couldn't stop from going to him.

"Thank you." I put my hands on his chest. "You didn't have to do that," I said softly where only he could hear.

"I know," he answered, rubbing my upper arms with his palms, "but I wanted to. You haven't seen her much lately, what with me stealing you away and all," he grinned, "and you told me she's leaving for school soon, right?"

I nodded and reached up on my tiptoes to kiss him, a quick, gentle peck. "Thank you. You're awesome."

"You're welcome."

"Ok, ok!" Beck shouted and flounced to us. "I can't believe you cut your hair. It's so frigging cute!"

"Thanks," I said and let her believe what she wanted.

"You have to take us somewhere, Caleb. Somewhere that is littered with celebrities and all-you-can-drink bars."

"Uh..." Caleb's eyes flicked to mine, "I'm not sure."

She wants to go clubbing the entire time she's here, doesn't she?

Ahh, you know my friend so well already.

I smiled at him to show my amusement.

"Well," he started again, "I went to a few clubs with Zeke last summer. We can try one tonight if you want. Then tomorrow night, I have a gig. You're more than welcome to come out and see the show."

"You play, man?" Ralph asked.

"Yeah, sort of," Caleb said modestly.

"He's being modest," I said. "He can play just about anything, but in the show, he's playing bass."

"Sweet," Ralph said in appreciation. "Sounds good. Well, uh, can we get a shower or better yet, can we take a dip in the pool? I smell like a plane, dude, seriously."

"Sure. Bathroom's up the stairs, all the way to to the end of the hall. You can change in there."

They made their way up the stairs as he instructed them to go to the bathroom that I had not destroyed. I looked up to him as I walked into the circle of his arms.

"So we're going swimming?" I asked and ran a hand through his hair making his eyes close. "And then tonight we're going clubbing?"

He groaned before answering, keeping his eyes closed.

"We don't have to, but it might work to keep your mind off things. Beck should do a pretty good job of entertaining you."

"Yeah," I agreed and twirled my fingers through his locks. He groaned again and laid his head against mine. "Ok, I guess I'm going to go put on my suit."

He nodded, but held me tight. "Are you all right?"

I nodded too and smiled when he kissed my nose. He went to put his suit on and I went to put on mine.

"Holy crap! A pool, a hot tub, a volleyball net and the beach in your backyard. Dude, I'm never leaving," Ralph spouted to Caleb before playfully shoving him and taking off to do a cannon ball.

He splashed Beck, lounging in her hot pink bikini by the poolside making her squeal and feign retaliation. We all knew she wasn't getting up. This had been the same scene for over half an hour now. Caleb and I were sitting on the side of the pool beside each other. Ralph swam and jumped in, beckoning Beck and egging her on.

Caleb was worried about me still and hadn't left my side. Although I was overjoyed to see Beck, I was upset about what had happened in the bathroom just a couple hours ago. My father's words came back to me, lancing through me with painful realization. I was a freak. This wasn't normal. Even the Aces didn't know what was happening to me and my mind reeled with scenarios and unforeseen events still out before us. I knew things were going to change but this whole Visionary thing was blindsiding us.

It was causing things to be muddled and even more complicated. I was becoming very disgruntled about it all. I looked over at Caleb to see him watching me with concern. He wasn't having any fun either. I felt even worse. We were on vacation for goodness sake...sort of.

I took a deep breath, pushing away images of breaking glass, tinkling shards on tile, energy ribbons dancing in the air, disappointed brothers, overprotective fathers and most of all, my own body turning against me.

I smiled and slid off the side into the water. Caleb's eyes lit with relief, hearing and seeing me, and he slid in with me wrapping his arms around me as we bobbed in the water.

"Mmm, there's that smile again," he praised and kissed me on the end of my nose.

"I'm trying."

"I know. I'm sorry that all this is happening. I wish I could stop it."

I shrugged and refused to say another word about it. I bit my lip and kissed under his chin.

He gave me a look that said I was starting something, especially in that bathing suit, but I just chuckled and splashed him before taking off across the pool. He gave chase and we all ended up in a splash war, even Beck, who decided it was pointless to try to stay out of it anymore.

Kyle soon joined us, not having gone with his parents and my dad.

"Mind if I join you?" he asked but he was looking at me.

I remembered the last time we were in here together, but knew he would never try anything with Caleb right there. "Sure," I answered. "Let's play volleyball," I suggested.

"But we're uneven," Beck whined.

"What?" I scoffed. "You scared, Rebecca? Let's do Caleb and me against the rest of you." I looked at him and he nodded, rubbing his hands in challenge. "How's that for fair?"

I laughed at her face as we all took our places as Kyle pulled the net across the pool and clicked it together on the other side.

"Oh, you are so going down now, little miss perky. Ralph, set me up," she said in determination, but her pink frilled bikini was refuting her tough-girl stance.

He did and she served a wide ball that knocked over my glass of tea on the table.

"Hey!" I yelled.

She looked surprised at first, but then smirked. "See? Mess with me and you get the horns."

I rolled my eyes at her mistake and her bravado and we began to play. Beck was ok for someone trying not to break a nail the whole time and Ralph's competitive spirit matched Caleb's. Kyle was just normal Kyle. It was so nice.

We lost by one point. But that point made all the difference and the smack talk ensued as we went inside to get ready to go out to the club Caleb told us about.

Twelve

Once Caleb and I made our way down to the foyer to wait for Beck and Ralph – we invited Kyle, but he said he had plans with Amber – I told Dad where we were going. He wanted us to take Bish with us.

"Dad, please. I can't deal with this tonight. I want to go out to get away from Bish and everything else."

Maggie, I don't feel safe with you-"

"I'll be with Caleb," I argued. "I'll be as safe as I can be."

"I'm not knocking Caleb. I just think the more bodies, the more protection. You and Bish could spend a little time together."

I took a slow, deep breath and spoke low with calm and conviction.

"Did you not see what I did to the bathroom upstairs? I can't, Dad. He's making me too crazy right now and none of us would have any fun. I *need* some fun. I need to take a minute and just be a teenager."

"But, Maggie, you wanted this remember? You wanted this life with Caleb and all the things in it."

"I'm not blaming you, Dad. I'm just saying I'm going out and without Bish."

"I can't allow it. I think he should go, end of discussion," he said and went upstairs to fetch Bish, I saw in his mind.

I stood there and seethed. Caleb said my name, but it sounded weird, muffled. I looked at him and there was a wall of energy ribbons between us. He gave me a surprised look.

"Calm down, baby, it's ok." He walked through them. It was the strangest thing to see all those wormy little strings going through his skin. When he reached me, he touched my cheek to draw off my anxiety. "Breathe, Maggie." I did as he said and slowly the ribbons dissolved away. "It'll be ok. I'll keep you occupied and away from Bish, I promise."

I needed to control my thoughts, my emotions. I nodded and tried not to think about it as I heard footsteps down the stairs and then their thoughts.

Ugh, Maggie looks so fantastic. What the heck is she doing to her skin? It's like flawless. And her arms are so toned. No wonder Caleb can't keep his hands off her – crap, forgot my handbag. I wonder where we're going. I wonder if I can trick the bartender into serving me. Worked in Chattanooga. Now where's the bag...there. Ok. Good. Ready. Now focus, Rebecca. She has something to tell you, she's been hiding it for weeks. She's gonna spill it tonight. I can feel it. She's probably pregnant, so school your face and don't let it show how you think she's ruining her life and is a complete idiot.

She took a big mental breath and descended the stairs. I shook my head at her and looked at the wall clock in anticipation. Bish joined us along with Dad, and to my dismay, Jen was with them as well...and she was dressed to go out.

"Dad, what's up?"

"I figured Bish and Jen should go and be chaperones."

Ah, no. I heard Caleb groan in my mind. *Now what?*

"Where are Peter and Rachel?" I asked.

"Oh, they went shopping. They always go to this little place when we come here," Jen answered.

"Ok, fine, let's go," I said, not willing to dwell or think about any of it.

We went outside and I looked at the cars. We'd have to split up. Crap!

"How do we do this?" Bish asked.

"Why don't you ride with us," I offered to Bish and Jen.

"But we don't know our way around," Beck said, "and I missed you and I want to ride with you."

"Ok." I thought fast. "Why don't we ride girls and guys?"

Caleb's dislike of that idea was evident in his mind, but everyone else was fine with it. Beck was ecstatic, and Jen and Bish were relieved, fearing they were going to be stuck riding together.

I kissed Caleb quickly and pulled Jen's arm gently to guide her with me as we got into Peter's rental Beamer and the guys piled into the Jeep. I sat in the back so Beck wouldn't feel left out and Jen drove.

"So, Jen, how have you been? Oh, wait. I'm sorry, this is Beck, my friend from home, and this is Jen, Caleb's sister." After their "Nice to meet you"s, I got back to my point. "Anyway, how have you been? How's Maria?"

"She's great. She's staying with Gran."

"Oh, boy," I laughed. "She's gonna be so rotten by the time you get back."

Jen laughed, too, and nodded. "Yeah," she groaned playfully, "I know. That girl loves her some Gran."

I saw how Beck was looking very lost so I changed the subject. "Ralph is very sweet lately, Beck. How are you guys doing?"

111

"Awesome. He told his parents off and he's going to school with me."

"Really," I gasped and laughed. "That's awesome, I think."

"It is. You know how he is about his parents. He stood up to them and for me." She pressed her lips together to keep from smiling or crying, I didn't know which. "Maggie, I am so totally falling in love with him."

"Aww, Beck, I'm so happy for you." I reached over the seat to grab her arm. "Ralph is a good guy."

"Yeah, he is. I mean, I don't want to move too fast. We're not gonna live together or anything, but the fact that he wants to go to school with me has to say something, right?"

"Yeah, I think so," I said slowly and heard Jen's thoughts of longing and disappointment, but she kept her smile in place as she looked between us and the road.

Dang it. It seemed every subject we went to was making one or the other uncomfortable. So, I told them all about Caleb's gig the next night and how he'd been practicing all week. Beck thought Zeke was hilarious and fabulous, couldn't wait to meet him, while Jen concurred with my assessment that he was crazy.

Once we arrived downtown, Jen pulled into the parking lot of a big warehouse looking place. It was dark, dank, dirty and disturbing. There was no indication that it was a club and not an abandoned warehouse used for illegal operations and squatters, except for one neon sign on the front that read 'Lively Pony'. The Jeep pulled in right behind us and the guys jumped out quickly to meet us.

"Omgosh, look at this place," Beck said and shivered with excitement. "It's so mysterious! Let's go in!"

The thump of the music was barely heard as we made our way through the parking lot almost overflowing with cars. We were a train as we zigzagged through the parked vehicles. Caleb towed me behind him with my hand firmly in his, then Beck was being guided with hands on her hips from Ralph. And Bish, if he realized he was doing it or not, walked closely behind Jen and had a hand out to the side slightly, as if to steer her if she tried to go the wrong way.

The bouncer was a strangely gangly guy, not the type you'd expect from a place like this. There was a small line that was started at the underground stairs to the door. That's why you couldn't see them from the street.

"I said no. Once we've reached a certain capacity, I can't let in the good looking challenged. Sorry," the bouncer whose nametag read 'Toad' said blandly. "Next."

The two guys he turned away were blinding mad, their minds blaring obscenities and anger. I cringed into Caleb's side and tried to force their thoughts

112

away. He put a hand on my head to press my face into his neck and sent me warm calm. When I lifted my head, I saw Beck watching us. She was smiling, but she looked confused.

"Why did they turn those guys away?" I asked to distract.

"Did you see all that metal in their mouth? And I'm not talking about tongue rings," Ralph explained. "And that one guy had on suspenders under his blazer."

"Poor guys. That's so mean." Everyone chuckled slightly and I looked around confused. "What?"

"Honey," Beck said slowly like I was a toddler, "that's what happens at these things. You can't just throw on any crap you want and not fix your hair and expect to get in. It is important to have a certain look. This isn't a honky tonk bar from Chattanooga, ok?"

I looked down at my jeans and heeled boots with a little black chiffon top and camisole. I'd put on the new earrings I'd bought the last time we went out. No one had said anything when we left, so I assumed I looked okay enough for this.

"So, how do you know if we'll get in?" Everyone chuckled again and I felt like I was seriously missing something. "What?" I said with more force.

"Have you looked in the mirror lately, sweetheart?" Ralph said and laughed again. "Don't worry about us lowly, " he bent to bow at the waist with his hands out, "tools basking in your glow. They always let the guys with the babes in on principle." He looked around at Beck and Jen grinning and winked.

Beck looked smug and Jen smiled, bemused. I just shook my head. Then it was our turn to meet Toad. My heart pounded for some reason, fear that maybe he'd take one look at my little seventeen-year-old self and turn us away. Caleb pulled me to him.

"Hey, man. Six of us," he initiated.

Toad looked around and his face never changed. "Cover is thirty for the guys, ladies are free tonight."

"Awesome," Caleb spouted and paid the man, waving Ralph's money away. *Focus on me, Maggie. You'll definitely overload in a place like this.*
Yeah, thanks.

"Go ahead," Toad spouted.

"Really?" I asked puzzled. "You're not going to check our IDs or anything?"

Toad looked back to me and smiled as he gave a slow once over that had Caleb gritting his teeth.

"I'll check anything you want me to, sweetheart."

"We're good, thanks," Caleb almost growled and pulled me through the big black and gray door as I heard Ralph and Beck laughing loudly behind us.

I was blasted with bass climbing from the floor into my toes and smoke so thick it took a second to catch my breath.

"You're not going to check our ID's or anything?" Beck said in a singsong, mock voice. "Ha! Maggie, you're so hilarious. You need to learn to be hot, honey," she said as Ralph dragged her away.

I had no idea what she was talking about and looked at Caleb. He was smiling and laughing silently. He pulled me to him with a hand on the back of my neck.

"Oh, my gosh, I love you," he muttered huskily and kissed me before pulling me to meet everyone else at the bar.

"Ok, I don't care what you do," Jen started, looking at us sternly, "but I will be watching the bar and if I catch any of you trying to score, so help me-"

"We won't," Caleb assured, rolling his eyes.

She gave him a 'duh' look and then turned her gaze on Beck and Ralph.

"Oh, come on!" he complained, but Jen's eyebrow shot up ever so slightly and it was amazing how she suddenly looked so menacing. "Ok, fine."

"Great. See you guys later," she called and then made her way through the crowd and strobing lights.

Bish watched her with great interest. In his mind, he was wondering if she was going to dance with anyone. He hated that he even cared.

I turned away from him and looked up at Caleb. "Well, are you gonna dance with me or what?" I said playfully.

"Yes, ma'am."

He grinned as he pulled me to the growing crowd of thrashers and shimmyers. I figured we would be so packed in there he wouldn't be able to tell that I couldn't really dance anyway. I was right. It was worse than sardines, but I was not complaining about being pressed against Caleb. The music was playing loudly, some techno generic club stuff that was very *Night at the Roxbury*.

We found Beck and Ralph on the dance floor. Beck immediately pulled me to her and started twirling me under her arm. I laughed as we danced together in between Caleb and Ralph.

Everyone's thoughts around me were disturbing to say the least as I slowly let them creep in. It was all sex, sex and drugs and strangely, local bands and eateries. The ones close to us, some were even thinking about me, looking at me and Caleb in ways I'd prefer not, so I quickly moved my focus elsewhere.

Eventually Ralph claimed he needed a drink and dragged Beck away, but I could pick my friends out among the crowd, I guessed because I was so attuned to them already. Beck and Ralph were dancing and snuggling by a large column in the middle. Beck's thoughts were floaty and sweet as she wrapped her arms around

Ralph's neck. And Ralph - well, he was still in love with her, like he'd said that day. He was ready for anything she wanted to give and couldn't wait for them to get to school and get a few months under their belt so he could propose. I felt teary-eyed listening to it.

Then I felt it, heard it, whatever. Bish was somewhere and his mind was burning with jealousy. I looked up and around for him and saw him, leaning against the bar, glaring at Jen and some guy. They were dancing on the edge of the crowd and the guy was pretty much all over her, but Jen was moving, eyes closed, just into it.

In her mind, she needed to just get away from everything, just be young for five minutes and forget about thinking about Bish, about anything. In his mind, he was freaking upset and wanted to strangle the guy, though he didn't know why.

I sighed and tried to push them out.

Relax. I looked up to find Caleb watching me. *Don't be the Visionary for tonight. Don't be an Ace; just be you. Push it all out and just focus on me.*

Caleb's face was so close and so sincere. I pushed all the attention of my mind and thoughts on him only as I stared into his deep blue eyes that were so focused on me. His mind was filled with everywhere his hands were at the moment and I felt flush all over. One, for not realizing that they'd been there the whole time and two, because of where they were. He had one knee between mine, one hand on the back of my thigh and the other arm wrapped around my waist tightly. I'd been so wrapped up in listening to everything around me that I forgot to pay attention to us.

He was so ready to move on with our lives; to not have to hide, to not have our family around all the time in the same house, to have to stop kissing or more when people walk into the room. He was so ready to do more than just touch me, so ready to Mutualize and have my name miraculously tattooed on the inside of his wrist by his crest, however that worked. He was ready for us to be us and nothing else. I had to agree.

I wanted to take him somewhere private right then and finish what we'd started.

He groaned in my mind and pressed his head to mine.

Ah, baby, don't.

What? I said in fake modesty. *I just thought that I'm pretty disappointed we never got to continue-*

Not here, please. Think about something else.

I giggled slightly and bit my lip. It was amazing how much I could fluster him.

Oh, I'm flustered all right. He smiled beautifully and sincerely, rubbing a thumb over my cheek. *You still have no idea how much pull you have over me. I'm completely captivated. I'm enraptured with you, Maggie. You're all there is for me. Ralph was right, too. You don't know how insanely beautiful you are. I'm the envy of every man in here, I guarantee you that.*

You're insane.

My argument had no real gusto because I'd heard the things people were thinking about me and it was strange. I'd never really been pretty before.

Yes, you were. You were always gorgeous. I hate to say this, but the thing I noticed first on the street that day was your freckles, how adorable you looked. Your hair was blowing around you and it was dark, making your freckles stand out under the lights. You were the most captivating creature I'd ever seen.

*Caleb...*I took a deep breath and tried to slow my heartbeat. I put my hand over his heart, feeling both our hearts together; one strong and steady as always and one galloping like a runaway pony. *You are so off the mark. You're the one who had me stunned. I was a stammering idiot trying to tell you I was ok. You were so close and your eyes...were so focused on me. I'd never been looked at that way before.*

And I'll never stop.

I hope not.

Then he was kissing me, moving us back to the shadows as he brought his hands up to hold my face and we continued to sway and move. It was so reminiscent of the time we danced on the beach at that party, before all the kidnapping and drama happened.

Caleb held tight to me and showed me his love and adoration with his lips and thoughts. I made sure to keep my mind on the outside of his and just listen. When I went digging, things happen, energy ribbons and breaking glass. I was sure no one here would appreciate any of that. When my fingers started to cramp from fisting the sleeves of his green and white polo for so long, I pulled back slightly and licked my lips to taste him there. He chuckled and breathed a happy sigh across my face.

We were bumped, jostled more than just by accident, by someone and I looked behind me to see a big guy with a black leather jacket and dark sunglasses on.

"I need you to come with me."

"Excuse me?" Caleb pulled me behind him. "Who are you?"

"I need the girl to come with me. It doesn't matter who I am." He looked back to me, or I assume he did because I couldn't see his eyes. "Come on, I don't have all night."

116

"Like hell," Caleb growled.

"I don't need this from you, boy. She's waiting and I'm not going to explain to her why I took so long. The girl is coming with me."

"Who's waiting?" I asked and the guy growled, reaching for my arm and I heard his thought.

I'm done waiting.

Caleb's hand snapped out to stop him, gripping him so tightly the big burly guy actually winced in his mind. It shocked me to see it as he bent down almost to his knees under Caleb's pressure. How was Caleb doing that?

What the-

"You better think again," Caleb said and I caught my breath at his control, but obvious seriousness. "You're not going anywhere with her. Answer her question. Who's waiting?"

"Someone you want to see," the man groaned and tried to pull his arm away. "You're breaking my arm, man."

"You reach for her again and I will."

Wow, somehow…Caleb did have some power. I'd have to tell Peter later. Maybe that will help him in the search to learn why Caleb didn't get his ascension ability.

"Fine, both of you can come, I don't care, just let go," he pleaded in a harsh tone. Caleb pulled his arm away, it going back behind him and around me while keeping his eyes on the man, now rubbing his arm like a sullen child. "Outside."

"Why would we? What's it to us?"

"Believe me," he said snidely and shook his arm out. "You want to come with me. She said to tell you that you'd find answers to your latest questions."

Caleb looked back at me.

What do you think? Your call.

I think we should go with him. What could it hurt? He looked at me like I was nuts. *What? You almost snapped that guy's arm. I know you can take care of me if something happens.*

He gave me a look that said he didn't like this, but was humoring me.

The first sign of trouble, we're out of there. No arguing.

I nodded and he waved his hand for the guy to lead us. He took us all the way through the back of the club to the alley. Caleb and I both became suspicious, but the guy stopped at a limousine. He turned to look at us and opened the door, beckoning us in.

"If you think I'm putting her in that car, you're crazy," Caleb said.

117

"Now, Caleb," a woman's voice crooned and I stiffened. The voice seeming familiar, but no thoughts were coming to me from inside the car. "Come on now, I won't bite."

Caleb's arm tensed under my hand and I could take the suspense no longer. I leaned to look inside and saw someone I not only never wanted to see, but never expected.

"Marla?"

Thirteen

Marla.

Marcus's sister who had cleaned me up when I was kidnapped and told me the story of the supposed beginning of all Aces; the guy down the well, which was the basis for Sikes putting me in the well to begin with. Here she was in the flesh and wanting to speak to us. I freaked because she'd see the mark on my neck and know what I was. I pulled the collar up on my neck and covered it with my curled fingers.

"What are you doing here?" Caleb said breathlessly, fighting for control, and pulled me behind him once more as Marla exited the limousine to stand in the open door. "Wow, you have some nerve," he spat out.

"I'm here to help you, believe it or not. I had to wait until you were away from the house, away from your parents, away from the others. I know my brother visited you in the echo." She rolled her eyes and muttered under her breath. "Idiot. Well I'm here to...elaborate. Please, sit inside with me for just a minute."

"A limo," I scoffed. "This is a little bit too much Godfather, even for a Watson."

"I drove here straight from the airport," she reasoned, like that explained it.

"How did you find us?" I asked. "Does your uncle know?"

"No, he doesn't, but how I found you doesn't matter; the fact that I'm here is important. Please," she asked again and held her hand out for us to enter.

I climbed in and Caleb climbed in closely behind me. Marla sat back in her seat and shut the door, but we didn't go anywhere. The guy who came into the club to get us came and got in the other side to sit beside Marla. We sat in the still limo and stared at each other for a minute before anyone spoke. Finally, Marla sighed and crossed her ankles, her hands in her lap.

Keep it covered, Maggie. She can't find out that you're the Visionary.
I know. I will.

I kept my hand curled on my neck, putting my chin on my hand to look casual.

"Ok, look, I know you have no reason to trust me, but think about it. When did you see me with them? I never agreed with your kidnapping. I only complied with them because I had to. I helped you. They wanted to just leave you in there and not let you bathe at all but I told them that was too cruel. So I went in against my uncle's wishes."

"Oh, that makes it alright?" Caleb roared. "They tortured her and because you weren't the one to actually do it, that makes you innocent?"

"No," she cried, "but I didn't have a choice."

"Yes, you did! You chose when you sat there and let them do that to her!"

The big guy scooted closer to her, as if to shield her if Caleb meant to hurt her.

"What was I supposed to do? They're my family but they're... evil." She covered her mouth and my heart skipped for her.

Why couldn't I hear her thoughts? Why was her mind shut to me when everyone else was a wide-open book that I read whether I wanted to or not?

"Oh, stop the water works," Caleb muttered and I chastised him silently.
Caleb. She's here. Let's hear her out.

He sighed harshly and unhappily, squeezing my hand.

"What do you want?" he asked her more softly.

"I want to help. I want to let you know what they've planned, give you a heads up. I at least owe you that."

"Yeah, you owe her more than that." Caleb looked around and between the two of them. "Ok, fine. What?"

"Sikes is furious. He wanted nothing more than to stop your ascension." She pressed her lips together and looked between us. "You know I'm pretty jealous myself. It's amazing, you two. I hope you appreciate what you have."

"I absolutely appreciate it but get on with your point."

She blew a long breath and smoothed her board-straight raven hair.

"Sikes is convinced that you're going to be the end of him. That...for whatever reason, you two have something between your abilities that's too powerful. You're a Seer and Caleb's a..." she paused and looked at him but he kept silent, "a what?"

"My ability is none of your business. So now what? What does he want to do to her now?"

"Well, you remember he took Maggie's blood," she started. "He's..." she sighed, "he's trying to find a way to use it. He's been experimenting on humans." I gasped, but she kept going. "He messed with your blood and gave it to three humans, all females, to try to spark some kind of reaction out of their bodies. But so far, he hasn't come up with anything. He...well, he disposed of them. Now, he's moved on to giving your blood to Aces."

"Wait, he's trying to make people have abilities just spring up because they have my blood in them?" I asked incredulously and completely grossed out.

"You remember the story I told you. It's not so far-fetched."

"So, what does this have to do with us?"

"Well...he ran out of your blood so...he's looking for ways to get more. He's talking about reward money to the first person who can bring you to him alive. A lot of money."

"I thought all the Ace clans were rich? Why would they want or need the money that badly?"

"Not all clans are as prominent as the Jacobsons." She made a face at Caleb. "The Watsons, for instance, have been heading downhill for years. It's gotten so bad that a few clans had people break off and go on their own; rogues."

"How come I've never heard of this?" Caleb butted in.

"Well, you're not exactly who we lowly, underprivileged Aces would tell our problems to, now are you?"

"What does that mean?" he said, scowling.

"It means that you and your family have always worked hard and built up your little empires, played it safe. You've always been well off and you don't take risks; the Watsons do. In fact, the Watsons are all about risk."

"I know," Caleb said impatiently. "The Watsons run the stock market, so what?"

"We lost everything," she whispered, like it was shameful. "My uncles and father ruined us. They put everything our clan had into one stupid venture and it's all gone, just so they can be lazy and not work, we're finished. And to top it off, we just learned our grandfather put up a second mortgage no one knew about on the land, the land where our compound sits. It's in foreclosure."

"How is he going to pay a reward if you have no money?" Caleb asked suspiciously.

"He doesn't actually plan to pay it," she said, guarded.

"Then how...never mind," I said once I'd thought better of it.

"Ok, well." Caleb wanted to feel sorry for her but couldn't muster it. "What does that have to do with us, besides them coming for Maggie?"

Like hell.

"My uncle's plan is to take Maggie again and ransom her to your family, after he's taken lots of her blood, of course."

"Ransom," Caleb grit out angrily. "What?"

"We know you're loaded, everyone does. He figures your family would give a few million for her."

I shivered thinking about it and Caleb's pulled me into his side.

"So you only came to warn us?" I asked.

"Yes, warn you that if I can find you, so can Sikes, eventually. I suggest you leave soon and go somewhere out of the country."

Like the Reunification?

I don't think that's a good idea anymore, Maggie. The Watson's would be there, so would every other clan, all clans are invited. If they put a reward out for you, it wouldn't be safe to go. Clans have sanction there. We wouldn't be able to harm them.

"Wow. Look at you two, going at it like old pros," she muttered, breaking our talk.

"What?" I asked, baffled.

"The mind chatter, I can see it in your faces." She smiled sadly. "My parents *used* to be like that. Anyway, I just wanted to give you a head's up and now I've got to get back before someone notices I'm gone."

I guessed that was our cue to get out.

"Ok. Thanks...I guess," I muttered.

"Don't thank me. I'm not your friend, I'm not on your side, and I won't help you again. It's too dangerous for me. Now we're even."

"Fine," I said.

"Be careful. Sikes is old and slow, but persistent and patient. Don't let your guard down."

I climbed out, making sure to cover my neck as I did so and accepted Caleb's hand to help me.

"Oh," she called, leaning out her window, "and I still wouldn't sleep by myself if I were you, not like you'd have a problem with that," she said, pursing her lips and looking at Caleb in a way that had me barking mad. She licked her lips and I swear I even heard her purr. Purr!

"Hey! I'm right here," I said hotly.

"Oh, sorry," she said and she didn't sound a bit sorry. "Anyway, Marcus isn't going to leave you alone so I'd make sure you always slept with hunky here."

"Fine. Bye."

"Oh," she laughed. "One little look at your boy toy and I'm dismissed? I told you before that it's dirty to mess with rival clans, but it's fine to look," she explained, her eyes shifting back to him.

"We're done here. Thanks for the help. Come on, Caleb."

"Gladly," he said and I heard him chuckle low in my mind.

You are freaking hot when you're jealous.

I rolled my eyes and smiled up at him.

You're crazy.

"Oh, and one more thing, Maggie," she yelled in a singsong voice. "Though these guys have to bring you back alive," I turned around to look at her once more, "that doesn't mean they have to be nice about it. My advice is to don't get caught."

"Got it," I answered.

Then the limo drove off with a small squeal of tires that totally reflected my mood. What the heck was going on? The universe was hell bent on not making anything about this easy.

"It's ok." Caleb wrapped my arms around his neck and his hands went to my hips. "We know and can prepare now, its fine. I'm not going to let anything happen to you," he assured me for the hundredth time, but for some reason I still needed it and I sighed long and loud.

"What about you and Jen, Kyle, Bish and Dad? What about everyone else?"

"We're fine," he insisted and pressed his forehead to mine. "My family can take care of themselves. If someone so much as tries to touch you, I'll…" He growled and shook his head. "Man, this isn't getting easier. My body is screaming right now."

"I'm sorry."

"Don't you dare." He pushed my hair back and looked in my eyes, the glow of yellow streetlamps lighting the blue in his. "I don't know what her real motive for coming here was, but we'll take the information. We'll be extra careful from now on. No one will get to you." I nodded and he looked at me sternly. "I mean it. You feel safe with me, don't you?"

"Of course," I answered.

"I won't let *anything* happen to you," he whispered and kissed my forehead.

"I know." I looked around at the alley and wondered how long we'd been gone. "We better get back."

"Yeah, we better. You ok? Marla picked a heck of a time to unload something like that; in a dark alley, in a limo, at the back of a club," he said wryly.

"I'm fine. We just need to go back in there and act normal. Act like we weren't just dragged into an alley and told that I was going to be put up for a ransom reward, while sitting in a limo," I said with a playful tone, trying to lighten the mood even though I wasn't really feeling it.

My veins started to burn a little as I saw a few ribbons dance in my peripheral as my emotions got worked up. No matter how hard I tried, I was losing it. Caleb put his hand on the back of my neck and I felt his calm invade me.

"Hold it together, baby, a little longer," he said soothingly and I saw the ribbons begin to fizzle and crack away.

Wait, she said they dispose of them, the humans. He kills them, kills the humans once he tosses them aside for not producing his results. All that because of me. Caleb's touch no longer cured my rage and it burst forth in an audible buzz and heat, the light bulb to the backdoor of the club in the alley burst and shattered to the pavement. I barely heard it.

"Maggie, it's ok," he soothed though he was looking around in frightened awe. "We'll get him. We'll fix this."

It didn't matter, nothing worked. I felt Caleb's hands all over me, my arms, my neck, my face.

People died. I caused someone's death.

"No, you didn't!" He jerked my face to look at him, framing my face with his big, warm take-charge hands. "Maggie, listen to me. It's ok, calm down and let me help you."

My skin was buzzing with energy. We didn't need the light bulb anyway because all the blue energy glowed around us, lighting the alley and street in an eerie way. Caleb pushed into my mind, breaking through my barrier. I saw through him that my barrier was pure devotion and adoration for him. I felt him tug my chin up and his lips crashed down on mine with delicious force that was totally different from any way he'd ever kissed me before. He was almost rough, frantic, hard and deep in his kisses and in the way his hands gripped me tightly. Soon, the limo and its wicked guest were long gone from my mind and I felt all the energy die off around me. It was like they cancelled each other out. One huge emotion took over the other.

I pushed him back a little to breathe and his mind was wide open. It was the only thing he could think of, kissing me, to bring me down from the tidal wave of emotions. It worked, but now I was on fire for other reasons as I licked my lips. He was, too, and we were practically feeding off each other's reactions and thoughts, fueling an already blazing fire.

I was still confused as to why this was happening. I wasn't like this before so it had to be a Visionary thing.

He ran a thumb over my bottom lip. "Better?"

"Kind of," I said breathlessly.

124

He laughed softly. "Yeah, me, too. But we better go inside."

I grabbed his hand in between mine. "Thank you. I'm sorry, Caleb. I can't control what goes on in my own head anymore. I didn't mean to get so upset. I don't know what's happening."

"I know that, it's ok," he said sweetly and repeated his thumb over my lip. "We'll work it out. I'll always be here to take those lips when you get too far gone," he said jokingly and winked.

"Caleb," I groaned, wishing we were home right now, on our couch bed.

"Maggie," he groaned, too. "Don't say my name like that if you want to make it back inside," he warned.

I laughed brokenly and pulled him to follow me. "Come on, bodyguard. Maybe we can get another dance in before it's time to go."

"Oh, I'll guard your body all right," he said playfully and I laughed loudly, it echoing through the brick tunnel of the alley and freeing my mood a little.

"Do girls usually fall for that?"

"Only one," he said, dripping with sugar.

I smiled, knowing that even though we were playing, he was completely being honest, too. "I love you."

"I love *you*," he said and pushed my hair behind my ear. Then he reached behind me and opened the back door, ushering me in. *Now, find everybody so we know if they missed us or not.*

K.

I searched in my mind and found Bish right off. He was still trying not to watch Jen and had been approached several times by girls of all colors, sizes and variety but he remained firm in his resolve for relationship celibacy. He was so ready to go home and wondering where I was and was just about to look for me. Jen was at the bar, the bartender chatting her up. Beck and Ralph hadn't left their necking spot.

We better go see Bish first.

Caleb nodded in agreement and we made our way over. I accidentally nudged a girl's arm and was blinded by a vision of her coming home to a burglary. She was beaten and shot, barely made it to the hospital. She gasped and I reached my arm out to steady her.

"Don't go home tonight," I rasped.

She nodded, having no idea what happened, but she couldn't deny what she had seen through me. She stumbled away and Caleb held me tightly from behind to keep me from falling over. The onset of the visions was swift, unpredictable and I felt everything they felt in them. It wasn't fun.

"Are you ok?" Caleb asked into my hair.

"Yeah, it was just so real…I can't control the visions." I turned to him. "I'm ok," I said, wiping my eyes and face. "It just sucks, I feel everything-"

I know. I felt it too.

You did?

I didn't the first time. Maybe it's because I was touching you this time. I'm sorry, Maggie. I know you don't want this and I hate it that it hurts you.

It's the Visionary's to handle. I'll be ok.

We're a team, you said so yourself. You and I can handle this.

I smiled gratefully up to him.

"Hey, Bish, having fun?" I asked as we approached, playing off as normal as possible.

"Where have you been?" he roared over the music. "I've been looking everywhere for you."

"Oh, I'm sure," I spouted sarcastically without thinking and kept going. "Since when do Jen and I look alike?"

I stopped and grimaced. I looked up at him and he was red with embarrassment, having no idea how he'd been caught.

"Whatever. Are y'all ready?"

"Not really."

"Lighten up, man," Caleb said easily. "Come on, it's a club. Why don't you go ask that girl to dance?" He pointed to a young girl, brunette, who was glancing our way. She saw she'd been caught and turned, biting her lip. "She's definitely into you. Go for it, man."

"Nah," he said but looked over at her and smiled a little when their eyes met.

It's not like I'll ever see her again, pointless, but maybe they're right. Maybe I'm too uptight and need some fun. Everyone else is certainly having some.

In his mind was a picture of Jen. She was the one having fun, the one most annoying to him. His gaze traveled over to the end of the bar where Jen was and he watched, pained, as she sipped her non-alcoholic drink from a little pink straw and laughed at something one of the guys there was saying.

Fine, she obviously doesn't care and I have no idea why I do.

He got up without another word and walked over to the brunette that was looking at us before. Her smile was genuine and surprised when she turned to see who tapped on her shoulder. He sat on the stool next to her and immediately ordered a drink.

"So, I'm Jessica," she was saying to him, I heard in their minds.

"Bish."

"That's unusual, I like it."

"Thanks. My mother gave it to me."

She laughed, tucking her hair behind her ear. Caleb took my hand and started to tow me away, but I stopped him. "Wait. I want to see if he's ok."

"Would you want him sitting around listening to us?"

"No," I answered truthfully, "but it's…" I sighed in defeat. "Ok, fine. I just feel so bad for him and Jen."

And as if to prove my point, the second Jen decided to notice Bish, I felt a thorn of unease and disappointment go through me from her mind as we passed her. Caleb stopped in his tracks, feeling it, too.

~ Fourteen ~

Just keep going. I can't listen to this anymore, Caleb muttered.

Yeah, I wonder what Beck and Ralph are...never mind. I guess we won't visit them either. Well, you wanna dance with me again? I promise not to step on your toes this time.

He pulled me into the circle of his arms and moved me with the music beat and pulse. He spoke to me, reassuring my turmoil.

They'll be fine. They just need some distance.

Would it be so bad for them to be together? I thought carefully. *What if she never imprints?*

Maggie, we've been over this. The rule has a purpose.

I know it does, but what if she doesn't? Do you really want her to be alone forever? Maria never to have a father?

It doesn't matter what I want. It's what's best and what's the safest for everyone.

I know it's risky, but what's love without risk anyway? Life is about risk. I hate to see two people who are so clearly attracted to each other not be able to have something that could be really good for them. What if you and I had never seen each other again after that first time? Would you have just forgotten about me?

Maggie, I can't talk about this. It doesn't make me feel good to think about it. I love my sister and I know you love Bish. I feel it, what they feel, but it's not worth it to break the rules for it. Where does it stop? Who decides what rules are ok to break and what aren't? Take Sikes, what he's doing isn't right but they've become so desperate, they'll do anything. It probably started with something small, but built up to this big thing. Once you open the door, it's hard to close it.

I know, I nodded. *You're right. I just hate it and it's easy for us to say for them to follow the rules when we already have each other.*

I know.

He sighed and rubbed the end of my curls in between his fingers with a contemplative expression on his face. I felt his guilt, though it wasn't our fault that we imprinted. He still wished there was something we could do and I was right there with him. His mind also flashed with images of the Watsons. They were trying to sneak into the house, grab me. Marla in the limo, looking all too eager to help but something just didn't add up. Sikes with his demented mind so focused on aiding his clan and ending ours. Marcus...

I hated to see him upset so I ran my hands up his neck to his hair and massaged and rubbed, trying to take his mind off everything but me. He closed his eyes, leaning his head against mine. This was exactly what he'd done for me not an hour ago.

Hey, I shook my head 'no'. *Stop. Don't do that.*

I need to think. I need to be focused on keeping you safe, to be one step ahead of them at all times. I won't let them get close to you and I won't hesitate the next time I see Marcus.

Just don't, we're a team now. You and me, remember? We don't need to drive ourselves crazy with worry about it all. We're powerful enough to make them scared, so don't worry. We'll handle anything they throw at us.

I placed my cool hand on his cheek and he sighed. Then nodded and smiled sadly in gratitude and I was happy he was trying at least.

You ready to go home? I asked. *We can take Ralph and Beck surfing in the morning and get them out of the house.*

You just want to show off your new skills.

Yeah, so.

He laughed and squeezed me to him. His blue eyes latched onto mine, all the lights and noise and bodies fading away around us.

Gah, I'm sorry, I don't want to bring you down, but I can't help what's in my head.

Don't worry about it. Nothing's going to happen to me. I know you. You'll take care of me. You're a really good dancer, by the way.

It's pretty easy with you.

It's easy with you! You make me look good.

Baby, that is not possible.

I rolled my eyes. *Let's find the gang.*

129

Gang?
Shut up!
He laughed as I poked his stomach.
All right, gorgeous, let's go home.
You had me at gorgeous.

He smiled and led me through the throngs of thrashers with a firm grip on my hand. We found Bish and Jen together at the bar and from across the room they seemed to be arguing. Caleb looked back at me curiously and I opened my mind to focus on them. That's when I realized what was going on, that they weren't arguing with each other but someone else. Bish was defending Jen against the guy she'd been talking to at the end of the bar.

It was aggravating trying to pay attention to their voices and their thoughts but as we tried to push our way through to get to them, Caleb encouraged me to try harder.

It seemed that the guy had asked for Jen's phone number and when she explained she didn't live here and was just out having fun, he apparently didn't take the news well. He tried to coax her to go home with him and when she refused, he got angry and threw his shot glass. Bish had been watching her on the sly and when he saw the guy, he got up from his seat – mid sentence with the girl he was talking to – and went to stand in front of Jen. She'd been so taken back from his gesture that she was standing behind him, leaning on the column with a hand on her chest, trying to catch her breath. Bish was holding his own to a very drunk guy who was practically in his face, yelling.

Crap.

If he swung, that'd be it and Bish would let him have it. Caleb emerged just in time to catch the guys arm as he made a clumsy try for a swing. He grappled with Caleb but eventually stumbled to defeat on a stool as the bartender threatened to call the cops. I assured him we were leaving and took Jen's arm as Caleb and Bish looked for Beck and Ralph. We found them near the bathroom and told them it was time to go.

As we made it through the door, Jen's arm linked through mine. Toad winked at me and made some comment about coming back to see him. Caleb turned and gave him a look that suggested otherwise but we kept walking. Once to the cars, Beck asked what was going on and Caleb told them about the little altercation. While he was doing that, Jen turned to Bish, who was standing beside me.

"Thank you," she said softly. "I don't know what happened. One minute we were telling stupid jokes and then next he was…" She choked up a little and I saw flashes from the little bit she remembered from when she was raped. Just bits and pieces was all she remembered, but it was enough to rile her. "I'm sorry."

"It's ok," I assured her and gave her a sideways hug, trying to keep the images from reaching Caleb.

"Hey," Bish said quietly and smiled. "It's ok. It's good for the heart to get pumping a little bit. I haven't been in a fight in a long time."

She laughed a little and sniffled. "Well, I'm glad I could help. Thank you."

"You're welcome."

And then, feeling soft towards her, he moved in to give her a sideways, friendly hug. Something took over me. I just knew I couldn't let them touch. Something would happen – bad or good, I didn't know which. I didn't understand it, but I went with my gut, not like I could stop it, when my hand shot out and the words 'No, don't,' blurted out of my mouth. I clamped down on Jen's arm, pushing her behind me. Bish looked confused and his eyes traveled back and forth between mine and Jen's. Jen was, unfortunately, more perceptive.

Maggie? What? What did you see?

I turned to look at her sadly, having no answer, but knowing exactly where she was going with it. She thought I saw her imprint with Bish.

"I'm sorry. I'm just really ready to go. I'll drive."

She looked unconvinced as she handed the keys over. "What is it?" she asked in a whisper. "Please tell me."

"It's nothing. It's not what you think."

She looked at Bish with the saddest expression, longing and want etched on her face as she closed her eyes and tried to hold her tears back. She thought I was lying, but couldn't bring herself to touch him, to find out for herself. She was just lonely.

Caleb came up beside me and asked the silent question as well. What did I see?

Nothing, I just had a feeling. I...I just couldn't let them touch each other. I don't know why. Something...something happened.

Caleb's eyes roamed the parking lot, as if it contained the answers and then back to me.

Let's get out of here and go home. I nodded. *Be careful. Follow me.*

As I drove, I tried to focus on Caleb and not listen to Jen's inner monologue of self pity, but Caleb was just as bad. His eyes shifted and he looked in the mirror for me every five seconds. He was thinking about his dad hiring someone to watch the house at night and installing a newer security system. He regretted bringing Beck and Ralph here because they'd just cause more distractions and make them and us vulnerable.

Beck was anxious for the rest of our trip and mad because I hadn't told her I'd cut my hair as she glanced at me from the passenger seat. Mad that I didn't ask permission, like it was girl-code or something.

When we pulled into the huge house's driveway, we got out and by the time I reached the porch, after listening to all their ranting, I was pretty upset by it all. Feeling and hearing someone else's thoughts was exhausting and it messed with me, made it hard to tamp down on my own feelings. I felt close to losing control like before and I saw a few energy ribbons bounce in my sideways glance.

"Lightning bugs," Ralph muttered and kept walking, not realizing that I had frozen in fear at the fact that he had seen them.

Caleb took my trembling hand as everyone else went inside.

"There's something we need to do first," he said and I knew he'd seen what just happened.

"What?"

"We need to practice."

"Practice? Practice what?" I asked puzzled as he towed me to the garage.

"That Marla is pretty, right?"

"What?" I asked and heard my voice take a harder note. Why the heck would he say that? "What are you talking about?"

He shrugged, rolling his shoulder and sticking his hands in his pockets.

"I was just saying that she was pretty. I haven't seen her in a while and she's sure gotten a lot hotter since I last saw her. And there's going to be tons of girls at the reunification I haven't seen in a year. I wonder if everyone is gonna be able to make it. Hope so."

"Ok. That's nice," I said still confused but feeling a ping of unease as to why he was bringing this up.

"You know you were right. There are a lot of girls who are going to be upset to see you with me. Last year was the worst," he groaned like I should feel sorry for him and leaned against the big chest freezer behind him. "I spent the whole time fending off phone numbers and offers to visit other clans." He clucked his tongue. "I guess this year will be different, huh? Oh, well. I'm sure we'll still have fun, even without all that female persuasion."

I looked at him closely. His mind was closed, cut off from me so I couldn't see anything, but I sensed something. Why was he bringing this girl stuff up? It seemed there was a point somewhere but as my skin began to tingle with annoyance and energy, I had a feeling I was missing it.

"I'm sure we have bigger things to talk about."

He quirked a brow and seemed to be a little annoyed.

"I bet Ashley would love something like that."

I froze and stared at him. Really? Did he just say that? "What are you doing?" I asked in accusation.

"What? I'm just thinking that Ashley would fit right in with the rest of the clans. She's just like them in some ways and they'd probably really like her."

I balked and glared at him. "Ok," I bit out, feeling my breaths begin to shallow.

"I can't wait to take you to London and show you off to all those significant-less jerks." He walked slowly to me and put his hands on my hips suggestively. "My girl. My hot, sexy girl that only I can have. They'll be so jealous," he crooned.

"Caleb, that's terrible. Why are you saying that?"

"And Bish and Jen. Wa, wa, wa," he said, making horrible baby noises. "Get a life already! I'm so sick of hearing them complain."

I pushed away from him and looked at him incredulously. I felt and saw a few ribbons of energy dance in the background. My fingers started to shake.

"Caleb, what are you doing?"

"Nothing. I'm just saying out loud what we usually don't. Like the fact that your brother hates me. The fact that Kyle's in love with you," he growled.

"Caleb, stop," I breathed and felt the air shaking around me, too warm and too blue to be normal.

"The fact that you feel sorry for him, the fact that every man I pass looks at you like they have the right to. Like you would enjoy them looking at you."

"Caleb-"

"The fact that if you'd never met me, you'd probably be dating that tool Chad, again."

"Enough!" I said loudly and the light bulb above the counter burst, then another above the trash as the air around me turned scalding.

"Finally, took you long enough," he groaned in relief and came forward.

He wrapped his arms around my back, pressing me to him, and kissed me fiercely as he gathered me up into his arms and lifted me, setting me atop the freezer. He stood between my knees and they clamped onto his sides automatically as I saw the blue energy ribbons writhe and dance in a haze, me letting my focus shift. But I was mad...right? Confused was what I was. I pushed him back a little.

"What are you doing?" I said through puffs of breath. "Why did you say those things?"

"I needed to get you riled up," he explained and let his palm drift down my neck to my chest. "We need to practice you taming the emotion, when you get overwhelmed like you did in the alley."

"You said all that just to get me riled?"

133

"Yeah. You didn't think I'd ever say those things for real, did you?"

"No," I admitted. "But you're a good enough actor," I answered wryly.

"I'm sorry," he said and nuzzled his way into my neck, kissing my throat and pulling me closer. "But we have to do things we don't want to sometimes, for research purposes."

"Research," I repeated breathlessly and anticipated his next move. Then he pulled away and crossed his arms, out of reach, leaving me cold and strange feeling sitting there. "What?"

"So, what are we gonna do about Bish and Jen? He's really suspicious."

"Now you're talking about Bish? Caleb…you're driving me crazy."

"I know," he said poignantly. "*Feel* it. We need you to feel and let it take you over, then we'll reign you back in. Practice. We can't have you breaking light bulbs and making energy strings out of thin air every time you get upset."

Ohhhh… I got it. He was purposely trying to piss me off, to help train me to control it. And boy was it working. I focused on what he said, Bish and Jen. That whole situation was aggravating and sad. I thought about it, how I'd feel if it was me, if I were Jen and had to watch her little brother imprint instead of me. After everything that happened to her, she deserved to be happy. And Bish's story was even worse…I saw the ribbons start to appear, Caleb noticing them too. Bish had a life no one should have to endure…the glass on the car window started to rattle and Caleb quickly stepped forward to capture my lips with his, rubbing his hands down my arms.

His touch soothed away the anxiety quickly. I pushed him back a little.

"Ok, let's go again."

"Good. This time try to pull yourself back to normal."

"Ok," I agreed as he moved to stand just out of reach of touching.

"Think about something you don't want to," he said, the protectiveness in his voice spiking at the idea.

I nodded and bit my lip, thinking. I thought about what Marcus had done to me, cutting my hair after making me trust him. I felt the energy and my skin started to tingle. The air felt hot and crackly around me as I picture strands of hair falling around my shoulders. Then I pulled back.

I took a slow, deep breath, closed my eyes, and thought about Caleb and I on the beach when we'd slept on the sand. I was sitting in his lap; he was being very sweet and about to ask me…a very important question. I felt the warm energy in the air cool off.

My eyes peeked open and looked up at Caleb to see him grinning.

"You did it." He came close, putting his arms around me. "It's amazing to watch. I always feel it with you, but to just sit back and watch it…it's amazing.

The air is so blue, but I can still see you through the fog. The little strings move around you and through you. Wow." He touched his lips in awe. "You burned me earlier, when I kissed you."

"I did?" I asked, the thought oddly horrifying.

"No, it's ok. It's just that you were so hot when I touched you. It was crazy, but I didn't want to break the spell. I thought that day that I pulled you from the shower that you were so hot from the water, but it wasn't that. It was just you."

I blew an exasperated breath and ran my hand through my hair. "I don't know if I'll ever be able to control it, Caleb. I feel like such a freak, I'm all over the place."

"A hot freak." I gasped and then laughed as he tickled me. Then he got serious. "I'll help you. Don't worry about that. If you can't rein it in, at least we know," he moved to nip my chin, "that I can kiss you senseless and that'll do the trick."

"You're insane," I giggled and accepted his kiss.

"Maybe we should try something else, too. Don't you usually see the ribbons when we, um…when we get excited?" he asked.

"Sometimes, when it's intense-"

He cut me off with a kiss and I saw his plan, to push me beyond excited, beyond wanting, beyond frustrated and have me pull back from that, too, to see if I could. It was dangerous for us to be careless around others. Ralph saw the beginnings of my ability tonight and it could have been so much worse.

He pushed me to lean back a little on the freezer and leaned with me, against me. I knew the best way to build the intensity would be to get him even more excited than me. I totally loved it when he lost control and I drove him crazy. So, I lifted his face with a nudge from mine to reach under his jaw. A surprised noise came from his throat as my smiling mouth moved from under his chin, to his neck and then his collarbone as I pulled the collar of his shirt down.

He leaned his head back, his breaths became faster, a low growl of a noise coming from his throat. His fingers dug into the shirt on my sides as my legs wound themselves around him for leverage. Then his heartbeat began to beat its way into my chest. Usually, I only felt it if I was focusing on him or if he was really, really anxious or upset…or excited. Now, it beat strong and fast beside mine.

I saw the first signs of our melding; the little energy sparks in my side view. I pulled back some from my mental grip on him and returned to his lips. He wasn't letting me have any leeway though. He immediately began his own assault and as his lips wasted no time on mine, his hands moved to hold my face. I pulled him closer by his collar, forcing him to brace himself with a hand on the wall behind us.

I had completely forgotten what we were doing except for this. There was only him and what was in his head was agreeing with me. The way he wanted me…the way he loved me and vice versa, was enough to take us both to places we'd never been.

I felt him messing with the buttons of my shirt with the other hand. In no time, it was undone and my cami was all that was left as I felt the warm air hit my arms as he pulled my shirt down my shoulders to my elbows. He kissed my skin there, and then he wound his arm around my lower back to press me to him as he took my mouth again. I'd never wanted anyone as much as I wanted him right then, so I took my hand and let it graze up his skin under his shirt. He chuckled huskily. "I thought you were supposed to be the responsible one."

I giggled as he continued to kiss me. I didn't hear the thoughts of Kyle and Bish until they were almost through the garage door, so the first thing I yelled to Caleb was 'Stop!'

Well, that was a mistake and Caleb didn't have time to obey before it was too late.

When Bish opened the door and found us like that and I yelled 'Stop', he was livid. Caleb looked up and immediately pulled my shirt closed for me, even though I was wearing a cami, the gesture was sweet. Bish didn't think so, given by the heinous glare he was giving Caleb.

I'm gonna kill him. He finally gave me a reason to kill him.

"What's going on in here?"

"Just, uh…fooling around," Caleb explained and gave me a helpless look. "Sorry, man, we didn't hear you coming."

"Maggie," Bish pleaded, taking a step forward and imagining his fist connecting with Caleb's jaw repeatedly. "Come here."

He wanted to get me to safety first.

"I'm fine, Bish," I said, reading his misinterpretation of the whole thing. "I wasn't in trouble. We were just playing around."

"Did you have something to drink tonight, Caleb?" he asked suspiciously and inspected him with his gaze.

"Nah, man, I don't drink. I told you that." He sighed. "Look, I'd never hurt Maggie. We were just playing around. I promise you, I'd never hurt this girl. I love her more than my life."

My heart jolted at his words, but Bish wasn't moved.

"Pretty words don't mean jack. Actions are what make us. It didn't sound like playing to me." He turned back to me and stepped even closer, holding his hand out. "Maggie, I promise you I'll get you out of here and you won't have to see a soul. You won't be embarrassed or whatever. He won't touch you. Don't feel bad about it. If he's pushing you to do something you don't want to-"

"No," I said and knew right then what I had to do.

Are you sure?

Yes, I answered and nodded my head, not caring if Bish saw or not. I'd had enough and I was gonna lose him if I didn't start to produce answers. He may call me a freak or run away, but so be it. At least my conscience would be clear. I looked at Caleb imploringly. He nodded.

I told you I'm with you, one hundred percent.

Ok, I'm going to tell him, but I think I need to tell him alone. He won't be like my dad, he'll be furious with you. I don't want him to fight with you.

You're doing the right thing, no matter what happens.

I nodded. "Bish," I said softly, "let's go take a walk."

I knew it! "I knew it, you little bastard! What did you do to her!" he roared and came at Caleb, prompting me to jump down and stand in front of Caleb. Caleb quickly changed my plans though and put me behind him, mentally chastising me and forbidding me to do that again. "I'm gonna murder you."

"I want to walk because I have something to tell you. Not because I'm trying to get away from him," I said quickly around Caleb's arm, gripping his shirt for support.

Dad, Peter and Jen had come to the doorway; all had heard the ruckus.

"Button your shirt," Bish sneered.

"I have another shirt on underneath," I said, but still found myself buttoning up anyway. "We weren't doing anything inappropriate. He's my boyfriend, Bish."

"Inappropriate," he scoffed at me like I was the most naïve girl he'd ever seen, and then turned his glare back on Caleb. "You better pray that she doesn't tell me that you hurt her, even a little. I will break your legs," Bish growled. "Let her go."

"Bish, enough!" I yelled.

"I'll let her go with you when you calm down," Caleb told him. "I want you to talk to her; I'm not worried about that. I told you I'd never hurt her. You've been so mad at her this whole time because we were keeping something from you. I'm surprised you aren't jumping at the chance to learn what it is."

"Don't act like you know me! Move!"

He pushed Caleb's chest and it was too much for me. I came forward, ducking under Caleb's arm and grabbed Bish's huge forearm in my little hand, but I knew I was no longer a normal little girl. I pushed through my thoughts to make him stop, for him to feel my power, the sting of my touch when I wanted something my way.

It worked.

He jumped back with a yelp, prompting a gasp from my father who tried to come our way, but Peter stopped him. Bish looked at me with a strange expression.

"You shocked me."

"Yes, I did."

"Static...static electricity," he mused.

"No, not static, me. Don't touch Caleb like that again," I told him firmly. I heard Peter's proud thoughts that I was protecting his son and, in his eyes, I was fierce. "Now stop being an idiot and come take a walk with me." I glanced over at Dad quickly. "I'm sorry, Dad. I can't do it anymore. I'm going to tell him."

"Are you sure you want to do that?"

"Yep," my one word clipped answer explained it all.

"Peter?" he asked, hoping for a little help, in in his mind.

"It's Maggie's decision. I trust her judgment."

"What in God's name is going on here?" Bish boomed. "What are you all talking about?"

I decided to give him a taste, if nothing else to shut him up. Feeling Caleb's hand on my arm to steady me, or more probably to keep me away from Bish's raging form, I let all my feelings come to me, felt all the aggravation at Bish, at being interrupted, at having to explain myself and saw the energy right before I felt it hum. I saw a few ribbons dance in between us and he sucked in a quick breath.

I'm imaging things.

"Nope, you're not imaging things," I answered and let the energy on my skin activate the air. The blue haze and energy was everywhere. When the windows started to rattle in the car, he just stood, gawking at it, looking back several times to see if everyone else was seeing what he was seeing. Dad gave him a sympathetic tilt of the head and Kyle smirked at me, a glaring 'show off' in his mind that I had to ignore and focus. "Go for a walk with me."

"Are you asking," he asked looking back to me with a new intensity, "or telling?"

"Asking."

"Just you and me?" Bish asked.

"You scared of little old me?" I asked playfully, but it was one of my fears.

"No, I don't want Caleb to come," he said pointedly, glowering at him over my shoulder.

"Fine with me," Caleb said, not unkindly.

"Let's go," I suggested.

He started to make his way to the door and I turned to Caleb.

I'll keep my mind open to you. I know you'll freak if I don't.

He sighed gratefully and touched my cheek.

You know me so well. Be careful.

I'll be ok.

I know. Just remember that if he doesn't take it so well now, he will eventually. Just give him time and don't jump to conclusions. I'll be right here, waiting for you if you need me. Just call me.

He kissed my forehead and I heard Bish growling in my mind, making me sigh and pull away from Caleb. I gave Dad and Peter a smile to assure them as I followed Bish out into the night.

~ Fifteen ~

"Ok," he said.

His mind was a total blank; he had no idea what to think.

That was the big silence breaker after our long, slow, quiet walk to the shore behind the house. And that was it, he didn't say another word. He watched me as he walked backwards and sat in the sand with a plop of exhaustion. It was like now that I was gonna let him in on the big secret, he was no longer sure he wanted to know.

"I love you," I started off, startling him, "I just want you to know that. I have always appreciated you looking after me." I moved to sit on my knees in front of him, not too close. "You are my brother. I don't care what some piece of paper says, you always were my brother. I didn't tell you about everything that's going on because I was trying to protect you. It wasn't not trusting or not wanting you to know."

"Ok," he ventured cautiously. I'd never seen him so cautious before. "I'm listening."

I began to unravel the story. I started from the beginning, about meeting Caleb, and imprinting, all the way to now. The words seemed jumbled and rushed to me. Over the span of, I didn't know how long, I laid it all out and he just sat back and listened.

"I met him...touched we imprinted...my soul mate...have to be together.... Kyle's mad or jealous... hurt me in echo dreams... Marcus and his hateful family... ascension you get these abilities... kidnapped by Watson clan... theories and this well.... got away and Caleb's family found me... abilities in a dream... family loves me... I love him... airplane to escape... beach house... my hair... you've been so…. and Kyle is acting so… Dad understands that I need… have to sleep together to keep me safe… I want you to know…. Caleb loves me, he'd never hurt me… his mind is laced with protectiveness… hear everyone's thoughts… lose control… trying to figure this all out… Visionary, some kinda leader… freaking me out… but, Jen is off limits…but I love you, so much. Please don't hate me."

I had felt Caleb checking in on me several times, so I figured it had been a while. I assured him I was alright, just needed some more time. Bish watched me and I waited for the thought to come. The same thing Dad had wanted that day, for me to prove it all, to demonstrate my powers, but it never came. He believed me completely but wanted to get me away from it all. Like Dad, he wanted me safe and happy and thought there was no way for that to happen in this life. I was a little surprised at how well he took it all and believed me so easily.

So, Caleb knew if you touched him, this would happen?

"No," I answered his internal question. "No, he didn't. The imprints have been dormant for over twenty years. He had no idea. But it happened and it wasn't anybody's fault. It's not a bad thing."

"Debatable."

"No, it's not actually." I crossed my arms and looked at him sternly. "I didn't tell you all this so you'd have more ammunition against Caleb. I told you so you'd be aware and stop trying to find reasons to pummel him all the time and to get off my back."

"So, you're saying Jen can't date anyone, unless they touch each other and sparks fly or something," he said the sarcasm evident.

"Yes. It wouldn't be fair-"

"That's the dumbest thing I've ever heard. You're telling me that no matter if I like her or not, no matter what she might feel for me, she and I can never date? Never try to be together if we wanted to?"

I was blown away.

"Out of everything I said, that's what you chose to fight about?"

"You're such a hypocrite," he spat with vehemence and stood, brushing sand from his pants angrily. "You're telling me that you and Caleb are meant to be together, that it's life or death, that you need to touch him or you have a fit or something, and that's all ok, but the ones who haven't magically touched anyone are just out of luck? No chance at having a life?" He scoffed. "Easy for the ones who have someone to say that, huh?"

"It's not my rule," I grumbled, agreeing with him. I'd said that to Caleb. "The rule has a purpose. You just don't understand how imprinting works. What if one of the people who got married and had kids imprinted with someone later on?

141

They wouldn't be able to help what they feel and they'd have to be with that person. What happens to the wife then?"

He groaned, but hadn't thought of that. I felt so bad.

"Look, I know about what happened to you. I've seen it all. I hate it, Bish. I hate that it happened to you. I hate that you feel the way you do about yourself. You are so…" I walked up to him and he held up his hands to ward me off.

"Don't, Maggie."

"Bish, you didn't deserve that and didn't do anything wrong. I saw enough to know that." I had to talk louder to speak over his protest to stop once more. "I love you and you don't have to do this to yourself. You're not a bad person, not a monster and you don't have to stay away from people because you're spoiled or tainted."

"You don't know what you're talking about. Everyone has just loved you all your life. You've never done anything to deserve what I got."

"Neither did you, but Mom left and it wasn't all Dad's fault, according to her. I didn't appreciate her. I wasn't what she wanted."

"That's not true."

"She told me, Bish."

He looked at me sharply.

"She said that to you?"

"Yes."

He shook his head and gritted his teeth angrily.

"Well…she was just trying to justify her leaving. She's was just…"

"No, don't make excuses for her," I spouted, crossing my arms over my chest to stop the wind chills.

"She loves you," he insisted in a whisper that somehow carried to me in the crush of loud waves.

"She left," I croaked.

"I wish I knew why she did. I wish I knew where she went," he muttered to himself.

"California, but I don't know where, she's been living with other guys, Bish. She doesn't care about us."

"What?" he asked softly. "She told you that?"

"Yes, I talked to her a couple times. She just bragged about how happy she was and how she wished we'd be happy for her too."

"Maggie, I didn't know all this. Why didn't you tell me?" he said taking a step closer to me.

"I didn't want you to feel bad, too. Now I'm really glad I didn't tell you. It would just have given you one more reason to hate yourself."

He rubbed his face and I heard him grunt into his hands.

"Maggie...I know that some things weren't my fault...but my real mom was beat on because of me. My dad hated me and then hated her for having me; that's my fault."

"It's not your fault you were born. You had no choice in the matter."

"It's doesn't matter if I had a choice, neither did she!" he yelled. "And then she hated me too because of it. I have never been with someone who wanted me before, never, until your parents decided to take me in. I still don't know why they took me but we were fine. Then for some reason, Mom left. I don't know why but maybe the stress of having me and worrying about my school in New York was too much for her."

"Bish, she left after you did. You got a scholarship, they didn't need to worry about you. It wasn't anything you did."

"I'm not a good person, Maggie. It really doesn't matter about Jen because...I wouldn't be good for her anyway. I'm like a disease. I infect everything I touch-"

"Stop it!" I insisted and went to stand in front of him, touching his arm.

He was shaking with fury. I went on my tiptoes and still couldn't reach his neck very well but I hugged him to me. He resisted for a split second before crushing me to him in a hug that hurt in more ways than one. His mind ran wild with painful past memories and future wants. He was so tired of feeling alone and all by himself. He thought this whole time I was pulling away from him because I no longer wanted to be his family. Like when Mom left, she took the glue for our family with her.

"That's not true," I told him firmly and heard the strain in my voice. "She doesn't matter. She has nothing to do with you and me. You will always be my family and I'm sorry," I said and couldn't hold my tears anymore. He placed my feet back to the sand. "I'm sorry that I'm not a normal girl. I'm sorry I lied to you about it and made you doubt us. I'm sorry and I love you."

"I love you too, kiddo. Ah, come on, please don't," he pleaded as he eyed the tear sliding down my cheek.

"I know it's no excuse, but I've been so worried about you, freaking out really, that you'd find out and...I'm not sure what I thought you'd do. I just didn't want you to get hurt and Caleb's family has never told humans what they are before, ever. Do you understand? Their family trusts me with their secret. So that I could tell you and Dad what we are."

"You said 'we'."

"What?"

"You said what *we* are, not what *they* are," he said quietly.

143

"I am what they are, Bish. They are my family now, too. I wanted to keep you and Dad in my life, no matter how naïve I was about you finding out or being suspicious of who I was. They are sacrificing everything…for me, so I can keep you in my life."

He blew a breath out of his pursed lips, his hands loosely on his hips. His thoughts were shifting, almost against his will. He didn't want to like them, didn't want me to be bound to them. He knew he had no say and he'd have to either like it or lose me. He looked up to see me watching him and gave me a wry smile.

"You can hear everything I'm thinking right now, can't you?"

"Yep."

"So you know my answer then."

"You'll try to let me be even though you still don't like it?"

"I don't like Caleb, at all. I think he's manipulative and-"

"Nope, that's not trying in my book," I told him. "Everyone is included in this; his whole family and even Dad. We are what we are. There are gonna be things going on that are weird, unexplainable and supernatural. I can't have you throwing a fit about my safety or anything else every time something comes up. Agreed?"

"Your safety is not negotiable," he said hotly.

"Yes, it is. Caleb is my protector now. He's in my mind, my body, my… soul. He can feel my heartbeat in his chest – literally in his chest, Bish – all the time, and it tells him when I need him. As a matter of fact, he's checked on me a few times already since we've been out here."

"I haven't seen him." I pointed to my head for an answer and he opened his mouth in realization. "Oh. I should have known. So you guys can speak to each other in your minds?"

"Yes, and he keeps everything bad away while we sleep. His touch can cure any cut or broken bone or disease. I'll never be sick again, never hurt again, never be safer than I am with him."

"I can't like him Maggie. He took you from us."

"Why is it so hard to believe that I'd go and get a boyfriend one day? Get married and move away?"

"It's not hard to believe, but that's not what happened. For one, you're only seventeen. For two, he didn't date you and ask you; he took you."

"I took him, too. That's how it works. We bonded to *each other*. It has to work both ways."

"Says him," he spouted just as I heard Caleb in my mind, checking on me once again.

You ok? You seem to be getting pretty worked up.

144

I'm fine. He's just being difficult. I'm defending your honor, so to speak.
I heard him chuckle.
Thanks. I'm sorry, babe. I'm sorry you have to do this.
It'll be better this way. I promise I'm all right.
Ok. Just...please calm down if you can. Your heartbeat is making me crazy.
I'll try.
Would it be better if I came out and helped you convince him?
No, definitely not. It's ok. I'm wearing him down, I think.
All right, I'm here if you need me.
I know.

"Bish, you don't have to like him. But you do have to be civil. I love you, but I promise you that if you keep trying to interfere and make Caleb feel worse about everything than he already does, I'll have to leave with him. We have a lot going on right now and I can't concentrate when I'm worried about you and him."

"So...this Visionary thing? You're like their queen or something?"

"No," I groaned. "I'm not really sure what it is. I'll find out soon. We're heading to London to their council for them to meet me."

"London?"

"Yeah."

"What's going to happen?"

"No idea. In the vision I had," I looked at him to see if his face would change at my talking so freely about it, but he just listened, "I was told that they'd lost their abilities because of pride and greed. I'm not sure what they're going to say to that."

"So my little sister is going in to tell an ancient family of people with powers that they are full of themselves."

"Pretty much."

"Hmmm, that should go over well coming from you. Maybe that's why you were chosen, because you're so cute."

I laughed happily, free from the burden of this thing over Bish and me. No more lies, no more sneaking, no more pretending. It was awesome.

"Maybe," I say coyly and he laughed. "Are you ready to head back inside now?"

"Yeah, I guess."

"I noticed how you avoided my request earlier. I need you to promise me."

"Promise that I'll be nice to Caleb, look the other way when you're all over him, stop hounding you about everything and let you do whatever it is you're supposed to do?"

"Nicely put. Yes, exactly."

145

"I don't like it," he said pointed a finger, "I just want to make that perfectly clear." He sighed. "But I promise that I'll back off and won't talk to Caleb at all. I will try to tame my brotherly comments to a minimum about you and Caleb sucking face. How's that?"

"As good as I'm going to get, I guess," I muttered.

"I'm glad you told me," he said and put his arm around my shoulders as we walked through the sand. "I can't believe all this is happening. I can't believe more that you thought I'd disown you over it."

"It's not just that. I wanted to keep you safe. If the other clans find out that we have humans who know about us, that's not gonna go over very well. It's not just us that we're risking."

"There's no risk," he insisted and squeezed me. "It's not like anyone would believe me anyway," he muttered wryly under his breath.

"I know that, and I know you'd never jeopardize me, but the council doesn't know that."

"I promise they'll never know. I'll keep my big mouth shut and keep pretending to be the disgruntled, ignorant brother. Which isn't going to be too hard."

"Thank you."

"You're my sister," he said, as if that statement alone was explanation enough to cover it all.

And it was.

"So, why did you send me out here with them?" Bish asked Dad, who met us at the sliding glass door on the patio. "You knew I couldn't protect her from…whatever it is that's going on. What did you think would happen?"

"Peter needed his family home. He needed the ones with abilities to stay with him and try to work out everything. We figured you'd come and keep an eye out and just be here. I had no idea you were having such a hard time out here, son. I mean, Maggie said you were a little over the top, but I thought you were just being protective, being you."

"Well, it's done now," he said, just as Peter, Caleb and Jen came through the door to greet us.

Ralph and Beck were sound asleep upstairs. Bish and Jen locked eyes and I waited. Caleb stood by Jen and glanced between the two, as did we all.

"So, you knew all along, too. I'm the only one who didn't know what was going on?" he asked her.

"I'm sorry," Peter answered. "It get's complicated when humans are involved."

"Yeah, I heard," Bish said, not taking his gaze from Jen. "So, you don't have any abilities right? You can't read my mind or anything?" he asked her.

"No," she breathed. "You don't get your abilities until you ascend, and you don't ascend until you…imprint."

"The universe has a wry sense of humor," Bish muttered and scoffed in anger. "I don't like this. I don't understand it and don't like it, but it doesn't seem like I have a choice." He sent a blazing gaze to Caleb, making me step closer to my significant protectively. "And I don't like you. Let's be clear on that. I promised Maggie that I'd let you and her be, and I will, but I don't have to like you."

"Fair enough," Caleb answered and he hated it that Bish was still angry. He was hoping everything would work out completely. "But my only concern right now is your sister. Her safety is the most important thing to me."

"I understand. I won't stand in the way, but don't get in mine."

Bish took one last look over at Jen, and she squirmed under his gaze, before leaving and heading to his room for bed. We all kind of stood in a lump of exhaustion and release. Caleb walked to me, took my hand to calm me, and I sighed, laying my head on his shoulder at the release of tension.

"Well," Dad spoke finally. "I guess it went well?" he asked.

I twisted my lips in thought. I wasn't sure if 'well' was the right word. "It went better than expected."

"I'm glad. I'm glad you told him and that whole mess is done. Now we can focus on all this other stuff."

That reminded me of Marla and her message to us at the club.

Caleb and I looked at each other in unison and thought the same thing.

Crap.

This was going to be a long night.

Sixteen

The next morning I was awakened by knocks on the door. I peeked up from the igloo of blankets we'd made last night and glared at the door. Peter and Dad had been furious last night when we explained about Marla's little visit. They yelled, they chastised, they paced. They asked the same questions over multiple times.

How come we didn't call them? How could we not tell them the second we got home? How could we be so calm?

I told them that Caleb and I had agreed to be more careful, and would probably be leaving the beach house the following Monday after the weekend gig and concert we had already planned. They thought we were nuts and insisted we leave that moment. We declined, advising them that we were in control of the situation. We were ascended and weren't helpless.

That didn't go over well and we were up, with Jen, Bish and Rachel as well on our case, forever. The hours ticked by and eventually I stated that I couldn't stay awake another second, and dragged Caleb with me to save him. Dad was spouting and sputtering as we left the room, but I didn't care anymore. I went and put on Caleb's *Death Cab for Cutie* shirt and climbed into bed with him.

They wanted to treat us like adults, pretend like they were ok with us and everything that needed to be done with me being the Visionary, but at the first sign of trouble, they baled on that and a parental takeover ensued.

Now, glaring at the door, I realized it was not our room door, but the front door and someone was pretty angry. They weren't using the doorbell and the knocks were becoming more insistent. A glance at the clock showed six forty five. What?

"Ah, make it stop," Caleb growled and pulled me to him back under the covers.

"I better get it. Everyone else is upstairs and can't hear it."

He huffed and pushed the blanket down, looking at me in a cute daze of annoyed sleepiness. His mind flashed with scenes of Marla and Marcus.

"No, I'll get it. Stay put," he slurred and climbed over me to the door.

"Ok," I said, noticing he had no shirt on with his Vols fleece pants, but figured that he didn't remember or just didn't care.

He opened the door and I saw through his mind that it was Amber. She looked scared and had been crying.

"Hey...Amber, what's up?" he asked, crossing his arms self-consciously.

"I...I'm...please, I just can't....I..." she mumbled and wrung her hands.

Caleb was at a loss as to what to say to her as she shook and sobbed uncontrollably. I slipped from the bed and padded my way there. "Amber?" I asked and came around Caleb to see her, fully broken and in a state of hysteria. "Amber, what's wrong?"

"Not you," she insisted and backed away, "anyone can help me but you."

"What?" I asked, bristling as to why she didn't want my help.

"Where's Kyle?"

"He's asleep, it's really early."

"Good. I can't ever see him again."

"Amber-" I started, but was hit with a vision of her past.

I saw bits and pieces of her as a child in school being picked on for having glasses, then having no friends to sit with at lunch. That all changed in high school. I saw her standing at lockers, laughing with friends. She hated it all, pretending to be happy about anything they did. A guy pinched her behind on the way to the bathroom and inside she cringed and wanted to slap him, but on the outside, she gave him a coy little smile and winked at him. It was her role in the play, her fake enthusiasm for being a puppet and popular and she hated it all.

Then she was talking to someone in her backyard. They had her pushed up against the backdoor, catching her coming home one night. I couldn't see his face but he was big and brawny and he spoke harshly into her face.

"You will do this or I will kill every person you know. Understand?"

"Yes! Yes! Just stop, please." She started sobbing. "Let me go."

"We'll be watching to make sure you do as we say. Get the blood and give it to us."

"Ok, ok, I'll do it."

"There's a cottage on the beach by the pier; an old run down place behind the dunes. Leave the blood in the mailbox and then call this number." He shoved a piece of paper into her jean front pocket. "Leave a message saying you've done your job." He patted her cheek condescendingly and she squeaked and turned away. "And then, you'll be free and never hear from us again, deal?"

"Yes," she whispered.

He released her and she sank to the floorboards with a thud. I saw it all. They wanted her to get the blood of someone to them and he had shown her through the window her father and brother watching television. He had threatened them. He gave no names and I never saw his face, but I saw whose blood they wanted.

Mine.

From the first time she met me at the pier, they'd been after her. She had apparently gone home sometime that night she stayed with Kyle but came back after they cornered her on her back porch and took the napkin with my blood on it, from when I'd cut my finger, from the trash can. It all came together; the trash all over the floor, Kyle cleaning it up the next day, her strange behavior ever sense.

"Did you give it to them?" I asked softly and Caleb, seeing my thoughts, moved forward to my side, taking my arm.

"No," he growled his hopes.

"I'm sorry, I had to," she answered, but I'd already seen her answer.

"It's ok," I assured her as she leaned on the doorframe in defeat.

I bit my lip and tried to remain calm. They had my blood, again. Marla had said Sikes was looking for a way to get more of my blood. And he found it by torturing people I barely knew. Was no one around me safe?

As my breaths accelerated, the doorknob rattled beside us and Caleb rubbed my arm. My lungs reached for a ragged breath and I felt Caleb's arms come around me, my face pressed into a warm, wonderful smelling neck and a flood of calm all around me. He kissed my forehead and placed his palm on my cheek. I looked up to him and he shook his head a 'no' to me.

Nuhuh, you're not doing this. You're not going to play martyr. I'm here and will keep you safe.

But everything is falling apart. I didn't even know her and yet she was threatened because of me.

We'll figure it out. We'll send her away somewhere for a while to keep her safe, just in case.

What about everything else, everyone else? Every time I think we might get a few minutes to breathe something else happens. I don't think I can do this.

Yes, you can. Look at everything we've been through. We're still here.

I shook my head, not knowing what else to say. I looked back to Amber when I heard a shuffle and saw she was turning to leave. Caleb's hand whipped out and he gripped her wrist gently, but quickly, with speed I'd never seen from him before. It was inhuman and it made me wonder, but he never said anything to my internal debate.

"Wait, Amber, come inside. We'll help you."

"How can you help me?" she asked as he pulled her inside and we all walked into the den.

"Do you have family you can stay with that's not here?"

"I have an aunt in Cincinnati."

"Ok, great. I'll make some calls and you can get your stuff and your family and get on a plane to go see her for a while, ok?"

She gave him a look that was as incredulous as it was stupefied.

"Why are you helping me after what I did?"

"You were protecting your family." He looked back and me and squeezed my hand. "I know what that's like."

"I'm sorry, I am," she pleaded,

"We know. Just sit tight for a bit. Go lay down; you'll be safe here."

She nodded and curled up in the chair like a child scared from a nightmare.

"What are we going to do?" I asked a little hysterically after he shut the door. "That could've been anyone coming to get my blood. Sikes put the reward out and people are apparently coming to collect."

"Well they'd expect us to pack up and leave right this second so we'll do the opposite. We'll stay and leave a little later like we planned."

"Yeah...you're probably right about that," I muttered as he got on the phone.

He made arrangements as he promised her and then went to wake her up. He told her to call her dad and tell him to pack a few things and come get her. It took some convincing with her father and Caleb eventually had to get on the phone himself and use his stern voice. He came quickly, within ten minutes, and Caleb gave her a little money.

"Now, don't tell anyone where you are. Just go and stay for a while."

"Thank you," she said to him and sniffled, looking over at me. "I'm sorry."

"It's ok, be safe."

She nodded as she left and we both sighed like we'd accomplished something but we really hadn't. We were still knee-deep in the thick of the mess.

"What are we gonna do?" I asked again.

"I'm not sure what we're going do, but right now, I'm going to make breakfast."

I followed him into the kitchen, clearly thinking I'd misunderstood him.

"You're making breakfast?"

151

"Yep, we all have to eat and there's no way I'm going back to sleep now."

"But…don't we need to…" I sighed and braced my hands on the counter in defeat.

"Come here." I walked slowly around the counter to where he was and he wrapped a hand around my wrist, running a thumb over the soft skin there, making me sigh again, but in release this time. "Help me. It'll take your mind off."

"What are we making?" I said in resignation.

"My aunt left a quiche recipe here. It's so good, you'll forget about everything else."

I looked up at his face, his blue eyes so focused on me and willing to do anything to make me feel better and keep me safe. How had I gotten so lucky?

"I'm the lucky one," he muttered under his breath and kissed my forehead, lingering there for a moment that I knew was for him. To feel me against his skin and keep his own anger and concern in check. "You wanna chop mushrooms or beat eggs?"

"Mushrooms," I said and reached up to kiss his dimple before heading to the fridge.

When everyone woke, except Bish, Beck and Ralph, they were pretty surprised that breakfast was ready, especially Rachel, who was impeccable in her slacks while everyone else slouched around in sleepwear, even Peter. I wondered what she looked like in a bathrobe, but figured I'd never see that. Peter was almost comical in his pinstripe silk pajama pants and white t-shirt. Even his pajamas were somehow business-like. I must've chuckled out loud because I felt breath on my neck and arms around me.

"What are you laughing at?"

"Nothing. Thank you for this. I do feel better."

He nodded and rubbed his nose on my cheek as I looked back at him. Then Bish made an appearance and everything stopped. We all waited for…something. Caleb released me and took a step away, which made me give him a look that said he didn't have to do that. Bish came and stood in front of me before giving me a big, hard hug. That's when I realized why Caleb had moved away.

"Morning, Mags," Bish muttered as he moved away and sat at the table. Caleb and I followed, and Peter dug in. That was the signal for everyone and we all started. It was awkward and silent. Bish must have noticed, too. "Everyone just stop already. I'm not going to break like a porcelain plate if you talk or move around me, ok? Can someone please pass the salt?"

Peter asked me in my mind if Beck and Ralph were still sleeping. I nodded. The clear crystal salt shaker went from one side of the table to the other in a slow slide, but no one touched it. Bish caught it in his fingers and looked around with wide eyes to see if anyone else saw it, too.

"I don't really have a name for what I do," Peter explained without prompt. "I'm the first of our kind to be able to find and move earthly elements, like salt."

"All right," Bish said easily, hesitating only a moment before sprinkling a little salt on his quiche. "Anyone else want to lay it all on the table, so to speak?" he said dryly.

"I can command metal," Rachel volunteered with a cheery smile, and I read Bishs' first thought.

Magneto.

"That's her nickname," I told him, reminding him of my ability, too.

"It's fitting," he said and smiled at her. "Do you...do you mind if I see it?" he asked shyly.

Her answer was to smile and remove his chain from around his neck, the cross he kept under his shirt. It came easily from around his head, hovering in the air for a second and landing in his outstretched palm. He flashed a surprised smile and looked at her with new eyes.

"Awesome," he muttered. "Anyone else? Jen?" he asked, even though he'd already asked her this last night.

He was doing it just to talk to her again and she smiled despite it all. "I don't have one. I'm not imprinted, remember?" she said softly.

"Oh, yeah," he answered, looking at her closely. He sent a small smile, which she returned. "That's right."

His mind was thinking it was a shame that she was alone, that she was so incredibly beautiful and smart and sweet, and he'd give anything to be another person in another life. She was thinking pretty much the same thing about him. Then he looked around at us all.

"Caleb?" he asked, just a little bit harder than needed.

"I don't have one either. I'm an imprinted freak," Caleb said with a smirk, but he was feeling a new sting at having to start telling people that he didn't have an ability.

"What?"

"Caleb, don't say that," Rachel scolded and turned to Bish. "Caleb didn't get his ability. We don't know why."

"Bad karma," Bish mused and chuckled.

"Bish," I said.

"Just kidding. So, Dad, have you drank the Kool-Aid, too?" he asked, laughing, which prompted us all to laugh.

He was taking it all in stride, a complete turn around from last night.

153

"No, afraid not. I'm still just little old me."
Bish nodded and took a big bite, smiling as he chewed. It was amazing.

Seventeen

Beck and Ralph came down shortly after that, bouncing and nuzzling each other as they walked into the full kitchen. Beck stopped mid-giggle and straightened up.

"Morning," she chimed brightly and turned to hide her blush as she grabbed a glass from the cupboard.

Ralph took a seat at the counter on the stool and eyed the quiche beside him.

"So what are we doing today since we apparently aren't going home like we should," Dad said and glanced at me meaningfully.

"Well…we need to talk, but later, not now," I said thinking of Amber's confession.

"Let's go surfing," Caleb interjected to force a subject change. "Maggie's gotten pretty good at it."

"Oooh," Beck replied happily, "but I don't have a board."

"We have plenty in the back."

"Yes, let's," Peter said and stood. "It'll be good for everyone to focus on something else for a while."

Beck and Ralph looked at each other. "Sorry, did we interrupt something?" she asked, biting her thumbnail.

"No, you're fine, just stress. Let's all go get suited up for the beach."

As he and the rest of them filed out, I got up to stand beside Beck. "Caleb taught me to surf after we'd been here a few days. It's so fun."

"I wish I knew how. Like, if I could find a genie to teach me to surf in like, a minute," she mused. I heard Caleb's cough and chuckle behind me as he and Ralph headed upstairs to get ready. "I don't want to spend my whole time learning, but oh well. At least we'll get to strut ourselves on the beach right?"

"Yeah, Beck. Sure."

I smiled as I grabbed her hand and towed her to get ready.

"It's freezing! Like ice!" Beck complained.

"Babe, just get in already," Ralph yelled, exasperated, as he sat on the board in the water. "How am I gonna teach you to surf if you won't get in the water?"

"Fine!" she yelled as I watched her plunge in and sputter when she got splashed in the face. She came up with a piece of seaweed on her neck. "Ooooh!" she squealed while she fluttered it off with swinging arms. "It got in my hair!"

"It's just seaweed!"

"I don't see you with seaweed in your hair!"

I laughed and turned to see Bish and Jen sitting on the sand with their shorts and t-shirts on. They were close enough to talk, but not enough to touch with Bella in between them. I'd long since tuned them out. The inner rant of misplaced feelings was too much to handle. She laughed at something he said and he smiled in enjoyment.

I bit the side of my lip and pondered what to do. It was really getting out of hand and it seemed that warning Bish about her was only making him want her more.

Men.

"Hey," Caleb said starting towing me into the water with him. "Not all men."

"You're not worried about this?"

"Yeah," he sighed, "but…it kills me that she wants it so badly and can't have it. I want her to be happy."

"And I want him to be happy. But at what cost?"

"Ok, enough. Where's our stress free bubble anyway?" he said and wrapped his arms around my waist.

"I think it popped when Marla made an appearance."

"Well, we need to get back to it and just relax for the last few days we're here."

"That's not possible with everything that's happened. Plus, I know you're not going to relax, so why should I?"

He screwed up his lips. "Touché. But," he grinned, "I have a show tonight. Don't you want me to be calm and ready for it?"

"Guilt," I said and giggled. "Really?"

"Whatever it takes," he rebutted in amusement and pulled me into the freezing water.

His mom and dad were right behind us and surfed like pros. I gawked at Rachel in her little swim suit, so different from her slacks she always wore, and she could glide and paddle with gumption.

Beck finally stopped whining and I heard her laughing several times as Ralph tried to teach her stay on the board. Dad swam around, forgoing a board, and got a workout. Kyle, poor Kyle, stayed pretty much to himself and eventually went and lay in the sand. Bish and Jen stayed on the beach the whole time, never once getting in the water.

"So, what's the star for?" Beck asked Caleb, us four sprawled out on towels on the sand. I was on the verge of sleep when Beck roused me with her question. Caleb kept a hand on my back as I lay on my stomach in case I fell asleep. It had been a long night.

Caleb rubbed his shoulder where the hollow green star was inked into his skin.

"Um...It's kinda silly, I guess. I'm a night owl." He shrugged.

"I get it. Cool. I like the other one, too. The swirls are neat. I always wanted a tattoo. Maybe Ralph and I will get one before we leave for school."

"Nuhuh," Ralph said and put an arm over his eyes, "I'm not marring my pretty skin. No offense, dude."

"None taken," Caleb said bemused.

Kyle was walking by, heading to the house his mind said, so I stopped him. "Come sit with us, Kyle."

He looked between Caleb and me, ready to keep going, when Beck helped me, unbeknownst to her. "Yeah, Kyle, you're so sullen. Sit."

He sighed and sat down, throwing the towel over his head and shoulders to shield himself from the sun. He was in my line of sight. I couldn't help it as I looked over his chest and stomach, hard and tan like all the Jacobsons were. He had a little trail of hair down the middle, too. I saw something right under his navel, peeking out of the top of his swim trunks. I squinted to look closer and heard him.

I told you I had a tattoo in an interesting spot. It's an eagle. I got it when I turned sixteen and it hurt like a mother.

I smiled and laughed silently. He liked my reaction and smiled, too, his eyes showing a little bit of happiness that hadn't been there in days. Caleb, however, gave me an odd look.

"Ok, everyone," Peter called, and I saw in her mind and felt Beck's eyes bulge as she looked up at Peter with only his swimsuit on. Those Jacobson men

157

had the no-shirt look down. "We better all go in and try to shower before Caleb's show tonight."

Everyone agreed as we trudged up to the house. Beck and I got dressed in the room where my suitcase was. Peter couldn't get anyone to fix the shower stall yet but had bought a shower curtain at least. I still felt bad but he assured me everyone understood and it was all fine.

After Beck and I showered and were fixing our hair, I heard her internally debating how to bring up that she knew I was hiding something. She figured it had something to do with my kidnapping and had been waiting for me to explain it. She was done waiting.

"So...you never told me what happened with you being kidnapped," she asked easily as she slid the flat iron down her locks.

"It was these guys," I said, my mouth in a wide 'O' as I put on mascara. "One of them was stalking me. They took me to their house and eventually I escaped. Caleb and his family had been out looking for me, combing the woods, and he found me. That's about it."

"So you saved him and then he saved you. You guys are so meant for each other," she said in a swoony voice.

"Yes," I smiled, "we are."

"So...are you pregnant?"

"What? No!"

"Well, you're just acting so weird, and everything seems so secretive about you guys coming here and all. I thought your dad sent you away to have the baby or something."

"No, we just came here because the guys never got caught that kidnapped me." She gasped and her face scrunched. "I know. It's ok, though. Caleb's always with me and I'm perfectly safe."

"You guys are sweeter than a sugar rush, Mags." She pumped her lip-gloss and talked through her application of it. "Goodbye Chad, hello Caleb, mister meaty, tanned, tattooed boy."

I laughed and sat on the bed to put my shoes on. "Beck, jeez. So how are things with Ralph?"

I knew the answers, but needed to be the friend right then. She spilled all the details. I mean all! I was blushing and eventually told her I'd had enough description for one night. She laughed and swayed her hips as she sang 'Dream' by Priscilla Ahn very badly and off key as she finished getting ready. Gosh, I missed her.

158

Ready, Maggie?

I smiled at Caleb and wished I could do something to ease him. His strain and nerves were coming to me from him, coating his words.

Yep. Be down in just a second. You're gonna be great, babe, stop worrying.

I can't. I'm freaking out a little bit.

I can tell. I giggled inside. *Be down in a sec.*

"Beck, we've got to go."

"Ok." She made smooch lips to the mirror and then smiled at me. "It's shameful to look this fabulous, isn't it?" she said, making me laugh.

"Absolutely, just shameful."

The boys met us downstairs. Caleb was rubbing his chin and sucking his bottom lip in and out, making me sigh with the warm familiarity of it. He smiled when he saw me. *Gorgeous.*

You look pretty good yourself. Very...rock star.

Ha. Ha.

He looked like he always did. Jeans and a black Foo Fighters t-shirt, his hair spilled over his forehead and around his ears. I pushed my hand through it. "It's perfect. It's you."

He grinned, shaking his head. "Zeke told me to wear leather, lots of it."

"And you're rebelling?" I said through a laugh.

"I'm telling him subtlety to screw himself."

I laughed again and turned when Peter entered the foyer.

"Ok, Caleb, we'll come later, right before you go on stage, ok?" Caleb nodded. "In case I don't see you before that, you're gonna kill 'em."

"Thanks," Caleb said and rubbed his neck in embarrassment. "Alright, if you're riding with me, let's go," he said and pulled me with my hand in his, not giving me the option.

Beck and Ralph came with us. Kyle was coming early, but said he was picking up Amber first. I didn't know what to tell him about her so I said nothing. And Bish....well Bish said he had no interest in seeing Caleb play so he was staying home.

Everyone else was coming later after the opening bands were done. Caleb grumbled that opening bands were the future of music and mostly the best part to see in the show anyway. If they got famous, you could say 'I saw them open for (Insert artist here) a year ago!' He thought they were crazy for not helping to support small local bands. I agreed, but didn't understand why he didn't just tell his parents all that. He didn't ever do anything to disappoint them or upset them.

In the car, Beck and Ralph sat in the back. The club, Stage Fright, was across town so we had a little bit of a drive to get there. Caleb turned on a Weezer CD and blared *Say It Ain't So.* I wasn't sure who started singing first, but we all joined in, badly I might add, screaming and singing at the top of our lungs, laughing. Ralph was drumming his hands on the back of my seat and Caleb was playing air guitar while he steered with his knees. Then 'In the Garage' came on and then the whole album played by the time we got something to eat through a drive-thru and made it to the club.

The parking lot didn't have many people in it because it just opened. I shielded my mind from everything before we went in. Once again there was no hassle with the doorman and we went in, getting an *I'm with the band* wristband in the process. As I stepped in, I looked around. The carpet was red and the walls gray with neon dragons and flames, shining under the black lights. The stage was short and shallow against the back wall with an open area in front for a mosh pit.

Caleb was using one of their basses in the show so he didn't have to bring anything with him. There was one band going on before them and he needed to head into the backroom to warm up as the opening band was about to go on already.

"You're gonna be so great," I told him and straightened invisible wrinkles on his shirt front. I could feel his unease about this. "I don't know why you're so worried. Remember when I went to see you practice?" He nodded and sucked his lip in and out. "Remember that look on my face that you love so much?" He nodded again and smiled a little. "Well, I'm going to have that look on my face all night, because not only do I love you, but you are awesome on that bass. And you could tell if I was lying."

He chuckled deep in his throat, his gratefulness sweeping over me. He looked at me, his eyes roaming my face with adoration. He pressed our faces together, noses touching, cheeks touching, and spoke to me.

Thank you. I love you, Maggie. I couldn't live without you, you know that?
Ditto.

He smiled against my cheek and blew a steadying breath before straightening and looking around.

"Stay where I can see you, ok?" he said, back to being the loving tyrant for my safety.

"Sure," I answered and Kyle came up beside us.

"You don't have to set up and all, man?" he asked.

"I do. I need to go, but…"

Caleb was backing out. He hadn't thought all this through and felt like an idiot for not thinking about what he was going to do with me during the show. He couldn't leave me alone, not with people after us.

"I'll stay with Maggie if that's what you're worried about," Kyle chimed in opportunity.

I figured a fight was coming, but Caleb was relieved. "Thanks, man, I appreciate it."

"No sweat," Kyle said and shrugged. "I'll get us a soda."

"Ok," Caleb turned back to me. "You ok with this?"

"Yeah, of course."

"Ok. Come see the guys before they start warming up."

As we made our way through the hall, I caught Kyle's eye and pointed to show him where I was going so he wouldn't look for me. He nodded and turned to Beck and Ralph as they hopped on the stools by him.

Block them out, remember?

I nodded to Caleb just as we went through the back room door.

"Maggie!" I heard and looked around Caleb's arm to see Spence, grinning and beating his drumsticks on his leg. "Hello, my little Tennessee muffin."

"Uh, hi?" I said or asked or something. I wasn't sure what to say and they laughed, making me flush.

"Caleb," Zeke called loudly, "what are you wearing, man? I thought we said to-"

"*You* said. Number one, I don't own any leather," Caleb explained with the fingers he was naming and pointing at Zeke. "Number two, you'll never get me in any."

"He looks fine," Spence said and pointed to his own KISS shirt with a drumstick. "Vintage T-shirts are the way to go, man. Leather is out."

"Bollocks," Zeke muttered under his breath. "We need to get started."

"Ok. Are you alright?" Caleb asked me in a low voice.

"Where's my honey tea?" I heard Zeke say behind us. "Someone swiped my honey tea!"

"Yeah," I said as we laughed at him.

"I never thought I'd say this, but stay with Kyle," he said sternly.

"Caleb, stop worrying."

"I can't stop. My veins are about to boil right now. This was dumb. It's so dumb to leave you unprotected so I can play some stupid show."

"It's not dumb. We have to live. We can't just leave everything behind and forget what we want. I'm not letting them do that to you or me. And besides, I'm not a little human anymore, remember? I can take care of myself."

"I know you think that-"

"Caleb, I'm the Visionary," I said a little harder to drive my point in. "I'm ascended and I'll be right here in front of you the whole time."

161

He sighed and I heard him thinking that he had actually almost forgotten; who I was and what I was. It almost made me smile.

"You're right, I'm sorry." He raised his hand. "Tyrant, remember?"

"Yes," I laughed. "Don't worry about me so much, babe, I'll be fine. I'll stay with someone at all times. There's no way they'd try to take me with all these people here. I'll be the one cheering very loudly in front," I said in a sugar sweet, playful voice.

"Ok," he laughed.

He held my chin between his fingers as he bent his head to kiss me. I could feel my heartbeat flutter under my palm on his chest within just a second of his lips on mine. Zeke made a noise to get our attention and we looked over at him.

"Come on then," he insisted as he waved his hand. "Groupies and wives hang outside while we prepare."

Eighteen

Caleb scoffed at Zeke and smiled at me as we listened to Spence start to bang a beat on the drums. "I'll see you after."

I nodded and he took me to the door. His gaze combed the bar until he found Kyle. He nodded to him, then kissed my temple as he turned me and pushed me with his hands on my back. *Stay with Kyle, please.*

Yep. Have fun.

I'll try.

I had to push through people to get to Kyle, who was waiting patiently in the back. The bar was filling up now, people's thoughts projecting that they were excited about the show. I smiled thinking about Caleb being so nervous for no reason. He was so good and the band already had quite a following.

"Hey," Kyle said and grabbed my hand to pull me through a couple who wouldn't move. He spoke into my ear. "What's so funny?"

"Nothing."

"They warming up back there?"

"Yep."

"Here." He handed me a cup and smiled. "I got you a drink."

"Thanks."

"So, are you excited?" I nodded. "There's going to be lots of girls here pawing all over him after the show, ya know."

"Yes, I'm excited. And I'm not worried about girls, Kyle," I laughed. "But thanks for trying."

He had a devilish grin and chucked my chin. "You got it."

"Where's Beck and Ralph?"

"I'm afraid to wonder." I scrunched up my nose, shaking my head at them, "And Amber's MIA. I haven't seen her in a couple days and when I went to pick her up for the show, no one answered the door. She won't answer my calls either. Guess that's over."

"I'm sure she had good reason," I mused over the music.

"What? I thought you hated Amber?"

"I don't *hate* anyone," I rebutted.

"You know what I mean. I know for a fact that she wasn't on your favorite people list."

"True, but that doesn't mean anything. We're about to go home anyway. It's probably good that it ended now, right?"

"Yeah, yeah, you're right," he said quietly and nodded. "Bish and Jen are pretty obvious, huh?"

"You noticed that, too?" I asked, but knew he was right about them being obvious.

"Everyone noticed. It sucks for them. Especially when we go home and he meets all my uncles. All those Jacobsons together won't stand for our Jen being pursued by some commoner."

"Commoner?"

"Not Ace."

"It's because they aren't imprinted, not because he's human. Your family's not that petty. I think I'm proof of that."

"Still, Bish better watch his back. He puts those googly eyes on her in front of Uncle Ben, he's sure gonna wish he hadn't."

Ok, subject change needed. "So what's the reunification like? Caleb told me some about it."

"It's basically a week long indoor picnic with drawn out speeches from the council and games and dances and stuff. Girls following the guys around like kittens, hoping and praying they'll imprint before everyone goes home."

"Sad."

"It didn't used to be. Mom said it used to wild and fun. There wasn't all the strain and desperation there is now. People enjoyed it and if they imprinted, they imprinted. No biggie," he scoffed and smiled sadly. "It was going to happen one day anyway, and people were happy."

"I'm sorry, Kyle."

He looked at me sharply. "Why are you sorry? It wasn't your fault. You didn't do this on purpose."

I felt my eyes go wide and my mouth open. "Wow. That's quite a change from what you usually say to me," I said softly, leaning in so he could hear me.

He shrugged one shoulder and smiled a small, sad, crooked smile. "It's not your fault, I was just mad. But I realized something in the pool that day." I gave him a look that said not to bring that up. "Just listen." He grabbed my upper arms gently. "I know you and Caleb are meant to be together. I do. And if it was me instead of him, he'd be happy for me." He bit his lip and looked a bit pained, but pressed on. "I am still in love with you." My breath caught. "That hasn't changed and I don't see a change coming anytime soon. But it's ok. I can love you and still be your friend. I can love you and be your family."

I looked up into his eyes. His mind was so wide open and honest, and he was waiting for me to tell him that it was ok. That this was an arrangement that we could both deal with; him in love with me from afar and me knowing it, but loving Caleb.

"It sounds like torture to me," I whispered, but somehow he heard me.

"I want it this way. I'd rather be with you as a friend than not at all."

"Maybe…I should go home to Tennessee…and you stay." He started to interrupt but I stopped him. "Kyle," I sighed. "It doesn't make me feel good to see you like this. To know what's in your head and not be able to…I don't like it," I said shaking my head and trying to move backwards, but he wasn't giving me any leeway.

"I do. I didn't tell you this so you'd run off without me. I told you this so you'd know I was going to back off and let you be. I'm not going to…be inappropriate with you anymore."

"But you're miserable," I said in truth, not vanity. His face was a clear picture of it even if I wasn't in his mind. He was miserable, inside and out. "I don't want to hurt you."

"And I don't want you to hide from me. We're friends, that's all. I can deal with it."

"By moping around and hardly speaking to anyone," I replied.

"I didn't have anything to say," he muttered lamely.

"Kyle," I protested.

I looked around us at the growing crowd and found Beck and Ralph still at the bar trying to coax the bartender into giving them drinks, who was internally debating kicking them out. I turned back to Kyle and looked at us. His big, lean hands were still wrapped around my upper arms gently and intimately. We were so close, our legs were touching, and some time I'd placed my hands on his chest, probably when I had been trying to retreat. Kyle was working overtime to remove the want to kiss me from his mind so I wouldn't see it. He just wanted to kiss me once, he thought. If he could kiss me once, then he'd be able to control himself around me. Just one kiss.

That idea was ludicrous, but in his mind it was sound logic.

"Kyle, I hate that you're so upset about this. I wish I could take it from you somehow-"

"I wouldn't want that. I want to feel what I feel," he said gruffly.

"But I don't want you to." His face fell further. His mind said something about me being disgusted by him. "I'm not disgusted, I'm sad. You're my friend. You've been my friend for years and I don't ever want you to be unhappy, especially because of me. If there was a way for me to snap my fingers and make a girl appear right now that you could imprint with and live happily ever after I would. I'd give a lot to make that happen, so you wouldn't hurt anymore."

He smiled and slowly traced my cheekbone with his thumb. "One more reason that I love you."

Before I could say anything, a group of college kids came piling through the door and knocked me into Kyle. His arms went around me to keep me from falling, his feelings smashing into me as well. He wanted to pull me to him and press my face into his neck, keep me there. I pushed away quickly, my hand feeling his fast heartbeat under my palm, but not before Kyle's lips brushed against my temple in a soft kiss that he hoped I thought was accidental.

I leaned on the wall, to move out of the group's way and also to get some space from Kyle, but he followed me. He was trapping me to the wall with his cage of arms as his palms went to the space near my head.

"I could've kissed you five times already, but I haven't. I'm trying to do the right thing, but I want to be honest, too. Will you stop trying to get away from me all the time and let's go back to the way we used to be? Just Kyle and Maggie, friends. I'll keep my thoughts to myself, and you and Caleb can do...whatever you want. I'm done with trying to come between you two." He smiled and waited for me to do the same. "Don't worry about me. I'm a big boy now," he said and grinned, begging me to agree.

"Oh, I see," I said and laughed. "Well, I'm not the same little girl you always knew either. I can kick your butt now."

"Doubtful," he laughed and pulled the ends of my hair playfully. I grabbed his forearm in a tight grip, letting him feel my strength that wasn't human any longer and smiled smugly. "Holy moly," he muttered. "What the...Mags," he grunted and tried to twist my arm the other way.

"Scared of a little girl, Kyle?"

"Jeez...ok, ok, truce!" He rubbed his arm and grinned at me with new respect. "Is that from the ascension?"

"Yep, and I'm just awesome," I shrugged and said in a bragging tone.

He laughed and put an arm around my shoulder as he pulled me away. "True."

I stopped him. "Kyle."

"Yeah," he said cautiously, like I'd renege on our agreement.

"Thank you," I said sincerely.

He nodded slowly before looking down to meet my gaze. We looked at each for a few seconds before I broke it and let him steer me as we walked to the bar to find Ralph and Beck, sucking down a couple bottles of water.

"Where have you been?" Beck asked me and eyed Kyle suspiciously. "And you. I thought you said you were bringing a girl?"

"I was. She bailed."

"Her loss," I chimed, ending that part of the conversation. "This band's pretty good, huh? Caleb told me they're still in high school."

"They are good," Ralph said and turned up the bottle to get the last drops. "But what does Caleb's band sound like?"

"Um," I thought, "you know…I can't really describe it. It's good though, just different."

"Well, you're about to find out, Ralph," Kyle said and we all turned to the stage as the previous band waved and headed off stage. Then, as luck would have it, the rest of our family came walking through the door. I gawked. Peter and Rachel both were in jeans and t-shirts. Hair was still coifed to perfection but casual in a way I'd never laid eyes on. "You made it right on time."

"Good," Rachel said eagerly and smiled. "Let's go get up front before they come on so we can see." She grabbed my hand and then Beck's. "Come on, girls."

I laughed with Beck as Rachel pulled us along. This side of Rachel was apparently going to be fun. We stood right up by the front speaker and were soon being crowded from behind. Peter and the rest pushed their way to stand at our backs. Rachel was practically bouncing on her toes. It was freaking adorable.

I heard Kyle and Peter talking about the business behind us. Kyle was asking questions, since he was starting school in a few weeks, about the job and things. Peter was proud that Kyle was interested and I got an inkling of disappointment from him because Caleb hadn't asked anything about it. He didn't seem interested at all and after what Kyle had said about Caleb at the picnic that day, about wanting to go to Arizona instead of working the family Architect business, he was worried that Caleb didn't want to continue the family business at all. Little did he know what Caleb was going to sacrifice for his family.

I felt bad for Caleb and understood his position to go to school, work for his family, and do what they wanted him to. He would be the only one not following along with it if he rebelled. They offered financial security, family protection and safety and he would be offering the same to them. I could see it, the importance of it, but it still sucked that he couldn't do what he wanted to do.

Kyle caught me staring and winked at me, pulling me from my thoughts. I smiled and turned back to the stage when everyone started cheering. Caleb was first on the stage and he looked out at the crowd as he made his way to stage right. I put my fingers over my mouth to stifle a giggle. He was so adorable. Then the rest of the guys came out, Zeke last, and he waved his arm in the air dramatically.

Caleb shielded his eyes and squinted until he saw me right in front of him. He smiled bashfully and sent a little wave before pulling on his borrowed zebra-striped bass. Zeke grabbed the mic, bending it forward, and spoke low.

"We are Metal Petals. Prepare to be rocked."

The crowd cheered as Beck and I laughed at him and the music started. It was a cover of *Ride* by The Vines. Then they did a few original songs before doing another cover, The Ramones *I Want to Be Your Boyfriend,* making the girls up front screech and bounce. Rachel practically glowed with pride and Peter wrapped his arms around her from behind, kissing her cheek. It was one of the sweetest things I'd ever seen as they watched Caleb, their son, my significant, totally in his element.

They then began another cover that I'd heard at practice that day, *The Way You Are* by The Afters. Zeke belted out the lyrics and crooned in a growl that totally worked. When he reached the second verse, he locked eyes with me. As he sang the words, he pointed at me and beckoned me to him with a crooked finger. I looked around me to the others, sure he was pointing at someone else, but no. I could hear his mind loud and clear. He was about to pull me on stage with him. I looked around me once more for a way out but we were too jammed in. Beck was laughing and pushing me forward when my eyes drifted back to him, he nodded and waggled his fingers for me to come. I shook my head a 'no'.

So he came down the stairs on the front of the stage and grabbed my hand as he sang. I begged him with my eyes to please, no, stop, anything! He didn't listen as he continued to sing the words and sway as he walked backwards up the stairs singing to me as the crowd cheered louder and louder with each step up I took. I wanted to die right there from embarrassment. Caleb looked halfway between laughing and punching Zeke as he strummed. Once Zeke had me on stage, he kept my hand in his and the mic in his other. He sang and shimmied towards me as he belted it out, my face flaming. "And after all this time I've come to find my soul's fragility, but you rectified my frailty by your strength. It's like the sun swallowed up by the earth, like eternity falls in reverse. As if the glass could contain the sand, that's the way you are in me! That's the way you are! Now you're with me, and now I see what it means to me, to be a part of such a mystery."

He twirled me under his arm, danced with me, turned me to face Caleb. Caleb smiled and shook his head as Zeke whipped me back around. I hoped he wouldn't pull me too close, because Caleb would have snapped, but he didn't. He did however grin like the Cheshire cat and wink at me, acknowledging my discomfort so I finally gave in and danced with him, much to his delight.

The crowd loved it but I was still fighting the heat in my cheeks.

The rest of the band laughed and I heard whistles too. Once the song ended, he kissed the back of my hand and bowed to me before helping me off stage. I covered my face with my hands as my friends and family heckled and joked.

"Don't do that!" Beck said pulling my hands away. "It was awesome, frigging awesome!"

"It was embarrassing," I countered.

"It was hot!"

I rolled my eyes and looked back to the stage to see Caleb watching me.

Sorry, he's a jerk.

It's ok. I'm alive, I joked.

You looked seriously hot if that helps.

I just laughed and shook my head at him.

"Look at you two," Beck observed. "You're so cute. It's like you're having a conversation with your eyes or something."

"They practically are," Kyle butted in with before I could say anything. He bumped my shoulder with his. "It's just disgusting."

He was smiling when I looked up at him. He was trying, really trying, and it made me want to sigh with relief. I bumped his shoulder back with mine and he laughed. Beck had Ralph bouncing up and down to the beat of the next song and I smiled as I focused on Caleb once again. He was doing that thing again, where he played so perfectly but his eyes were perfectly locked on mine at the same time.

I smiled before glancing over at Dad to see him and Jen talking over the music and laughing. I saw in his mind that he was telling her a joke about a guy walking into a bar. I shook my head at him. Then I picked up the thoughts of a girl next to me. She was looking at Caleb and imagining snagging him up after the set, going dancing or sitting at the bar and then whatever else he wanted to do. I glanced at her she smiled at me.

"Oh, my they are so hot, aren't they?"

"They are, yeah. Especially mine," I inched.

"I know! The leather is hilarious!" she said laughing. "I love the bands here. They are always so eccentric and crazy!"

In her mind, she assumed that since Zeke pulled me on stage he was the one I was talking about.

"Um, no, the lead singer isn't mine. That one," I said, pointing at Caleb and she balked.

"He's your boyfriend?"

"Yep."

"Well-" and the next word that came out of her mouth I had never used before and didn't have any plans to.

Then she turned without another word and stomped straight out the door of the club. What had just happened? I looked back to the stage to see Caleb trying to stifle a laugh. I glared at him, making him laugh harder.

Beck all of a sudden grabbed my arm, almost jerking it out of the socket.

"You have to come to the bathroom with me!"

"I do?" I asked sarcastically.

"Yes!"

"Whoa, wait," Kyle interjected, "I'm coming too."

"To the little girl's room?" Beck asked with her hands on her hip. "Even you can't finagle your way into the ladies bathroom, Kyle."

"I need to stay with Maggie."

"What, why?"

"I just do," he answered firmly.

"Kyle," I said and gave him a look, "I think it's ok if we go to the bathroom without you."

"Caleb asked me to watch out for you."

"He didn't say follow me to the bathroom!"

"I'll wait for you guys in the hall."

"Whatever, let's go," Beck yelled and whined as she pulled me behind her, Kyle right behind me. "Jeez. Why are you so precious all of a sudden?" She looked back at me and smirked but you could tell in her tone she was irritated and her mind was confirming that. "I wish I had every male in a half-mile radius gawking after me."

"What are you talking about?"

"Did you not see? Every guy in this place has his eyes glued to you like you're only wearing a corset or something."

"Beck."

"I'm serious."

She walked into the bathroom door, pushing it until it banged loudly against the wall behind it, skipping two girls who were already in line.

"I'm sorry, she's... I'm sorry," I told them and bolted in the door after her. "Look, everyone is just a little on edge because of everything that happened with the kidnapping, that's all."

"That has nothing to do with all these guys out there that don't know you or anything about you, Mags." She went in her stall but kept talking to me, to my embarrassment. "And the lead singer of Caleb's band," she yelled from her stall, "pulling you on stage like that, ugh. I'm telling you, Mags," toilet flushed, stall door opened, "you've seriously changed since high school, ok? You have no idea what you look like, do you? You're like a movie star or something."

"Beck, high school was only a couple weeks ago."

"I know! That's what I'm talking about!" she yelled and I stopped washing my hands to look at her. "You are so different; confident, pretty and important." She sighed. "You hardly even talk to me anymore. I was the last person you called when you got home from being kidnapped."

I could feel my mood start to plummet, the thoughts of the other girls jammed in the bathroom coming to me against my will.

"Beck," I said softly and went to hug her, but I bumped into a girl who was coming to the sink. "Excuse-" I started, but before I could finish, I was hit with a vision, right there in the middle of the crowded ladies room.

~ Nineteen ~

The girl who touched me was a small, waif of a girl. She was young, just graduated from high school too, and was going through a rough time. Her dad was a drug addict and they were being evicted. All she wanted was to get away.

In the vision, I saw her being woken up in the middle of the night and yanked by her hair from her bed by someone who had come to collect money her father owed him. He thought if he threatened his daughter's life that her father would pay, but he didn't know that her father could care less. He was in too deep, too far into the addiction. The girl I was looking at was going to be kidnapped tonight and killed as revenge for her father's transgression four days from now.

As I watched it all play out so did she, as they did when the visions hit. She was dazed and her breathing was ragged. I gripped her arm to keep her steady and realized we'd both somehow sunk to the floor together. Beck was attempting to get our attention by snapping in front of us and waving.

I saw Kyle pushing his way through the girls at the door to get to me. He bent down, grabbing my arm gently to steady me.

There were a couple energy ribbons bouncing behind Beck's head. Oh no, no! What could I do? Everyone was going to see and I couldn't stop. My body was too worked up. I looked at Kyle helplessly, knowing there was no way to explain or make him understand. And he looked back, knowing there was nothing he could do either. I hid my face and took a deep breath. Kyle pulled my face back to look at him with a hand on my cheek and I didn't think, I just acted, or reacted rather.

I remembered Caleb and practicing reining it in, and kissing seemed to have worked, so without any thought to consequences for Kyle or me or Caleb, without any wonder to what Beck would think about seeing me kiss Kyle, without any thought at all really except to keep everyone from seeing what I was...

I reached up from my knees on the floor and kissed him.

I held his collar for stability and though Kyle's mind was shocked and unsure, his hands definitely knew what to do. They snaked themselves around my waist and he had an inkling, an after thought really, that there was more to this. That there was a very good reason I was kissing him that had absolutely nothing to do with my wanting him, but he didn't give a flip at the moment. This was what he had waited for for two years and he was going to savor it.

He kissed nothing like Caleb. His lips felt all wrong and not like the love I felt all through me when Caleb took my lips. All I saw and felt was Kyle's want and desire for me. With Caleb, there was love, protection and adoration mixed in with a need to make me happy and comfortable, but with Kyle, he was solely focused on the fact that he'd wanted me for so long and could never have me. That thing inside me that told me that what I was doing was so wrong was pulsing and screaming uncomfortably. I pulled back, hoping the short kiss had been enough to stop the uncontrollable Visionary inside me.

"I'm sorry," I told him quietly, looking up into his unbridled eyes. "I was losing control. I couldn't think of anything else to do."

"Maggie, what happened?" he asked breathlessly.

"I had a…" I looked at Beck sitting there waiting for her own explanation with wide, unbelieving eyes and knew I couldn't give him an answer. Beck's mind screamed the fact that she was confused at why I was kissing Kyle. "It was nothing."

I turned my gaze on the girl and begged her with my eyes not to say anything. Her eyes swept over me with a look of fright. I needed to talk to her. She couldn't go home.

"It wasn't nothing!" Beck yelled and stood. "That was definitely something. Why the hell did you kiss Kyle? And the lights flickered and they must have some kinda glow-in-the-dark paint in here because everything was glowing blue." She looked at the girl. "You saw it, too. What happened?"

The girl looked at me for an answer but I didn't know what to tell her. I motioned with my eyes to the door and hoped she realized I wanted her to come with me. I let Kyle help me up and it didn't escape my notice how his hands seemed to lock themselves to my waist from behind as his mind warred with the want to wrap me up and run with me, and the fact that he knew I didn't belong to him. I took the girl's hands and stood her up beside me. I kept her hand in mine and looked back at the door to see if Caleb was there yet. I knew it wouldn't take long until he realized something was wrong.

"Beck, I need some air. I'm going to go outside for a minute, ok?"

"I'm coming with."

Dang it.

"Will you just go and make sure Dad isn't looking for me? He'll worry if I take too long."

"You don't want me to come with you?" she said, but instead of being hurt, she sounded extremely peeved about it. "Really, after everything that just happened?"

"Beck, I'm sorry, just-"

"Fine."

She made her way out, pushing through bodies, and didn't look back.

She'll be ok. You did the right thing.

I looked at Kyle and smiled sadly. "Yeah, but that doesn't make me feel better."

There was a growing crowd outside the door and I saw in some of their minds that they had heard a scream and had come to see what had happened. I took the girl's hand and pulled her behind me. Kyle stopped me and went first. He pushed and excused us as we went on, and when we got to the hall, I saw Caleb coming.

We were separated by a sea of dark and skimpily dressed girls.

I can't get through. What happened?

I had a vision in front of everyone.

His mouth opened slightly and his mind ran with scenarios that were all bad.

It wasn't that bad, but I have to get this girl out. She's gonna die tonight if I can't get her to go somewhere other than home.

Ok. Um...just wait. I'll...

Kyle must have understood better than I thought, because he put a hand on my shoulder to get my attention. "I'll take you out this exit and Caleb can go around, out the front door, and meet us in the alley."

Caleb heard Kyle's plan through me and nodded. His gaze held mine for a moment longer and I saw in his mind that he knew. He knew that I had kissed Kyle, and he'd seen it all and felt it in me. He knew why I did it and how I had felt about it, but it didn't make it any easier. I felt my lips part as if to say something, but he just smiled sadly and turned to beat his way through the throngs of people.

I heaved an aggravated sigh. I was aggravated at the whole situation and still had to try to explain all this crazy mess to the scared girl gripping my fingers like a vise. I pulled her along behind me as Kyle pulled my hand to follow him.

"Hey!" we heard behind us. We turned to see a stocky and very overweight security guard. "You three, did you see what happened in there? All the girls are going nuts about something."

"Nope, sorry," Kyle answered and tugged me with him.

As soon as we busted through the back door, I was hit with water droplets. It was raining and the alley had standing water already, covering the ends of my shoes. The girl gasped and whimpered, lifting her short dress hem and muttering about it being silk.

I turned to her immediately. She was shorter than I was, and her blonde hair had long chunks of purple streaks on the ends. Her eyeliner was thick and her purple silk dress was short and completely contrasted to the big black boots she was wearing.

"Listen. You saw what I saw. You can't go home," I told her firmly.

"What are you?" she whispered but I still heard her. And I heard her thoughts. She was terrified of me and needed my comfort all at the same time. She gripped my hand tightly, but also wanted to run the other direction. I smiled a little to hopefully ease her nervousness. It didn't. "Are you psychic?"

"No."

"Are you a vampire or something?"

"No," I answered her and any other time would have laughed but the girl was freaked. "But I have gifts. I'm not going to hurt you."

She looked up at Kyle questioningly.

"Does he have gifts, too?" she said and her huffing breath made smoke in the rain.

"Not yet."

"Yet?"

"I can't explain it to you. Do you have somewhere else to go other than home? A friend's?"

"No. None of my friends are trustworthy enough to stay with. I don't exactly hang out with the Honor Society."

"No one? No relatives?" Kyle butted in and asked her as he stood close to us.

"No. There's just me and my pops."

"Ok, um…" I tried to think of a solution, but Caleb ran around the side of the building.

His father and everyone else were right behind him. I dropped the girl's hand and ran to him. My legs moved and I had no thought to the notion but that I had to get to him. Once I reached him and felt his arms around me, I was grateful for it. I pulled back to look at him.

"I'm so sorry. I had to. I didn't know what else to do." His hands came up to frame my face as the rain pounded us. "And I was losing it and…I'm sorry."

He stopped anything else I might have said with a thumb over my lips. Drops of rain ran down his cheeks and he licked one that ran down his lip.

175

"I know, I saw. I knew what happened the second he touched you. I understand," he sighed. "We just have to be more careful in the future. And work on controlling it better, that's all," he said a little harshly.

"It meant nothing," I assured him, needing to explain my betrayal further.

"I know," he said, but his jaw was tight.

"It didn't feel like nothing to me," Kyle muttered behind us.

We both turned to look at him stunned.

"What did you say?" Caleb asked in a low voice.

"I said it didn't feel like nothing to me. Maybe Mags was just using that as an excuse to kiss me," he said quietly.

"Shut up, Kyle," Caleb said, effectively dismissing him and turning back to me.

I looked at Kyle closely. What was he doing?

"Caleb, we need to go," Peter said from behind us. "They may not realize what they saw, but those people saw something. We need to get out of here."

He was right. We had other things to think about right then. I looked back to see the girl watching the whole display with pursed lips and trembling hands. Kyle stood close to her and watched her with an odd expression, but I tuned him out. I turned back to look at us, my whole family and my friends piled in the alley under the streetlight. We looked like a force to be reckoned with, dangerous. I shuffled my way over to her and tried to smile again.

"You'll come with us tonight if that's alright. Then tomorrow, you can go somewhere and stay for a while."

"I can't go anywhere. I don't have any money," she whispered.

"We'll help you," Caleb chimed from right behind. I should have known he'd shadow me. "Don't worry about that. Come on." He put an arm around my shoulders. "Let's go to the car. You're soaked to the bone."

I grabbed the girl's hand and she came willingly, at a loss of what else to do. As soon as I turned, I realized what a mistake I'd made and I had no way to fix it. Beck was gripping Ralph's hand tightly and looking at me like she didn't even know who I was anymore. She shook her head and her fogged breath came out in long spurts into the rain as I sloshed through the water.

Her mind questioned me. As a friend, as a girl in love, as someone she used to know. She thought I'd let my good looks go to my head. She thought I was becoming superficial and arrogant, and involved in something she didn't even want to know about. Why else would I be dragging a girl I didn't even know to my house after collapsing on the floor with her in a club bathroom?

I couldn't say anything, couldn't refute her thoughts. I just looked away and closed my eyes as Caleb led me to the Jeep and spoke softly in my mind.

She'll understand. Once all this blows over, she'll forget all about this.

I don't think so. Not this time. I'm sorry. I was stupid and naïve to think I could keep her as a friend with everything going on. I was just selfish and wanted my friend.

You're not to blame. I'm the one who brought her here. Normally it wouldn't be an issue but, with everything going on with the Watsons and your new abilities...I'm sorry.

I'm going to send her home. It's the best way, I think.

Well, Dad said we're all going home. He booked flights for everyone for the first thing in the morning.

But, why?

I told him about Amber.

Really, but he's been so mellow all afternoon.

He didn't want to worry your father, and especially Bish.

Aha.

He opened the door for us and pulled the seat for her to climb in the back. I went ahead and climbed in with her. Jen rode with us as Caleb took off towards the beach house. I saw Beck climbing in with Peter and Rachel and tried not to worry about her right then. She needed to hate me and be mad at me. That way she would go home and not contact me for a while and hopefully, all this would blow over and I'd be able to get her to forgive me later.

"It'll be ok, Maggie," Jen soothed from the front seat.

"Yeah, I can't wait for that part to come true."

"Can someone maybe tell me what's going on now?" the girl asked beside me.

"What's your name?" I asked her.

"Ecstasy." I gave her a questioning look and she sighed. "My father really loves his drugs, ok. Ecstasy Lynne Parker."

Then her mind filled with images of him doing said drugs. He was doing plenty of other things that a small daughter should have never seen. I winced when she got to a particularly bad part with him hitting her with a spatula across her legs. She was thirteen at the time.

"Stop, please," I begged her.

"You can read my mind," she guessed and leaned forward intrigued. "Can you see my future? I mean...other than what you saw tonight?"

"I can sometimes, but it just comes to me."

"What kinda crappy gift is that?"

"Hey," Caleb barked.

"Just saying. Have you ever tried?"

177

"No," I answered and knew right where she was going with it. "No, I'm not practicing on you."

"Why not? I'm a willing guinea pig!"

"No."

"Maybe you should," Jen said and turned in her seat. "You can use me, too."

"What? No. I think we've all been through enough tonight."

"Maggie, you're my sister and I love you," she said and I bit my lip at hearing her say that to me, "but the reason that we had to go through all that tonight was because you haven't controlled your ability yet. You need to learn," she told me softly, but firmly.

She was right, but it still stung.

"Jen," Caleb warned.

"No, she's right," I said. "I need to control this. I can't be turning things blue and breaking stuff every time I bump into someone."

"Breaking stuff?" Ecstasy asked.

"Yeah, when I get upset or mad or…" I drifted off and met Caleb's eyes in the mirror. He smirked and winked at me. "Anyway, things break; glass, mirrors and light bulbs. Light bulbs are usually the first to go."

Twenty

"Wow. So you're like a superhuman heroine or something? You see these horrific things happen to helpless people in bathrooms and snag them up before it happens and save them," she said, but I heard the condescension.

"I'm sorry about your dad. He shouldn't treat you that way."

She scoffed and folded her arms over her chest. "Whatever, I don't need him. I've been doing fine on my own."

"Yeah, well, here's your chance to start over for real. Not just pretend you're alright, but to actually *be* alright."

She opened her mouth as if to say something, but stopped herself and leaned back in her seat, looking out the window. And I was freaking a little bit, sincerely. *Caleb,* I whispered in my mind.

Yeah?

I'm scared.

We're almost home. Just hold on, ok.

I don't know if I can. I don't know if I can do this. Every time this happens, I see all these horrible things...

Baby...I'm sorry.

He pulled into the driveway. The headlights showed Bish sitting in the swing on the porch. He stood when he saw us and made his way to the Jeep with a large golf umbrella. He looked funny at Ecstasy but opened the door and offered his hand to Jen to help her out. I felt that same tingling anticipation that I felt before and reached quickly to grip his hand instead, and climbed out. He quirked a brow at me, but smiled.

"Did you guys have fun?" He crooked his neck. "I see you brought home leftovers." I punched his stomach making him 'ooph' as he laughed.

"Bish, this is Ecstasy. Ecstasy, this is my brother Bish." She eyed him appreciatively and then bit her lip, trying to look all cute and seductive. I thought

Jen's eyes were gonna bug from her head so I pressed on. "So Ecstasy came with us because, uh...she uh..."

"She and Maggie have some girl stuff to talk about," Caleb rescued me. "They met at the club and clicked."

"Ok," Bish answered and looked at Caleb. He was trying to school his features. "So...how did it go?"

Caleb blinked in surprise. "Fine."

"Yeah, I saw that guy pull you on stage. It was hilarious," Ecstasy chimed.

"Caleb pulled you on stage?" Bish asked.

"No, Zeke did," I answered. "He was trying to be funny."

"Did Caleb try to stop him?"

"Why would he?"

"Because even I know you'd hate that."

"It's fine, Bish."

He looked at Jen. "Did you have fun?"

"Sure," she said. "It could've been better."

They looked at each other and smiled slowly. I was getting pretty exasperated with trying to play referee to those two. I sighed loudly, not even trying to stop my annoyance.

"Jen, can you take Ecstasy inside and get her settled until we come back in?" Caleb asked and took my hand as he stood in front of me. "I need to talk to Maggie."

"You guys need to come inside. Maggie doesn't need to be out in the rain," Bish insisted.

"I got this, man," Caleb said a little harder.

Bish stopped and turned back to look at us. He gave Jen the umbrella and waved for her to take Ecstasy inside.

"Dude, you apparently don't *got this* if you think it's ok to keep my baby sister out in the rain. She'll get sick."

"She won't get sick because I'll heal her, because *only I* can heal her."

Bish scoffed, "So smug."

"Oh, my gosh, I'm so sick of this!" I said, but neither of them looked at me.

"I'm not doing this with you again, man. I told you before that I'll take care of Maggie. Right now, I need to talk to her so, please."

"So take her inside and talk to her," Bish growled.

"We're going to sit in the Jeep, Bish. Jeez, chill!" I yelled at him and went to open the car door, but he slammed it, taking it right out of my hand. "Bish!"

Caleb pulled me next to him.

"I've always held back," Caleb started, "because you're her brother and I didn't want there to be problems between us, but, dude, enough is enough. Maggie is my responsibility. Mine. I don't know what your problem is with me, but it has nothing to do with her. I think she's smart enough to decide whether she wants to go inside or not."

"Shows what you know, college boy. Maggie's young and naïve, and however you tricked her into joining your little family with…gifts or whatever is one thing, but this isn't her. Right now, she's looking pretty stupid to me."

I gasped and Caleb pushed me behind him almost out of instinct. It set Bish off. His eyes bulged to half dollars and he stepped forward, pushing his chest to Caleb's.

"Don't call her stupid," Caleb said easily.

"Man, you are making this whole not-liking-you thing so easy," Bish said and smiled cruelly.

"I don't care if you like me."

"That's clear as a bell."

"But Maggie is not a little girl anymore."

"Is that what you tell yourself so you can screw my sister in good conscience?" he sneered and pushed Caleb's chest.

"Bish!" I yelled, but Caleb had had enough.

He pushed Bish's chest back and I put myself in between them to stop them, but Caleb just pulled me back behind him on the other side, so I just circled him. Then Peter and Dad pulled up, thank God.

"Bish," I heard Dad yell as he ran over. I saw Ralph and Beck make their way into the house without even looking at us. Kyle seemed to notice the tension and thought it better to go inside and play Halo. "What's going on?"

"Nothing. We're just having a friendly conversation."

"Answer me," my father said in a tone he hadn't used on Bish since we were kids.

Bish looked at him, then to me and his face changed. "Nothing. I'm going to bed."

"After all that?" I yelled. "What was the point in that? What's the point every time you try to start a fight with Caleb?"

"If you want to ruin your life, Maggie, go ahead. I'm done. No one just falls in love in five seconds, ok. No one."

Dad ran after Bish and Peter and Rachel came to us.

"Are you ok?" he asked, and I heard in his mind he was asking Caleb and not me.

"Sure," he said gruffly and looked at me. "Sorry."

181

I shrugged and saw Bella padding her way down the driveway. "He pushed you. What were you supposed to do?" I told him.

"Come inside," Peter said started to tow a still stunned Rachel inside.

"Maggie and I need to talk," Caleb said and scratched Bella's head.

"Can't you talk inside?"

"No, Dad, we can't. Can I please just talk to *my* significant without everyone jumping on my case about it?"

Peter looked back in shock. I heard him mutter in his mind that Caleb had never talked to him that way before. "Sure, son, I was just trying to-"

"I know that, Dad," he said softly. "I know you were trying to protect Maggie and help me and guide us, but everyone needs to just calm down a little bit. Maggie is the Visionary, or has everyone forgotten that because she's so lax with the titles?" Peter and Rachel both looked at me a little bashfully. "And she is mine, my significant, and everyone is constantly telling me and even Maggie what we should do. I know we're young, but the imprint chose us for a reason. Please try to remember that. I got this, Dad," he said pointedly and firmly, but gently. "I got this."

Peter nodded his head and rubbed his chin. "Ok," was all he said.

"Peter," Rachel said insistently. "He's just a-"

"Don't say it, Rachel," he said softly and not unkindly. "Come on, Bella."

Then he nodded to Caleb and towed his stricken mother away. Caleb looked about as bad as I felt.

He ran his hands through his hair, leaned his back on the wet Jeep and groaned in frustration. I leaned against him and put my head on his chest. His arms, as if attached to my moods themselves, wound around me and he sighed into the top of my head as the light rain continued to come down on us. We were already soaked anyway.

"I'm sorry," he repeated.

"No need. I'm sorry."

"No need."

"Everything is so screwed up, but I'm really proud of you."

"What in the world for?" he asked softly, like it was so hard to believe.

"For standing up to Bish and Peter. You never do anything to upset anybody." I lifted my head to look at him. "Sometimes, you just have to do what needs to be done. People aren't always going to like it, but it's your life. It's *our* life and we both need to start taking responsibility for ourselves."

He chuckled and wiped at my cheek. "Still amazing," he muttered as if to himself. We smiled at each other and then he sighed, his smile draining away. "Bish was right though. I should take you inside out of the rain. Are you cold?"

182

"I'm fine. If I didn't want to be out here, I would have said so."

"I know. I'm just so tired of everyone telling me how to take care of you. Dad and Mom are always on me about it."

"They're just trying to help," I said softly and lay my head back down.

"I know, but it's just like you with the Visionary stuff. You hated it when I was trying to tell you how you should handle it."

"Touché," I muttered and smiled against his shirt. After we sat for a minute in thoughtful silence, I broached the subject of the club. "I'm sorry I kissed Kyle."

"I already told you I understood."

"I know, but I feel the need to apologize again."

"Don't worry about it. Things at the club would have been way worse if you hadn't."

"Yeah, but I hate that you want to punch Kyle even more now."

He outright laughed at that. "Yeah, I really do, seriously."

"Caleb."

"Yeah."

"I feel like I'm messing everything up." I looked back up to him. "I feel like I'm not this person I need to be. I can't do this." For some reason, everything seemed to just crash down on me at that moment. I started to cry as I croaked out my explanation. "I mean, every time I see a vision or someone's past comes flying at me, it's always bad, horrible stuff. I don't wanna see it. I don't wanna know it. I don't wanna lose control anymore. I don't...I don't..."

"Don't what?" he said softly. "Why are you blocking it from me?"

"I don't want you to be disappointed in me," I explained and sniffed.

"I would never," he held by face by my chin, "be disappointed in you. What is it, Maggie?"

"I don't want to be the Visionary," I told him in a whisper.

"Baby, I know that."

"You do?" I squeaked.

"Yes. You're not exactly a closed book," he said with a slight smirk.

"But I thought you'd be angry, like I was rejecting your family and abilities or something."

"Maggie," he chuckled, "I can't really be mad at you, in case you haven't noticed."

"I know, I know. The bond," I said begrudgingly.

"No, not the bond. It's you. You're so sweet and you care about everybody. You hate it when people are upset with you. You love cream soda. It's kind of hard to be mad at someone who's like that."

183

"But right now, I don't feel that way," I continued on and didn't play into his joke. "I was almost angry when that vision hit me tonight. I didn't want to...help her. I knew I was going to see all those horrible things about her and then I'd have to figure out a way to help her get away and have to use your family's money to do it and I just...didn't want to."

"I think you're being a little hard on yourself," he chided quietly and ran his hand down my wet hair.

"I think you're a little biased."

"Oh, I'm definitely biased," he said with a smile, "but it's also true."

I looked up to him, my rock star, my sweet guy, my open book significant. He stood up for me with Bish and his dad and Kyle. He always took care of me even though everyone made out like he didn't.

"I am so in love with you," I told him.

He smiled graciously and pressed his nose and cheek to mine with a hand on my jaw. "I'm so in love with *you*."

"I know," I said happily and smiled through the rain on my cheeks. Maybe there was some tears mixed in, too, but right then, I didn't care.

He bent down the last inch and kissed me. He kissed me, and kissed me, and kissed me until my bones were noodles and my troubles forgotten for the moment. As the rain fell, my spirits lifted. My significant was perfection for my needs.

Twenty One

By the time we made it back inside, everyone was pretty much packed and getting into bed. I listened for Beck as Caleb went to get us a couple towels but she must have been asleep already because her mind was quiet. Rachel was at the table with Ecstasy who was chowing down on a bowl of ravioli.

"Hey," I said to announce us as Caleb handed me my towel and I dried my arms.

"Are you all right, honey?" Rachel asked me.

"Yeah."

"Caleb. You all right?"

"Yeah, Mom, I'm fine. I'm sorry about earlier." She nodded and he sat with a plop in the chair across from Ecstasy. "Ok, so have you thought about where you want to go?" he asked her.

"Um," she mumbled, "not really. It doesn't really matter, I told you, I don't know anyone anywhere. I don't have any money. It doesn't really matter to me."

"Well, we're leaving in the morning so why don't you just come with us to the airport. We'll figure it out then."

"Whatever."

"Ok, kids, I'm going to go to bed." Rachel came to hug Caleb around his shoulders from behind and he patted her hand. Then she hugged me, long and hard. "It's all going to be ok, Maggie. You have to know that, right?"

"Sure, thanks."

She pulled back to look at me. She smiled sadly and said her goodnights. Bish and Jen moseyed in through the other door right at that moment. I saw in

Jen's mind that she had taken him for a walk on the beach to calm him. She looked up embarrassed because it might look to Caleb like she was taking sides.

Bish and Caleb stared at each other. Neither of them seemed as riled as before, but they were far from BFFs. I did the only thing I could think of to keep the peace, take the focus off of them and put it on me.

"Ok, Ecstasy, I'll take you up on your offer to practice if you still want to."

"Yeah, absolutely."

"Me, too," Jen chimed.

Bish looked at her and put a hand out in front of her to stop her, but didn't touch her. "Whoa, what? Practice what?"

"My ability," I answered and threw the towel across the chair.

"You're not *practicing* anything on Jenna."

Jenna? Even I didn't know her real name was Jenna. I bit my lip to stop the smile. Bish had it bad. I looked at Caleb, who had turned red in the face. Oh, boy, I didn't think we could stop them anymore. It was only a matter of time.

Caleb shot me a look to say he wasn't thrilled with my thought. I just shrugged at him.

They don't want to be told how to live their lives anymore than we do, Caleb. I shook my head and took his hand. *How hypocritical have we been?*

He sighed and nodded, pulling me to him. He kissed my forehead.

My family is going to be so pissed.

His words rang with harsh truth, but he laughed. I looked up at him and smiled. When I looked back to Bish, he was watching us.

"So, all those times you two were being weird you were talking to each other…in your minds?" Bish asked with a fascinated look on his face.

"Yep," I said with a smirk.

"Ok," Ecstasy sang and stood from the table. "This is all accommodatingly awkward. Can we move on to my being target practice, please?"

"Let's take it to the garage so we don't wake anyone up," Caleb suggested and towed me behind him without waiting for someone else to say anything.

I heard them following us. Bella followed too and I heard Jen tell her to stay as she closed the door.

We had to walk by the chest freezer…the one Caleb sat me on when Bish found us with my shirt open. I gnawed my lip as my cheeks flushed at the memory. I looked up to see Caleb grinning at me in standard male satisfaction.

He touched my cheek, tracing the crimson pattern.

I hope the day never comes that I can't make you blush.

I felt the flush burn hotter and blaze down my neck.

Enough, you.

186

He laughed as we made our way to the center.

Bish wasn't as intrigued by his memory of this garage as we were with ours. He glared at the freezer and then at Caleb.

"We were practicing that night, too," I told Bish.

He had the good grace to look a little embarrassed. "Yeah...Jenna told me told more about what goes on after you're bonded. I still don't understand, but I know that things are really different. And...I'm sorry. I overreacted. I always overreact, but Maggie you don't know what it was like for me. My parents...as a kid-"

"Actually, I do."

"What?"

"One of my abilities is to see the past, remember? I saw more than I wanted to see of yours," I told him quietly.

He blanched and shoved his hands in his pockets. He rocked on his heels and his shame blazed like a fire through me. It was almost as if I could feel the heat from it. I was confused as to why he felt so responsible for everything that happened.

"It wasn't your fault. I saw everything."

"I'm not going to talk about that right now. Now," he said back to business and crossed his arms over his big chest, "what exactly do you think you are going to do to Jenna?"

I caught her small smile at his protectiveness beside me. I glanced at her and she glanced at me. Her smile melted and she begged me with her eyes.

"Please don't read my mind right now, Maggie," she whispered.

I nodded. "I'm not trying to," I told her gently. "Let's just do this, I guess."

"Hello, Mags!" Bish said exasperated.

"I don't know what I'm going to do, Bish. Try to focus and see what I get from them. We had an issue at the club tonight."

"Issue?"

"Yeah," Ecstasy chimed in too happily, "she saw me die." She smiled cruelly, but I saw what was in her mind. She was scared.

"Ok," he dragged out. "Well, you're still kicking, so I assume that's why she brought you here?" She tipped her head to him in answer. "So you're just going to look into her mind, that's it. You're not going to use any magic on Jenna?"

It didn't escape my notice how he kept saying her name and talking about her instead of to her.

"Oh, don't worry about little old me over here," Ecstasy said sarcastically and put her green polished nail hands on her hips.

It was scary how much she reminded me of Kyle and his snarkyness.

"No, I'm not gonna use magic on her," I said and rolled my eyes. "I don't possess any *magic* that I know of."

"You know what I mean. Ok. I mean, if she's ok with it," he conceded.

"I am," Jen, or should I say Jenna, confirmed.

"Me first," Ecstasy said.

I swallowed. I had no idea what to do or how to start. Caleb pulled two chairs into the middle of our circle and sat me down in one. Ecstasy sat in the other.

"Most people I've had visions for, I touched."

She held out her hand eagerly. I noticed her eyes were also eager and bright, lit with the hopes that I would tell her something awesome and life changing. I hoped I didn't disappoint.

I touched her hand and it was surprisingly soft as I tried to focus. I felt Caleb's hands on my shoulders as he tried not to worry behind me.

"I've already seen your future for tonight and the next few days. I'm going to try to see your future after that."

She just stared at me expectantly. And I stared back. I focused on her face, her pulse beating under my fingers in her wrist, her eyes barely blinking.

Nothing happened.

I cleared my throat in annoyance and focused again. Her mind was so focused on me and waiting that I saw nothing else in her mind. I breathed slowly and deeply, but got nothing. Dang it. I huffed and slammed back in my chair and the lights flickered. The light bulb above us glowed brighter and then dimmer. Ecstasy eyed it speculatively and then looked back to me.

"I don't think I can just will it like the other things-" I explained but Ecstasy cut me off.

"What other things? What do you mean 'will it'?"

I decided to show her. I sent my thought to turn the light out above us. I also thought about how it felt when Bish pushed Caleb. The light went out with a low keening hum and we were submerged in darkness. All I could hear was her breathing.

"Um…ok, I get it," she said and I heard her annoyance.

"You asked."

"I hate the dark. Please turn it back on," she said evenly, but she was serious. The dark scared her.

So I repeated my process and turned it back on. Bish was looking at me a little wild-eyed. I sighed and gave him a look.

"Are you really surprised?" I asked.

"Yes. You just keep coming up with all these things you can do."

"I don't come up with them," I muttered but he was still going.

"What do Peter and Rachel-"

"No, Bish, stop." He looked at me funny. "Ecstasy doesn't know *everything*."

"What do you...oh. Well, you kinda just let the cat out of the bag, sister."

"No, I didn't! She doesn't know-"

"Ok, ok," Caleb ordered softly and rubbed my neck. "She knows something is up but she doesn't know what. Let's keep it that way."

"Yeah," I reiterated. "That's what I was getting at."

Bish rolled his eyes at me, but smiled in tolerance.

"Anyway," I accentuated. "I'm different apparently."

"She's special," Caleb said and ran his fingers down the mark on my neck that Bish or Ecstasy couldn't see. "She's pretty much royalty for us."

"Really," Bish said in awe as I fought not to roll my eyes. "Hmm."

"Ok. Let's get back to this and get it over with. I'm ready for bed," I insisted.

"Ok."

We tried again and again for the next half hour and nothing happened still. I'd had it. I was tired and in a foul mood from too much channeling of bad thoughts and feelings, trying to force a reaction. I no longer wanted to try anymore.

"That's it. I'm done. I'm going to bed."

I started to get up and go, without waiting for anyone, but Caleb grabbed my arm to halt me. I had a second's thought, a moment of weakness, where I thought about zapping him in my annoyance, but stopped it immediately and felt guilty. Caleb heard my thought and released my arm quickly.

"I'm sorry," I told him. "It's just thinking about all these bad things..."

"I know," he said, but didn't make a move to touch me again. "Let's go, Ecstasy, you can sleep on the couch. Come inside and I'll get you set up in the living room."

I turned back to leave, but Jen was there. She grabbed my hand to say something about trying another day but that was it. That was all it took for some reason. I was smacked with another vision but this time in was Jen's. It was her future not her past, and there was blood everywhere.

189

~ Twenty Two ~

I gasped and pulled my hand away in reflex, but the vision kept coming. I vaguely felt Caleb's arm around me from behind. He was shaking as he watched the vision with me. Jen and Bish were standing together later on in the future, not tonight. It was dark. I couldn't see their surroundings, but they were...touching, murmuring into each other's ear and in their minds in an embrace. Jen laughed and as she leaned her head back in her glee, Bish took that opportunity to kiss her neck. There were gunshots. Bish and Jen both looked around and suddenly Jen bent over with an agonizing scream. Bish followed her, but when he took his hand away, it was red with her blood. Then he, too, was hit in the shoulder with a bullet...then the stomach. They fell in a heap on the ground and writhed in pain together, their bodies unable to heal the other's, until they stopped writhing. They were both dying and couldn't be saved.

I screamed as I watched the so very life-like scene play out. Their blood was so red, their eyes so wide and white against the dark, their hands entwined as they knew death was coming. I fell to the floor and Caleb caught me in his arms. We both sank down. When it was over, I turned and sobbed into his shoulder as he tried to keep his emotions in check.

"No, no, no, no," I heard myself say.

Then I realized I wasn't the only one chanting those words. I looked over to see Jen on the floor, too. She had her arms wrapped around her stomach and she was rocking and chanting, tears running down her face. She had seen the vision, too. Then Bish's voice boomed above everything else going on and called all of our attention.

"What the hell was that?"

"What...you saw that?" I squeaked.

"Yes, I saw it."

"Did you see it?" I asked Ecstasy and she just shook her head and looked at us.

"What was it?" he asked and balled up his fists to stop the shaking.

"A vision. I...Bish..."

"A vision. You're saying that what we saw is going to happen... to us?"

"Yes, I guess. I don't know."

"What do you mean you don't know!" he bellowed and Ecstasy flinched.

"I don't know!" I yelled back. "I'm new at this. The visions just come, and I can't control them."

Bish looked down at Jen and she looked up at him. For a split second, I saw their look of longing. They were going to imprint. Bish's breathing was ragged as he bent down and reached for her hand. She jerked back and slid backwards on the floor in a hasty, frightful attempt to escape him. He looked shocked.

"Don't touch me," she begged. "I have a daughter and I have to think of her. Please, don't touch me."

In her mind, she was sorrowful. Finally, she had confirmation that she was going to imprint and now, that was all taken away. She couldn't let him touch her because then she'd imprint and the vision would come true. She'd leave Maria motherless. Otherwise, she thought the trade off was worth it. To have your significant, to know real love and be completely happy, even if for a short time, was so worth it to her. But that dream was shattered now in her thoughts. She *was* going to die...just old and alone.

"Jen," I soothed and scooted to her, pulling her into a rough hug. "I'm so sorry."

"Wait," I heard Bish mutter behind us. "You're saying that Jenna and I...we're going to...imprint?"

"In the vision you were imprinted," I said softly.

"Bish," Jen said softly looking at him unabashedly. Her tears ran down her face, but her eyes spelled her feelings for him. "I'm sorry. I can't. I want it, like nothing I've ever wanted before, but I can't leave my daughter without a mother. If I never touch you, then we won't imprint, and if we don't imprint then the vision won't come true. Right, Maggie?"

"I don't know, Jen. I've been able to stop them before, so I guess so."

"How did you stop them?" Bish asked.

"Well…there was a girl at the club we went to. I told her not to go home because her apartment was going to be broken into. She was going to beaten almost to death."

"But how do you know that she didn't go home?" Jen reasoned. "Or that she wasn't hurt in some other way that night? Maybe you see what's supposed to happen and you can't stop it."

"Well, I can't be sure. I never saw her again."

"How do you now that I'm not going to be kidnapped tonight?" Ecstasy asked. "Maybe that's why you couldn't see my future, because I don't have one. Maybe I'm supposed to die and even though you told me about it, something's still going to happen, like that movie 'Final Destination'."

"This isn't a movie," Bish growled.

"I'm just saying."

"Well, don't. Jenna-"

"Bish, please don't. I'm going to bed."

Caleb helped her up and then me. She and Caleb hugged each other fiercely, almost like they were saying goodbye, but neither of their minds wanted to voice it. She sniffed and smiled sadly at me. We stood and watched her go. Bish started to follow but I stopped him.

"Bish no, she'll freak. She needs some time to think."

"I won't touch her. I just want to make sure she's ok."

"It's hard on her, Bish. She's wanted to imprint every since she was a little girl. She's known about it her whole life and thought she never would. Now she found out that she could, but she'll die. Just don't, not tonight."

He exhaled and I felt the pain from it through him to me.

"It's probably just as well. She's too good for me." His mind reeled past a lot of stuff I'd seen before, of his childhood, how he thought he was worthless, but he spoke again before I could protest. "Is that why I've felt so weird around her?" He looked at us. He looked at Caleb's hand locked around mine as he spoke. "Why I felt so protective and fuzzy around her?"

"You feel some of that stuff before the imprint," Caleb explained. "You always feel something for the person."

Bish nodded and slumped into the chair Jen had vacated in defeat.

I turned to Ecstasy.

"Ok, let's get you situated on the couch."

"It's not like I can sleep anyway. I'm just going to stay awake and wait to see if you stopped the vision or not. See if someone's going to sneak in and grab me."

"We'll keep a watch out," Caleb assured her. "I'll make sure the alarm is set before we go to bed."

"Well, I'm not thrilled to be the guinea pig to see if you can stop a vision but I guess I don't have much choice. You got any booze to lighten the mood?"

"How old are you?" Bish asked, leaning his elbows on his knees.

"Eighteen."

"Then, no, we don't have any booze."

"Nark," she muttered as she made her way through the door to the kitchen. We followed her, but I turned to look at Bish. "Are you coming?"

"In a minute."

I nodded and we went to make up the living room couch for Ecstasy. Caleb explained to her where everything was and that he and I were right in the next room. She nodded and sat down numbly on the couch. She was trying to put up a big front but in her mind, she was scared.

"It'll be ok," I told her. "I'll get you some clothes." I brought her some jammies and some clothes for in the morning. "Alright, our door will be open if you need anything."

"Ok." Caleb started to turn the lamp off as we went by. "Please leave it on," she pleaded.

"Ok."

I didn't even speak to Caleb, just threw on one of his t-shirts and climbed in bed. He pulled the lamp string and climbed in with me after changing and I latched myself to him, begging for sleep to find me quickly.

I woke several times during the night and so did Caleb. I felt like a mother hen watching over Ecstasy, who conked out so deeply that she never even cracked an eye at us as we kept getting up to check on her. Even after she spouted that she'd get absolutely no sleep.

In the morning, I woke with a start. I ran into the next room to find the couch ruffled and empty. Caleb ran in, too, and went to the door to check the alarm but then I heard her singing in her head, in the shower.

She was singing the words to Sesame Street, which made me chuckle. Caleb said he needed to go for a quick swim to clear his head for the day, so I went to greet Rachel and everyone else in the kitchen. Bella was lounging at Dad's feet, chewing on some bacon.

The coffee smelled heavenly and Rachel made honey buns. I smiled in thanks to her. Then, for some unknown reason I hugged her and kissed her cheek.

She smiled brightly and kissed mine back. "Thank you, honey."

I scratched Bella's head as I passed and went to sit by Dad and Bish. Bish still looked grim, but everyone else was oblivious to what we had seen last night. I put my head on Bish's shoulder and nibbled my honey bun. We had to figure this out. I couldn't lose Bish.

He took a big sip of his black coffee and I could taste the bitter taste in my mouth from it as I heard his thought. *Are we going to talk about last night?*

I shook my head, no. "Not right now," I whispered.

He pulled his arm up and over me to lay it on my shoulders. I lifted my knees to press against the table edge as he continued to sip his coffee and look at nothing on the wall.

"I'm glad to see you two made up," Dad observed. "I was thinking it was going to be a warzone all day long."

"No worries, Dad," I assured him.

"Good."

"We need to get a move on," Peter said. I saw him pat Rachel on the bottom, making her smirk as he passed her behind the island counter to get more creamer.

I giggled and Dad gave me a funny look. I just shook my head but then my jaw dropped as Ecstasy shuffled into the kitchen. The purple in her hair was gone and she had brushed it out straight. She had no makeup or eyeliner on. She looked so different, like a completely different person. She fingered her hair and shrugged bashfully when we all continued to gawk.

"I washed out my hair color. Temporary." She looked at me. "Thanks for the clothes."

"No problem, Ecstasy."

"And you can call me Lynne, my middle name. If I'm starting over anyway, I may as well get rid of that ridiculous name, right?"

Everyone chuckled in agreement with her.

"That's a very grown-up outlook, Lynne," Rachel said and directed her to the huge plate of honey buns.

"Rachel makes the best homemade honey buns," I told her.

She shrugged and went to grab one. "I usually don't eat breakfast," she took a bite, "because I'm not ever...oh, my gosh!" She looked at Rachel. "These are the best things I think I've ever had!"

"Thank you."

"Can I have two?" she asked tentatively.

"Of course, honey."

"Thanks." She grabbed another one and came to sit beside me. "So..." she began.

194

"We're leaving soon," I told her.

"Good," she muttered under her breath.

Jen came in then and accepted the good morning kiss from her dad. She glanced our way and tried to smile. Her mind said she wanted to try to be normal. She wasn't mad at Bish and didn't want him to be upset, or me. So she smiled sadly at us and then sent a small wave as she went back upstairs with her honey bun.

Bish never moved but his breathing changed when he saw her and when she left, he sighed. I rubbed his arm under the table.

I looked over at Lynne and saw she had icing drip down her chin. She wiped it on her hand, then grimaced and looked around for a napkin.

"I've got it," I told her.

I focused just like Caleb and I had on the beach that day. I pushed forward the thought for the napkin to lift from the counter. I also had to tack on a bad thought to go with it. The first one to pop into my head was the vision I saw last night. I winced, but went ahead and when I saw the napkin lift from the holder, I smiled. Bish's arm tightened on mine in surprise and Dad's eyes rounded. Peter and Rachel watched in fascination, too, but it was Lynne's reaction I enjoyed the most. She watched it stoically as it made its way in the air down the length of the table. Once it reached her, she grabbed it and wiped her mouth and then took another big bite as if nothing at all had happened.

She saw us all watching. "What?" she muffled around her bite defensively. "I'm hungry."

We all just laughed for a long time. It was funny that she seemed to be so ok with everything. She wasn't freaked about a napkin floating to her. She was just weird.

"I'm still here," she said a few minutes later. "So I guess your theory holds some water after all. You can change the visions."

"I guess."

"What theory?" Dad asked.

I explained to him everything that happened, except the part about Jen and Bish's vision, and then said I was going to shower and get ready.

I bumped into Kyle on the way out.

"Hey, Sorry, I-" He stopped when he saw Lynne at the table. "Is that Ecstasy?" he asked with inflection.

"It's actually Lynne now. And yes, that's her. Quite a change, huh?"

"Yeah," he said absently and looked at her for a moment longer. Then he looked back at me almost...guiltily, as if I would be mad that he was checking her out. "So, um." He pulled me to the little nook by the stairs. "I'm sorry about being a jackass yesterday in the alley, about you kissing me. You see, I had to do something to make Caleb think that I don't want you like I do. If I just sat there and wasn't myself, then he'd know something was up. I have to do it, Maggie. If he and I are ever going to be friends again…he can't know that this wasn't some crush. If he knew I loved you for real…he'd take you away from me."

"Kyle," I whispered. "You can't talk like that, ok?"

"I know, but I just needed you to understand. I wasn't trying to start trouble between you and me. I was serious about what I said to you in the club. I want you any way I can get you."

"Ok, Kyle. It's fine."

"Friends?" he asked and held his hand out to me.

"Friends."

I shook his hand and he grinned. "Awesome."

He waltzed into the kitchen, slung his arm over Rachel's shoulders and kissed her cheek. She smiled at him and handed him a glass of juice. I couldn't help but think that I missed the smart-alec Kyle; the clown cut up guy who had been my friend for years.

I wondered if things would ever be the same again.

~ Twenty Three ~

Within an hour, we were all packed into the cars and headed to the airport. Beck and Ralph didn't come down for breakfast and just walked straight to the cars when we yelled it was time to go. I felt horrible about it all but I couldn't talk to her. I'd just get emotional and it wouldn't make her feel any better because I wouldn't have any answers for her.

Caleb slung my bag into the back of the Jeep and then patted the floor with his hand in back for Bella to jump up into. He shut the trunk and followed my line of sight.

"You're right, just let her go," he told me gently.

I nodded and we all got in, fitting between the three cars we had. Lynne and Kyle rode with us. She immediately started asking us about Tennessee and snow. She's never seen snow before.

"Well, there won't be snow for a couple months," Kyle told her.

"What's it like to grow up like that?" she asked softly. "Normal families and holidays, snow outside your house that isn't falling apart. Parents actually giving you gifts instead of taking your paycheck at Christmas."

"I don't know. I've never known any different. What happened to your mom?" he asked her.

"She left."

"Mine, too," I told her.

"Really. Why would *your* mom leave?"

"Same reason as yours probably."

"I doubt that. Anyway, so, what's the plan?"

"Well," Caleb took over, "the last time we did this we just gave her some money and she took off, but with you, I think it'll be better to fly you out somewhere."

"The last one?" Kyle asked Caleb and Caleb cursed in his mind.

"We had a problem before with another girl," I explained. "We had to get her and her family out so we sent them away."

"Who? Was it just like this? You had a vision?" Kyle asked.

"Kind of," I said, and even I heard the odd tone in my voice. I wasn't the world's most fabulous liar.

"What does that mean? Who was it?"

He'll just be even madder, if we don't tell him now.

Caleb nodded and looked at Kyle in the rearview mirror.

"It was Amber. Sorry, bro."

"What? Why didn't you tell me?" He looked at me. "She didn't stand me up, did she?"

"No. I'm sorry. I thought it'd be better for you to just forget about her."

"What happened?"

I told him the whole sordid story, beginning to end. He listened but his mind poured on the guilt. He felt like he'd dragged her into our mess. I assured him it wasn't his fault and she was safe now. For some reason he was angry at Caleb. But I wondered if he was just playing his part, like he said before.

"You could have told me, dude. I'm not nine. I think I could have handled it."

"Yeah, totally," Lynne chimed in. "No offense, but crappy move. Who doesn't tell someone their girlfriend skipped town?"

"Exactly!" Kyle said and pointed at Lynne to drive home his point.

I just giggled in my seat. How would we survive if we had to live with them both; two Kyle's...Ugh...

After we returned the cars, we went and stood at the ticket counter. Caleb was encouraging Lynne to look at the flights and decide where to go. She wanted to go with us.

"Why can't I just go to Tennessee? What's the big deal?"

"We're not out of the clear yet. We have lots of trouble coming our way and it wouldn't be very smart to bring you right to it," he told her.

In the end, it was Kyle who convinced him.

"She knows Maggie's secret. It would probably be a good idea to keep her close, right? Plus, the four days Maggie saw into the vision, up to the part where she dies hadn't happened yet. We need to keep an eye on her until then."

"Where is she going to stay?"

"With me," Kyle announced, smiling smugly. "We have plenty of room at my house and Mom would love a project."

A cute little project.

His gaze shot to mine after his thought and he looked as if he should be guilty or something again, just like earlier. I just grinned and shook my head at him.

"Thank you, Kyle," she said and smiled at him. "If it's ok with everyone else, I don't want to wear out my welcome."

"That's a good idea I think," I said. "Although, Peter isn't going to be so easy to convince," I told Caleb.

"I know. Oh, well. Let's get you a ticket," he said to Lynne but Kyle stopped him.

"I got this."

"But she's our responsibility," Caleb reasoned.

"Uh, hello, standing right here!" she complained. "Besides," she grabbed Kyle's jacket clad arm and started to the counter, "I think the single one is more interesting anyway."

In her mind, she was very intrigued with Kyle, and the thought of staying at his house was more than interesting. He looked down at her and grinned.

"Seriously," Caleb said with animated hands. "That just happened? Kyle is spending his money on something other than Halo?"

I laughed at him. "Come on. Let's go break the news to the family."

It didn't go so well and once again, we were left pulling rank. Well, I was. I hated to use the Visionary card, but it seemed to be the only reason anyone would listen to us.

We sat in the chairs at the gate and as I rested my head back on the seat backs, I felt Caleb's fingers running down the Visionary mark on my neck. My eye peeked at him.

"It won't rub off, you know," I teased. "I'm still the Visionary."

He chuckled. "I thought you were asleep."

"I wish. I am so tired from getting up all night."

At that, he grabbed my hand to help fill me with his touch. I sighed and closed my eyes on his shoulder. As I sat, I listened to the thoughts around me. Kyle and Lynne were sitting by each other and he was telling her about playing football. She told him she played volleyball in high school. They were both pretty engrossed in their conversation and I felt my lips quirk at the thought. Good old Kyle didn't stay down for long.

Dad was talking to Rachel and Peter about something over a newspaper. Ralph was playing his DS and Beck was reading a magazine someone had left behind. She was still mad.

Jen and Bish were sitting across from each other and pretty much just staring miserably into each other's eyes. How had no one else but us noticed the strain on their faces all day?

I lifted my head and looked at them. I didn't think I'd ever seen a more pitiful pair. I wished there was something I could do. I tried to think of anything but that. I smiled when my mind flashed to the 25 Hour Skillet and Big John and Smarty. I chuckled and Caleb smiled as he saw the day Big John chased him with a meat cleaver in my mind.

"You're enjoying that memory a little too much, I think."

I laughed and then remembered the bracelet; the bracelet that the Watsons took from me. I rubbed my wrist at the loss. Caleb sighed beside me.

"What?" I asked.

He cocked his head to the side and smiled. "Well, I was going to wait until your birthday to give this to you."

"What?"

He reached in his bag, gave me a little white box with a red ribbon and leaned forward to whisper in my ear, his lips touching my lobe. "Happy early birthday, Maggie." I looked at him funny and opened the lid to find a bracelet...with a star charm, the exact replica of the one that was stolen from me. I looked back to him and he smiled, lifting his hand to wipe a tear from under my eye. "I wasn't trying to make you cry."

"Thank you, Caleb. This bracelet means a lot to me."

He took it out of the box and clasped it gently on my wrist. He looked at it and then lifted my hand to kiss my wrist.

"Perfect," he whispered.

"Thank you, babe," I said and hugged his around his neck tight.

"You're welcome." He chuckled into my hair. "I would have given it to you when I got it if I knew you'd be this happy."

I had a thought. "That day...that you went into the store and left us in the Jeep; you were doing math in your head so I couldn't see what you were thinking."

"Pretty smart trick, huh?"

I nodded. I reached up and right before I touched his lips, they called our flight number over the intercom.

We both sighed and sat back.

"Come on, gorgeous."

He grabbed my bag and his and we made our way to stand in line. Bella was somewhere in the back with the luggage. Beck came right up behind me and sniffed in a way to get my attention, but to show me she was peeved as well. I couldn't help it. I turned around to face her.

"Beck, look, there are so many things going on right now that you don't know about and I can't tell you. But know that I love you and I wanted to spend time with you but there are some things I have to do first. Please don't be mad at me."

"You kissed Kyle," she hissed quietly to me. "The Maggie I knew would never have kissed someone she wasn't dating and then drag some drug addict home with her."

"Beck, please. It's not what it looks like."

"Says every person ever caught doing something they shouldn't," she sneered.

"Lynne was in trouble, but not the drug kind. We're taking her with us to keep her safe."

"Uhuh. And kissing Kyle? The same Kyle that you promised me nothing was going on with."

"That's it, isn't it?" I realized. "You're mad because you think I kept it from you that I was seeing Kyle, which I wasn't."

"You kept everything from me!" she yelled, but bent her head when everyone in our vicinity looked at us curiously. "You cut your hair and didn't tell me, you slept with your boyfriend and didn't tell me, your dad *lets* you sleep with your boyfriend and you didn't tell me! You left for California and didn't tell me until you were already here. I was the last person you called when you got back from being kidnapped and you haven't even tried to tell me about it. You barely speak to me anymore."

"You didn't ask anything about it," I rebutted lamely.

"I shouldn't have to. I'm your best friend, or I was. Now I guess you have a cuter, more male version," she said and rolled her eyes at Caleb's back.

"That's not fair, Beck, you have Ralph."

"Yes, but I don't talk to him!" She turned to him. "No offense, babe." Then she turned back to me. "I have plenty of things to tell you about, but now I'm going away to school and you're gonna go get married or something and have babies, and I'll have no part in it."

I took a chance and pulled her to me for a hug. She resisted for a split second before she gave in with a begrudged sigh.

201

"I was taken by some jerks who wanted something I didn't have. I'm not traumatized about it but they're still after me. That girl right there," I pointed to Lynne who was oblivious and still talking to Kyle, "her father is a drug addict and she was looking for a way out. I know that sounds crazy, but I had to help her. I just sleep with Caleb, nothing else." I lifted my eyebrows to accentuate my point. "And as for kissing Kyle, it was stupid, I thought it was helping. I know that makes no sense but... I'm sorry."

"You know you really didn't answer any of my questions. Not one," she said but her steam seemed to be dissipating.

"I know, but I'm trying."

"Are you in trouble?" she asked and grabbed my arm gently. "You're not pregnant are you? You're sure?"

"No," I whispered so I wouldn't yell.

"So you and Caleb are seriously serious."

"Yes," I said and heard the laugh entering my tone.

"Are you going to marry him?"

"Yes."

Her eyes bulged slightly, but she kept it together. "Are you still going to college?"

"Mmhmm."

"Will you promise to tell me everything one day?"

"If I can," I said carefully. "So you and Ralph, are you seriously serious?"

She cracked her first smile. "I think I love him," she whispered and looked over her shoulder at him as he talked to Caleb. "I've never said that to anyone and it's a little scary but...I do. I love him."

"Have you told him?"

"No, are you crazy!" she said incredulously.

"If it's true, you should tell him."

"Do you love Caleb?"

"Beck, I just told you I was going to marry him someday."

"That is so not an answer."

I laughed in exasperation. "Yes. Of course I love him."

"Have you told him?"

"Yes."

"What?" she said loudly. "It's been like a couple of weeks or something."

"I know, but it is what it is."

"Aww... Mags. You love him," she said sweetly.

I scoffed. "So marrying him is no problem, but my loving him is something to shout about?"

202

"Yes! Oh, I love you, Maggsie." She hugged me again. "I'm sorry I got mad. I just want to be in your life. I'm gonna be your Maid of Honor, right?" She looked at me with a look of horror with the thought that I could not choose her.

And I wasn't going to have a real wedding so I just smiled. "I love you, too, Beck."

"Rebecca, it's our turn, babe," Ralph called back to us.

"Ah, I love it when he calls me Rebecca," she groaned and we giggled as we made our way to the boys.

"I see you're back in her good graces," Caleb said into my ear from behind me. "I guess I was wrong to tell you not to try."

"It was a whim and I went with it."

"Well, I'm glad. I hope it lasts."

"Me, too."

The plane was similar to last time except for there was no sweet confessions or story time for Caleb and I, and I didn't freak out about the plane taking off. Caleb and his family had once again opted for First Class and we were all piled into the left side together in rows of three. Lynne was next to me in the aisle seat and was going on and on about how First Class was so awesome as she drank her third glass of free orange juice. In truth, I just wanted to sleep, but it didn't look like that was going to happen. Caleb on the other hand was dozing next to me, his seat back with one arm behind his head and the other in my lap as Lynne talked endlessly to me.

"This is the best orange juice I've ever had, I think."

"It's pretty good," I told her and I tasted the sweet/sour of the pulp in her mouth in her mind to mine.

"I know I've been saying it a lot, but you guys live the life!" she said and laughed in genuine happiness.

She was in complete awe of her surroundings.

"It's not all glamour," I muttered under my breath.

"I can't wait to get there," she said absently. "Kyle's family sounds awesome." She turned to me. "Thank you. You saved my life."

"It was nothing," I said and she grabbed my hand.

"Yeah, it was. I know you're tired and I know you checked on me all night. Go ahead and go to sleep. I'm going to watch the movie. They're about to show *Airplane*." She laughed hard. "Hilarious, right?"

I just laughed as I leaned over to press against Caleb. He sighed when I did and pulled me closer, kissing my forehead in his sleep. I closed my eyes and couldn't wait to be home.

203

Twenty Four

We all parted when we landed. Dad and Bish went back to his house and Beck and Ralph went to theirs. Bish and Jen's goodbye was bittersweet. It was strange to have everything out it the open and yet it such a sad and sticky situation.

"I guess I'll see you later?" Bish asked her.

"Mmhmm," she answered. "I'm sure you will. Maybe I'll see you before we leave for London."

He swallowed painfully. "Yeah," he said gruffly and rubbed his upper arm self-consciously. "I'll come by your place and see Maggie, maybe."

She waved and went to wait in the car with her parents.

I hugged him and Dad. Dad wasn't happy that I wasn't coming home with him. I explained that we'd spent every night with him so far and had never spent time at Caleb's home.

He let me go but I figured it was only because he didn't think he could stop me.

We put Bella in the SUV and I climbed in with Kyle, Lynne, Caleb, Peter, Jen and Rachel. We would drop Lynne and Kyle off at his house after someone explained everything to his parents.

I checked my phone messages in the car and was surprised to find one from Chad. I listened to it and he told me about getting his apartment ready and how much he missed me. He asked me to call him soon. I closed my phone and bit my lip.

I glanced at Caleb and saw him trying not to look annoyed. I just didn't say anything. When we pulled into the driveway, Uncle Max came out and greeted us. I hoped that they didn't make a huge fuss about me being the Visionary.

As soon as I got out Uncle Max greeted me with the bow. Ugh. Caleb immediately told him to stop, but Max's eyes were glued to the mark on my neck. I begged them to please not treat me differently, and after some persuasion, they agreed.

After introductions, I showed Lynne where the bathroom was and when we were coming back down the stairs, she tripped on the bottom step and grabbed my arm to stop her fall.

And I was blasted, to my dismay, with yet another vision for her.

The vision was of her and a guy. They were standing in a kitchen together but the background was fuzzy and I couldn't really see it that well. He was wiping something from her face, flour I thought. They were laughing hard and grabbing onto each other as if they would fall over if they didn't. The guy was turned and I couldn't see his face, but as they got serious, I saw in her eyes that she loved him. He pulled her closer and kissed her gently. She dropped the bowl of flour from her fingers to the floor to grasp his arms. And when they pulled back, they both said 'I love you' at the same time.

I gasped as I came back to myself. Caleb was already there behind me holding me up. Lynne had fallen to the floor and Peter was helping her up. She looked at me with expectations. "What was that?"

"I saw you...you were imprinted, too," I said in quiet awe.

"Too?" Peter asked. "What's going on, Maggie?"

Don't, Maggie. Caleb begged and Jen did her own begging at the same time. *Please, no, Maggie.*

"What's imprinted mean?" Lynne asked me.

"You imprint with your soul mate. I saw Lynne imprinted with someone, but I couldn't see his face."

"She's going to imprint with someone?" Kyle asked almost angrily.

I looked at him and he was seething. Jen beside him was discreetly wiping her eyes.

"That's what I saw."

"Great," he muttered. "Awesome, frigging awesome."

"Kyle," Lynne said softly, having no idea what we were talking about, but knew he was upset about something.

He just shook his head and left the room.

"What's going on?" Uncle Max asked. "What's wrong with Kyle? What has he done?"

"Nothing, Uncle Max, they just met," Caleb assured him knowing exactly where he was going with it.

Neither of us mentioned Amber though. Lynne leaned against Peter in her shock. I could see her shaking and went to her.

"I'll take her. Uncle Max, where can I put Lynne for the night?"

He didn't say anything so I turned to look at him and he was smiling. "You called me Uncle Max."

I felt my grin spread at his enjoyment of it. "Yeah."

"Put her in the room you stayed in with Caleb," he said and came to stand next to us. He rubbed her arm soothingly and kissed my forehead. "It'll be alright, girls. We'll figure this out."

I nodded and took her to lie on the bed. She seemed to be in shock or something. I tried to explain as best as I could what imprinting was and how it all worked. She listened but didn't say anything for a while.

"You kissed Kyle at the club, but you're in love with the beefy one."

"Yes, I kissed Kyle for a reason, but I don't love him. We're just friends. I was trying to control my ability."

"But he likes you. He watches you."

"He seems to like you an awful lot, too."

She scoffed. "Boys like that don't like girls like me."

"What does that mean?"

"He knows about me, my family, where I come from. I'm trash. He's a nice guy. They ride in on their white horse, nurse you back to health and make you fall for them, then move on to the gorgeous girl to spend the rest of their life with. That's just the way it is."

"I saw you in the vision. You were imprinted with an Ace," I argued.

"Yeah, well, maybe we'll do something to stop that vision from coming true, too," she said dejected.

I left her there to sleep and went downstairs.

When I came back down and heard them talking, I stopped on the steps to listen.

"So the Imprints are returning," Uncle Max said and I heard the relief in his voice.

"It looks that way, if Maggie's vision is correct," Peter said. "I wonder who it will be."

"Well, she's a darling girl," Rachel explained. "Anyone would be lucky to have her. She's just had a rough time lately."

"So, any news on this ransom business?" Max asked.

"No, nothing. The Reunification is in two days. We just have to keep her safe until then," Peter said. "Surely the Watsons wouldn't have the gall to show their face there."

"But they will be under protective sanction. If they do come, you can't harm them, you know that. Just like you couldn't harm them when they kidnapped her the first time."

"Well," Caleb cut it, "I think that's bull. None of this would be happening if we'd taken care of them the first time."

"Son, we have to follow the rules. We aren't allowed to harm other clans."

"But they aren't following the rules!" he yelled. "And they harmed her!"

"I know, but we aren't like them," Peter said with conviction. "We are nothing like them and I don't ever want to be. We'll do this the proper way. We've never had a clan denounced before but once they are, they're fair game. And they probably know it and will run like scared children."

"It's not supposed to be like this," Caleb muttered and I heard his footsteps. He found me sitting on the stairs and grabbed my hand to tow me. "We're leaving," he called. "See you at the house, Dad."

He took me outside to the garage, to his bike. I smiled looking at it and laughed out loud when he ran a hand down the length and sang to it.

"Ah, I've missed you, Lolita."

We climbed on after he put on my helmet. When it rumbled to life, I felt giddy. I'd missed the bike, for sure. He pulled out of the driveway and we rode all the way to his house in comfortable silence. He drove slowly to savor the feel of the ride.

When we pulled onto his street, I noticed his gate was open. He stopped the bike in the middle of the street and looked around.

The gate is never left open.

Nothing looked out of order. He pulled into his driveway and stopped. He got off the bike and took off his helmet to look around. We heard whining motors coming down the street. I cocked my head to figure it out but Caleb tensed.

He ran to the call box and pressed the button, calling for Randolph but he never answered. Then two riders all in black pulled up in the driveway on motorcycles. Caleb pushed me further back behind him and stood straighter.

I had a sudden feeling that I needed to stop them. I pushed my hands forward to command the gates. They closed in a frightfully fast swing, knocking both the men from their bikes and sending them skidding on the asphalt.

They got up quickly and came to the gate. One of them shook it angrily but the other one just grabbed the mad one by the collar and jumped, clearing the fence and gate in one quick leap. They landed on their feet in a graceful pounce on our side.

We waited for something to happen. They never spoke but then all of a sudden, without warning, they ran towards us.

Caleb turned and pushed my lower back with two hands. "Get in the garage!"

"I'm not leaving you!"

"Go, Maggie," he demanded harder.

I obeyed…halfway. I didn't go to the garage but I ran further away from them and watched as the horrific scene unfolded. One of the men took his hands palms up and made the ground beneath Caleb lift and shake, making a little hill that eventually opened up into hole under Caleb. He jumped and reached for the edge just in time and clung for his life as the mound raised higher and higher and the hole got bigger and bigger. Then the other one huffed and pushed the one working in aggravation. His mind said he was mad because he should have taken care of Caleb already and he was ready to take me for his reward money. I saw it in his mind what he was doing before he did it but him pulling the gun out of his jacket pocket shocked me into shivers.

He climbed the mound and pointed it at Caleb. I couldn't see Caleb's face but I heard him.

I love you, Maggie.

That was it for me.

The man got one shot off before I pushed my hands forward and the guy's gun went flying back behind him. I used my other hand and imagined lifting Caleb up and over the mound to land in the grass and that's exactly what happened. The men cursed and one ran for me. I pushed through the thought to move his bike, to send it skidding and crashing into him and when it carried out my commands, I closed my eyes to to the sickening crunch of bones and tearing of flesh on the concrete driveway.

When I opened them, the other man was making a swift advance to me. Caleb was hot on his tail but wouldn't reach him before the man reached me. I tried to think of something to do, anything, but I froze and the guy reached his hands around my neck.

"That was my bike you wrecked, you little twit," he growled in my face, not worried about his comrade at all. Then his eyes drifted to my neck and his grip loosened a little in his shock. "The Visionary."

Caleb pulled him off and slung him backwards. He skidded in the grass on his back, leaving a trail and indention as he went with the force. Caleb was shocked at his strength but didn't dwell on it. The man got up and went to grab the gun that was near him as he roared with aggravation and cursed some more.

Then something happened that I never expected. Caleb held his hand out for the gun and it flew threw the air just as the man reached for it, straight into Caleb's hand. The man ran at us full speed with his clear intentions blaring though his mind to mine and then to Caleb. He was going to kill Caleb and take me to Sikes. Without further hesitation, Caleb lifted the gun and pulled the trigger.

The man stopped mid-run and flew back from the force of the shot. He lay still on the ground and Caleb turned, throwing the gun to the ground. He pressed my face into his neck.

"Don't look."

Caleb had killed the monster for me.

It was then that I felt him, his pain. I had no idea why I hadn't felt it before, but my body recognized the injury and began to heal him. I pulled back, though he tried to stop me, to see a huge red spot on his t-shirt on his stomach. I pulled his shirt up to see a gunshot would on his right side.

I screamed as my heart beat painfully for him.

"It's alright, baby," he soothed and grabbed his chest a little, like he could feel my heart and it was as painful for him. "You're healing me already. It's ok."

I held his arm under mine to steady him and we watched together as the wound sizzled and burned, closing up and becoming tan again instead of red and angry. Caleb groaned as the bullet pushed itself out and fell with a dull thud to the ground.

I knelt on my knees to inspect closer and ran my fingers over it in awe. I hugged him around his middle, pressed my cheek to his stomach and burst into tears.

"Why didn't I see that coming? Why didn't I get a vision for this?"

"I don't know."

"You could have died," I croaked as he rubbed my hair then he bent down with me and pulled me to him. "What if I hadn't been here, you would've-"

"Shh, don't. Shh." He lifted my chin and kissed my lips softly once. "We'll always be together."

"What was that?" I asked and felt the cool wind on my wet cheeks. "How did you do that, Caleb? Did you get your ability?"

"I don't know what happened. I just felt like it told me what to do and I did it."

It was then that we realized someone was watching us. I looked behind us and saw Marcus standing in front of the garage.

He clapped and smiled cruelly as Caleb and I stood up.

"Bravo. Bravo, really, a spectacular show. I think you've gained some new abilities that we never-" His eyes moved to my neck as well and his arrogant steps faltered. "No. No, that can't be. You're human trash!" he roared. "You are not our Visionary!" He shook his head furiously and balled his fist. "It's a trick. They painted that on you to trick us." He made wide, angry strides to us. "I'll see for myself."

Caleb once again shoved me behind him and I waited in fright, but also fascination, as him and Marcus sparred. There were no abilities for him either so it was a fair fight. I wanted to help, but was afraid that I'd just distract Caleb or hurt him somehow. As it turned out, he didn't need my help.

I saw in Caleb's mind as he fought the moves he learned from Uncle Max as he went along. Some he knew already, but some he learned as he went, his mind teaching him. If I wasn't so scared, I would have been fascinated to see it as it happened in his mind.

Caleb didn't have to fight long. He had the advantage of knowing how to fight that Marcus didn't. Marcus would make for a punch and Caleb would rear back to evade and then land a blow to his jaw or chest. Then Caleb kicked a booted foot to Marcus's chest, sending him flying several feet away from him.

I put my hands up to hold him off as he started to run back to us but it wasn't my power that stopped him. We looked behind us to Peter and Rachel there. Rachel was holding him in place with a murderous look on her pretty face. Marcus's belt chain, buckle and ear gauge were straining and pulling as he groaned.

"No man should wear all that metal," she said and threw him aside to slam into the side of the garage.

He lay there motionless and Rachel ran to Caleb.

"Oh, my! What…" she said with her hands fluttering without any idea of where to start.

"Maggie took care of me, Mom. It's fine."

"What happened?" Peter boomed and looked around. "Are you alright?" He moved forward to inspect me; grasping my arms gently and leaning down into look in my face. "Maggie? Are you alright, sweetheart?"

The yard was destroyed with the huge mound hole and dirt everywhere. There were bike parts and I turned away when I saw a leg sticking out from behind a pile of mangled metal.

"Yes. They were waiting for us," I explained. "They must have been Aces because they had abilities. Then Marcus came from inside the garage."

Peter paled. "Randolph," he muttered and took off running.

Rachel and Jen both ran in after him. Bella trotted up to Caleb, sniffing his shirt and whining. He bent down and patted her head. "It's ok, girl."

Then we walked slowly inside and as I had suspected, it was confirmed when I heard Rachel's keening cry. Marcus had killed Randolph, their butler, jack of all trades, security man and family friend.

Caleb sat solemnly on the back steps and I rubbed his back with my hand inside his shirt to soothe him. I felt responsible. They were after me. This was all happening because of me.

"Stop it, Maggie," Caleb commanded. "This would have happened to anyone who imprinted. We'll get them. This isn't over and it's not your fault."

I nodded and heard Peter on the phone with the police. Randolph was a human. This was a human murder and had to be handled by human authorities, but what about the mess outside?

I left Caleb there on the step to go and try to clean up a bit. I felt horrible and sickened, but it had to be done. I bit my lip so hard I tasted blood when I used my power to scoot the bikes and their owners into the hole in the earth they had created and tried to bury Caleb in. Now they were buried in it instead.

I pushed the ground closed and the dirt back down as much as possible in my mind and tried to make it look normal. You could tell something had happened, but it didn't look suspicious.

I had forgotten all about Marcus as I suspected they had.

I whirled around quickly only to find him gone. Crap. He knew. He knew I was the Visionary and now all my enemies would know. I went back inside and told them Marcus was gone and he had seen my mark. Peter cursed up a storm and shoved all the items off the counter in the kitchen to the floor with a roar. Rachel tried to calm him with soothing words and touches. I saw him wrap her in his arms and they just held on to each other as Caleb pulled me from the room.

The police came, I saw them out the window, but Peter took care of all of it. He told them the mound was the beginnings of a pool. Caleb and I just took showers and went to lay in his room in silence. I wanted to comfort him somehow, to make it all go away, but I felt like he just wanted me to be there, that that was enough, so that's what I did. I made sure to touch him somewhere and we just stared at the ceiling together and tried to make sense out of everything that had just happened.

Twenty Five

We woke a little later to Peter. We were still on top of the covers just as we had been before and at sometime had finally fallen asleep. Peter sat on the bed next to me and told us that he had hired a cleaning crew to come and take care of the place. He didn't think it was safe to stay when someone had breached the security. We would all go stay at Kyle's until it was all fixed up.

So, we got up and got dressed again. Everyone seemed calmer and steadier now and Caleb insisted on driving his bike, though I suggested that maybe he shouldn't drive. He smiled and said he was fine. So we trekked right back to Kyle's after only been gone from there a couple hours.

Everyone was still up when we returned and there were a few other people there to greet us, Gran being one of them. She smiled big and hugged Caleb and me at the same time. I smiled widely because she was the first Ace I met since becoming the Visionary that didn't bow to me. She murmured all kinds of sweet things to assure us that all would be well and she was glad we were safe.

Maria ran to her mother and squealed loudly.

Kyle also greeted us and I saw genuine relief when he looked at Caleb and they bumped fists. Then he hugged me and squeezed me extra tight. Then he pulled away and sat on the other end of the room by Gran. I heard Jen ushering Maria to bed in the hall.

We all sat in the living room to have a pow-wow.

Lynne had come down and she too seemed better. She came straight to me and wrapped her arm through mine. She smiled at me.

"You look like crap, if it's ok for me to say that."

I laughed. "I'm so glad you're back to yourself."

She shrugged and sat down next to me and stared straight across the room. I felt Kyle glancing my way several times, his interest and longing pouring to me through his mind, but I shut him out and focused on Peter.

Peter told them all what had happened and they gasped and uproared over it all. Uncle Max reiterated his earlier point about harming other clans. Even though they were after us first, the council forbade true harm to other clans and to take a life was grounds for denouncement of the guilty individuals, and sometimes of the entire clan.

That was when it truly hit me. I had taken a life. Caleb had taken a life for me too. Even though they weren't truly human and they were trying to kill me – well, kill Caleb and take me to be tortured – it still felt odd and wrong. Everyone assured us that they would fight the council for us. They'd stand behind us and we did the right thing, but as I clung to Caleb's arm, I'd had it. I was just done with the Watsons and all their mess and didn't want to talk about it anymore.

Everyone dispersed, some going home, some going upstairs. A few people bowed to me, kissing my fingers and then touching their foreheads with them, but most respected my wishes and just tried to tame their looks of awe.

I stopped Peter to ask him about why I hadn't gotten a vision for Caleb being shot or us being attacked. He said that you can't see visions for yourself nor your significant. Great. I then told him about what Caleb did in the fight and his gaze shot to Caleb.

"I still don't feel anything, Dad," Caleb assured. "It was just right then, at that moment, now...nothing."

Peter sighed.

"Well...I don't know. This is just getting more complicated," he said before heading to bed.

We went to stand in the kitchen with Lynne, Kyle, and Jen.

"Have you told your dad what happened yet?" Jen asked me.

"No," I sighed. "He would just worry all night. I'll tell him when we go see him tomorrow."

"You're going over tomorrow?" she said hopefully, but cleared her throat and ducked her head.

"Yeah, I think we should all go see them before we leave for London," I said and saw her grateful look at including her in coming with me.

"Well, what about me?" Lynne asked. "Where am I going to go when you all leave?"

"Don't know. I haven't thought that out yet," I said in frustration at the never ending problems coming our way. Caleb put a hand on my neck and squeezed in a massage. I leaned into him and didn't know what I'd do without him. *What are we going to do with her?*

No clue. Maybe she can stay with your dad?

Maybe. I'm so tired of thinking right now. I just want to rest and not have to worry about everything for just a minute.

I know. By the way, thanks for saving my life...again. You were so incredible back there.

So we're even I think. I smiled up at him. *You were pretty good, too. Your karate is almost as good as mine.*

He laughed out loud and kissed my forehead.

"Oh, this is so going to your pretty little head," he said with a smirk.

I turned back to see Lynne watching us.

"Are you talking to each other? In your minds?"

"Mmhmm, all significants can."

"Wow." She cleared her throat shrilly. "So, why do you keep getting visions for me and no one else?"

"I have no idea, Lynne. I'm as confused as you."

"Hmmm. Ok, well, I guess I'm going to bed."

"Goodnight," Kyle said beside her and smiled. "I'm right next door to you if you need anything."

"Ok, thanks," she said softly and looked away from him, feeling flush for some reason that she didn't understand. She started to walk away, but stopped. "I don't want to be a burden to you guys. You've been so good to me already. I can just find somewhere to crash. You don't have to worry about me. You got me away from my dad, that's enough for me."

"No," Kyle said vehemently. "We like having people here. Don't worry about it." She nodded and turned to leave again. "Lynne. Still be here when we get up the morning, please."

She turned and looked up at him. She was pretty short and seriously thin. She just looked so small and fragile next to him and he looked at her with an odd expression. One I recognized and I felt my heart spike at the realization.

She was staring at Kyle earlier across the room during the meeting and he wasn't looking at me during the meeting either, he was looking at her! I had blocked him out to pay attention and just made assumptions! I felt Caleb turn my way in recognition of my thoughts right as Kyle reached out to touch her arm.

And then it happened.

Kyle and Lynne imprinted right there in the kitchen in front of us.

It was amazing. Their faces registered the shock of heat and lightning in their veins. Her face was in awe but somewhat frightened by it all. I imagined my

214

face looked exactly the same when it had happened to me. His face was elated. I saw a couple of their future visions but they happened at the same time so it was so hard to concentrate.

I saw a piece of one where Kyle was twirling her under his arm, her red dress flowing around her legs, in a big yard at night under the stars.

Then another short look at her putting something away in a tall cabinet. He came up behind her and lifted her so she could reach. When she turned around you could see her small belly bump and he rubbed it gently.

The last one I could make sense of was of the two of them standing in a big, grand, gold room in front of hundreds of people.

When she finally gasped, I knew it was over and looked around. Caleb's grin was broad and he was gripping me to him with affection. Jen was trying to paste on a smile, but was utterly devastated inside. She so wanted this for herself.

Kyle's mouth was open and he looked the happiest I'd ever seen him in my long time of knowing him. He closed the short distance between them and framed her face with his hands.

"It's you," he whispered, and it made me smile at my own memory of this exact moment.

"It's me," she said through her happy tears and smiled.

Then he kissed her. I balked and looked at Caleb accusatorily.

You could have kissed me right then and instead you tortured me for days.

Kyle's not a gentleman like I am, he said clearly enjoying the whole thing.

Caleb, I sighed and let him wrap me up in his healing arms. *It's actually happening. The imprints are coming back.*

I know. And it's all because of you.

And you.

He smiled as he kissed me, but it didn't last long. Kyle's mom came in and gasped at the scene.

"Kyle! What-" In her mind she saw it all over their faces and knew what had happened. "Oh, my...thank you, God!" She ran to him and embraced him tightly, dragging Lynne in with him, but she was willing. "Max! Peter! Max!" she yelled and everyone who was left ran in to see what happened, their minds flashing with thoughts of attacks and ambushes.

What they saw brought Uncle Max to tears.

"Dad," Kyle croaked and Uncle Max stumbled to him and bawled in a way that only a grown man could, big and loud. "Dad, it's ok."

"I know, son. For the first time in a long time, it's all going to be ok." He hugged Lynne to him and they all just huddled for a bit. I noticed that Kyle never let Lynne's hand fall from his.

Gran was still there and came up behind Caleb and me, putting an arm around each of us.

"Now ain't that a sight."

"Yes, ma'am," Caleb whispered.

"I wonder, did you both look that goofy when you imprinted?" she said with a teasing glint in her eye.

"I'm sure we did," Caleb said good-naturedly, "probably goofier."

"And how are you doing with everything that's been going on?" she asked me as she tossled the ends of my hair.

"All right, I guess," I answered. "I'm pretty sick of the bowing, for sure."

"Well you better get used to it, Miss Priss. You're the Visionary and those old coots on the council won't stand for breaking tradition. Come the day after tomorrow, you're gonna have three hundred people bowing to you."

"Ugh," I groaned and bit my lip. "Well, I'm going to try to change that. We have a lot of changes coming our way."

"I heard. I also heard you found my Raymond's book."

Without another word from her, I ran and got it out of my bag in the car. When I came back, we sat at the counter together with Caleb and looked at it. The brand new imprint celebration was still going on on the other side of the kitchen, but we gave them some privacy.

"Oh, look at us!" she exclaimed at she saw the picture he had pasted in the cover. "How young and handsome was he?"

"You were pretty smoking, too, Gran," Caleb joked and she slapped his hand gently.

"Now don't go throwing your lies at me!"

She ran her finger over Grandpa Ray's face and then turned the page and started to read. When we got to the last page she got up without a word. When she came back, she had a long feather pen in an ink well.

She called attention to everyone.

"I think we have a few additions to make. Caleb," she turned to him, "I nominate you as Jacobson family historian and record keeper. All in favor, say aye."

"Aye," a chorus rang out.

"Wait," Caleb said. "What does that mean?"

"It means you keep our records for us; births, imprints, ascensions. And it seems you've got some catching up to do." She took the long black and white feather in her hand and placed it across her palms. "This was the very first historian's pen. This belonged to your Grandpa Ray as well. Everything in this book is written with this pen." She gave it to him and he held it, as if testing the weight. "And now it's yours. It'll be your job to keep track of everything and your job to find a predecessor when you're done with it all."

"Thank you. I'm honored, Gran," Caleb said and his thoughts flashed to a time when he saw Grandpa Ray writing in it once when he was little.

Maria bounded around the corner and hid behind Caleb, peeking around him for her mom in her cute pink pajamas.

"I'm sorry Grandpa's not here to give it to me," Caleb said to Gran as he hugged Maria to his side.

"Me, too, sugar," Gran said and I saw her rub her wrist tattoo absentmindedly.

"But Grandpa Ray is here, Gran. Right here," Maria said and pointed to Gran's heart and her own.

Gran smiled brightly and hugged her.

"You are so right, sugar. What would I do without you?"

"Um…be bored?"

Everyone laughed.

"You don't know how true that statement is."

Twenty Six

Unfortunately, we didn't get much time with Maria because by this time, it was after midnight. So Jen carted her off to bed, but I knew I'd see plenty of her in the week to come because she'd be going with us to the reunification.

It was hard, I could tell, for Kyle's parents to move away from the new significants. It was like if they stopped looking at them, it would go away and be a dream. Eventually, Kyle coaxed them enough to tell them he was taking his significant to his room. They were tired and ready for sleep.

It was kind of funny watching Kyle tow Lynne up the stairs. Everyone looked high like they were drugged.

"Sleep tight, you two," Gran called to them.

"That's not all they're gonna be doing," Caleb muttered behind me and laughed when I elbowed his gut.

"Caleb Maxwell Jacobson!" she reprimanded. "For shame."

"Maxwell?" I asked. "How did I not know your middle name?"

"There are still a few things you don't know about me," he muttered low in my neck. "But I actually take the time to look for these things in your head, Maggie Camille Masters."

I gasped. "Not fair," I muttered.

"Alright you two, that's enough of that." But then she looked at us closely. "Have you been being careful? You remember what I told you before about Aces getting pregnant the-"

"Gran," Caleb protested and held a hand up. "We talked about this."

"I'm just saying."

"Bye, Gran." He scooped me up fireman style over his shoulder and carried me up the stairs with Peter and Rachel chuckling and Gran sputtering, scandalized once again.

When we passed Kyle's door, we could hear them murmuring in there and Caleb chuckled at being right.

"You're cute when you're smug," I said once he put me on the bed.

"Then I'm cute all the time."

I laughed and covered my mouth, then groaned when he lay on top of me gently and began to kiss my neck. "You're not tired?" I asked.

"Not after all that, no. Are you?"

"A little."

His mouth moved to ear and all my breath left me. "You don't sound very tired to me," he said in a tone that told me exactly what he had up his sleeve.

"Caleb, we're in your uncles' house," I chastised.

"Yeah, in our room. Nobody's going to come in. I'm ready to do this, Maggie."

"I am, too," I realized. I was ready to Mutualize with my significant. I bit my lip. "Do you know exactly…what to do?"

He smiled genuinely and caressed my cheekbone with his thumb. "Oh, yeah," he whispered.

Then he kissed my mouth and let his hands drift down to grab my arms. He pushed them to the bed over my head and held them down gently as he continued to kiss me ardently.

Then we heard a knock at the door.

"You have got to be kidding me," Caleb muttered against my lips. "What?" he said in aggravation and leaned back, pulling me up to sit by him.

The door swung open to reveal little Maria. "I'm sorry. I'm scared."

He softened and patted his lap. She slowly came and let him pull her up.

"What's the matter, M? Where's you mom?"

"She's talking to Nana," she explained. Nana was Rachel. "She was crying about something. But I heard Uncle Max talking about you getting shot with a gun. And someone shot at Maggie, too," she said wildly.

"But we're fine," he soothed. "See?"

"I'm scared. Can I sleep with you?"

How could you refuse a face like that? "All right," Caleb sighed and stood, throwing her on the bed, making her laugh. "Hop under the covers."

"Yay!" she squealed.

He turned to me and pulled me close to him. "We are going to finish this if it's the last thing I do," he growled and I giggled.

"Agreed."

"Alright, scoot over, Maria. You can sleep next to Maggie, ok?"

"Ok."

Caleb spooned behind me and fell asleep pretty quickly for someone who had claimed not to be tired. Maria snuggled into my chest facing me. I smiled at the feeling of being completely surrounded, literally, by the people I loved.

In the morning, I woke first. I slid out from between them both and bumbled my way into the kitchen to find it empty, which surprised me. Usually Rachel was up cooking something yummy and with this many people in the house, you'd think there'd be one person awake. The clock said it was 6:55. That probably explained it. I decided maybe I should contribute for once.

I pulled out a bag of grits and two packs of bacon. How hard could it be, right?

Fifteen minutes later, I had burned grits to the bottom of the pan and had a plate of undercooked bacon with a few black pieces thrown in on top. I felt like an utter failure.

That's where Caleb found me.

"Something smells…oh." He tried not to laugh, I'll give him credit for that, but he didn't last long. I gave him a sulky look. "Ahh, it's ok. Cooking isn't everyone's forte."

"I think boiling grits and making bacon is pretty basic," I muttered.

He wrapped his arms around me from behind. His hair was still slightly wet and I figured he'd grabbed a shower. "It's fine. We'll just grab something on the way to your dad's."

"But what kind of wife am I going to make if I can't even make bacon?"

I felt him still behind me. I hadn't even realized what I'd said. He turned me slowly in his arms and looked at my face closely.

"What are you saying, Maggie?" he asked with hope and eagerness lacing his voice.

I sighed and gave in with a little smile. I'd known what I was going to say when he asked me ever since that day when he *almost* asked me on the beach. "I'm saying yes."

"Saying yes to what?" he said with a little grin.

"Well, you were going to ask me to marry you, weren't you?"

He pulled me to him and lifted me from the floor, knocking the spatula and plate to the floor in the process. He laughed and squeezed me.

220

"Yes, I was. Oh, my...Maggie, I love you." He pulled back, but didn't put me down. "Really, you want to marry me?"

"More than anything," I responded.

He kissed me and laughed at the same time. It was a feeling like nothing else to have put that smile on his face. They must have heard the plate fall because Rachel and Peter made their way in to see what was up.

"What happened?" Peter asked, clearly confused about the situation as he looked at the mess on the floor.

"Maggie said yes," Caleb explained through a massive grin, but didn't take his eyes off mine.

They knew exactly what he was talking about. They rushed us with grins that matched Caleb's.

"Oh, Maggie," Rachel squealed with tears on her cheeks. She cried more often than any other mother I've ever met. Then I thought of my own mother. She'd never see me married. I pushed that away and focused on the now. "Honey, I'm so happy for you."

"Me, too," I said truthfully as I heard Peter congratulating Caleb. Then he turned to me and hugged me just like my own father would. I wondered how my dad would take the news.

"You proposed over a plate of burned bacon?" Rachel asked and looked around in laughter. "Caleb, honey, we need to work on your timing skills."

Everyone laughed and neither Caleb nor I refuted her explanation. He'd actually proposed to me on the beach, even though he never finished the words. In my mind, that would always be how he asked me to marry him. Caleb nodded at my words and then sobered a bit.

"I've got something for you. Come on." I followed him to his suitcase in the living room. He pulled a small box out and twirled it in his fingers. "Our kind doesn't do engagement rings. Rings are a really sacred thing for us-"

"Your mom told me."

"Oh. You talked to my mom about the rings?"

"And the wedding."

"Oh." He seemed to like that a lot. "I was going to tell you about it, but you were so freaked out about the marriage thing I thought I'd just wait." I nodded my head in agreement. "Ok. Well, then as I was saying, I don't have a ring for you. I can get you one if you want, but you don't really seem like the big rock type to me." I bit my lip to tell him he was right. "I bought this a while back. I wanted to be ready for when I could finally ask you, so..."

I took the box he offered me. It was Tiffany blue and that alone made my heart spike. But he said it wasn't a ring so I took a deep breath and lifted the lid.

It was a small black and silver hinged box.

It was made out of glazed obsidian and had the filigree markings on it, just like on their fences and his tattoo in silver. The Jacobson crest was on it as well with our names filled in on both sides to make a whole. Just like our tattoos would be if I had one. It was beautiful. I said as much.

"It's beautiful." When I lifted the lid there was a note and key ring inside. The key ring matched the box in color and intricacy. I started to pull the note out, but he stopped me.

"That's my vows. You keep those until the night before the wedding," he explained and I nodded, but then picked up the key ring.

"But Caleb, I don't even have a car let alone keys to put on it."

He pulled me to the couch and knelt in front of me. "Traditionally, the wedding present from the husband is a house or a piece of land somewhere. So, I figured I could give you something to put our very first key on."

I sat stunned. Then I wrapped my arms around his neck.

"Caleb," I breathed. "Thank you for being so you."

He chuckled. "Well, I'm not sure what that means."

I pulled back to look at him. "You always know exactly what I want." I looked at the oval key ring in my hand. "And this is the sweetest thing I've ever gotten from anybody."

He smiled in a way that made my heart skip. "I'm glad you like it. I was a little worried that you'd think I was being presumptuous."

"I said I'd marry you, didn't I?" I grinned. "I don't expect us to keep living in Uncle Max's guest room."

He blew a sigh of grateful relief. "Thank you for not making a fuss over me spending money on you."

"Well…I guess things have changed a little bit lately. I guess maybe I'm a little more open to being spoiled," I said and rolled my eyes and smiled.

"I am so in love with you, Maggie," he sighed, repeating my words to him from the other day.

"I love you, too."

I was surprised when he just kissed me on the nose and left it at that. Soon we were greeted with others who had heard the news and wanted to congratulate us. After several minutes of being petted and told all about what the dedication would be like, and how fun it was to be surprised with a house of our husband's choosing, we told them we needed to leave.

We went to get dressed to go to my dad's, to tell him the good news and see him before we left for London in the morning. We passed Kyle and Lynne on the way in the kitchen as they stepped down from the stairs.

"Hey, guys," Caleb said and smiled. "Did you sleep ok?" Lynne blushed and smiled into Kyle's arm. Kyle laughed and that made Caleb laugh, too, "I didn't mean *that*," he insisted.

"Yeah, we slept great," Kyle told him. "In fact, it was the best sleep I think I've ever had in my long life. I didn't wake up once."

Caleb looked at me and smiled.

"I know." He turned back to Kyle. "So...Maggie and I are getting married."

Lynne gasped, her eyes immediately went to my ring finger, and she frowned. Kyle's eyes were huge, but when he looked at me, there was only the love of family and friends. It was true. The significant replaced everything else before them. So they were telling the truth. If an Ace who was married imprinted with someone else, he wouldn't be able to stop his feelings.

Kyle was elated and smiled. He moved forward to hug me and kissed my cheek. I pulled back to see his face and he was smiling, then he sobered a bit.

I'm sorry about everything that happened in California. I was out of line. It's kind of funny, really, that the same day I confessed all that to you, and told you I was going to let you be, that we find the girl who I was going to imprint with.

"I don't think so. I think it all happened for a reason and purpose."

He nodded and seemed to understand.

Destiny is a meddlesome wench, isn't she?

I laughed and nodded. "I guess."

"You can't outrun destiny," he chimed in a sarcastic rhythm.

"So I've heard," I said dryly.

He laughed and went back to lace his fingers with Lynne. She looked at me and smiled.

"Congratulations."

"You, too. I told you, didn't I?"

"You did," she agreed with a grin that wouldn't stop.

"Alright," Caleb started, "well, we're going to go tell Maggie's father." Kyle came forward to inspect Caleb's face closely. "Dude, what are you doing?"

"Just memorizing your pretty face before it gets all mangled."

Caleb laughed and shoved Kyle, who laughed, too. "Shut up, man."

"Hey, it's not Jim I'm worried about. You think Bish is going to be thrilled about this?"

Caleb shrugged. "I guess we'll find out."

He took me up the stairs and as we made our way, we heard Kyle making a trumpet with his lips, playing Taps. Caleb shook his head and yelled down to him. "Shut up, man!"

We heard Kyle laughing as we turned the corner to our room.

Twenty Seven

Where else could we go for breakfast but the 25 Hour Skillet? The memory of Caleb coming there the first time played again in my mind. I giggled on the back of the bike as Caleb took off my helmet.

"I hope your old boss keeps the cleaver to himself today," he muttered.

I laughed again as I pulled him with me through the revolving door and heard it chime. It was so familiar and felt like I hadn't been there in months. I saw Smarty come around the corner, her pencil on her ear, and she didn't even look up.

"Two of ya, doll?"

"Yes, ma'am."

"Ok, follow- Maggie!" she yelled and hugged me tightly. "Oh, honey," she touched my hair, "your hair is to die for! So chic."

"Thanks." I pulled back some. "You remember Caleb?"

"Of course. You don't forget a face like that easily."

He thought she was going to shake his hand, but instead she pulled him into a hug. Her mind reeled as she felt his arms and how lumpy and rugged his was. Big John was lumpy, but for other reasons and she was remembering how he used to be. She leaned back and smiled just as I heard my name brusquely behind me.

I turned to see Big John wiping greasy hands on his already disgusting apron.

"Sweat Pea, you get your butt over here and give me a hug right this second."

He slammed into me, making breathing a request instead of a given, squeezing the life out of me.

"Big John," I rasped. "It's ok."

"It's not ok. You were kidnapped. It was on the news! And then not a word from you and you just show up in the diner? What happened?" he yelled, causing

224

some of the customers to look our way. "Is it him?" He looked at Caleb and then back to me. "Is he got you mixed up in something?"

"BJ," I said softly. "No. I'm ok. It was…that person that I told you about that was stalking me. He took me. But Caleb found me and brought me back. He's been watching out for me."

BJ looked at him, but didn't say anything. When he looked back to me, he sighed ruggedly.

"How's your dad taking all this?"

"Better than I expected," I said truthfully. "Bish came home. He moved back in. We're fine, I promise. You don't have to worry."

"Ok. You still going to school?"

"Yep. Planning to."

"You keep in touch," he ordered. "And you do what you set out to do, you hear me? You be the person I know you can be and don't let them ruin you with their crazy ideas and persuasion. You stay true to who you are and make sure you come back and see me now."

I rolled my eyes good-naturedly and smiled tolerantly at him. "Of course. You're worse than my dad."

"Well, somebody has to look out for you."

"Problem solved," I said and pulled Caleb's arm, as he was studiously giving Big John a wide berth, to stand beside me. "You remember Caleb?"

"Of course I remember," he sang and crossed his arms. "Bike boy."

"Nice to see you, sir, minus the cleaver, of course," Caleb said with a smile and I smashed my lips together, but couldn't keep in the giggle.

Neither could Smarty as we both broke out into laughter. Caleb even chuckled, but BJ remained stoic and eventually walked back to the grill with a smirk.

"Follow me, hunky," Smarty said through a giggle. "I'll get y'all a table."

"Yes, ma'am," he said, always the respectful gentleman.

He let me pull him as we followed her and sat across from each other. We told her to bring us both coffee and she ran off to get it.

"So, what are you getting?" I asked.

"Why don't you order for me," he suggested and leaned back in his seat relaxed. "You let me order barbeque for you."

"Ok," I said carefully. "What about-"

"Nuhuh," he stopped me with a smile. The smile that turned my stomach to pudding. "Just order it. I'll eat it, I promise. You know me well enough to order my breakfast."

225

I hoped so, so when Smarty came back I ordered us both a bacon and cheese omelet- extra bacon. Caleb grinned and nodded as I ordered. Once she left I moved to his side of the table. We just got engaged for goodness sake and I didn't want to be away from him, even across the table.

"I agree," he said and sighed as we leaned back against the booth. He leaned his head back as his arm came around me. He seemed pretty happy and relaxed even though we were about to tell my dad that we were getting married. "I'm not worried," he said in response to my thoughts. "Your dad likes me. He knows I'll take care of you."

"You're awfully cocky," I said playfully looking at him. "What makes you think he won't freak? He *is* my father and I'm his only little girl."

"Betcha five bucks."

"Deal," I said with a laugh. "He is gonna freak and I'll take your money and buy a honey bun with a diet cream soda and I won't share with you," I sang.

"You're going to be singing a different tune in a little while. I hope you're not too full on omelet to eat crow."

I laughed and leaned against him. I hoped he was right. I didn't want to disappoint Dad or fight with him. I just wanted to be with Caleb and everyone be happy. Who cared if I was being a little fairytale naïve about it? A girl could dream, couldn't she?

We ate our omelets and after hugging everyone and promising to come back soon, we took off and made the ridiculously short ride on Caleb's bike to Dad's house.

Caleb parked the bike in the garage because it looked like it might rain and we went in, but neither Dad nor Bish was there. I decided to grab a few things from my room for the trip the next day. I was going through my closet, looking at dresses and clothes to take to London, when I felt Caleb's hands on my waist.

I turned to him and looked in his blue eyes. The dresses fell to the floor from my fingertips. He was sucking his lip in and out, and thinking about what I'd look like in a red dress on our wedding day.

"Did you find what you were looking for?" he asked and looked at the dresses on the floor.

"Yes," I whispered. I reached up and put my arms around his neck, bringing him down to kiss me.

He made a little surprised noise, but my mind was wide open and he knew *exactly* what I was doing. I reached one arm to the side to my door and turned the lock. His eyes popped open and he stared at me, his breathing heavy and loud.

I want this, you know that. You're not just doing this because of the engagement are you?

No, but who cares if I am?

I pushed his chest so he'd go backward toward the bed.

I do. I want you to do it because you want to, not just because you know I do. I want you to want it as much as me.

I am and I do.

His legs stopped at the mattress side.

You have no idea how much I need to do this with you right now.

I have a pretty good idea. I thought and giggled.

I'm not just talking about that. My body is twitching on the inside. My blood is about to boil out of my skin with the demand to consume you. When you look at me like that...it's like kerosene on a fire. You have no idea what you do to me.

I felt a pull in my chest, an ache so good, and I knew it was the exact match to Caleb's. It was my body saying finish this, do this, be together, be consumed and do the consuming, feel everything there is to feel between each other, know everything, learn everything, take our time, create a frenzy and focus on nothing but our significant.

Caleb put his palm on the middle of my chest.

Your heartbeat is my favorite thing to listen to. When you look at me and your heart rate jumps... He smiled. "It's the best feeling in the world to know that I'm in the heart of the most important person to me and the proof of that is literally right under my fingertips."

I licked my lips as I fought for breath, my chest rising and falling dramatically under his hand. He placed a warm palm on my cheek and I turned my face to kiss it. His heartbeat made its way into my chest and it was just as erratic as mine, in a good way.

He continued to caress my jaw and cheek, letting the pad of his thumb swipe my lips. I closed my eyes and let it all wash over me; the way I felt, the way he felt and the way he was everything in every way. I was no longer one person. I was a half to make a whole. And my other half was making me feel scorched and jagged on the edges.

Don't be scared of this. I won't hurt you.

I know that without a doubt.

Jagged on the edges doesn't sound so good.

Oh, it's good.

I pushed him to sit on the bed and turned the light off with a flick of my fingers and my over-stimulated mind. Even though we were mostly in the dark, it was like I could see him. I could sense him and knew exactly where to put my hands to touch his arms, his neck, his lips. Without any bumbling or error, I found his mouth and pushed him down to the bed.

His breaths seethed between us and his hands found my waist in a second. He let me have control for a moment. He let me feel the rush of commanding and dictating someone who was utterly at your mercy. Someone who would do anything you wanted.

But I soon found myself under him without even realizing I'd been put there. He repeated his earlier actions and brought his hands down to grasp my wrists, placing them over my head and pressing them to the mattress. His mouth continued on mine with a sweetness that reassured and made me feel more than loved before he eventually settled his forehead to mine. I felt him press into my mind, no longer asking permission, but taking what was rightfully his; all of me. I opened my mind as far as it would go. He didn't have to press, I'd give it to him.

His protective barrier was ever strong and at attention. As I passed everything that made up him – his love, his adoration, his need for my happiness – I saw things I'd never seen before and began to feel the melding of our minds taking place as the energy ribbons came in full force.

I saw him with Vic at a party, just wanting to go home more than anything. I saw him and Kyle talking about me after we'd imprinted, Caleb asking all sorts of questions and Kyle rolling his eyes.

I felt Caleb's skin as if it was my own just like before. It felt like I was looking down at myself and feeling the opposite touch and then I was me again, wading in a sea of everything Caleb.

He moved one of his hands in his mind to my leg and then back up my side. I moved mine in my mind to grasp in his hair.

Then I saw Caleb the day Maria was born, the look on his face of pure wonder as he looked at the baby in his hands. I wanted to see that look on his face again…one day. I felt a zing go through my entire body, a strange hot and cold that jolted from one side to the other before I even had a chance to realize it. I felt Caleb's surprised breath on my face and knew he was feeling the same.

I saw us together, bits and pieces and jumbles of kisses, him watching me when I wasn't looking, him catching me watching him, him feeling my heartbeat for no reason at all except that I loved him.

I made my leg move against his side in my mind and felt him retaliate with a hand in his mind to my cheek and jaw and it rubbed a caress that made me shiver.

I felt another zing and felt every inch of my skin burn and tingle. I gasped at the pleasure of it. It burned me in places I never thought about and even my eyelids felt super sensitive and super alive. Caleb leaned down to kiss each one slowly, like each one was important, and then groaned into my skin when another zing came. Caleb's skin was freezing cold, but cooled me in a sensual way, and then it was as if we traded places.

My skin and veins were ice, but Caleb's hot skin was the perfect match for mine and when he kissed me again, it was like imprinting. All those strong sensations of being jolted with electricity and tingles were a full force assault on our senses and minds. I heard my breathing take a turn for uncontrollable and then I held my breath as the fireworks started, so to speak.

The energy ribbons were non-existent when I opened my eyes as the entire room was aglow. Blue filled the air and then zings filled me, making me curl my fingers into my palms. Caleb coaxed my hands open to lace his fingers with mine as the cold and hot zings mingled in us and between us and built into something we could no longer stop nor control.

Caleb released my lips only to moan softly against my mouth as the end neared and the pleasurable zings became almost painful as they consumed us. Then the burst of fire in my veins made me shriek with the force of it and the blue around us turned blinding white as everything was drowned out but my significant. I could taste him, smell him, feel him, his every thought, his every want and every need from me was available for my taking. And I took it.

I had just experienced something no other human but a handful would ever know about. It was better than anything I'd ever felt and couldn't see anything being better. It was better than chocolate! It was better than honey buns! It was better than kisses and touches and sweet words combined. I was enraptured.

When I finally settled back into myself, I realized I was still holding my breath, but Caleb's blasted fast and loud against my cheek. He lifted his face to look at me and I saw his cheeks were flushed as if he'd exerted himself, but we were still right where we had been the whole time.

He unlaced our hands and brought his to my face. I noticed they were shaking slightly. "Breathe, Maggie."

It was so much like that first day, the first time he said my name as his significant.

I took a deep shuddering breath and when I let it out it was a moan of utter happiness and satisfaction.

He continued to look at me as we fought for breath and shared the little bit we had between us. In the minuscule light from my curtains, I saw his face and it spelled satisfaction and love. The corner of his mouth rose. Then the rest joined it in a genuine smile that told me everything. It was good for him, too.

He chuckled at my thought. "Yeah," he agreed with a sigh. He kissed me softly once more on the lips, my cheek, my jaw. "You're making me the happiest man there is."

"Then we're even."

He laughed at that, too, and rolled to lie back on the bed to catch his breath. He pulled me to lean against him and ran his hand down my arm. My body continued to tingle and I felt like I'd been given a shot of morphine. I was buzzing and calm, like I'd float away.

I'd always hated that expression, but now understood the feeling completely. "Are you ok?"

"What kind of question is that?" I asked and laughed, hearing the breathlessness of it.

He laughed, too, and spoke into my hair. "Thank you, baby."

"Caleb," I started to protest.

"I mean for everything. You accepted me and love my family, you love me despite everything that's happened, you're going to marry me… Thank you. If you had a goal to make me happy, you've succeeded."

"I'm glad you're happy. It *is* what I want."

A few seconds later, I felt a searing pain in my wrist. Caleb jumped, too, and I thought it was because he felt my pain and heartbeat, but he hissed at his own wrist. To see what was going on, we brought them up together into the air above us.

There in the dark, in my room, on my bed with the man I loved, on my wrist in the same place as Caleb's…was my Virtuoso tattoo. It burned a bright orange, like it had been branded into my skin. Caleb's burned bright, too, and I saw my name around the edge of his. And mine, had his beautiful name around the edge, too. We instinctively put them together and I poorly held back a happy sob when they lined up perfectly. Two halves to make a whole.

Caleb was no longer in awe and my protector took over.

"Ah, Maggie, I know it hurts a little. I'm sorry."

"It didn't hurt," I insisted. "I wanted this so bad." I sniffed and he wiped under my eye. "I've been thinking about going and getting it done myself."

"I know."

"Then why don't you know how happy this makes me?" I said through tears and a smile. I looked at my tattoo once more and frowned slightly. "What's that?"

He looked back up and frowned, too. In the middle of both of our half moons was an infinity symbol – a sideways eight looking thing – but I knew exactly what it was.

"Infinity," Caleb muttered beside me in awe. "I've never seen that on our family's tattoos before."

"It means things are about to change," I told him and grinned like a complete fool.

"Maggie," he sighed. He put his face against mine. "You are so amazing," he whispered into my skin and kissed me, slowly and languidly. He took his time at showing me how much he thought that. Soon, I was breathless again, and I felt his thoughts flit through his mind about wanting to Mutualize with me again…like right then. I smiled into our kiss and broke it unwittingly. He smiled, too, and leaned back a little to trace the pattern of the tattoo on my wrist with his thumb. "Do you want to see a vision?" he asked carefully.

"What?"

"Do you want to see one of my visions, from when we imprinted. I figure, since you already agreed to marry me, it couldn't hurt to show you now."

"Yes," I breathed. "Please."

And when he pressed his head to mine once more, I saw us in a big yard at night. It started with dancing, bare feet, and worked its way up to black pants to red dresses. Caleb was holding me close as we danced slowly. He lifted my chin higher and kissed me as everyone cheered and egged him on behind us, then he told me I was beautiful in my mind. I turned to see Kyle and Lynne, just as we were, near us dancing. She smiled at me and when I looked back to Caleb he lifted my hand to kiss my ringed finger, but my hand was blurry so I couldn't see a ring he had placed on me. I smiled and when I looked around for Dad, I saw him watching us. He was crying, trying to wipe his face on his sleeve.

Caleb pulled back and I felt the cool of wet on my cheeks. He wiped them away again.

"Those better be happy tears."

"They are." I sniffed. "Thank you for showing me that. What else did you see?"

"Nuhuh, cutie, not so fast. One thing at a time," he whispered playfully.

"Do you know what I saw?"

"Nope."

"Do you want to?"

"Are you trying to make a trade?"

"Yes."

He laughed. "Then no. Mine are good enough to last me."

"Boo," I groaned and he laughed again.

"Are you ready to pick out your dresses now?" he said into the skin under my ear.

"No," I groaned again.

He moved to kiss my neck. "Well…I'm sure we can find something to do," he told me, his voice low.

"I never want to move from this spot again."

"Agreed, we'll stay right here forever," he said and put his head on his arm as a pillow.

Sadly, forever didn't last long as I heard a car and then the front door.

Twenty Eight

When I got up and turned the light on, I looked in the mirror and did a double take. I looked like I'd run a marathon. My cheeks were flushed and my hair was a mess. The crying hadn't helped. Caleb came up behind me, wrapping his arms around me, and looked at us in the mirror. He was a mess, too. We both laughed at our reflection and I flushed an even brighter red at why we looked that way.

"I look terrible," I said.

"No, you look like someone who's been loved on."

"Yeah, I know. And Dad's gonna totally know what was going on up here." He gave me a look that said otherwise. "Well, not *exactly* what was going on." I sighed. "I feel like a teenager about to get caught with her boyfriend in the house while her parents went on vacation."

"You *are* a teenager."

"A teenager who's getting married," I countered. "I have to stop worrying so much about what my dad is going to say about things."

"You're right. And you're going to be eighteen in just a few days."

"Yeah," I replied.

"Then he won't be able to say a word."

"But I still don't want to disappoint him."

"I know. Well, let's start right now, by telling him that we're getting married. Don't let him freak you out, just tell him that I asked and you said yes and that's all there is to it. And that we're leaving for London tomorrow morning and he can't come with you."

"Yeah, he's really not going to like that one."

"I know. I'll let you break that one to him."

"Thanks," I muttered.

He smiled and turned me to look at him, framing my face with his hands, his thumb ran reverently over the Visionary mark on my neck.

233

He kissed me quickly and then ran his fingers through his hair to tame it before heading downstairs to let me try to fix myself somewhat. I giggled as I thought about what we'd just done. He was right in his explanation. It wasn't sex, I mean we barely moved the entire time and our clothes were on, but it was so…perfect. It felt like there was no way to be any closer to Caleb than that and I felt everything he felt and thought. In honesty, I couldn't wait to do it again.

But for now, I had to get myself ready and tell my father that his little girl was not only going across the sea to save a non-human race of people but that she was also getting married, the second she turned eighteen. I smiled. What had I been so scared about?

I put the clothes I'd grabbed up off the floor and some extra shirts into a little burgundy rolling luggage that my parents got for me when I went on a fieldtrip to D.C. for a competition with the cheerleaders in ninth grade. I left the bag by the door because that would be a little dramatic I thought, to bump down the stairs with my luggage before even telling him he couldn't go with us. The council wouldn't stand for humans being present.

So I brushed my hair and changed my shirt. When I was swiping on some lipgloss and face powder, I caught a glimpse of my tattoo in my reflection. I looked down at it, the black ink weaved in delicate calligraphy and Caleb's name so perfectly aligned and involved around the outer rim of the half moon. I smiled. I got my tattoo. I must've been doing something right.

I made my way down the stairs and heard them talking. I almost stopped to listen but I had been doing that too much lately. So I pushed on and smiled when I got to the bottom to see them all sitting in the living room together; Caleb, Bish and Dad.

And no one was dead yet.

"Hey, baby girl. I'm surprised to see you here today," Dad said as he stood and kissed my cheek. "You look very pretty," he observed.

"Thanks, Dad."

I went to sit between Caleb and Bish on the couch and hugged Bish's arm. He patted my hand but ultimately I gravitated to Caleb's side and welcomed his calming touch as he put his hand on my knee.

I decided to just out this thing, right there and then.

"Caleb asked me to marry him."

Bish and Dad both looked up, but they didn't seem too surprised. In fact, Dad nodded.

"I figured that was coming. And I'm assuming since you're sitting here that you said yes?"

"Mmhmm." He glanced at my finger and frowned and I heard his thought. "They don't do engagement rings, Dad."

"Huh," he said in a disapproving way and I wanted to laugh at how differently this was going that I thought it would.

"The husband gives a house," Caleb clarified. "The day before we're married, I'll give Maggie the keys to the house I picked out for her."

Great, I heard Bish. *One more reason Jenna's better off without me. There's no way I could buy her a ring let alone a frigging house.*

I looked at him and he knew I had heard. He clenched his teeth and refused to look at me so I pressed on.

"Yeah."

"Wow, a house," Dad said and clucked his tongue.

"Yes, sir," Caleb said in his respectful, but firm manner as he rubbed his chin.

"The women are ok with the husband's picking out a house for them, without them even seeing it?" Dad said with a questioningly raised eyebrow.

"Yes, sir. It's just like an engagement ring. The woman doesn't pick that out either," Caleb countered.

"True…but she's not going to live in her engagement ring."

"It's tradition. It's what we've always done, even back to my ancestors. See, back then, you couldn't marry until you had a place to take your wife after the wedding. So, they worked days and nights to prepare for her to come and be with him. But, regardless of imprinting, the catch back then was that you had to build it by yourself. It was a show of commitment and faith that you planned to work your hardest and do whatever was necessary to make her happy and take care of her."

My father blinked in surprise. "Well, then. What can I say to that? Have you found a house yet?"

"No, sir. It's hard for us to keep things from each other." He pointed to his head to demonstrate. "So, it kind of has to be last minute to keep it a secret."

Dad nodded and took a deep breath, leaned forward and steepled his hands. "Ok. Well…I mean, you know the usually spiel. I'm your father and I think eighteen is too young to be married, but I also thought twenty four was the perfect age and look how it turned out for me," he said, but he wasn't bitter or upset, he was just stating his case. "I still can't completely grasp everything that goes on with your family and this imprinting stuff, but from what I've seen with my own eyes, I can't say that it's not true."

"Jim, I know I've said this before, but Maggie is in good hands. I won't let anything happen to her and it's not just because I wouldn't anyway, but because my body won't let me. Your daughter's heartbeat is in my chest," Caleb said firmly, "and it's the most precious thing I have."

I looked at him, biting my lip at his sweet words. Dad was stunned silent, with his mouth and mind, and Bish was same old Bish. He wasn't happy about it and still agreed that people could say anything they wanted to and it didn't mean it was true. But he had told me he was going to back off and he was. He knew it was inevitable. He just hoped I'd be ok and that I'd come to him if I needed him later.

"I will," I told him. "But I won't have to, not for that."

He smirked. "I'm not sure I'll ever get used to you being able to read my mind," he said dryly.

"That's what I said," Dad said smiling.

I looked around at them and marveled at the fact that everything seemed to be falling into place so peacefully. Like puzzle pieces that were cut so perfectly.

Then the doorbell rang. "I wonder who that is?" Dad remarked.

"Maybe Jen," I said and felt Bish jerk. "I told her yesterday she could come, but with everything else that happened I figured it'd be best to come by ourselves. I'll get it."

As I made my way to the door, I heard the thoughts of a woman before I reached the knob. At first I thought it was Jen, then Beck maybe, but I froze with my hand on the knob.

It couldn't be...

I jerked open the door, letting it bang against the wall, to prove myself wrong, but no. She was right there, flesh and blood.

My mom.

Caleb ran in behind me, feeling my heart gallop, and wrapped a hand around my wrist. Whether to calm me or restrain me I wasn't sure and I wasn't sure if he was either.

"Sarah?" I heard Dad say in disbelief behind me.

"Hello, Jim," she said and it had been so long since I'd heard her voice that I barely recognized it.

She was thin – so thin – not in a sickly way, but like she had made herself that way. Her hair was dyed a deep black, her tan dark and her makeup too much. We just stared at each other. Her eyes perused me with clear relief but also surprise.

She's finally taking care of herself. She's lost weight and cut that dreadful hair. And who's this...

She eyed my significant with a twinkle of interest in her eye and I knew right then, there'd be no reconciliation for us. She hadn't changed. She had no interest in coming back to be our family again.

236

"What are you doing here?" Dad asked her harshly.

"Jim, we talked on the phone, you know why I'm here. I'm ready to come home," she said, her tone impatient and embarrassed. Like how dare we question her when she was on our doorstep.

"No can do, I'm afraid." Dad moved to stand beside me. "We just don't have any room for anyone else right now."

"Are you seeing someone?" she said and laughed like it was impossible.

"No, I'm not seeing anyone. I've been a little busy taking care of my daughter."

Mom's face turned red, her eyebrows rose in anger. "Our daughter,"

"Enough," I shouted and the chandelier above us started to rattle in response to my anger, but I felt Caleb's squeeze of my hand and I took a deep breath. "Enough, Mom. What are you doing here, for real?"

I'd already seen in her mind that her boyfriend left her. She had been staying at his place and had nowhere else to go. She refused to be a waitress and that had been the only job she could find, so she figured she could say she wanted to make sure I was ok after my 'ordeal' and that she wanted to come home.

Home wrecker.

"I told you-"

"The truth," I said.

She sighed and made a dramatic show of pulling off her shades and smoothing her hair before pasting on a huge fake smile for me. "Honey," she crooned and took one step towards me. "I missed you."

When she touched my hand before I could jerk it away, I saw it. Her little secret. Her dirty indiscretion that would have destroyed everything I knew up until that point and could also from now on. She really was a home wrecker.

In a vision, I saw her giggling. She was young and the man she was with was young, too. At first I thought this was college or something, but I noticed the house she was in...this house. They were in the kitchen and doing disgusting things on our kitchen counter together. She glanced at the clock and effectively ended his perusal of her.

"My husband will be home soon," she said to him.

"Tomorrow, same time?" he asked, his back still to me.

"You know it."

She kissed him long and hard and then the vision flew to another one.

She was crying in the bathroom, a slender white stick in her hand that held her fate. She apparently wasn't happy with what it told her. A man knocked softly on the door, and she sniffed angrily and rolled her eyes, but the voice she used was sweet and innocent as she wiped her face and put on a smile.

"Come in."

Dad was so young and handsome back then, looking at her with a face full of concern.

"Are you ok? What did it say?"

"I'm pregnant," she whispered.

Dad looked shocked but not in a bad way. "But…we were careful…we used protection."

"It's not always one hundred percent, Jim."

He smiled hugely and pulled her from the tub side laughing. "We're going to have a baby!" He laughed. "I know you said you wanted to wait a while, but…wow. We're going to have a baby."

"Yes," she said happily, but her eyes were dead behind his back. "We are."

Then the vision changed to my mother crumpling a piece of paper into the trash. It was a result, for some blood test I had as a kid when they thought I might have Meningitis. She tossed it in the trash as if not a care in the world. When I glanced closer, I saw the one sentence that would ruin everything. The one sentence that would change my life even more than it had already.

Dad was not my biological father.

Twenty Nine

I gasped back to reality with a warm, calming hand on the back of my neck and my face pressed into a neck that smelled like my whole world. I sobbed loudly and clung to him as he held me up, doing the only thing he could do.

How could she? How? Why?

How had she pretended to be happy and love us all those years when she didn't want me at all? She didn't want Dad, our life, or our house. She hated it all, endured us. How could she do that to Dad? I had no idea what to say.

Gah, Maggie. I'm sorry.

He can't find out, I begged him and looked up to his face. *He can't find out. This would kill him. He can't...*

Caleb nodded and then I heard an exasperated sigh from the devil herself.

"I think you're being a little dramatic. It was just a graduation, I'm sure your father took lots of pictures and I'll look at them." The glass in the door next to her started to rattle, but she didn't even notice. "I'll even get you a gift if you want one." I looked over at her blankly, in awe of her utter gall. I saw a few blue ribbons behind her head and tried to breathe and accept Caleb's calm as he discreetly kissed the back of my neck, desperately trying to keep me from showing my mother what I was. "That's what this is show about isn't it? You're upset because I didn't come for your graduation?"

I glanced at Dad to see what his face looked like because his mind was blank. He looked regretful, mad and sad all at once, but he was just waiting for me to say or do something. He was at a loss for words.

Bish had been awfully quiet through this whole thing and she never said a word to him. I looked at him too and he was pretty much the same; just totally not understanding her at all.

239

I looked back at her and just stared in contest.

Her eyes shifted to Caleb and she smiled.

"I'm sorry, my daughter is being rude. I'm Sarah, Maggie's mother." She held her hand out to him. "And you are?"

"Caleb," he answered, but made no move to shake her hand, "Maggie's fiancé."

She scoffed. "What?" she hissed and looked at me. "You're marrying him?"

"Yes, ma'am, she is," Caleb said stiffly.

"This," she started again with the sweet voice to Caleb, "juvenile tiff between my daughter and me has nothing to do with you. You don't have to hate me by association."

"Leave," I said, startling everyone.

"What did you say?" she whispered as if hurt, but her face was murderous.

"I said leave," I told her, my voice finally calm and I felt in control of myself. "We've been fine here without you."

"This house is half mine, you know. I made this house a home. I took care of both of you and you never gave me anything in return."

"Gave you anything like what? A new hair color, a new diet?"

"Maggie, I am your mother. Now I already talked to Jim and he-"

"I never said you could come back," he said softly. "I said before anything else you needed to work out your problems with Maggie, but I never said you could come back."

"Well, I'm trying."

"Little too late, I think."

"Jim," she squeaked as if hurt and made a step as if to touch him.

I put my hand out. "Don't touch him. Leave!"

"I am still your mother and you can't talk to me that way."

I moved forward, as close as I could stand it, to whisper to her where no one would hear. Her excessive high dollar perfume gagged me.

"I know what you did. I know about my father and the kitchen counter."

"Your dad and I-"

"No, not him, my *father*," I enunciated the word so she'd catch my meaning. She did. She paled and fidgeted with her earring.

Not possible.

"That's why he's so upset with me? You found out and told him?"

"No, he's upset because you're heartless."

She opened her mouth to say something, but thought better of it.

How can she know?

"I know lots of things," I said and she went wide-eyed. "Just go. We were fine before you came."

Without another word, she picked up her suitcase and started to turn away. Dad caved, looking at her dejected face.

"Why don't you come in for just a minute, Sarah?"

She looked back and didn't smile. "It's not worth it."

Then she left and I closed the door softly. Too softly, so Dad wouldn't see how incredibly angry I was. I let him think I was upset because Mom hadn't come to my graduation, that was better than the truth, and once again, I was stuck looking one way to people, but the truth being different.

I leaned on the door and heard the buzz of chatter around me, but I was so caught up in my own mind that none of it got through. Then when I looked up, I realized they were all talking to me. And when I let them into my mind to see what they were saying, I was bombarded with an overload of concern. Caleb was bent down looking into my face, holding my arms and Dad and Bish were right behind him.

I squeezed my eyes tight and heard a groan escape my throat. Caleb was telling them to stop thinking so loud, to turn it off for a second. I took a deep breath and opened my eyes.

"Are you ok, baby?" Caleb asked me and framed my face. Dad looked at him sharply. He'd never heard Caleb call me that. Never heard anyone call me that but himself.

"Yeah," I answered and looked at Bish. He was leaning on the wall beside us and staring at the floor.

She didn't even look at me, didn't say a word to me.

I nodded to Caleb and went to hug Bish. We were closer now than ever. Both of us were in love with a dad who loved us back fiercely...but wasn't our real father.

He accepted me easily, but hugged me with gusto.

"I'm sorry, baby girl," Dad said, but looked at Caleb and frowned at calling me that now. "Maybe I should have let her come home when she asked me to before."

"Nuhuh, that wouldn't have helped."

"But you're so upset-"

"Because I could see right through her bull crap, Dad."

Dad said a silent 'oh', forgetting once again about my ability. "I'm sorry," he repeated. "I'm so sorry, kids, that she couldn't...that she wouldn't..." He shook his head in frustration as how to make us understand and be ok.

"We still have you, *Dad*," I said firmly, emphasizing the *Dad* to affirm to myself more than anyone that he was my father, no matter what some piece of paper said. "It's ok, we'll be fine. It was just a shock to see her, that's all." I pulled from Bish's grasp and asked Caleb the silent question. He nodded. "Dad, do you mind if Caleb and I stay here tonight?"

"Of course not," he insisted and started towards the kitchen. "I'll order a pizza." Bish grunted in a funny pattern that indicated something was amiss. Dad smiled as he looked back. "I meant I'll order four pizzas."

We all laughed uneasily, trying to get out of our funk, and Bish nodded his head in agreement and approval. A little while later we all sat around the table and laughed eating our pizza, one with no olives, as Bish told us all about New York. He said he passed the Naked Cowboy everyday walking to work. He had to schedule his boss to get a pedicure, manicure and highlights done every two weeks.

He said he was the most girly, yet manly man he'd ever seen. He would parade girls through the office daily for lunch dates and other events, but he took more care of his looks and personal hygiene than any men he knew all combined.

Dad asked Caleb more about the house situation and the wedding. When Caleb explained the wedding, how it wasn't done in the traditional human way, and that humans had never been to one before, Dad balked, but Caleb assured him he was sure his family wouldn't mind them coming since they knew everything anyway.

Then they started talking about Vols Football. Dad and I had always been UGA Bulldog fans, even though we'd never lived in Georgia, but Caleb and Bish were extreme UT fans.

It was very good to see my future husband, my dad and my brother all sitting and talking about mundane, totally human things civilly and even with jokes and normal goading and prodding.

Mom wasn't brought up once.

But we had to tell him what happened at Caleb's house, though I didn't want to. I did want Dad to be on alert. He stood and fumed, as did Bish, who slammed his hands on the table. I told them what happened; that Caleb had saved me like always and Caleb insisted that I have saved him. When he described how the bullet came out of his stomach by just my touch alone, Bish and Dad's eyes were as glued to him as ever.

Eventually they calmed down and we explained we were leaving in the morning anyway and it would be fine. When I told Dad they couldn't come, they weren't happy but they seemed to understand mostly. I think Dad just wasn't thrilled to be in a room with three hundred Aces. I echoed his sentiment.

Then we told him the part I dreaded most, the part where Kyle imprinted. And the reason I dreaded it was all over Bish's face. He was thinking the same thing that Jen had been thinking. He was happy for Kyle but knew it would never be him and never be Jen. Dad was just plain fascinated.

When I yawned, Caleb took over and told them we were going to head to bed. I stopped and looked at Dad. He had the sleep-on-the-couch rule, but before I could say anything, he answered my internal question.

"You two respected my wishes in California. I trust you to sleep in your room." He got up and smiled at me, putting a hand on my cheek. "Plus, you're going to be married soon. You're growing up way too fast, girl. I guess I can't stop you anymore."

"Dad, you're gonna make me cry," I said and smiled, but could feel the tears pricking the back of my eyes.

"Ok," he conceded, "goodnight, baby." He grimaced at his words again and thought to himself that was going to be a hard habit to break. "Goodnight, son." He shook Caleb's hand. "Thank you again for keeping her safe."

"You don't ever have to thank me for that, sir." Dad nodded at that. "No one knows we're here so we shouldn't have any problems, but you might want to set the alarm."

"Oh, yeah," Dad thought. "You know, I don't think I've set that alarm more than five times the whole time we've lived here."

He set out to find the manual and after I hugged Bish, we went upstairs. When we came inside the room, I felt my cheeks flush once more as I looked at the bed. Caleb chuckled softly behind me as he shut the door.

"I just promised your father no funny business." He moved to kiss my neck from behind and whispered his words into my skin. "You're safe for tonight." I shivered as goose bumps ran rampant down my arms and he caressed them, satisfied by my reaction. "Alright, you. Let's get to sleep."

He texted his dad to tell him where we were and after I put on some cherry print sleep shorts and a cami, which I hadn't worn in forever, we climbed into bed.

Caleb's hand rubbed my hip over my shorts. "I like you in my t-shirts, but I kinda miss your fruit shorts."

"You do? Which is your favorite?"

"Right now, these," he said and moved his palm again, making me giggle. "But I really love your bananas."

"They're my favorite too. I'll be sure to bring them to London."

"You do that."

I smiled, but sobered as I remembered all the events of the day; some happy, most nerve-wracking, some downright heart breaking.

243

"We won't tell him," Caleb assured me.

"I don't care what some piece of paper says, Caleb. He's my father. That doesn't change anything. I don't even feel anything different for him. He'll always be my dad."

"I know."

"Promise me."

"Promise what, babe?"

"Promise that he won't find out, and we'll be ok in London, that Bish and Jen can be together, that everyone will be safe and that everything is going to be figured out and we'll get happy endings."

Caleb sighed in sympathy for me. "I can't promise that, but I can promise you that we'll try like hell," he said firmly.

I nodded and snuggled closer. "That'll do."

Thirty

In the morning, we ate breakfast that Bish cooked for everyone and then made our way back to Kyle's. It looked the same but there was a lot of mind chatter on the inside. At first, I thought our family had come to all go to the airport together, and there were some of them there, but then I realized as I reached for the doorknob that it wasn't. My skin crawled with slime and as the door swung open, I knew who I'd see.

Sikes.

"Maggie. Caleb," Sikes said seriously. "Good of you to join us."

Caleb yanked me behind him without even thinking about it.

"Sikes," I muttered and looked around at the ten or so other Watsons lined up around him.

"Caleb," Peter bellowed from the front of the line where they had everyone piled in the living room. He stood front and center like a shield for his family. "What are you doing here?"

"What do you mean?"

"Oh, I believe I can clear this misunderstanding up," Sikes said. "You see, I told them that we had taken you both hostage and if they put up a fight, we'd kill you both. And they believed me."

Peter fumed, looking at Sikes with disdain.

I should have killed you when I had the chance. The code of the council be dam-.

I tried to block out Peter's rant and focus on Sikes' mind to see what he had in store for us. I knew they knew already. I was sure that Marcus had told them and I saw him smugly standing in the corner, though I didn't see Sikes' wife. I took my jacket off and lifted my chin in defiance, but also, to make my mark known beyond a shadow of doubt, no hearsay. They'd see it for themselves.

A few Watsons gasped, but most just stared at me. There was a reason I was the Visionary and I didn't know if it was for this purpose or another one, but I had to do something. As I looked over and saw Jen and Gran looking so scared, I knew I had to do something.

Kyle and Lynne were there, too, in the back. Sikes didn't know they were imprinted I realized. He would have been livid about that one. One more imprint for our family and none for his that he thought was so deserving of it.

Lynne looked at me and chewed her lip. She glanced unsettled around me and I saw the light above me honing in and out of bright to dark as I got worked up. I looked away, unable to comfort her.

I was mad enough to make my power work without much effort and when I slammed the kitchen door, smacking one of them with it in the back and he fell unconscious to the floor, I almost smiled. I heard Jen's scared thoughts but didn't understand why until...they brought out Maria. They had her and the one who held her had a blue blazing fire in his palm. He grinned at me as if they'd won already. I had to keep myself in check so as not to throw something at him.

Caleb took my arm from behind him and I felt him shaking with rage.

"Villainy 101; always have a backup to your backup," Marcus said happily and laughed at the look I shot him.

"What do you want?" Peter asked Sikes, back to business.

"I want Maggie to come with us and for you all to not put up a fight. I figured this was the only way to do that. Now...what do I have to do to get you to understand that I mean business?" He tapped his finger on his lip like he was thinking and I yelled a 'no' before he even finished his sentence. "Kill Caleb maybe? That way there'd be no reason for you to come after her."

"Take my blood," I told him, begging, "I don't care, just leave them alone."

"Ah, Maggie, so quick to try to resolve things. No, my dear, I'm afraid that won't do. I need a steady supply until my experiment can give fruition."

I could no longer hold my anger in and the blue ribbons bounced and writhed in the air around us, glowing brighter than usual. The Watsons looked uneasy, their eyes roaming the room in fright and wonder, but Sikes was a rock of calm.

"Sikes," Peter barked, "you know this won't work."

"It will, or she will die while I try."

"Like hell," Caleb growled and moved me behind him further.

"Ooh, I love to see a newly mated couple. So feisty." And then he glanced at our wrists and his grin turned up even more and he laughed almost as if he was happy for us. "And feisty you are. Already got her to Mutualize with you, I see. And how was it, boy?"

The Watsons laughed and cackled all around us as Caleb's arm tightened protectively around me.

My face flamed, even in the circumstances, and our family's eyes searched our wrists, their faces wanted to smile at the revelation. I held my wrist to my chest as if in protection of it. My mom and Sikes were trying to ruin all our happiness with their doom and gloom.

"Even Maggie, a human, gained a family tattoo. Hmm," Sikes hummed not sounding too thrilled about the idea, but Peter and the family's thoughts were fascinated.

Maria whimpered near us and I saw the man putting his fire palm towards her face and then taking it away, over and over. I saw that it was only his left hand and he couldn't do anything but hold it in his palm. I remembered what Kyle and Marla had told me about their abilities being lame. And I'd had enough. I had a strange feeling coming over me; an 'urgency' that told me exactly what to do.

Caleb, we can do this.

What?

We can take them. I know it.

Maggie, I see what you're thinking but I don't have my ability. That was a fluke before-

Not a fluke. Trust me. Please, please, trust me. I can feel it.

Alright...I trust you, tell me what you want me to do.

Just feel it out. I'm going to take out fire-boy, just follow my lead.

At that, before they realized we were plotting, I grabbed a vase of flowers with my mind next to Maria and the man and flicked my fingers to send it flying into him. It busted against his chest, soaking him with water, and putting out his hand blaze. He snapped trying to make it come back but the water wouldn't let it. I flicked my fingers on one hand again to make Maria career as gently as I could toward Jen, who caught her easily, and used my other hand to send him flying into the china cabinet. Porcelain plates, cups, and gravy boats rained down around him and I felt a twinge of guilt for wrecking Kyle's parent's house.

Then we had a full force war going on. They all piled in to start in on us and Peter bellowed for some of our family to stay back, the ones without abilities. He came forward taking out one easily with a too quick to be human powerful uppercut with his palm to the man's nose.

"No!" Sikes roared and looked around at his plan falling apart.

I saw Rachel pushing one hand forward to throw silverware off the table across the room at two men charging her family. One knife and then one fork, alternating her hands as one piece of hard metal flew, then the other. The men were stabbed several times by several different pieces before they finally fell to their knees and groaned. I turned away when one pulled a butter knife from his chest. It was buried half deep and he screamed in pain as he yanked it free before collapsing to the ground.

Sikes roared and lunged for me.

Caleb stopped him easily, lifting his hand out and holding him in the air by just a thought. Caleb's face beside me was fierce and he couldn't even be surprised at himself. He was in his element and in the moment, his hand strained in his control. Peter gasped and looked at Caleb as proudly as a father could. He thought he'd gotten his ability, though in truth, we had no idea what was going on with him.

Then another Watson made a move to stop Caleb. Caleb used his free hand to call a vine from the yard. It burst through the window, showering Caleb and Sikes with glass shards and then wrapped around the man's neck and torso, slamming him forcefully into the wall and holding him in place. Caleb's uncle, the one who's ability it was to do that, gawked and glanced confused at Peter before doing almost the same thing to another Watson.

Caleb still held Sikes in the air and I stopped another one by flicking my fingers to crash the couch against him and smash him to the wall. The rest of them that were left just stared as if they had no idea what to do now.

I answered their internal questions.

"I suggest you run."

One did run. Marcus ran right out the front door like the coward he was, but the couple of others that were left seemed torn.

Sikes' choking and gagging noises were beginning to be annoying in the silence of the aftermath. Caleb lowered him slowly to the ground as we all surrounded them.

I wasn't the only one wondering what we were going to do with them, especially Sikes, the leader of my lynch mob. It was one thing to use self-defense, but to outright just kill them...

Out of nowhere, the absolute last thing I ever expected happened.

One of Sikes' men jumped forward from behind him and shoved one of the silver, long, sleek knives that Rachel had thrown at them into Sikes' back. His eyes went wide in surprise and then he fell, lifeless to the expensive tile floor in a very anticlimactic end.

Everyone was more than shocked when the man threw his knife down and fell to his knees, looking right at me.

"I'm sorry, Visionary. He was my family, my clan, my Champion. I felt like I was obligated to follow him but I... He was wrong," he said firmly and his thoughts were of a tree; a big, leafy old tree that's branches had grown and intertwined into a wrought iron filigree fence. It didn't make sense to me but I listened. "Please forgive me and take this," he motioned to Sikes's lifeless body, "as retribution. Let me go. I'll go far away. Please."

He bowed his head low and kept thinking about this strangely mangled and beautiful old tree. I figured it was from his home and he missed it and was ready to go back.

I nodded to him and watched as he got up and walked slowly out, my family parting to let him pass. I nodded to the other two as well that just stood there, waiting for punishment. They ran to catch up to the other one and I turned Caleb to me.

"I told you," I said in relief and hugged him tightly. "I knew it would work."

"What happened?" Peter asked Caleb and came to the center. "How did you do that?"

"I still don't know," Caleb said and leaned back. His took my wrist in his hands and ran his thumb over my tattoo. "Maybe it has something to do with this."

He turned my wrist to show them and they gasped and came closer. He showed them his wrist too and the reaction was the same.

"What is that?" Uncle Max asked.

"Infinity," Caleb answered.

"I've never seen that before," Max continued, "and Sikes was right. A human getting the family tattoo had never happened before."

"And," Peter asked, "when did you...um...how long have you had..." Peter was having trouble getting his question out.

"Oh for goodness sakes," Gran cut in. "When did you do the deed?"

"Gran!" Rachel said appalled.

"What? We all see the tattoos. We know that they Mutualized, it's not a secret. It's natural isn't it? I remember when you and Peter came over after the first time you Mutualized-"

"Gran, please, no," she begged.

"Oh, whatever. Anyway, what your extremely old fashioned parents are trying to ask you is when you Mutualized."

"Last night," Caleb answered softly and tried not to laugh, but failed when Kyle and Uncle Max chuckled. Even I found myself trying to stop laughing. This whole thing was just ridiculous as we stood in the debris and talked about intimate events. "What does that matter, though?" Caleb finally asked.

"I'm trying to pinpoint when the change happened in you," Peter explained.

"It's not that," I told them and I looked at Caleb. "Yesterday at your house, you didn't have the tattoo then, and before when that guy grabbed me at the club. You held that big guy's arm with no effort at all."

"I don't get it," Caleb said, hopeful and intrigued.

"Peter's ability is to detect earth elements. Go ahead, try to focus on something in this room and see if you can find anything."

"I still don't get it."

"Trust me," I whispered and smiled.

He closed his eyes immediately and cocked his head to the side. Peter watched spellbound as Caleb's eyes scrunched and he moved his head around. When he opened his eyes and looked dead at the ring on Gran's finger, Peter clapped his hands once and laughed.

"Incredible," he said in wonder.

"What is it?" Caleb asked. "I can...see something, like a sparkle."

"Yes," Peter concurred, "Gran's ring is sapphire. Wow." He grinned ear to ear. "What does this mean?" he asked me.

"It means," I explained, "Caleb can borrow our abilities." I turned to Caleb and spouted my revelation proudly. "You were doing it this whole time with me. You just thought you were reading everything through me because I'm your significant but really, you were borrowing my ability when you were around me."

"So I'm a...poacher?" Caleb asked, but he was happy. So happy.

Everyone laughed and clapped him on the back and hugged us.

"That's why you never felt the urgency we feel for our ability. Wow," Peter continued, "I'm so proud of both of you. You saved our lives, I hope you know that."

We looked around at the mess and I apologized for starting the demolition. Uncle Max waved me off and said it was fine. He was just glad everyone was alright. We also had to go soon. Our flight left in two hours. I tried to come up with an idea on how to fix their house. And we still had Watsons to dispose of.

"Go," he told me. "Me and the wife will deal with all this and leave tomorrow. You need to be there now."

"If you're sure..." I inched.

"We are."

"I'm really sorry."

"Not another word about it," he commanded and hugged me. "Now, you all get going or you'll miss your flight."

Thirty One

After the guys got the luggage from upstairs and we loaded down the cars, we convoyed our way to the airport. Peter handed me my passport right before we got out. I started blankly at it. I'd never even thought about my needing one before that but he apparently had. And he somehow had connections to get one for me. Hmm.

They must have bought every seat on the plane to fit so many people flying at once. And that was exactly what they did. We rode a huge Boeing all the way to London, a straight shot, with a plane full of Jacobsons. I shook my head at them, the uncles bantering with the stewardesses and Gran yelling about her orange juice being powdered and they were trying to kill her.

I laughed as I turned back to my seat.

"What's so funny?" Caleb asked beside me.

"Nothing, I'm just happy."

"Good."

"Hey, love birds," Kyle said as him and Lynne took the seats beside us. "We sure know how to party, huh?"

"Yeah," I said. "Lynne, are you ok? That's not a very good way to be introduced in to the family is it?"

"I'm ok," she said softly. "It was pretty scary though. It's not always like this is it?"

"Lately, yeah," Kyle said but soothed her by rubbing his thumb over her knuckles. She sighed deep and I bit my lip, remembering how drugged and calm I felt at Caleb's touch those first few days of being with him. Caleb read my mind and rubbed his thumb over my knuckles too, winking. "But don't worry. We're

251

going to London. The reunificantion is just a big party really, and with us coming with our significants to show off, it's gonna be even better. Nothing bad ever happens at these things."

She smiled at him and they put their heads together to take a nap. We had a long flight so I leaned into Caleb and did the same.

When we landed and did our extremely long and exhausting trek through customs and security, we were met by another convoy, but this time it was a row of sleek black Range Rovers. We all piled in and Peter led the way. Caleb drove behind him and the rest followed us.

We drove for about an hour and a half before we reached a small road that took us up into the green hills. It was absolutely gorgeous. There were huge rocks and boulders everywhere, and green vines with the greenest grass. We went up and up and just when I was about to ask Caleb how much further, we pulled into a stone driveway and into a big yard with a little cottage.

Peter didn't stop though and was headed straight for a big long wall of bushes. I figured he'd turn at a driveway or something near it, but no. And when he went through I heard my little shriek and then it was our turn. Caleb's mind was blank.

"Caleb!"

I squeezed his arm and braced for...something, but instead we went straight through it, like a big curtain that swayed around us and into a big garage looking thing. It went down and around like a parking garage and there were some other cars there, too, already nestled into spots along the back wall. We pulled into a spot beside Peter and I heard Caleb and Kyle chuckling.

"You could have told me," I said.

"What would have been fun about that?" Kyle asked and got out, pulling Lynne out his side with him.

"I'm sorry," Caleb said with a smile that said he wasn't. "Forgive me."

"Maybe, after some persuasion."

He leaned forward with a grin and kissed me. I sighed at the rush of calm I got and felt him pull me a little closer over the gearshift. Someone tapped on the window.

Maria.

"Come on, guys!" she said muffled through the glass. "Everyone's going in and you don't want to be left out here alone, do you?"

I bit my lip as we laughed and even though we very much wanted to be left alone for a minute before making my debut, we got out and walked with her. We walked back to the yard through a door off the side and everyone made their way to the cottage.

I felt confused as to how everyone would fit in there.

"The guardians live here year round," Caleb explained. "They live in the house but the council palace is underground."

"Palace," I whispered.

Then I saw the tree from that Watson's mind. It lined the side fence. It was massive, and just like his memory, it had wound its branches and limbs into the filigree work along the top of the fence. It looked old, like it had been there from long ago.

When we crossed the threshold behind everyone else, I saw an older couple holding open one door that lead right to another, down into a dark hallway. They ushered us in and shut the door, locking it behind us. I felt my heart rate pick up.

"It's ok," Caleb soothed. "It's always this way. This hall takes us down to stairs to the council meeting place. They hide it so there's never any chance of someone seeing us or wondering what all those people are doing all together like this, you know."

I nodded and he wrapped his arm around me and kissed my temple. We reached the stairs and started our descent. It was a very long way. Maria was going on ahead of us about the fight today and how awesome it was. How Caleb and I kicked butt, she said. Caleb chuckled, his thoughts affectionate for her. He'd been scared today, watching her in the clutches of the Watsons. That had been one reason he had been so focused and honed into what he had to do.

At the end of the stairs was a door and I could see the glow from the ones going in already ahead of us.

My heart skipped again in anticipation.

I didn't want to be a freak show. I didn't want to be on display.

"It's ok, Maggie. This first day will be bad, I won't pretend it won't be but, after that, it'll be fine and they'll get used to it. But you have to remember, you're like a miracle to them. You represent what they've been waiting for."

"Caleb's right," Peter said. I hadn't realized he had stopped to wait for us. "And unfortunately, they are very traditional in the old ways. There are some things you'll be subjected to that you'll just have to endure, I'm afraid."

"Like what?"

"Like the bowing, for one."

"Oh, come on," I groaned.

"I'm sorry, dear. But they will think it a disgrace and insult on anyone who doesn't treat you as the Visionary should be treated in their eyes."

"Ok," I conceded. I didn't want to fight with Peter or disappoint him. And I didn't want to stomp on their tradition. I just wanted to be normal. "I promise I'll behave accordingly," I said all proper, making him smile in amusement.

"I'm so very proud of you, Maggie." He kissed my forehead. "We'll be with you the whole time. We'll get through this together."

I nodded and gladly accepted Caleb's firm grip on my hand as he towed me into the bright light from the room. It was just like his memory; a big golden room, like a ballroom, with high ceilings and no windows. The walls had gold moldings and sparkling gold chandeliers. The floor was gold too and it was intimidating. There were so many people in there and as if they sensed me, every eye in the place turned to me. I cringed and Caleb pulled me closer.

"You're ok. You're just going to have to get used to people seeing you as I see you. Amazing."

Please don't leave me alone here.

You will not be able to get rid of me, he promised.

As we turned to follow Peter I saw something that stood out among the nicely dressed people; a girl with black hair, dressed in a long purple dress with a small train and her skin white and gleaming. She had an entourage of about fifteen people behind her. One of them looked awfully familiar to me but the girl I recognized right away.

Marla.

"Maggie," she crooned and came to us.

Peter had stopped too and eyed her curiously. A few others of our family made their way to stand at our backs.

"What are you doing here?" I asked her.

"It's a Reunification. I'm supposed to be here."

"But…Sikes attacked us. He-"

"I know all about what Sikes did." She turned to one of the men. "And thank you, Lionel, for disposing of him for me. He was becoming very bothersome."

The guy bowed slightly to her in acknowledgment. He was the one who stabbed Sikes. He had been thinking of the tree so I wouldn't see into his mind what he was actually doing. I still couldn't read Marla's mind even now and I didn't understand why, but I got the implication of what she was saying.

"You knew Sikes' planned to attack us," I accused.

"Yes, of course. That's why I sent Lionel with them to make sure that if you didn't have the stomach to finish my uncle, then the deed would still be done."

"Why?"

"Because he was ruining everything!" she yelled and came closer, walking as if she was being caressed. "He was wasting our chances on humans. Humans!

254

They didn't deserve what he was offering them. Your blood, your precious, gifted blood. And little did he know how precious it was. He had no idea you were the Visionary. So I disposed of the humans to keep them in the dirt, where they belonged."

Caleb's hand squeezed mine painfully, but I didn't care. She was confessing all. She had waited for this moment and was now reveling in the reveal of her secret.

"You killed those humans?" I croaked as the others started to come forward to witness our heated discussion. "Then why the charade? Why come to us and tell us it was Sikes?"

"To put you off my scent, of course, and it was Sikes'. He planned to kill them once he got his results but I didn't wait for that. I didn't care if the humans could gain abilities or not. I just cared about me. So I took your blood for myself."

"You mean you-"

"Yes. I drank it in a poultice, along with the others, but he didn't know. He didn't realize what I was doing or what I had done until it was too late."

"Why, Marla? What purpose did it serve?"

"Well, you can't hear my thoughts, can you?" I didn't answer, but she knew already. "I know you can't and the reason why is because your ability doesn't work on yourself. You can't see your future or visions for yourself. And now, you're in me. I'm half you. So, you can't read my future or my mind either. Lucky me, I get to keep all my secrets."

"But why?" I asked again more forcefully.

"Because Sikes was ruining everything and taking us down with him. He destroyed our family and now we have nothing. So I got rid of the ones who were loyal to him and brought along the ones loyal to me and our true family." She looked behind her and I held in my gasp when I saw Marcus among her followers. She turned back to me and pasted on a pretty smile for the onlookers who were coming but not close enough to hear. "I intend to raise my family back up and take what was rightfully ours to begin with. Power. Now that Sikes is out of my way, the only thing still standing in it, my dear sweet, pretty Visionary...is you."

The End......for now.

Oh, the thank you's could go on for miles. Thank you to my God, the readers who have picked up this book and my others as well, you are the reason I do this. It's been SO much fun getting to know all different kinds of people from all over the world who have read something of mine. It's humbling in every sense of the word and I thank you for allowing me to be a little piece of your world. You guys are the best and I love to hear from you! You rock!

Be sure to look for **Defiance**, the next installment in the Significance series due out Spring of 2012.

Shelly's Other Series

Collide
Devour
Stealing Grace
Wide Awake
Smash Into You

PLEASE FEEL FREE TO CONTACT SHELLY AT THE FOLLOWING AVENUES.

www.facebook.com/shellycranefanpage

www.twitter.com/authshellycrane

www.shellycrane.blogspot.com

Playlist

Now, when I write, I picture it in my head like a movie, complete with a cast and soundtrack. So… I figured I'd give you the soundtrack as I see it, if this was a movie. Each song will have a description next to it if it pertains to a certain scene. Hope you enjoy!

1. Opening Credits – "Break The Same" – Mutemath
2. "The Mall and Misery" – Broken Bells
3. Shower cry- "Open Your Eyes" – Andrew Belle
4. "Leaves" – Ours
5. "Simple Life" - Carolina Liar
6. "High On The Ceiling" – Anya Marina
7. Playing Xbox- "Mountain Man" – Crash Kings
8. "Tyrant" – The Bravery
9. Dancing with Bish at pier – "Shake Your Shimmy" – Living Things
10. "Around My Head" – Cage The Elephant
11. "More Time" – NeedToBreathe
12. "Constant" – House Of Heroes
13. "No One Sleeps When I'm Awake" – The Sounds
14. Maggie learns what she is – "100 Suns" – 30 Seconds To Mars
15. Maggie at ice cream shop – "If You Run" – Boxer Rebellion
16. Maggie driving back from Ice cream shop – "Cold Fame" – Band Of Skulls
17. Makeup scene – "Ocean Wide" – The Afters
18. "Oh My Stars" – Andrew Belle
19. "High and Dry" – Radiohead
20. "Lola Stars and Stripes" – The Stills
21. "Perfect Situation" – Weezer
22. "Fix You" – Coldplay
23. Maggie on beach with Rachel – "Never Say Never" – The Fray
24. "Inside Of Love" – Nada surf
25. Caleb and Maggie wake up on beach – "Just Say Yes" –Snow Patrol
26. "Show Me What You're Looking For" – Caroline Liar
27. "He Won't Go" – Adele
28. Maggie and Beck get ready – "Dream" Priscilla Ahn
29. Dancing in club – "ET" Katy Perry
30. Alley scene – "All I Need" – Matt Kearney
31. "For The First Time" – The Script
32. "Talking Bird" – Death Cab for Cutie
33. Garage scene – "Open Your Eyes" – Snow Patrol
34. "Mine Is Yours" – Cold War Kids
35. "Wish You Were Here" – The Sounds
36. "You Are Too Beautiful" – Hawksley Workman
37. Kyle and Maggie in club – "Gotta Be Somebody's Blues" – Jimmy Eat World

38. Maggie on stage – "The Way You Are" – The Afters
39. "24" - Jem
40. "Fences" – Phoenix
41. "Somewhere Only We Know" – Keane
42. "I Can Feel A Hot One" – Manchester Orchestra
43. Jen and Bish vision – "Lost Year" - Mutemath
44. "Oxygen" – Living Things
45. "Typical" – Mutemath
46. "The Only Exception" – Paramore
47. "Helena (So Long and Goodnight) – My Chemical Romance
48. "Saved" – The Spill Canvas
49. Kyle and Lynne kitchen scene – "Right Before My Eyes" – Cage The Elephant
50. "The Man Who can't Be Moved" – The Script
51. Maggie and Caleb bedroom – "Beautiful Love" – The Afters
52. Afterwards – "Falling Slowly" – Glen Hassard
53. "Duet" – Rachael Yamagato
54. "If" - House Of Heroes
55. "Maggie" – Rod Stewart
56. Maggie answers the door – "Run" – Snow Patrol
57. "I know What I am" – Band Of Skulls
58. "Odds" – Mutemath
59. "Butterflies and Hurricanes" – Muse
60. London airplane and car ride – "Safe and Sound" – Hawksley Workman
61. Meeting a new enemy – "A Beautiful Lie" – 30 Seconds To Mars
62. End Credits -

CPSIA information can be obtained at www.ICGtesting.com
Printed in the USA
LVOW12s1925230813

349371LV00018B/762/P